Anne Baker

LIVERPOOL GEMS

headline

First published in 2016 by
HEADLINE PUBLISHING GROUP

First published in paperback in 2016 by
HEADLINE PUBLISHING GROUP

3

Cataloguing in Publication Data is available from the British Library

ISBN 978 1 4722 2534 4

Typeset in Baskerville by Avon DataSet Ltd, Bidford-on-Avon, Warwickshire

Printed and bound in Great Britain by Clays Ltd, Elcograf S.p.A

HEADLINE PUBLISHING GROUP
An Hachette UK Company
Carmelite House
50 Victoria Embankment
London EC4Y 0DZ

www.headline.co.uk
www.hachette.co.uk

Anne Baker trained as a nurse at Birkenhead General Hospital, but after her marriage went to live first in Libya and then in Nigeria. She eventually returned to her native Birkenhead where she worked as a Health Visitor for over ten years before taking up writing. Anne Baker's previous Merseyside sagas are all available from Headline and have been highly praised:

'A heartwarming saga' *Woman's Weekly*

'A stirring tale of romance and passion, poverty and ambition' *Liverpool Echo*

'A fast-moving and entertaining novel with a fascinating location and warm, friendly characters' *Bradford Telegraph and Argus*

'A wartime Merseyside saga so full of Scouse wit and warmth that it is bound to melt the hardest heart' *Northern Echo*

'Baker's understanding and compassion for very human dilemmas makes her one of romantic fiction's most popular authors' *Lancashire Evening Post*

'A gentle tale with all the right ingredients for a heartwarming novel' *Huddersfield Daily Examiner*

'A well-written enjoyable book that legions of saga fans will love' *Historical Novels Review*

To find out more about Anne Baker's novels visit
www.annebaker.co.uk

By Anne Baker and available from Headline

I would like to thank Martin Kemp for the help he gave me regarding the training of chartered accountants in the 1930s. He was at pains to point out that, although he underwent his training in Liverpool, it was more recent than the 1930s. I hope I've understood correctly the facts he took such trouble to explain.

CHAPTER ONE

Saturday, 4 May 1935

C AROLINE COURTNEY WAS ONLY half awake when from the folds of sleep came the feeling that today was an extra-special day. As she struggled to open her eyes, her bedroom door opened and Aunt Prudence, already dressed, said in a stage whisper, 'Carrie, it's six o'clock, time to get up. We've a lot to do this morning.'

'Yes, of course!' She yawned and sat up obediently. Today was her twin sister Connie's wedding day. Aunt Prue had decided they would cater for the reception and it would be held here in their home.

'Let the bride sleep on; you can bring her a cup of tea later.'

All she could see of Connie was her mop of wild pale blond curls on the pillow of the bed alongside her own. Carrie had exactly the same hair, exactly the same everything really; they were identical twins. The family had always called her Carrie; that was Connie's first attempt at saying her name.

She dressed in her everyday clothes as quickly and quietly as she could. The main road outside led down to the Liverpool docks, and the house shook as a heavy wagon loaded with goods for a foreign port thundered past. There were fewer of

1

those since the Depression had tightened its grip.

Downstairs, Aunt Maud put a cup of tea into her hands and Prudence called from the living room, 'Carrie, come and help me move the dining table into the middle of the room. It'll be easier for people to serve themselves if they can walk round it.'

'Will one large tin of sliced peaches and one of pears be enough?' Aunt Maud was tipping the fruit into Grandma's cut-glass bowls.

'Yes, we have two trifles as well. Could you start whipping the cream to decorate them next?' Prue started arranging the food on the dining table.

Carrie set about washing lettuces, bunches of spring onions and radishes. The wedding was to take place at eleven this morning, and Prue's lined cheeks were already flushed. She'd worked all the family hard for the past few weeks, cleaning and cooking.

Carrie could feel an air of excitement in the bustle of preparation. She knew she should be pleased and happy for her sister, but she felt on edge and even a little sad. Connie was not here beside her and she'd be seeing a lot less of her from now on. Connie had been her constant companion and they'd done everything together until she'd started going out with John. Carrie had already felt the bonds that bound them loosening, and she knew she was really going to miss her twin.

Their mother had died when they were six months old, and Aunt Jennifer, their mother's widowed sister, had taken them to live with her. But only eighteen months later, Jennifer had been rushed to hospital needing a major operation, and had never recovered enough to look after them again.

Archibald Alan Courtney, their father, had not been in the country at that time. He'd fought in the trenches during the war and afterwards had found work in South Africa. Without being asked, his elder sisters Prudence and Maud had taken the girls in, and had brought them up on a strict timetable of regular churchgoing, frugal meals and hard work. Times had been hard, but at least, Carrie mused, she and Connie had always had each other.

They had left school at fourteen and their father had arranged for them to have a two-year course at Skelly's Secretarial College, where Connie had excelled at typing and shorthand; she was now a secretary for the council. Carrie had preferred bookkeeping and was now working in that capacity.

Connie came down in her dressing gown. 'I've had my bath and I've come to help. I don't like being up there by myself. I could hear you all chatting and laughing.'

'If you really want to help, butter those scones and ice the cupcakes Maud baked yesterday,' Prue told her.

Uncle George arrived. He was Prue's favourite brother, who lived in Preston and ran a hire-car business; he'd offered to ferry guests to and from the church. 'I've brought some beer, Prue.' He staggered in with a crate of bottles and lowered them on to the kitchen table. 'It won't do to run short today.'

Prue was indignant. 'Don't leave them there in everybody's way. Put them on the larder floor; you won't be wanting them until later. You can make yourself useful.'

'What d'you want me to do?'

Prue pointed to the large piece of boiled ham and the tongue that she'd cooked yesterday. 'Carve them and set them out on these platters.'

George came to get the carving knife and fork from the drawer near the sink. 'Carrie, my dear, when can we look forward to your wedding?' he asked. 'We all enjoy occasions like this.'

'I have no idea,' she said with a rush of impatience. She'd had that question fired at her dozens of times since Connie and John had become engaged. She'd heard it phrased in many different ways, all of them hurtful, because she didn't even have a boyfriend, which Uncle George knew very well. She'd never had a real boyfriend, but she was not going to let that upset her, not today.

'Never mind dear,' Aunt Prudence said consolingly. 'There's no need to be jealous, your turn will come.'

'I'm not!' Carrie was indignant; the last thing she felt was jealous of her twin.

'Well, envious then.'

Carrie shivered; perhaps she did feel a touch of envy. She too wanted someone special to come and sweep her off her feet.

Maud said briskly, 'You'll not have any trouble finding a husband. You're just as beautiful as Connie. Many people can't tell you apart, can they?'

They were indeed identical, with the same mass of tight curls, emerald eyes and lovely fair skin, but Carrie felt there had always been more spark behind Connie's face. She was very outgoing, had more to say to strangers and was full of fun. Carrie, twenty minutes older, had always felt towed along behind her twin sister.

At fourteen, Connie hadn't been interested in boys. She'd worked hard at school, learned the piano, and sung in the school choir. Everybody fussed over her; she'd always taken the limelight. At sixteen she had John Bradshaw as a special boyfriend. The aunts considered him suitable because they knew his father, who had played football with their brothers.

Connie buzzed with enthusiasm for one craze after another. She and Carrie had joined a cycling club some years ago, and rode for long distances on most summer Sundays. That was where they'd met John.

'You've plenty of time. You're only nineteen, after all. Connie is a very young bride,' said Aunt Prue. 'Personally, I think it better to wait until you're older. It gives the groom a chance to establish his career and so be better able to support a wife.'

That was a dig at John, Carrie thought. He was articled to a firm of accountants and not yet qualified, but he was twenty-one and had come into a small legacy from one of his maiden aunts, and was thus able to make his own decisions.

Aunt Prue went on, 'They should wait and get to know each other better. Save up, and not rush into marriage.'

'Connie reckons she knows him well enough after three years, and anyway, she'll carry on working,' Carrie said.

'She'll have to, won't she? It won't be a traditional marriage.'

Carrie knew that Connie was in love with John, and that he adored her. They'd be happy in any sort of marriage; the last thing they wanted was to wait.

Carrie longed to have a boyfriend of her own who thought about her the way John did about Connie. It didn't seem too much to ask; it was what every girl wanted, but for her, that special someone didn't come. She was beginning to fear he never would.

He hadn't come for their aunts. Both had strong features and must have been quite good-looking in their youth. They had the wild family hair, though it had turned iron grey now and tended to frizz. Aunt Prue was tall and stringy; she had thin pursed lips and was a bit of a disciplinarian. She was a retired secretary and managed the housekeeping and just about everything else. Maud was eight years younger and a little stout, and Prue kept her very much under her thumb.

Maud was still teaching in a primary school, though she was looking forward to retiring next year. She had a wider social life than Prue, often going out with her fellow teachers to concerts and theatres, and occasionally going away on holiday with one of them. She also had a beautiful voice and sang in a choir, often singing solos, and that took her out and about too.

She spent more on clothes, and even a little on cosmetics, and looked smarter and much younger than Prue. She often brought home little treats such as books, board games or chocolate, and during the school holidays she'd taken the twins out and about, and always to the pantomime at Christmas.

Maud knew how to enjoy herself and have a really good time, but sometimes Carrie had seen her look disappointed with her life. She found her more approachable than Prue, and always turned to her first when in difficulties.

She had heard that Maud's boyfriend had been killed in the Boer War, but nobody spoke of him. When Carrie had asked about him, her aunts turned the conversation to how few jobs there were for those who had fought and survived.

It had taken years of struggle for the country to get back on its feet; then a further economic downturn had started in America in 1929 and quickly spread round the world.

In Liverpool, output in heavy industries had plunged, and unemployment in the country had burgeoned to three million, while in most trades profits had shrunk to about half. They had been difficult years for everybody.

Her aunts had never left their mother's home and had changed very little in it since they'd inherited it. Carrie loved the spacious semi-detached villa, which had been built in 1902, pebble-dashed and with high eaves. It had a front room they called the parlour and which they used only at Christmas and on occasions like this.

The dining room was used as a living room because Prue thought it wasteful to light two fires, and the kitchen at the back covered the width of the house. The twins had spruced the place up for the wedding; they'd even whitewashed the back yard walls and grown a few flowers in tubs. It looked like being a sunny day, and the guests would be able to spill out through the kitchen.

Only the two families had been invited, with a few neighbours and one or two of the girls Connie worked with. 'We can manage perfectly well, providing we limit the number to twenty-five,' Prudence had told them. It had crept up to thirty-two since then.

At nine thirty, they all sat down in the kitchen to the breakfast Prue had made. It was what they usually had: tea with boiled eggs and bread and butter. 'On schedule,' she said, looking at the clock.

Afterwards, Carrie and Connie went upstairs to get ready. There were three generous bedrooms, a box room, and a bathroom with a large bath on legs that was developing green water stains in the enamel. Carrie only needed a wash, as she and Maud had been urged to have their baths last night so that there'd be hot water for the bride and for Aunt Prue this morning. Connie was in her bridal gown by the time she returned from the bathroom, and the only help she needed was to fasten the buttons down the back.

It took longer to remove the frizz from her overabundant curls and make them shine with a little brilliantine, a trick learned from Uncle Bob, who had similar hair. Connie looked radiant in her demure white gown, with faux orange blossom woven into her hair and her veil clipped in place.

Carrie, who was to be the only bridesmaid, quickly slid into her gown of primrose satin. Connie interrupted her application of face powder to button her into it. Carrie used brilliantine more lavishly on her own hair; it was the only thing that tamed it and made her curls shine, but neither girl admitted using it to their friends. Brilliantine was meant for men.

'Right, are we both ready?'

'I am,' Connie said, 'but I'm beginning to feel butterflies in my stomach.'

'I'm feeling more than butterflies,' Carrie said. 'Up to now we've spent our lives together sleeping in this room, but you won't be here any longer.' She looked round at the twin beds, the shared dressing table and the framed photographs of their mother and father hanging on the wall. Auntie Maud had hung them there years and years ago, and Prue had said, 'Just like the photographs of royalty in the town hall.'

'They'll want to know what their parents looked like,' Maud had retorted.

It was a good full-face studio portrait of their mother, but the image of their father had been blown up from a snapshot.

He was sitting in sunlight that was brighter than any they'd ever seen, and the buildings behind him looked exotic. He was wearing slacks, and an open-necked short-sleeved shirt with a sunhat. They'd never seen him dressed like that. It made him seem a stranger.

'I'll be on my own from now on,' Carrie said, biting her lip.

'No you won't. I'm not going far and we'll see each other often,' Connie told her briskly. 'I don't want to lose touch with you. Anyway, Dad is back for a while, so you'll have his company.'

That cheered Carrie, but only briefly. 'Yes, but you and I are close, and I hardly know him.'

'He'll want to take you out and about, won't he? Come on, let's go.'

'Do you want your veil down now?'

'No, I can't see much through it. I don't want to trip up.'

Carrie found it quite difficult to hold up Connie's train as well as her own long skirt to negotiate the stairs. Another goods wagon thundered past outside, but in a moment of quiet when they were halfway down, Connie asked, 'What's that strange ticking sound?'

Carrie listened: something was going *tap, tap, tap, tap*. 'I don't know.' The ringing of the front doorbell interrupted them and she ran to let the newcomer in. 'It's Dad,' she called.

'Hello, love. I daren't hug you now you're in your finery,' he said, pecking at her cheek.

Carrie had not seen much of her father. He'd come home every three years or so and he'd always made much of her then, but she didn't feel she knew him well. He was still a handsome man at forty-nine, having acquired a good tan and just enough greying hair at his temples to make him look distinguished. He'd always been very generous to both of them, and had provided Connie with enough money not only for the wedding but to launch her into married life.

'There you are, Connie. You look a picture; you make a beautiful bride.' He took both her hands in his and leaned forward to kiss her cheek. 'Do you want a drink?'

'No she does not,' Prue said indignantly. 'Not until after the ceremony.'

'There's tea if you want it,' Maud said from the kitchen. 'I'm just cutting another plateful of bread and butter. I was afraid there wouldn't be enough. After all, it'll be lunchtime, everybody will be hungry.'

Carrie filled two teacups. 'It'll spoil our lipstick, but we need it,' she said.

Connie peeped into the dining room. 'Aunt Prue, it looks a magnificent spread.'

The feast was all set out on the table. The wedding cake took pride of place on the tea trolley in the corner. Prue had baked three fruit cakes in special tins borrowed from Gladys, their next-door neighbour, who had spent her life working in the bakery she had inherited following her husband's death. She had iced and decorated them, making a thoroughly professional job of it.

'Thank you, everybody,' said the bride with a quiver in her voice. 'It all looks beautiful.'

Gladys was buxom, bordering on rotund, and often complained of feeling hot. Her cheeks were scarlet and always wreathed with smiles. 'We all want to do you proud,' she said.

Bob and Dilys came out of the kitchen to greet him. Bob

was her father's favourite brother. 'You haven't changed a bit,' Archie told him. 'You look quite athletic.' Carrie knew Bob was the only brother her father had kept in regular touch with, and there was a lot of hugging and back-slapping.

'I've got to keep fit in my job,' Bob said; he was a police constable. 'So I can chase after the lads when they nick things.'

'Not like George, who's running to fat now that he rides round in his taxi all day.'

'How long are you staying?' Dilys wanted to know. 'You must come to Sunday lunch. You look really well, Archie. Life in those foreign parts must suit you.'

Archie Courtney had started his working life in the Lancashire coal mines, but after the Great War, he had gone out to South Africa to seek his fortune. He'd found work in the gold mines of Pretoria, where he said life was good. Carrie had dreamed of joining him there one day, but it seemed that was not to be. Dad had arrived home the other day for Connie's wedding, but was being vague about his future plans. He said he might stay for a while; he might even settle here for good.

As the time went on, Carrie could feel the tension building. Prue was making sure their relatives and neighbours left for the church on time. Archie had bought himself a car, and today Bob was going to drive it. John's father had also offered the use of his car, which along with George's taxi gave them three cars to ferry thirty-six people to the church and back.

Bob had already taken two carloads. 'Wherever is he?' Prue worried. 'He ought to be back by now if the wedding is to start at eleven.'

'Here he is now,' Maud reported from the parlour window, and Prue ushered the remaining family out.

The house seemed suddenly quiet when they'd gone and only the bridal party remained. Connie was renewing her lipstick in the hall mirror.

Carrie said, 'Dad, Aunt Prue says you've taken a house in Allerton.'

'Yes, I've rented a furnished place. It's got most of what I need, but it's a bit bare at the moment. You must come and see it.' Since he'd told them he would be trying to make his living in this country, Carrie had been half expecting him to ask her to move in with him. Perhaps she wouldn't miss Connie so much if she had a different life herself.

'Dad, could I come and live with you?' she asked. It shocked her to see from his face that he'd never thought of it and didn't want it.

'Why?' he demanded.

She felt rebuffed. 'Well, children usually live with their parents, don't they?'

'But Prue and Maud have brought you up. I'm afraid it might upset them if you were to leave now. Besides, love, it would mean a longer journey to work for you.'

Carrie worked in central Liverpool and travelled in by tram; she'd checked and found it would take two or three minutes longer from Allerton but was equally convenient. She felt disappointed, but she made herself smile; she mustn't be anything but happy today. 'There's that ticking noise again,' she said. 'It sounds like a clock.'

'Ah, here's George coming back for us,' her father said. 'Come on, Connie, let's get you to the church.'

Carrie slammed the front door behind her and climbed into the back of the car beside her sister. Connie reached for her hand and Carrie knew she was feeling nervous. This was her big moment; she was about to move into an exciting and very different life. Dad was sitting in the front talking cricket scores with Uncle George.

'We're going to be five minutes early,' Carrie said, 'and the bride is supposed to be five minutes late.' She wanted everything to be perfect for her sister.

'I'll drive round again,' George said easily, only momentarily taking his mind away from the cricket.

When he finally pulled up outside the church, Carrie could feel the bride shaking slightly. She helped her out; once in the porch, she pulled down her veil and straightened the folds of her gown. Maud was waiting for them and went forward to signal their arrival and take her seat next to Prue.

The organ had been playing softly but paused now for a moment. 'I wish you every happiness,' Carrie whispered and squeezed her sister's hand. 'Both of you.' The organ struck up in joyful proclamation and Dad led Connie forward. Carrie fell in behind, blinking hard; she had a lump in her throat.

Auntie Maud was smiling up at them from under her new navy straw hat with cherries on the brim. Prue still looked stern and fraught. Carrie didn't miss the way John turned to smile at his bride as she drew level with him.

They made their vows in the age-old tradition. Carrie could hear Aunt Maud's lovely voice soaring above those of the rest of the congregation. The service and hymns heightened the emotions. It was a fairy-tale wedding.

As John slid the ring on to Connie's finger, her eyes were like stars. After they'd signed the register, the newly married couple led the way back down the aisle while the full-throated organ crashed out the triumphant notes of the Wedding March.

Carrie found herself out on the church steps in the sunshine, tears in her eyes, trying to smile at the photographer. She thought it couldn't have been a more romantic wedding.

CHAPTER TWO

Prue was herding Carrie with Maud and Dad back to George's car. 'Bob is going to bring the bride and groom. Gladys will come with me. We need to get home first and be at the front door to greet the guests,' she said.

When George dropped them at their gate, Carrie still felt in a romantic haze. Prue took charge. 'Archie, I want you to open the two sorts of sherry, sweet and dry, and Carrie and Gladys will help you fill up the trays of glasses that I've set out. Maud, if you would—'

'I need to spend a penny first,' said Maud, rushing upstairs to the bathroom.

Prue went on. 'John's father will push as many as he can into his car and he'll not be far behind us.'

Carrie followed her father to the kitchen; she'd poured only one glass of sherry when she heard Maud shrieking at the top of her voice. She stopped, cold shivers running down her spine. 'Something terrible must have happened,' she said.

'What could it be?' Beside her, Dad put down the bottle he was about to open and turned to go upstairs, but Maud was already hurtling down.

'Water . . .' She could scarcely get the words out. 'Coming through the ceiling. All over the landing.'

'What?' Prue's mouth had dropped open.

'Water! Everywhere is soaked.'

Archie shot upstairs and was down again in an instant. 'I think something's leaking in the loft. The stopcock? Where is it?'

'For heaven's sake, you and Bob fitted a new sink for us once.' Prue was impatient.

'That was ages ago. How am I supposed to remember?' Nevertheless, he went straight to the kitchen and opened the cupboard under the sink; moments later he was frantically turning the water off.

The front doorbell rang, 'We should all be lined up to greet the guests as they arrive,' Gladys said.

At the same moment, Prue screamed, 'The dining room! Oh my goodness!' Her face was purple with stress.

'It's all right,' Archie assured her. 'I've turned the water off.'

'No it isn't! Don't be so stupid! Everything's spoiled. What a mess,' she wept.

From the doorway, Carrie surveyed the damage. The once crisp white tablecloth now drooped and dripped water, the plates of bread and butter were awash, the cream was lifting off the trifles, revealing curdling custard and small pools of water collecting on the layer of jelly. Dad came to stand behind her. 'Oh my God!'

The doorbell rang again, and Carrie went to let the guests in. There were gasps of horror and dismay all round.

'We can't eat this food,' Prue wailed. 'It's all ruined.'

There was a wet patch on the ceiling, and water was still dripping on to the table. Maud and Carrie dragged it out of the way against the wall.

Archie went out to the wash house in the yard for the ladder, and one of the guests helped him carry it upstairs. Meanwhile, the rest of the family crowded round the dining table trying to salvage something from the feast. Plates of neatly cut bread and butter were drained over the sink and the residue was heaped on top of the six-foot yard wall for the birds. Bowls of sliced peaches were tipped straight down the lavatory in the wash house.

Carrie returned to the tray of glasses and began filling them; they were all going to need a drink after this. John took the tray and handed the sherry round.

Archie came downstairs. 'The cold-water tank has sprung a leak,' he reported. 'We need all the bowls and buckets we have up on the landing; I can't stop the tank emptying.'

There were gasps of alarm from some and sympathy from others. Carrie went out to the shed to fetch the baby bath that Prue used to wash sheets. Gladys went next door to get containers from her house and, puffing hard, took them straight upstairs.

Prue was going from room to room trying to assess the damage. 'The landing and the dining room below have caught the worst of it,' she wept. 'We should never have pulled the table to the middle. The twins' bedroom is wet too.' The ceiling had a big wet patch spreading from the wall. The guests who had followed her were pushing the beds away from the drips. 'What are we going to do?'

Carrie took the baby bath into her bedroom. Connie's bed was damp, but she wouldn't need it tonight; thankfully her own was still dry. Water was pinging into containers; the whole house was in chaos.

Her father rapped on one of the buckets for quiet. 'Does anyone know of a plumber? Preferably one living nearby. Someone who would come round now?'

One of Connie's friends said, 'I have an uncle with a plumbing business. He lives in Allerton, not very far.'

'He's on the phone?' She nodded. Dad was sorting pennies from the change in his trouser pocket; he pushed them into her hand. 'George, can you run this young lady to the nearest phone box? Tell your uncle I'd be very grateful if he'd come and sort us out.'

He brought out his wallet. 'While you're out, George, get a few bottles of white wine and some more beer. We're going to run out at this rate. I knew Prue wouldn't buy enough.'

'Everything's ruined. Everything's a write-off.' Prue sounded quite hysterical. 'We've worked so hard to make a good wedding breakfast for Connie and John, and now look at the mess! There's nothing left fit to eat. What are we going to do?'

Gladys put an arm round her waist. 'You mustn't worry, Prue. Archie is doing all he can. He's getting it under control, it'll be all right. Come and have a glass of sherry.'

'No, I couldn't possibly drink anything,' she wept, but Gladys pushed a glass into her hand and Prue ended up gulping down two glassfuls, after which she collapsed, morose and silent, on to a dining chair. She looked as though she might slide off, so Carrie took her upstairs to lie down on her bed.

'Prue is highly strung,' Dad was telling everybody, 'but underneath she's as strong as a horse. She'll be fine in fifteen minutes.'

John was carrying small tables out to the yard. 'Could everybody help to bring out the plates and any food that's still edible?' he shouted. 'It must be possible to salvage some of it.'

'Prue would hate to see all this wasted,' Maud said. 'It's clean water; it was heading straight for the cold tap.' She began scraping cream and water off the trifles. 'We can open a tin of evaporated milk to go on these.'

'No!' Connie was shocked. 'No, Maud, it's come through two ceilings and the landing carpet. There are specks of dust and dirt on everything, little hairs too. We don't want to poison people.'

Carrie hugged her. 'I'm so sorry it's spoiled your wedding breakfast.'

'It's all right.' Connie had a little giggle. 'Nobody is going to forget my wedding, are they? But it's lunchtime and we're all hungry. You could wash the salad again. That lettuce would be fine.'

'The water's off,' Dad reminded her, but Gladys was struggling in with a bucketful from her house.

Guests were patting food dry with tea towels and eating it. George returned with more drink and began distributing it. Fortunately, he had not carved up all the joint of ham, and there was a piece of tongue left too. Dad set about slicing them up. Everybody seemed relieved that the flood had been dealt with and the party could begin. Soon they were laughing and making jokes about the predicament.

Carrie went upstairs to see how Prue was. She was lying flat, staring up at the ceiling, looking decidedly morose. 'Come down, Prue, everything's going well now.' The buzz of conversation could be heard up here. 'It would be a shame to miss this after all the work you put into it.'

Later on, her father rapped on a table for silence. 'I had

prepared a speech for this occasion,' he said, 'but it's gone completely out of my mind. Anyway, I have to apologise to you all for the shortcomings of the wedding breakfast, and to thank you for buckling to and helping us.' George rushed round refilling glasses. 'So all I'm going to say is let's raise our glasses to the bride and groom, and as well as wishing them happiness, let's hope this is the worst disaster they'll have to face in their married life. All the luck in the world to Connie and John.'

Maud wheeled out the trolley with the wedding cake to applause. It was still in its pristine state and many hands helped her lift it down the step into the yard. 'Gladys has made a magnificent job of icing the cake,' she said. 'I'm so glad this hasn't been spoiled. Come on, Connie and John, you have to cut the first slice.'

It was Gladys who dismantled the three tiers and presented the bottom one for the bride and groom to cut, while cameras clicked. 'Forget the tiny bits of wedding cake traditionally given just to taste,' she said. 'Archie, you cut it into generous slices. Your guests may still be hungry.'

Carrie took the plate round. Everyone was appreciative, and even Prue relaxed and helped herself to a slice. There was laughter as well as a heightened buzz of conversation.

She whispered to Connie, 'It's going well now, isn't it?'

'Very well,' her twin agreed.

Shortly afterwards, Connie, all excited smiles, came looking for her and took her by the hand. 'Come and help me change into my going-away outfit. Time's going on and we have a train to catch.' The honeymoon was to be a week in the Lake District.

Carrie followed her up the stairs and squelched across the

landing to the bedroom they'd shared. Connie's green two-piece, bought specially for the occasion, swung on a hanger from the doorknob of one of the two large Victorian wardrobes. Connie sat down in front of the dressing table and tried to remove her headdress. 'Can you help me get this out of my hair?'

It took Carrie time to unwind the strands of faux orange blossom from her tight curls. Really, Connie didn't need much help once she was out of her wedding dress. Carrie changed, too, into the blue frock she'd kept for best for the last year.

Connie said, 'I'm leaving my bouquet here for you. I'm cutting out the tradition of throwing it for the next bride to catch.'

'It could be Aunt Prue who catches it,' Carrie said, and they both giggled. She knew her twin understood that she was a bit touchy about being considered the next bride in the family.

When Connie was ready to leave in her new outfit, they both took a last look round at the twin beds, each with a white candlewick counterpane pulled neatly up over the pillow. 'Mine is soaking.' Connie felt it. 'It's just as well I won't be sleeping here tonight.'

Carrie couldn't help feeling they were facing changes such as they'd never known before. 'It's the end of an era,' she choked.

'Oh, Carrie!' Connie threw her arms round her in a hug. 'I know it is, and I've caused it. I'm going to miss you. I almost wish you were coming with us.'

'On your honeymoon?' Carrie's lip trembled but she had to laugh too. 'I'm sure John would have something to say about that.'

'But we've never been separated before, have we? We mustn't get cut off from each other.'

Uncle George was waiting to drive the newly-weds to the station. He'd refused to let Carrie tie old boots and tin cans to the rear bumper for luck. The whole family turned out on the pavement to wave them off, but the car turned for the station and was out of sight in a moment.

They trooped back inside. Everything suddenly felt flat. It was all over. Great-Aunt Vera said she must go to catch her tram. 'I'll ask Bob to drive you home,' Archie said. Other members of the family began to drift away. Carrie stood between Prue and Maud, kissing everyone goodbye.

'A bit of an anticlimax,' her father said when the front door closed behind the last group.

Aunt Prue led them to the kitchen. 'Two bottles of wine left,' she said. 'Archie, I told you not to buy too much.'

'We couldn't have rescued Connie's party on one glass of sherry each,' he said.

Prue bent down to lock the wine into a low cupboard. 'We'll keep this for Christmas,' she said.

'Wouldn't you like another glass now?'

'No, we've all had quite enough, thank you. Now then, Maud, there's plenty of clearing up to be done, even if the water isn't on yet. Gladys has brought us two more bucketfuls. Carrie, if you fill the kettle and a couple of pans and heat them on the stove, we could start the washing-up.'

'For heaven's sake,' Archie said. 'It would be better to wait. The plumber says your cold-water tank is leaking because one of the joints has split.'

'A tank has joints?'

'Several, where the pipes come off. He's gone back to his yard to see if he can get you a replacement tank.'

'That sounds expensive. Couldn't he repair the old one?'

'He says not, but he'll put a new one in as soon as possible.' Archie opened another bottle of beer. 'I could do with a bit of a rest after all that.' He led the way to the parlour.

They all followed. Carrie felt shattered. Maud paused to pour wine from the only bottle that had not been drained. 'I think we should thank Archie for sorting us out,' she said to her sister. 'You and I wouldn't have known where to begin.'

'Of course, Archie,' Prudence said. 'We're very grateful for your help.'

'It was a bad start,' Carrie smiled, 'but Dad, you did get the party going eventually.'

'It was not at all what I intended.' Prudence would not be cheered. 'A big disappointment for the bride and groom; it spoiled everything for them.'

'I don't think so,' Archie said. 'Connie and John mucked in to help.'

Carrie wanted to smile. 'Connie said nobody would ever forget her wedding.'

Archie Courtney had been sitting in the window, watching for his brother Bob to return with his car. When he saw the brand-new Austin 10/4 pulling up to the kerb outside, he gulped down the last of his beer, leapt to his feet and kissed Carrie's cheek. 'Bye, love.'

His sisters got to their feet too; he kissed them dutifully. 'No need to come out,' he said. 'We're all tired now.' They trailed after him anyway, as he'd guessed they would.

Prue had always been a trial to him. She was eighteen years his senior, and as the firstborn in their large family, she was inclined to boss all her siblings. As the youngest, he felt he'd received the bulk of her attention, and now, at the age of forty-nine, it irritated him. One advantage of living abroad was that he'd escaped Prue, but she was nosy and wanted to know more than he was prepared to tell her. She caught up with him on the pavement.

Her pale grey eyes challenged him. 'You're quite a stranger here now, Archie,' she said. 'I thought you went out to South Africa to enjoy a better standard of living?'

'I did,' he said, wishing she wouldn't stare at him.

'What have you come back for, then?'

Archie didn't know what to say; he wasn't sure coming home was the right thing for him. 'I missed England,' he said lightly. 'Got a bit homesick.'

He had a very good friend – Rod, a businessman – who had asked him to come and help start up a new firm here, but he'd told him little about it and left everything up in the air. Marion had been keen to come over and work for Rod, and had persuaded Archie not to be left behind. 'It'll be fun,' she'd said. 'We'll have a good time.'

They'd both insisted on the need for secrecy. 'We don't want everybody to know what we're doing.'

Prue didn't give up once she'd started. 'Don't tell me you're tired of being waited on hand and foot by servants? Tired of the luxury life?'

'Prue, it wasn't all luxury. I had to work very hard.'

'Yes, so you've said.'

Bob was getting out of the driving seat. 'Don't go away,'

Archie told him. 'I'll drop you and Dilys off on my way home.'

'Thanks,' Bob said.

Archie held the car door open for Bob's wife. That did not deflect Prue's attention. 'We have to assume you made your fortune out there.' She could be more than outspoken, and she missed nothing.

'No,' he said, 'but I managed to better myself, pull myself up on my boot strings.'

'Archie, within a few days you've got yourself a fancy house and bought a new car. I hope you aren't going to spend all your money at once.' This was what he disliked about Prue. She always had to pry. 'While you were getting rich, Maud and I have brought the twins up for you. They're not children any longer; not the hard work they were. In fact Carrie could keep house for you. We've taught her to clean and cook.'

'No,' he said, 'she's settled with you and Maud, and she's reached the age when she can help you.' He couldn't have a grown-up daughter living with him; Carrie would see too much and start asking awkward questions. He looked round for her, hoping she wasn't hearing this. 'I'm very grateful for all you've done for the twins.'

'She'll be disappointed, I know. But Archie, I can't see you fending for yourself; that isn't your style, and certainly not after all those years with servants. If you don't want Carrie, it must mean you have a woman to share your life.'

That was a shock; how did she know? He took a deep breath. 'Yes, I have. She's on the way here now from South Africa.'

Prue's eyes opened in surprise. 'You've got married again and you haven't even told us?'

'No, but I'm hoping to persuade her.' He got into the driving seat. 'I came on ahead to find somewhere for us to live. Her name's Marion, you'll like her.'

Prue sniffed. 'Shall I come round and help you settle into this grand house you've found?'

'No, thank you.' He was exasperated. 'I am settled in. It's a furnished house. It's clean and shipshape, though a little bare.'

Prue had the sort of gaze that seemed to see into his mind. 'I hope you're going to invite us all round to see it,' she said.

'Of course.' He put the car in gear and made his escape.

'Smashing car,' Bob said enthusiastically. 'It's this year's model, a 10/4 Lichfield saloon. What would I give to have one of these?'

CHAPTER THREE

JOHN HAD GIVEN CARRIE a key to the furnished flat he had rented, and asked her to put in a loaf and some milk on the day they were due to return, as it would be late when they got back. The evening before, she took round some late wedding presents, and ran the carpet sweeper round to pick up a few specks of dust.

She'd helped Connie get things ready. The double bed was made up with new bedding, and a fire had been laid in the living-room grate. This was what Carrie really envied: Connie was now Mrs John Bradshaw and had a home of her own. They'd talked a lot about the stifling routine in Aunt Prue's house.

There was dried and tinned food in the larder, but very little else. On the spur of the moment, Carrie picked up one of the wedding present pans and took it home with her. On the way, she bought the ingredients for a stew and cooked it on Aunt Prue's stove that evening.

The next morning she took the stew to work with her. She bought the loaf and milk at lunchtime and called round again on her way home that evening. She was walking up their road when a taxi drew up and Connie and John got out.

Connie threw her arms round her in a great bear hug.

'We've had a marvellous time,' she said. 'I've so much to tell you.'

Carrie helped them carry their suitcases up to the flat. 'Everything was wonderful,' John said.

'I can see you've had the sun, John,' Carrie said. 'You've quite a tan.' She and Connie had such fair, translucent skin that they tended to keep in the shade, but even so, Connie's cheeks were pink and she had a luminous golden glow.

Carrie opened the bag she'd brought and took out the pan of stew. 'It only needs heating up.'

'Carrie!' She saw the look of delighted surprise on Connie's face before she gave her another hug.

'How kind of you,' John said, and kissed her cheek. 'We were having our first argument in the taxi. I wanted to have a walk round and look for a fish and chip shop, but Connie thought we should have beans on toast.'

'He said beans wouldn't be enough,' Connie laughed, 'though we've eaten huge meals over the last few days.'

'Thank you,' John said. 'Your stew will please us both.'

'Oh, I have missed you,' Carrie said.

John laughed. 'Connie couldn't stop talking about you, so you can take it she's missed you too. Sorry to come between you, Carrie.'

She pulled a face. 'Somebody was always likely to,' she said, 'and I'd just as soon it was you.'

'Look, why don't we have a day out next Sunday? Go to New Brighton and have some fun? I'll invite a friend to make up a four.'

Carrie forced herself to say, 'No, you'll want to settle in, do things together.'

'No, I mean it. Connie wants to.'

Carrie knew they'd both tried to include her in what they were doing, but this was making her feel a failure. She would have to face up to it.

'John, you must be scraping the bottom of the barrel when it comes to friends to introduce me to.' He'd been doing it over the past year. One or two had taken her to the pictures afterwards, but it had never gone further than that. 'You must give up trying to matchmake.' Pride made her add, 'I'll do it on my own sooner or later.' Though, to be honest, she was almost ready to give up hope. Maybe she'd been cast as another maiden aunt?

'Of course you will,' John said, as though he could read her thoughts. 'You're only nineteen, for goodness' sake. Being a twin must be marvellous when you're a child, but sooner or later you have to set off on your own.'

That sums it up, Carrie thought as she left to walk home.

It gave Carrie the occasional pang that John had started by being *her* friend. They'd had long discussions about bookkeeping and accountancy and the jobs they were doing.

One weekend last summer, she'd gone with Connie on an expedition with the cycling club, and they'd stopped in a park twenty miles from Liverpool to eat their sandwiches. They'd sat near tennis courts and Carrie had watched a game with interest, a doubles match. John had asked if she played.

'Yes, in the park at home.'

'Will you have a game with me next week?' he'd said.

'I'd like to,' she'd replied. Of course, Connie had gone with her, though she didn't care for ball games; she wasn't any good at them. But as with everybody else, John had been drawn to Connie and it was her he really took to. She was thrilled to be marrying him.

Carrie had had to tell herself that it was not betrayal on Connie's part; that she liked John and mustn't resent the fact that he'd chosen her sister. She very much wanted Connie to be happy. Marriage was the natural route through life, and they both wanted that. No way did either want to end up an old maid like Prudence.

One Saturday afternoon three months ago, Carrie had agreed to go shopping with Connie. She needed to buy her going-away outfit and said she wanted a couple of new nightdresses too.

John spent Saturday mornings having lectures, and he called in to see Connie on his way home to fix a time to meet her that evening. She stood talking to him in the hall for the ten minutes it took Carrie to get ready.

'Come on, Connie,' Carrie said when she came down. 'The shops will be closing before we get there.'

'Sorry, sorry.' Connie shot upstairs, leaving her with John.

'Come and sit down,' she said, taking him into the deserted living room. 'That's a huge load of books you carry around.'

He lowered his rucksack from his shoulder.

'Can I see?' Carrie asked.

'You're interested, aren't you?' John asked as she opened one of the books and sat down. 'They're accounting textbooks. I've got to revise. My exams are looming.'

'Yes, I'm interested. As a bookkeeper, they keep me doing the routine bits, and it can get a bit boring. I'd like to move on, learn more. Unless I do, I'll not get promotion.'

She met the gaze of his gentle grey eyes, expecting him to say: but if you want to get married, what's the point? Instead he said, 'You're saying you want to train to be an accountant?'

'I've been thinking about it,' Carrie admitted, 'but I'd have to sign up for five years, wouldn't I? That's an awful long time. I'd be twenty-four before I finished.'

He laughed. 'That's what I did to become a chartered accountant, but there are all sorts of other accountancy exams.'

'Why did you choose to be a chartered accountant, then?'

'Because it's said to be the highest accountancy qualification.'

'Then that's what I want to do. How do I start?'

'You'll have to talk to your father, ask him if he'll pay for you to be articled. I'm afraid that's necessary.'

'Is that what you did? Will it cost a lot?'

'Yes to both, but they'll pay you a little back monthly as pocket money, and after three years, when you're becoming more useful to them, they'll add a bit more to it.'

'Are there many girls doing it?'

'No, I did hear of one, but she only survived two years.'

'What happened, did she change her mind?'

'She wanted to get married.'

'Oh! They don't employ married women?'

'Of course not. She was asked to leave.'

Connie gave that some thought. 'What about the money that had been paid to article her? Did her father get part of that back?'

'I've no idea. She left the day she told them. We articled clerks heard nothing of the details.'

'Aunt Prue would have a fit if I did that to Dad. Such a waste of money.'

31

'If you go ahead, you'll find the work more interesting, but five years is a long, hard slog.'

Carrie pulled a face. 'It's a big decision to make, but a change of job would be a good thing for me now.'

Since Connie had been going out with John, Carrie had made friends with Edna, another bookkeeper who worked at a nearby desk; they went to the pictures after work and sometimes to the swimming baths on Sunday morning. She was afraid she'd lose Edna's friendship if she left her job, but there would be a whole new office staff to make friends with, and if she felt in a rut, which she did, then she must make an effort to get out of it.

The very thought made her shiver. 'With three million on the dole and men willing to do anything to get work, I feel I have to hang on to the job I've got.'

'Well, jobs are not easy to find, but being articled is a little different. You'd be another pair of hands for the firm, and your father would be underwriting the cost to them.'

'But could I find an accountant who'd take me on? As a girl, I wouldn't be anybody's first choice.'

'No, but you do have experience. Three years of double-entry bookkeeping under your belt means you'd be useful from the start. If you're really keen, why don't you make enquiries?'

Carrie tried to decide.

'Atherton and Groves, where I'm articled, is a good firm to work for. There are three partners, because Mr Groves's son was promoted to the partnership a year ago, and I reckon he'll take a pupil on this year. You'll find them all friendly and fair.' John smiled. 'No need to give in your notice until you know he'll take you.'

'I took English and commercial subjects at School Certificate, but will that be enough?'

'You don't have to reach any special educational level. If you get an interview, Mr Groves will be looking to see if you're reasonably bright, and how keen you are to sign up for five years of study. They see accountancy almost as a vocation, on a par with entering the medical profession or the Church. They have strong moral views and will expect the same from you. The firm rates honesty, loyalty and hard work very highly; they'll want to think you have integrity.'

'That's you, John. You have that.'

He pulled a face. 'No, no, I'm falling down on honesty, and I daren't admit it to anyone in the office. I haven't told them I'm getting married; they wouldn't approve of that until I'm qualified. Neither has Connie told the council, and she doesn't intend to, as they don't employ married women. We've had to do it, but I'm articled to Mr Jeremy Groves, and he'd see that as living a lie.'

'The same thing happens to all women,' Carrie sighed. 'It's very unfair.'

'It is, and until we get on our feet, Connie and I need all she can earn. But we men fare no better. Once married, we are supposed to support our wives for the rest of our lives.'

'And your children,' Carrie smiled. 'That's the way of the world, and right now, there's nothing we can do to change it.' She knew her twin was earning three pounds three shillings a week, while she herself was paid only two pounds ten shillings. That hurt a little too; it made her think she'd made the wrong choice when she left commercial school.

'You decide what you want to do, Carrie; go for it and put

your own interests first. I'm sure Mr Groves will think that for a woman, you're very ambitious.' He smiled. 'No doubt he'll warn you off marriage.'

Carrie pondered. 'Well, men aren't exactly lining up to propose to me. It doesn't look as though I'm going to follow Connie's example. At least as an accountant, I'd have a top-notch career.'

'You're too impatient. Sooner or later you'll bowl somebody over and they'll want to rush you to the altar.'

'If I did qualify as an accountant and then got married, would I be able to work?'

'How could I possibly know that?' he laughed. 'I don't know any married women who work: nurses, teachers, secretaries like Connie, they're all asked to resign as soon as they're married. They're said to be taking jobs away from the men.'

'It's a risk I'll have to take. I might have to live in sin, or do the same as you and Connie and keep it quiet.'

That afternoon, Carrie trawled through the big Liverpool shops with Connie looking at clothes, but her mind was full of very different plans for the future.

Things were changing at work. Another tabulating machine of the latest design was acquired for the accounts department, and another girl was taken on to do nothing more than check figures on it. There was plenty of that work for Carrie too, but she found it boring; the last thing she wanted was to do that all day.

Of course what she really wanted was to have what Connie had. Everybody else seemed to have an exciting life, while she was in a rut. At present, she was working in an office where there were fifty girls to every man, and most of the men were already married. It helped her make up her mind. If Connie was going to have a completely new life, so would she.

She went round to see John and told him she was going to take his advice. Together they drafted a letter of application to Atherton & Groves.

Carrie was kept busy at home. Aunt Prue had made a claim on her household insurance policy, and although they had agreed to foot the cost of the new water tank and make a payment towards the cost of redecoration, Carrie felt she had to offer to spend time during the evening and weekends whitewashing the ceilings.

They all bound up their hair and set about the job together, but Prue found she lost her balance painting ceilings, so Carrie and Maud did it together. They spent three weekends on the ceilings, after which Prue decided the walls of the landing, stairs and hall looked shabby and soiled.

They chose the wallpaper together but had to pay a man to come and hang it, as Maud said she couldn't cope with the height on the stairs.

One Sunday, some four weeks after the wedding, Carrie and her aunts were invited to afternoon tea by her father. 'It'll be to introduce his new lady friend,' Maud said.

Carrie was shocked. 'A new lady friend? He's said nothing to me. How long have you known about her?'

'That's your father all over,' Prue bristled. 'He said something at Connie's wedding. I expect he'll ask her too.'

'He met this lady in South Africa,' Maud volunteered. 'Archie came over first, in time for the wedding. She had to stay to sell her house and pack everything up.'

'Why didn't he tell me?' Carrie asked. 'Does this mean he's going to get married again?' It sounded very much like it. This must be why he didn't want her to live with him. He might have said; it wouldn't have seemed so much like a brush-off if he had.

'We don't know, dear,' Maud said. 'He doesn't usually marry them—'

'Maud!' Prue said sharply. 'Please watch your tongue!'

Carrie felt more surprised than ever, and very curious too, but Prue's stern face stopped her asking more questions.

CHAPTER FOUR

T HE COURTNEY FAMILY HOME was in the suburb of Aigburth. After Sunday lunch, Carrie and her aunts got ready to catch the tram to Allerton. 'Come with us,' Prue said to Gladys, who came to lunch most Sundays. 'It'll do you good to get out, and Archie will be pleased to see you.'

'I'll come another time,' Gladys said. 'I feel I need my midday rest today.'

Archie's house was detached, and larger than Prue's, with an elegant open porch and a well-tended garden, a handsome house in a good-class residential area. It looked over Calderstones Park and the name on the gate read 'Brackenridge'.

'Archie's going up in the world,' Maud said. 'This is very nice.'

'I hope he knows what he's doing,' Prue said in a doom-like tone. 'This is far bigger than he needs.'

'He said he was renting to start with,' Maud said, 'to find out if it suits him.'

'I can tell him now that a more modest house would suit him better, especially as he doesn't have a job yet.'

Archie came to the door smiling a welcome. 'Come in all of you and meet Marion.'

He led the way to a sitting room with two large windows. Connie and John were already sitting on the sofa talking to an elegantly dressed middle-aged lady. 'This is Marion Collard,' he said, 'a very special friend of mine. She arrived from Cape Town last week.'

'Hello, Carrie.' Marion stood up and came to kiss Carrie's cheek. 'It's lovely to be here and meet all Archie's family. I've heard so much about you. I was sorry to miss Connie's wedding.'

'You've caught up with us now.' Her father patted Marion's arm, and that gesture made it clear to Carrie why he didn't want her to live with him. It made her feel more alone than ever. Even Dad, at his age, had found romance.

Prue was fishing for information. 'I'm English,' Marion told her, 'born in Wigan. I come from a long line of coal miners, just like you and Archie.'

'Dad, we hardly know anything about your early life,' Connie said, 'though Maud did say you once worked under-ground.'

'Before you were born, I worked for seven years at the coalface in Parkside Colliery in Newton-le-Willows. They were hellish years. Our father spent his working life down a mine, and I was expected to follow in his footsteps.'

'Yes, and he was killed in one too,' Prue said. 'Just a small disaster, didn't make the headlines. An explosion of methane gas caused by a spark.'

'Two killed instantly and four more died later of their injuries,' Archie said. 'Mining is a dangerous business.'

'But we got compensation from the mine owner,' Prue said. 'That's how Mother was able to buy our house. She'd been brought up in Liverpool and wanted to come back.'

'But I couldn't live in it, except on my day off,' Archie told his daughters. 'I had to find lodgings and keep on working in the pit, and so did my brothers. Jobs were not easy to get in those days, and we knew nothing else.'

'But you were promoted to foreman,' Prue interrupted, 'and you did go to night school in the hope you'd get a job above ground.'

'Pie in the sky then, when I married your mother in 1911. Once the Great War started, I volunteered, that got me out. Got your uncles out too, Carrie, and none of us ever went back. We congratulated ourselves on escaping until we found that our experience meant we all ended up digging and maintaining tunnels and trenches for the army.'

'But nobody liked fighting in the trenches,' Carrie said. 'Were you not better off underground?'

'Yes, we soon realised we were safer, though a sniper put a bullet in my leg. That gave me six months at home in Blighty, so I didn't complain too much. Yes, George, Bob and I all survived the war for that reason.'

'Then you went out to South Africa?' Connie wanted to know.

'Yes, you and Connie were well looked after and happily settled with Prue. I had a friend who persuaded me to go with him. Neither of us wanted to cut coal again, if we could possibly avoid it. A great deal depends on who you know, and war threw me amongst men I'd never have met here.'

Marion said, 'My family went to South Africa after the Great War for exactly the same reason. They wanted jobs that allowed them to get away from working underground.'

'But it was the mining industry that employed us both when

we first went out.' Archie took over from her. 'In my case it was gold that was being mined, and for Marion's family it was diamonds.'

'Much more romantic than coal,' Maud said.

'There's nothing romantic about mining, however glamorous the goods being dug out. It's dirty, dusty work underground, but the jobs we were given were largely in the offices above.' Archie nodded at his daughters. 'It was my first taste of middle-class life, and I loved it.'

Marion smiled at Carrie. 'I started work in Kimberley, but after a year or so, I moved to Johannesburg to work in the retail trade. Selling diamonds is much more pleasant, and that's where I met your father. He'd made the same decision.' She was wearing a magnificent necklace of diamonds and pearls with matching earrings.

'I love the jewellery you're wearing.' Carrie had noticed their sparkle immediately. 'Absolutely gorgeous.'

'I love it too,' Marion said. 'Your father designed and made it for me.'

'Is that your job, Dad?' Connie asked.

'Yes, I'm a jeweller, but you knew that.'

'Not that you designed and made things as smart as that. Aunt Prue thought you worked in a jeweller's shop selling the diamonds and—' Carrie broke off as she noticed that Marion was wearing several diamond rings, and also a wedding ring. 'Are you and Dad married?' she asked in surprise.

'I've been a widow for four years,' she said. 'I suppose it's time I left off wearing his ring.'

'Are you going to marry Dad?' Connie asked.

'He's trying to persuade me,' she said with a disarming

smile in Archie's direction.

Carrie heard Prue explode with impatience. 'Isn't it time you got on with it, Archie?'

'Probably,' Marion said lightly. 'I'm ready for my afternoon tea, what about you?'

She served it with some style from a smart new trolley that she wheeled into the sitting room. There was an extravagant array of small sandwiches, scones and bought cakes, but the atmosphere was a little stiff.

When they got up to leave, Prue pushed her head into the dining room to look round. 'Another large, bright room,' she said, 'and a lovely big dining table, ideal for dinner parties.'

As they were making their way to the nearest tram stop, Aunt Prue said, 'I don't know what Archie is thinking of, getting involved with a woman like that.' Her tone was one of condemnation. 'She was dressed to kill, with more glitter than a Christmas tree. Poor taste.'

'I thought she looked rather nice,' Maud said. 'That blue dress suited her, and she was very pleasant to us.'

Prue sniffed, and flicked a bit of fluff from her drab brown coat. 'All those bought cakes, twice the price and not a patch on home baking, but she probably can't. It looks as though it'll take a pretty penny to keep her. Mutton dressed as lamb, and in the present state of the economy, where is Archie going to find a job that will support her too?'

Carrie knew better than to offer opinions that went contrary to Aunt Prue's, but Connie asked, 'Is Marion going to live there with Dad, then?'

'We don't know.' Prue's voice was heavy with disapproval. 'They aren't saying, are they?'

'I thought you whispered that you'd seen a double bed when you went upstairs to the bathroom?' Maud said.

'Shush,' Prue cautioned.

'But it looks as though—'

'We don't know.' Prue's voice rose an octave, and Carrie was left in no doubt that Marion was living with her father, and that her aunt, who considered her to be an innocent young girl with no knowledge of the wicked ways of the world, was trying to protect her from hearing about his moral lapse.

Carrie had been invited to spend the rest of the evening with Connie and John, and share their supper. Their tram came before the one her aunts needed to catch, and as soon as it pulled away, they had a fit of giggles.

'Poor Aunt Prue, she's shocked at what Dad is doing. You'd think Queen Victoria was still on the throne, wouldn't you?'

John sat on the seat behind the twins. 'She's afraid, Carrie, that you might believe it's all right to follow his example.'

Archie reflected that, with Marion listening, he hadn't felt comfortable telling his daughters about how he had met their mother, nor how much he had loved her. It was the summer of 1910 when Archie had met Greta Fielding, a fair-haired eighteen-year-old beauty, and fallen madly in love with her. She had filled his mind with dreams; life with her would be bliss. He couldn't really afford to marry, but he didn't care about money, he didn't care about anything else; he just wanted her. They married on a shoestring the following year and it was all he had hoped for, though they had to scrimp to get by, and Greta, who had never been strong, was frequently ill.

They had a son in 1913, but then it was even harder to

make ends meet. Robert was a frail child. He caught whooping cough that Christmas, and over the following months he fought for his life. In March, when they laid him in his grave, Greta was overcome with grief, and nothing Archie could say or do comforted her. All that summer, war threatened and Archie felt very low. Life had become a struggle.

When war was declared in August, there was a huge outburst of nationalistic fervour. Flags fluttered over hastily set-up army posts where men could volunteer to fight. Military bands played in the streets and children ran along behind. The Kaiser needed a kick up the backside, and every red-blooded man in the country wanted to deliver it. England needed them. The whole country was swept up in a heady mood of optimism. Young men signed up in hordes.

Archie Courtney was caught up in the enthusiasm and immediately felt more alive. All his mining colleagues said it would be their one chance to see something of the world and have a bit of fun, and anyway, the war would be over by Christmas. He and his brothers were in the first wave of volunteers.

They had not expected the army to find their experience useful, or to be directed to dig tunnels and trenches in France. 'This is worse than the south Lancashire coal fields,' they complained to each other. 'At least we had our families round us there and we could live at home.'

It didn't take long for all those who'd signed up to fight to become disillusioned. Life in the trenches was horrifyingly hard, and death seemed frighteningly near. The Courtney brothers could at least console themselves that it was safer underground.

Archie became friendly with Roderick Reinhart, a miner who came from St Helens and had a similar background. They spent the war in the same place doing the same work. They talked and argued both between themselves and with their officers, about the best direction for the tunnels to run, and how to shore them up.

When a sniper put a bullet in Archie's leg, he was hurt badly enough to be sent back to England, and after a month or so in hospital, he went home, where Greta nursed him back to health. After five months, he was declared fit enough to fight again and sent back to the front, but he left Greta pregnant with the twins.

She was ill throughout her pregnancy with a chesty cough. She left the rooms Archie had rented and returned to her family. They looked after her and took care of the babies when they were born. Shortly afterwards, her illness was diagnosed as tuberculosis and she never recovered her strength. She died when they were six months old.

Her sister Jenny took the twins to her own house, but when they were eighteen months old, she too became ill. Archie was given two weeks' compassionate leave to come home to see them, and was prostrated with grief that he couldn't hide.

Prue offered his daughters a home without being asked, and, so that she and Maud could continue to work, she arranged that Archie should pay a small wage to Gladys Nesbit to look after them.

They all knew Gladys; she'd been living next door when the Courtney family had first moved in, and had been firm friends with their mother. She was the nearest thing to a grandmother the twins had known. It was an arrangement that had stood the test of time. Gladys had become virtually a member of the family.

When peace came, Archie was more than ready to return to England. He was eager to see his twin daughters, now thriving and nearly two years old. Prue and Maud invited him to make his home with them, and he set about finding a job that was more to his taste, but there were hundreds of ex-servicemen seeking work, and he had no experience of anything but mining. Gladys continued to care for his daughters even when his payments faltered.

Thinking about that now, he was almost overcome by guilt. He couldn't forgive himself for abandoning Greta to join up, when he could have continued to work in the pit. Like many others, he'd thought that going to war would be an adventure that would get him out of working underground. He'd also abandoned their baby daughters by leaving their care to Prue and Gladys.

For years now it had been on his conscience, like a weeping sore, and guilt had dogged him ever since

Archie left the army having achieved the rank of staff sergeant, while Roderick had been promoted to warrant officer. They kept in touch, and Archie knew that Roderick was having the same difficulty finding work.

Roderick's father was Dutch, but he'd been killed when Rod was two years old. His mother, who was English, had brought him up alone. He was flamboyant in every way, and his voice was loud and carried far.

Rod stood out in a crowd; he was well over six feet tall,

three inches taller than Archie. He was broader, too, although a year younger. He had sapphire-blue eyes sparkling out of a tanned and weathered face, and there was always a slight smile on his lips. He radiated good humour and everybody liked him.

He suggested they meet in a pub, where he showed Archie an advertisement he'd torn from the *Liverpool Echo*, inviting applications for junior management posts in the gold-mining industry in Johannesburg.

The first thing Archie asked was, 'Are you sure that isn't underground work?'

'No, not if it's junior management. And think of the local population. It must be cheaper to employ them; they'll be doing the underground work. It'll get us away from the pits.' Rod was keen. 'It'll be a great adventure.'

'I thought joining the army would do that for us,' Archie said, 'but look where we ended up.'

'But we both survived, didn't we? Come on, let's try South Africa. It could be our big chance.'

Once out in Johannesburg, they'd spent three years working for the same gold-mining company. Yes, they did go down the mines, but only in the capacity of overseer. They were not required to spend all their working hours there, and had office desks too. But Archie rated the gold mines hotter, more claustrophobic and more dangerous than the coal mines at home.

He and Rod began discussing how they could find work that was better paid and more interesting. First Rod and then Archie went to work for the largest jewellery retailer in South Africa. They started behind the counter in the

Johannesburg shop to gain an insight into the business, but they also got experience in repairing jewellery and making up new pieces.

Archie enjoyed handling precious metals and gemstones, and a few years later he got a job with Gordon and Mayell, a company that manufactured jewellery for the retail trade and exported it all over the world. Rod followed him, and for another few years they worked as colleagues again.

Five years ago, Rod had resigned to start a business of his own, and Archie had seen him prosper year on year. He admired what Rod had achieved, but felt he'd done well for himself too. He was interested in fine jewellery and found he had a flare for designing it. He was holding down a job he really enjoyed. He'd started by making up his own designs, but soon he had three assistants working for him who did the easier jobs, and he was getting on well with Tom Bennett, his boss.

He couldn't say he was enjoying a millionaire's existence, but with a comfortable house provided by the firm, servants and a generous salary, he thought himself very comfortable. Most Europeans lived well in Johannesburg, but he could see that Rod now had a very lavish lifestyle: he'd become extravagant, was a big spender and was generous in the extreme.

'How d'you do it?' Archie asked him one day.

'I work for myself,' he said, 'while you are on a set salary. You're good at design and your work makes a profit for your firm, but they retain most of that.'

Archie wasn't sure he was right; he and Rod had friends in common. 'What about Alec Worthing and Tom Kendrick?

They aren't self-employed, but suddenly they seem to have money to throw at the wall too.'

Rod laughed. 'They do a few jobs for me on the side. Moonlighting, you know.'

Archie thought of all the luxury goods he could have if he earned more money. He could buy a house in England, go home to see his girls as often as he wanted, and treat them to anything they asked for. Even go round the world. He asked, half seriously, 'Do you have work you could push my way?'

'D'you mean that? I mean, are you really prepared to work for me?'

'Yes, of course.' Rod and his friends still seemed to have plenty of leisure. 'Why not?'

'I'd have to be able to trust you.'

'Of course you can! You've known me long enough. What would you want me to do? Oh!' He remembered. 'I've signed a contract to say I won't design jewellery for anyone else.'

Rod's bright blue eyes were staring into his. 'That's exactly what I would want. That's what you're good at.'

'Then I'd have to resign and work full time for you.'

Rod smiled. 'Would you need to tell Gordon and Mayell? I mean, you can work in your own home and bring your designs here when you come for a drink. You'd have no reason to alter your routine in the slightest. How would they know?'

Archie said, 'Every designer develops a style of his own, you must know that.'

'I like your style. It's modern, but I don't see it as being recognisably yours. There's lots of similar stuff about.'

'Well, thank you.' Archie felt a bit miffed.

'Come off it, Archie. Your stuff is popular, sells well, and everybody likes it. It's what I'm looking for.'

That mollified him. 'I've played it straight and honest up to now. I thought you did too.'

'Mostly I do.'

Archie said warily, 'Dare I ask what you occasionally do that might not be dead straight?'

Rod laughed easily. 'Well, I have been known to heat gemstones.'

Archie understood exactly why he did that. It was a practice that was forbidden, because genuine gemstones occurred naturally in rock and were sold as a raw material. However, jewellers had been illicitly heating them since medieval times, as that reduced small flaws in rubies and diamonds and made them shine more brilliantly, therefore increasing their value.

'All right, I'll do the odd job for you, as long as it isn't illegal. What exactly do you have in mind?'

He started by designing a few necklaces. He had to make them up at work to see how they turned out, but then he melted the gold down again and returned it to stock. Rod had them made up in his own workshop using top-quality gemstones, and they sold for premium prices.

'Excellent,' Rod said. 'I also want to make jewellery for the mid market, so I need designs to sell at relatively low prices: earrings, rings and necklaces. They must be simple and easy to make and weigh next to nothing. I'll have lots of copies made.'

Archie sometimes saw these designs displayed in shop

windows. He thought he was paid handsomely, and the extra cash was giving him almost everything he wanted.

But there was one thing he lacked, and that was a soulmate to share his good fortune. It had taken him a long time to get over Greta's death, and he found being a widower lonely. He'd sought the company of women when he could, and had had several short liaisons, but none that had stood the test of time. He wanted another wife, an enduring partnership.

He knew the business connection was drawing him more frequently into the glittering group that surrounded Rod. It had taken him time to realise that none were just friends; like him, they all had a business connection. They were Rod's trusted allies, and he was always organising something: weekend trips away to a wildlife park, or boating on some lake or river. He regularly gave parties at his home or hosted lunches and dinners at restaurants. Archie joined in and was enjoying life.

One Sunday, Rod invited him to a buffet lunch to be held round his own swimming pool. It was there that Archie saw Marion Collard for the first time. She had a striking face, and was slim, with an attractive tan and a relaxed manner. He thought she looked wonderful in her scarlet swimsuit and immediately took to her. She seemed to know a lot about diamonds, and she drank quite a lot, but she swam and danced like an athlete. He thought she must be younger than he was but found it difficult to guess her age. He didn't like to ask her outright, so when she left to get dressed, he asked Rod.

He laughed. 'Her age is her big secret; she doesn't tell anybody.' She returned in a red dress that had a quiet elegance about it, but Archie was not pleased when he noticed she wore a wedding ring. 'I see you're married,' he said.

'Not any more. My husband Graham died of cancer four years ago,' she told him.

'How awful!' Archie knew it took a long time to get over things like that. He told her about Greta, his own wife, and the twin daughters he rarely saw. 'One of them, Connie, is hoping to be married in a few months.'

The party went on until dusk and he monopolised her company all day. When the gathering was breaking up, he said, 'Can I drive you home?'

'Thank you,' she said, 'but I have my car and driver here. Can I offer you a lift? We have been given quite a lot to drink.'

'Yes, but I'm getting hungry. I was thinking of going to a little restaurant I know.' Archie took a deep breath. 'I'd like you to come with me.'

She smiled. 'Even better, there's plenty of food at my place. Why don't you leave your car here and take pot luck with me?'

He didn't need persuading.

It was Rod who told Archie later that Marion had risen in the jewellery trade to become an expert at valuing gemstones, especially diamonds, and that she was also doing occasional jobs on the side for him. Archie could see from her elegant grooming that she spent a good part of her income in clothes shops and beauty parlours.

Rod's business was burgeoning. 'I'm thinking of setting up a small offshoot in England,' he told everybody. 'It seems the right time.'

Archie could guess why. Diamond prices, like everything else, had dipped in the worldwide Depression, but now, in the mid 1930s, they were one of the few luxury items rising in value.

'I think we can thank Hitler for that,' Rod said. Like all expatriates, he was very interested in the news from home. 'Diamonds are valuable enough and small enough to hide in a person's clothes, should he need to get away in a hurry.'

Rod arranged a month-long trip to Europe, leaving his manager in charge of his factory. Archie missed the social life, but he had Marion as a companion. There was nothing he enjoyed more than escorting her about town; he was proud to have such an attractive woman on his arm, and thought he was falling in love with her.

His first tentative kisses sent the blood coursing through his veins. Marion was responsive, lifting her face to his, giving him hugs and smiles. They both had years of married life behind them and she soon banished any diffidence he'd felt about making love to her. Soon all their outings ended up at either her house or his, and he felt his life had new meaning. Within a few weeks he was utterly beguiled by her.

Rod returned with tales of the Amsterdam diamond trade. He told Archie he'd taken diamonds there to be cut. 'Make me a few designs for brooches, and I also want something really pretty for a bespoke customer. She wants a very special necklace. She's thinking of one big stone, say up to six carats, surrounded by a lot of small ones. She likes emeralds and rubies as well as diamonds. I'll show her your designs so she can choose.'

In the end, Archie made the piece up in Rod's workshop. He had never made anything quite so valuable before; he set the stones in platinum and worked slowly and carefully. Even he was pleased with the result, and Rod said his customer was delighted.

'I've kept on making up a few of the pieces at Gordon and Mayell,' Archie said, 'partly because I enjoy doing it, and partly because it has taken me a long time to hone that skill, so I don't want to lose it.'

'Very wise,' Rod said.

'Thank you for putting that work my way,' Archie said. 'I enjoyed doing it.'

Some months later, Rod asked Archie and Marion over to dinner. 'It'll be just the two of you,' he said. 'I want to put a business proposition to you.'

Archie was curious and tried to discuss it with Marion. 'He wants the three of us to go to England,' she said. 'It sounds very interesting, but I know no more than you. We'll have to wait to hear his plans.'

As usual, Rod was full of *joie de vivre*, and though Archie tried to steer him towards his business proposal, they had drinks on his terrace followed by a good dinner before he began.

'I've set up a new company in England called the Starbright Jewellery Company,' he said. 'My business has provided the funds, and I want you two to go over and help me start it up and get it running. I've made arrangements for several large jewellers in north-west England to use our services. We will do the work they require on their premises.'

'What sort of work?' Archie wanted to know.

'There'll be some repairs, but they'll also want you to design and make up jewellery to sell in their shops. I'm having diamonds cut in Amsterdam. Marion will be a great help to you – she can put a value on the work and help you make the pieces up – but I want her to concentrate on the paperwork. The jewellers will have to be billed for what you do. She will look after the money side of things.' Archie knew that Marion had done a course in commercial subjects at school but had wanted to work directly with diamonds.

'I've arranged for another man to join us in Liverpool; his name is Bill Dainty, and he's an experienced jeweller. His job will be to help you with the practical work. Archie, I want you to go over first and rent a comfortable house with enough room to accommodate the three of us, and I want you to buy a car so we can get round. Bill Dainty has his own rooms.'

'This is to be permanent, then? I'll have to resign from Gordon and Mayell?'

'Well, it's difficult to say at this stage. Could you get them to agree to a leave of absence? Say six months or so? Then, if Starbright founders, you'll have lost nothing.'

'I don't know if they will.' Archie was doubtful.

'I think they will,' Rod said. 'They won't want to lose you; they're making money from your designs. You've trained others to make them up, so they don't need you there for that.'

'What d'you think, Marion? Can you get leave?'

'It sounds exciting. I'm all for it. I feel in need of a change and I think I could always get another job here if I had to. And so could you, Archie; you've quite a talent for design.'

'When did you say your daughter was getting married?' Rod asked. Archie had spoken often of the twins.

'May the fourth.'

'I could arrange for you to go over in time to be there. It would fit in with what I'm planning, and it's time you had a rest and a decent holiday.'

Archie pulled himself up in his chair and agreed that he would love to see Connie get married.

'Join us, Archie,' Marion urged. 'It'll be great fun.'

'And financially rewarding if all goes well,' Rod smiled.

Archie made up his mind in that instant. 'Count me in,' he said.

CHAPTER FIVE

THREE WEEKS AFTER CONNIE'S wedding, Archie found himself waiting at Lime Street station. The *Union Castle* mail boat had docked in Southampton that morning, and Marion and Roderick were coming up by train. Archie had spent the last few weeks getting ready for them. He'd prepared comfortable bedrooms and stocked up with plenty of luxury food and drink.

He heard the signal drop; the train was about to draw into the station, and he felt a quiver of excitement. The new life they'd planned was about to begin. More important, he was about to be reunited with Marion; he'd missed her terribly.

Rod planned to stay in Europe for about five weeks. He had business affairs here and he wanted to go to Amsterdam to collect the diamonds he was having cut there. He also wanted to see his mother, who had been ill, so he'd only be staying with them for a few days on this occasion.

Rod was larger than life, full of bounding energy and off the train the moment it stopped. He was the first to engage the services of a porter. He wore a panama hat, though the Liverpool sun hardly warranted it, and his abundant blond hair sprouted from under it.

Archie was watching for Marion, but Rod drew him into

an enthusiastic bear hug and was patting his back. 'Hello, how are you? Good to see you. Has everything gone to according to plan?'

'Yes, everything's organised,' he said, and looked round in time to see Marion step down from the carriage, smiling at him and looking wonderful. He took her in his arms and kissed her. 'Marvellous to see you again.'

Rod took charge of everything, as he always did. 'So where have you parked the car? Will we get all this baggage of Marion's into it?' She had a trunk as well as several cases.

'I doubt it.'

Before Archie realised what he was doing, Rod had summoned a taxi and asked for the luggage to be loaded into that. 'It can follow us,' he said. He opened the car door for Marion and ushered her into the front seat. He himself climbed into the back and didn't stop talking all the way to the house.

'You've done well,' he told Archie. 'In a good-sized plot so the neighbours aren't too close, and it's well back from the road.'

'You said pick a quiet spot.'

'Yes, you have.' He approved of what he saw inside, too. 'You haven't hired any help?' They were all used to domestic servants in South Africa.

'You said not to, but I thought perhaps a cleaner?'

'No, better not, they can get curious and poke around.' Rod had also suggested they eat mainly at home rather than become regulars at the local hotels and restaurants.

Archie helped Marion carry her suitcases upstairs. 'There are four bedrooms,' he said, 'and they're all doubles. This is mine,' he flung open a door, 'and I'm hoping you'll share it with me. There are two wardrobes here. I chose it because of that.'

Marion cast a cursory glance round. 'Let me see the others. Rod expects us to have a room each. I'll accept an invitation to join you in that bed from time to time, but for now, I'll settle for this room.' She dropped the suitcase she'd brought up on to the bed.

Archie was disappointed. Rod understood that Marion was his girlfriend. 'I'd expected . . . This is our new life, after all.'

'Perhaps later, when Rod has gone. Is there a decent room for him?'

'Yes, with a big bay window at the front.'

Archie had known that, once Marion and Rod joined him, he'd be kept busy. Rod moved a chair to the hall table and opened a file on it. For the next hour, he commandeered the telephone, and his voice could be heard all over the house making appointments for them.

When he'd finished, he said, 'I must tell you about one special jeweller who is something of a friend. You'll like him. He's helped me get this group together and organise things. If you have problems when I've gone, he'll help you deal with them. He's anxious to meet you and has invited us all round to his place for something to eat and a chat, but I've rung him and he's a bit tied up at the moment.

'It seems his family lives in Wales but his wife and youngest son are in Liverpool, staying at his flat at the moment. We need to put off meeting him until they've gone back home.'

Archie had foreseen that it might fall to his lot to put a meal on the table on the first night; they wouldn't feel like going out after travelling all day. He'd been fending for himself over the last few weeks and felt he could cope with the English domestic routine.

'There'll be an extra person for dinner tonight,' Rod informed him. 'I've asked Bill Dainty to come round to meet you and Marion.'

Archie was glad he'd bought a leg of lamb for their first meal. He lit the oven and put the joint in with some potatoes to roast, then went upstairs to see if Marion would help with the cooking, but she was sprawled on her bed and seemed to be asleep. Her clothes and belongings were scattered everywhere, still waiting to be put away.

Some time later, the doorbell rang twice, and as neither of the others stirred, Archie left the beans he was de-stringing to answer it. The man on the doorstep looked a bit of an underdog. He was shabbily dressed, in his mid fifties, painfully thin and rather bent.

'Hello,' he said, 'I'm Bill Dainty.'

'Come in,' Archie said. 'We're expecting you for dinner.'

'Excellent. Rod didn't mention that, he just said to come. It smells good.'

Rod took over, ushering Bill into the sitting room and pushing a glass of Scotch into his hand. Marion came down to join them, and Archie could hear the three of them laughing and talking. It made him feel left out. As soon as he'd set the table, he made haste to join them. Rod, always ready to play host, pressed a drink on him, but Archie knew he'd be expected to serve the meal and couldn't relax.

Once the food was on the table, Rod took over the carving and became the life and soul of the party. Archie had bought a blackcurrant tart at a bakery to follow, and implied he'd made it himself. He'd also bought a variety of cheeses. Bill Dainty tucked into everything as though it was his first meal of the day. They all praised his cooking, though Archie saw lumps in the gravy.

While they ate, Rod explained his plans for them and the appointments he'd made for the next few days. 'I've arranged for us to visit the jewellers who've signed up for my Starbright business, so I can introduce you to the people you'll be working for and you'll know where their shops are. They need to know you and you need to know them. I hope they'll show you the stock they want you to work on, but in any case you'll have to go back to do it when I've gone.'

He produced a list of shops and opened maps across the tablecloth. 'You'll need to write down directions, Marion, so you'll have no trouble finding them again.'

'What sort of work have you arranged for us?' Bill asked.

'There could be a few repairs and some polishing up. It'll be well within your capabilities.'

'I'm sure,' he said drily. He looked in poor health, his face grey and his hair sparse and thin, but he had a good sense of humour and seemed to get on well with Rod.

'And for me?' Archie asked.

'The same, of course. You'll have to help with the general work as well. I'll fix up the bespoke stuff later.'

At midnight, the party was broken up when Bill said it was time he went. It was raining, so he put on a yellow oilskin cape and prepared to cycle home.

'We'll pick you up at ten,' Rod told him, opening the front door.

'OK, but don't come to the house where I have rooms,'

Bill said. 'I'll be waiting at the end of the road.'

Rod headed straight upstairs to bed, which didn't please Archie, because the table was still laden with leftover food and dirty dishes, but Marion helped him get things under control.

'Having no domestic help isn't going to be easy on us,' she said. 'It's asking too much. We'll eat out from time to time, once Rod goes away.'

'Come to my bed,' he invited as they went upstairs. After all these weeks away, he needed her presence.

'I'm whacked, Archie,' she said. 'Not tonight.'

The next morning, Archie muddled through making breakfast for Rod and Marion, but he didn't like the way they chatted at the table while he did it. Rod decided to take over the driving. They picked up Bill Dainty and drove through the tunnel under the Mersey. It had only been opened last year and they thought it amazing. He took them to a jeweller's shop in Birkenhead and introduced them to the owner, who unlocked his workroom and ushered them inside.

'This is where I do repairs,' he said. 'You'll find everything you need here.'

Rod said, 'Let's see what you've got for us.'

The jeweller brought out a box containing a mixture of rings, bracelets, necklaces, brooches and earrings. The others set about examining them.

Archie looked them over, feeling uneasy; this wasn't the sort of stock he'd expected. He was surprised, because Rod usually dealt in high-quality goods. 'Not top of the market,' he said.

Marion said, 'Normal stock for a shop like this.'

'It's not all in for repair?' Archie asked.

'No,' they told him.

'But it is all second hand?'

'Of course.' Bill Dainty looked at him in surprise. 'It's the usual stuff.'

'What d'you want us to do with it?' Archie asked.

'Polish it up, make it all look like new,' Marion said. 'No girl wants to think a stranger has worn her engagement ring before her, so there's practically no second-hand market.'

Archie knew that was true. He also knew it was impossible to sell second-hand rings as new ones.

'Right,' Rod said, 'we'll move on then.' They said goodbye to the owner. 'Marion will phone you to let you know when the boys will come and do the work,' he said.

Back in the car, he went on, 'There are two shops in Chester I want to take you to, and others in Nantwich and Warrington. Tomorrow we'll do Southport and Ormskirk. I'm not going to have time to introduce you to all the contacts on my list now, but there'll be plenty of work you can start on. As I've said, my mother is ill and I want to spend a couple of nights with her in St Helens before I go on to Amsterdam. When I come back, I'll have time to take you round the rest of the shops I've signed up.'

'Wouldn't your mother like to go back to Johannesburg with you for a holiday?' Marion asked.

While she and Rod discussed that, Archie sat on the back seat with Bill Dainty, musing on the collection of jewellery he'd just seen. He'd worked in the trade long enough to think he knew it inside out. He'd seen that Rod was making his fortune, and he'd already been persuaded to bend the rules in regard to his contract with Gordon and Mayell, but what he suspected now was going too far. He should have foreseen where this could lead. He should have started asking questions before now.

'Here we are, this is the next shop,' Rod said. 'It's Mr Ball here.'

'Mr Ball,' Marion said, writing it down.

Archie guessed that this visit would be much the same as the last. He knew that all he had to do was ask Rod where all this jewellery came from, but the words stuck in his throat. He couldn't bring himself to do it; he was scared he'd have his worst suspicions confirmed, and what would he do then?

He was very much afraid that what he'd seen was stolen jewellery; that he'd got himself involved in illegal activities. The service Rod's business seemed to offer was fencing. What a fool he'd been to get himself in this position, and what about Marion? He'd put her in danger too. He needed to talk to her about this, but they'd rarely been alone since she'd arrived. He wished he knew how to get them both out of this mess.

Carrie had to wait two weeks for a reply to her letter of application, but as John had predicted, she was invited to come for an interview. She showed him the letter. 'Yes, it's from young Mr Groves, Mr Leonard. If you get in, you'll be articled to him; he'll be your mentor and arrange your training. I like him, he'll be more go-ahead than the others. You might have struck lucky.'

When the day came, Carrie was a bag of nerves but told herself she must smile. She needed to look more confident than she felt. She wanted this chance.

Atherton & Groves had a suite of offices in a prestigious building in Liverpool's financial centre. She found her way up in the lift after studying the names printed in gold on a large board in the entrance hall. She let herself into their outer office six minutes before the appointed time.

John had explained that the first person she'd see would be Miss Woodford, the elderly receptionist. She was talking to a young man carrying an armful of files. Carrie introduced herself.

'Ah, yes, Miss Courtney,' the receptionist said, 'we are expecting you. Both the Mr Groveses will interview you; I'll let them know you're here. Please take a seat.'

The young man smiled at her. 'Are you coming for a job? We're definitely in need of new blood here, young people with a bit of go in them.'

Carrie smiled at him. He seemed friendly and attractive; he had thick, rather untidy chestnut hair in need of a trim. At first glance, he was the sort of man she'd be happy to work with.

'Come this way, please,' Miss Woodford told her. 'They'll see you now. They're in Mr Jeremy Groves's office.'

Carrie followed her to a large, rather dark office, where two men got to their feet to greet her. 'Do come in, Miss Courtney, and have a seat. We are the two Groveses – father and son. I am Jeremy Groves.' He was a stout middle-aged gentleman with a puffy face and bags under his eyes. He wore heavy-rimmed spectacles with thick lenses. 'And this is my son Leonard, who is now a partner in this firm.' Leonard was a tall, confident-looking man in his thirties, standing as straight as a guardsman.

'Good afternoon,' Carrie said. The two men sat down side by side; she was separated from them by the wide mahogany desk. Her letter of application was open in front of them.

The younger man spoke first. 'So you're hoping to be articled to me?' He had straight dark hair and intense eyes that seemed to miss nothing. 'Tell me a little about yourself. You're employed at the moment as a bookkeeper?'

That was the start of what felt like a grilling about her circumstances. They encouraged her to talk at length about her job and her training at Skelly's. They delved deeper to find out about her present employer and what she actually did.

'Do you use a tabulating machine? Often? You're fully familiar with them?' Carrie felt on firm ground with machines.

'What do you know about petty cash accounts? Tell me about the sorts of daybooks you are familiar with.' When one ran out of questions, the other started. All the time she was struggling to answer, she could feel two sets of eyes searching her face. She hardly had time to think.

'How far do you go with your bookkeeping? Can you manage an account up to the trial balance stage?' They went on to discuss profit-and-loss accounts and almost lost her.

Carrie was glad when they moved on to her interests and how she spent her spare time. She talked about tennis and was able to list cycling and music, thanks to Connie's enthusiasms. They asked about her friends and her family and whether her father would be willing and able to fund her training.

'I haven't yet asked him,' she said, 'but I think he'd be able to.' She told them she had an identical twin and they asked if she was a bookkeeper too. 'No, she preferred to do secretarial work and has a job with the council.' She told them she knew John Bradshaw, one of the articled clerks, because he was her sister's boyfriend, and that he'd advised her to apply. John had reminded her that on no account must she tell them he was her brother-in-law.

'Ah, John Bradshaw, a capable young man,' Mr Groves junior said. 'He's articled to my father.'

'He told me that this was a good place to work.'

'We'd like Mr Atherton to meet you,' the younger man said. 'I'll just see if he's free.' He pulled the telephone on the desk towards him and spoke into it. His father leaned back in his chair to rest; the puffy eyes were lost in thought.

Carrie was relieved to have a break and looked round. In this office, she felt she'd stepped back in time. The furniture was dark and heavy; oil paintings in ornate gilt frames almost covered the walls. All were of senior-looking executives dressed in formal suits, waistcoats and ties, like Mr Groves. She thought they could be retired members of the firm. Everything seemed very old-fashioned and bore little resemblance to the modern office where she currently worked.

Moments later the door flew open and in strode a much older man with a bald and shiny head. The puffy eyes opened. 'Ah, this is Mr Atherton, our senior partner. We all like to see and discuss any new entrant to the firm.'

He meant vet them, Carrie thought, and the grilling started again, covering some of the same ground. She told them about being brought up by her maiden aunts because her father had been abroad. Like everybody else, they were interested to hear that he'd worked in the gold mines of South Africa, and they gleaned from her every last detail she knew about what he did. Carrie had noticed that for those who spent their lives in the centre of dusty old Liverpool, the thought of living abroad and working in a gold mine seemed wildly exotic and adventurous.

Young Mr Groves came back to her first. 'Are you happy in your present job?'

'Yes,' she said, 'but I would like to progress, learn more about accounting, do more interesting work.'

'Should I decide to take you on,' he said, 'you would have to sign a contract of articles of clerkship. That means five years of study.' They all smiled at her benevolently. 'I'll think it over and let you know.'

Old Mr Groves said, 'Thank you for coming. I'll ring for someone to show you out.'

Carrie stood up, feeling dazed as well as exhausted. The interview was at an end, but it had taken more than two and a half hours. The young man she'd seen earlier with the receptionist came. She followed him down corridors to the outer door, which he held open for her.

His brown eyes blazed with golden sparks as they looked straight into hers. She felt a huge tug of attraction. 'When do you start?' he asked. She blinked at him. 'You did get the job?'

'Young Mr Groves is going to write and let me know,' she told him, 'when he's made up his mind.'

'He'd be a fool not to take you on.'

Carrie sauntered to the tram stop. She had another reason now to want to move to Atherton & Groves.

CHAPTER SIX

A S HER FATHER HAD A telephone in his new house, Carrie rang him the next day. 'When would be a good time for me to come to see you? There's something I need to tell you. Ask you, I mean.'

'Oh, what? Is something the matter?'

'No, Dad. I can't talk about it on the phone. Would it be OK if I came on Sunday?'

'Yes; better bring your aunts to tea or Prue will complain she's being left out. Unless, of course, you want to keep them in the dark?'

'No, no, I've talked about it to them. We'll come round about three then. Thank you.'

When Carrie told Aunt Prue of the invitation, she immediately jumped to the wrong conclusion. 'Archie is probably going to announce that he intends to marry.'

'No,' Carrie said, 'I need to ask him to pay for me to be articled.'

Sunday turned out to be such a sunny day that Prue got out her street map and they walked to Allerton. Marion let them in wearing her diamonds again, and looking every inch the lady of the house. The sitting room now appeared comfortable and elegant; tasteful lamps and ornaments had been added to the decor. The tea trolley was laden as before. Carrie thought everybody else seemed more relaxed, but she felt on edge. She wasn't sure that her father would be willing to pay out a considerable sum on her behalf.

'So what did you want to discuss with me?' Archie asked, beaming at her as he filled a plate with cake.

'I'd like to have more training,' she said. 'Become a chartered accountant. It takes five years.'

'Good Lord! Would you do that at night school?'

'Partly, but there's also lectures on Saturday mornings and a correspondence course, plus a weekend residential course once a year.'

'I'm all for you gaining more qualifications, Carrie, but five more years of study? What's wrong with the job you've got? I thought you liked it.'

'I do, but I want to advance, learn to do more. As a bookkeeper, I'll always be junior to an accountant.'

'Well, if you're that ambitious, I'd say go ahead.'

Carrie took a deep breath. 'Dad—'

Prue cut in with enthusiasm. 'I quite agree. One never knows what lies ahead, and if Carrie can become qualified and support herself at a professional level, that is to be commended.'

'Yes, well, I don't see how that involves me,' Archie said. 'You must know that if it's what you want to do, I wouldn't stop you.'

'Dad, I'm not sure yet whether I'll be given the chance to do it, but if I am, I'm afraid I'll need you to pay for me to be articled.'

'Articled? What's that?' Archie's slice of sponge cake was suspended halfway to his mouth.

'A sort of apprenticeship; I'll have to sign a five-year contract of articles of clerkship, and I'll need you to support me.'

'Good God! I thought I'd got you off my hands,' but he was smiling at her and she knew he was half joking. 'How much will that cost? '

'Quite a lot, I'm afraid, but most will be returned to me in monthly payments as pocket money.'

'Pocket money! That makes it sound as though you'll be working unpaid for five years. You're earning a wage now, with annual increments; do you really want to go back to that?'

'She does,' Aunt Maud said. 'She'll have long hours of study, and miss out on a lot of fun, but won't it be worthwhile in the long run?'

'Of course it will,' Prue said. 'You gave Connie money to get married; it's only fair you do this for Carrie.'

'It's not just the money, for heaven's sake, Carrie: by next year you'll want to get married as well.'

'I won't be allowed to, Dad. You know married women aren't allowed to work.'

'Then why put yourself in that position now? Won't you want to do what Connie has done? Isn't marriage and motherhood what every woman wants?'

'There are other things in life, Dad! Anyway, nobody is trying to rush me to the altar.' It hurt to point that out, but it was true.

'If no would-be husband presents himself,' Prue agreed primly, 'as happened to Maud and me, then wouldn't Carrie be in a much better position in life if she did this?'

'She's not even twenty, for God's sake, and a good-looking

girl. She's got everything ahead of her.' Archie had gone red in the face. 'Half the men of your generation were killed off in the war; that's why you and Maud didn't find husbands. It's different now.'

'It's what I want, Dad,' Carrie said quietly. 'It's what John did, and you rated him good husband material because of it.'

He turned on her. 'Did he put you up to this?'

She ignored that. 'I might not even be given the chance to do it. I've had an interview with an accountant, but he's yet to decide whether he'll take me on.'

'This isn't coming at a good time for you,' Maud said sympathetically to Archie, 'not when you're still looking for a job. We know you have all the expense of setting up a new home and settling in a different country.'

Marion smiled at Carrie, then turned to Archie and patted his arm affectionately. 'Darling, you know you should do it,' she said quietly. 'It's your duty as a father and only fair after all.'

Every eye turned on Archie. He smiled. 'Of course it is. All right, Carrie, if you can persuade this man to take you on, I will do my duty.'

'Thank you, Dad.' She leapt across the room to kiss him, but she knew she owed gratitude to Marion too. She wished Dad would marry her; she couldn't remember her mother, and would welcome a stepmother.

Archie had worried for days. Marion had not come to his bed, and worse, she and Rod seemed on friendlier terms than he remembered. Several times he heard them discussing the

71

system Rod wanted her to use to keep records of the work they were going to do, but he found it difficult to understand all the details.

At least in the mornings Marion helped him decide what food must be bought to provide meals for the next twenty-four hours, and it was she who got Rod to stop outside the shops they needed to go to. Usually they left Rod reading the newspaper in the car, and Marion and Archie would go into the shop. 'Those pork chops look nice,' she'd suggest. 'You know how to cook them? And perhaps we should get some steak for tomorrow.'

One day Bill Dainty wasn't waiting at the end of his street when they stopped to pick him up. 'What a bind,' Rod said. 'Archie, could you try and find him?'

'I think he lives at number forty-seven,' Marion added.

Archie looked down the street of small terraced houses. He knew he was in an area of Toxteth known as the Welsh Streets; his mother had had relatives living here once. It had been designed by a distinguished Welsh architect and built by Welsh builders in the 1870s, and had been largely populated by Welsh families who had come to Liverpool to find work.

The knocker on the door of number 47 was hanging loose but was still usable. The place looked dirty and run-down. The landlady came to the door wearing a soiled pinafore. 'Yes,' she said, 'Bill Dainty has a room upstairs, but I don't think he's up yet.'

At that moment, Archie saw him clattering down the bare boards of the staircase. He was half dressed, with a greyish towel over his shoulder and a piece of soap in his hand. He looked bleary-eyed, as though he had a hangover.

'Sorry,' he said, 'had a bad night.'

Archie felt sorry for him. 'Go back to bed,' he told him. 'We're only going to go round the jewellery shops where we'll later return to work. I can't see it matters if they don't meet you now.'

'No, I've got to keep this job. Hang on a moment, I'll just rinse my face and get more clothes on.'

'Don't worry. I'll tell Rod you're ill.'

'No, I'm coming. Really I am.'

'OK, as fast as you can then.'

Bill disappeared in the direction of the kitchen sink. Archie assumed there was no bathroom in the house. After his years in South Africa, this standard of living made him wince. He didn't want to see any more and walked slowly back to the car.

'Bill isn't well; he's overslept but he's coming now,' he reported.

Rod was bristling with impatience. 'I hoped he'd be more reliable than this.'

'Give him five minutes,' Marion said, stretching lazily in the front seat.

Bill came jogging towards them but had made no effort to comb his hair. 'Sorry, boss,' he panted, 'my alarm clock didn't go off.'

Rod was pursing his lips. 'Buy another,' he said. 'You've got to keep to time. We can't be waiting around for you.'

'I'm very sorry about this. It won't happen again.'

He was coughing so much, Marion handed him one of the cough sweets she kept in her elegant lizard-skin handbag.

73

Archie thought he looked pathetic, but, like him, Bill wasn't expected to contribute much to the rounds they did.

Once they returned home in the late afternoon, Marion would make a cup of tea for them all, and when Archie got up to prepare the dinner, she and Rod would drain the teapot and then carry on with a stronger drink. Archie was finding the days long and exhausting. Rod always wanted to stay up late, while Archie felt dead dog tired by eleven o'clock. He hated going to bed leaving them talking and laughing, but he had to do it or fall asleep in the chair. He'd hear them come up together very much later, and have the awful fear that Marion was going to Rod's room.

He was becoming stupidly jealous and imagining things. He had to tell himself that Marion would never do such a thing. She'd said she loved him. She'd shown it too.

Today was the day Rod had arranged to go off and see his mother, and for Archie it had been a long time coming. This morning Rod had brought his suitcase with him, and after a morning spent going round some shops in Manchester he said, 'You've met most of our clients now. We'll finish off when I come back from Amsterdam.'

Once back in Liverpool, Rod stopped to drop Bill off and said, 'Seven tonight all right?' To Archie he said, 'We'll have a bite of lunch and then you can drop me at a railway station so I can go home.'

It was almost one o'clock when Rod shook Archie's hand and kissed Marion's cheek and wished them luck. Flooding with relief, Archie got into the driving seat. Now that he was alone with Marion, he needed to explain why he was so anxious and see what she thought. They needed to sit down and talk.

They must decide what to do about things.

'Not now,' Marion said as she settled into the seat beside him. 'We need to go back to that row of shops we passed about half a mile back. There's nothing left to eat in the house. We need to buy eggs and bacon and get something to put in sandwiches. You heard what Rod said, he's fixed up for us to start work in that shop we visited in Woolton. We'll go home and have an hour or two on the bed. The owner is expecting us to work tonight.'

Archie felt terrible; there was only one reason why they were going to work at night. And worse, it shocked him to find that Marion fully understood the situation and seemed happy to go along with it.

'Yes, it's safer that way. No staff around wondering what we're doing.'

Archie had thought that, once Rod went, they could relax and not rush round so much, but Marion was equally eager to organise him. At six she got him off his bed and cooked him egg and bacon. He found it a struggle to get it down, but Marion ate with gusto. For work like this, Archie noticed, she wore no jewellery but her watch.

They went to pick Bill up from the end of his road; he'd always been on time since that first occasion. While Archie drove, Marion directed him to the jeweller's shop from the notes she'd scribbled when Rod had taken them there.

The owner locked the door behind them as soon as they were in, and took them upstairs to show them where they could make a hot drink. 'Will you stay until morning?'

'Very early morning,' Marion said. 'We want to be away before anybody else is up.'

'Good; wake me when you're ready to leave,' he told them. 'I've brought my sleeping bag. I'm going to bed down in my storeroom.'

He took them to his workroom, showed them where everything was kept, and brought out a tray covered with the sparkling jewellery Archie was getting used to seeing. 'Twenty-seven pieces, here's my list.'

'This should keep us busy,' Marion said. 'We'll need another chair, and another lamp so we can see what we're doing.'

She sat down at the workbench, opened the bag she'd brought and took out a pad of paper and a pencil together with her loupe. 'You can check them off on the list and note down how long we spend on each one.' She pushed the pad towards Archie.

'I don't like the idea of being locked in,' he said.

'It's the safest way.'

The owner returned with the extra chair and lamp, and Archie brought the tray of jewellery closer and sat down. 'These are all modern pieces,' he said. 'Average stuff, middle of the market.'

'Not so easy to trace,' Marion said. 'There's a lot of quite similar stuff. The assay marks are very small on jewellery; we can try altering them, the object being to hide the fact that they are stolen and, if feasible, make the piece seem more valuable at the same time. Or we can eradicate the mark and put on a new one. That of course means more work, so the piece has to be worth the trouble.'

Archie was shocked by her matter-of-fact manner. Did this mean she'd done it many times before? 'We're handling stolen property, aren't we?'

'Of course.' Marion glared at him. 'What did you think you were going to do?'

He had a sinking feeling in his stomach. 'The same as I did in Johannesburg.'

'You said you wanted more money, didn't you?'

'Yes, but I didn't realise . . .'

'Come on, Archie, you aren't that naive. Let's get going. This is one for you, Bill, to get you started.' She lifted her loupe to her eye. 'An eighteen-carat gold solitaire diamond ring. Modern, marked 1928 in London, round brilliant cut, clear white, about half a carat, with slight occlusions.'

Archie was a bag of nerves. He'd known Rod for over twenty years and had seen he was making his fortune; he knew he could bend the rules a little, but it hadn't occurred to him that he was fencing stolen property. That was a criminal offence, and now Archie himself was up to his neck in the thick of it. What a fool he'd been.

'Have you written that down?' Marion wanted to know. 'We've got to bill this fellow when we've done his work.'

Archie was all thumbs and had to ask her to repeat what she'd said. She'd given the ring to Bill; now she snatched it back, adding: 'Eradicate the assay mark.'

She picked up another ring, 'I hope you're good at this, Archie,' she said.

'I've never tried.'

'Well, you'll have plenty of practice now. We send it all to the assay office in Chester or Birmingham and they have to believe it's newly made. So you need to do a perfect job every time.'

Archie felt sick. 'If I don't?'

'Then you'll have to take the stone out, melt the gold down and start again.'

That week, Carrie received a letter telling her that Mr Leonard Groves was offering to take her on as an articled clerk. She was thrilled. He urged her to discuss the matter with her father and bring him to another meeting. A draft of the contract was enclosed, together with a document setting out the conditions, and she was asked to write a letter of acceptance.

It took time, more correspondence and several appointments to settle the matter, and Mr Groves did point out that written into her contract was the proviso that she must not marry whilst she was in training. Each time she went to the office she looked out for the attractive young man who had been so friendly, but she didn't see him again. At last the contract was signed and she had a date to start at Atherton & Groves.

The first morning, Miss Woodford said, 'Young Mr Groves will not be in the office this morning, so his father will have a word with you to start you off.'

Carrie was ushered into his presence, and he levered his bulk out of his chair to greet her. 'I'm pleased to welcome you to our firm,' he told her in his slow, pedantic manner, 'and to tell you a little bit about it.

'Atherton and Groves is a partnership of professional accountants. The senior members are all chartered accountants, and my son Leonard will oversee your training to become one. But you will also find certified accountants and cost and works accountants working here as well.

'We act as accountants to a large number of small local

businesses and as auditors to larger companies, both public and private, who employ their own accountants. All limited companies have by law to be registered at Companies House and file their audited accounts annually. Their taxes are based on those figures. Some of the work is done in our office, but it is usual for a team to visit the client's premises and work there.

'I have asked one of our managers, Mr Heatherington, to start you off. He will control the work you're given and answer your queries. We ask you to be flexible, tackle whatever job you're given, and apply yourself to your studies. As you've already had some training, and three years' experience of bookkeeping, you may find some of the work familiar to you, but do ask for help when you need it.

'I'll ask Timothy Redwood, another member of our staff, to explain our routine and show you where everything is kept.' He rang a bell, and the young man with the tousled hair appeared. Carrie was pleased to see him. He beamed at her.

'Miss Courtney is joining us. My son has taken her on as an articled clerk,' he said. 'She has the advantage of having considerable experience as a bookkeeper, and I've no doubt she'll prove to be an asset.'

To Carrie he said, 'Timothy has been working as an articled clerk for a few months; he'll show you round and introduce you to everyone.'

'Uncle Jeremy,' Tim said downheartedly, his smile slipping, 'I've been working here for over a year now.'

'Tut tut, of course you have. Time goes so quickly, doesn't it? I'd like you to look after Miss Courtney until she finds her feet.'

Tim's brown eyes surveyed her warily. 'I thought you were coming to replace Miss Haddon, Mr Atherton's secretary?'

She shook her head.

'No, Timothy, as I said, she's a fellow articled clerk.' Mr Groves smiled at Carrie. 'I'm sure you'll fit in very well, my dear.'

She stood up to follow Tim out of the office. 'I can't believe it,' he said, as soon as the door closed behind them. 'A girl like you articled to Len? Whose idea was that?'

'Mine, of course,' she said.

Carrie was afraid she'd been wrong about Timothy Redwood. He was the opposite of friendly this morning.

He eyed her wild hair. 'But you look like a schoolgirl who'd be more at home on the hockey field than in an audit office. I don't suppose anybody will take you seriously.' She was shocked.

They met John in the corridor outside his office. 'Hello, Carrie. Welcome to the firm. I'm glad I've caught you, I was going to take you out for a bite of lunch on your first day, but I'm being sent out of the office today. All the best.'

'You've got a boyfriend here?' Tim asked.

'No, my sister's boyfriend.'

He took her to a large room with a couple of dozen desks occupied mainly by men, though there were six women. They were all eyeing her with great interest. 'This is Miss Courtney,' Tim said in a loud voice. 'She's joining the firm as another articled clerk.'

'Carrie,' she said faintly, but Tim was reeling off the names of all the people there and they were nodding and smiling at her. The two secretaries, Miss Hancock and Miss

Markham, both seemed quite elderly to her, and something in the mould of Aunt Maud. There were four younger women: two comptometer operators, Phoebe and Ruth, and two typists.

'I'll have a desk brought up for you,' Tim said, 'but first I'll introduce you to your manager. His office is over here.'

Mr Heatherington was thirtyish, tall and good-looking. Carrie found him both patient and kind; his explanations of what he wanted her to do were clear and concise and he gave her some very easy work to start with. Too easy and simple really; as a bookkeeper, she'd moved well beyond this point. Her desk was squeezed in behind Tim's and in front of those occupied by Ruth and Phoebe.

The ladies made an effort to be friendly, especially Ruth, who told her that Mr Heatherington was married with two children, and that Tim Redwood was a spoilt relation of a senior partner. Carrie found her first day unnerving and felt a little lost. Some of her male colleagues came to chat her up, but not all repeated their names and she couldn't work out who they were or what they did.

Phoebe said, 'You're very brave to take articles and face five long years of study and exams. They won't let you get married, you know.'

Ruth added, 'We can't see the point of tying yourself down like that. Don't you want to get married?'

'Well, I want to eventually, but I have no one in mind.'

'But you could have, long before your five years is up.'

One man did make an impression on Carrie; he came to her desk and said, 'I'm Daniel Devereaux.' He had come-hither eyes that wouldn't leave her face and was flashily dressed.

'What a bit of luck to find they've taken on a girl like you,' he said. 'You and I could have some good times. Are you doing anything on Saturday night?'

'Yes,' she said, 'I'm booked up.' She didn't like the look of him; he was altogether too brash.

When he returned to his own desk, Phoebe came over. 'You haven't agreed to go out with him, have you? Danny Devereaux is the office Lothario, a fast worker. When he gets you on your own, you'll be fighting him off. He's tried it on with all of us. He's no great catch, either; he's a bookkeeper of twelve years' experience and always will be. Better to give him a wide berth.'

Carrie was summoned to see Leonard Groves, who explained that she would be given some work to do in the office, but mostly she'd be taken out as the junior member of a team of four clerks, all with varying amounts of experience, to work at the premises of a client. She would either help draw up the accounts of a smaller business, or audit the accounts of a larger one. The members of the team would keep changing, according to who was available and who had experience in the trade of the client.

Many of the clients had businesses in Liverpool, but some were in the towns of south Lancashire. Carrie thought she would enjoy getting out and about instead of being stuck in the same office every day, and she hoped she'd get used to working in factories against the clatter of machinery.

Her first week at Atherton & Groves passed slowly, and she started her studies by being enrolled in a correspondence course. Because she had three years' bookkeeping experience, she began by thinking it was easy.

The first time she was taken out was to a small factory assembling bicycles. She knew nothing about bikes and nobody in the team, but they were friendly and helpful. She felt she got on well with the other members, as her bookkeeping experience meant she could work quickly and had some understanding of what she was asked to do. She went on to help audit the accounts of a chain of shoe shops and then to draw up the accounts of a factory making matches. She really enjoyed seeing how different businesses functioned.

So far, all she'd seen of Tim Redwood was an occasional back view of him hunched over his ledgers if he was at his desk. They hadn't worked together in the same team. When she saw him on her tram one morning, she said hello, but he was staring out of the window and appeared not to see her. She had to pass him to sit further down the tram, and was conscious of what felt like his unfriendly gaze on her back throughout the journey. He made haste to get off as soon as they reached their destination, and she saw him stride away to the office as fast as he could.

He didn't always catch the same tram home in the evenings, but when he did, he ignored her then too, waiting in line engrossed in the *Evening Echo*. She didn't like that and couldn't believe she'd thought him friendly when she'd met him on the day of her interview.

But there was still something about him that she found attractive, and she thought the other girls in the office would too. She found they took a keen interest in everybody else, and it didn't surprise her to hear Ruth say that Tim was good-looking but stuck-up because he was related to the bosses.

Phoebe added, 'The men don't like him and tend to

ignore him when they can. He's quite peculiar, a bit of an odd fellow.'

The first time Carrie and Tim were in the same team, they were sent to a factory making jam. Being the two most junior members, they were given the job of physically checking the stockrooms, and counting both the ingredients ready for use and the finished product waiting to be distributed. By late afternoon, Carrie felt hot and sticky because they'd had to move cartons about to check on the different types of preserve. Tim had been quite gallant, insisting on doing most of the heavy lifting. They'd had a chance to talk, and she didn't think he had grandiose ideas about himself; in fact she thought perhaps he was shy.

'I've been given to understand,' she said, 'that you have a reputation for being stuck-up.'

He half smiled at her. 'I have? Who told you that?'

'More than one of your colleagues, and you've certainly put your nose in the air when I've seen you on the tram.'

'I'm sorry.' A flush ran up his cheeks. 'That must have seemed ill-mannered, positively rude really.'

'You were quite different on the day I came for my first interview – outgoing and welcoming. I thought you'd taken a dislike to me,' she said.

'No,' he said, 'not at all. In fact quite the opposite.' He took a deep breath. 'You see, I don't belong to the gang . . .'

'What gang? Surely there's no such thing at Atherton and Groves?'

'No, no, I just mean that group of young bloods who hang around together; I suppose you'd call them friends. Mostly they're Atherton clerks, but there are others; they take an interest in any girl that joins the firm. One of them, Danny Devereaux, told me to keep away from you.'

'You mean he doesn't want competition from you?'

His cheeks were crimson now. 'He meant leave the field clear for the gang. They did the same when Phoebe started.'

'It doesn't matter to me how clear you leave the field,' Carrie said. 'I wouldn't touch Danny Devereaux with a bargepole. I don't think he's head of the popularity stakes with Phoebe either, or Ruth for that matter.'

'That's good news.' He had a slow half-smile that she found very attractive.

They left the jam factory at the same time that evening and travelled home on the same tram. Carrie's home was in an inner suburb and she learned that Tim lived along the same route but several stops further out. The next morning, he'd kept a seat for her next to him. It seemed he could be friendly, but he was a bit odd, and he certainly wasn't one of the in-crowd at Atherton & Groves.

Two days later, they were given separate jobs checking figures, and she could see he was hesitating over what he was doing. 'Are you all right with that?' she asked.

'I'm not sure . . .'

She explained the point to him and saw a flush of mortification run up his cheeks. She hadn't meant to make him feel small. 'I'm just beginning to realise what an advantage it is to have done bookkeeping first,' she said.

Danny Devereaux was working nearby. 'Tim isn't the brightest spark, is he?'

Carrie saw Tim's cheeks darken to crimson and knew Danny had deliberately set out to belittle him. She felt sorry for him, but he turned on Danny and said, 'You're so much brighter than I am, Danny. You could have been running the firm by now if only you could face exams. Such a drawback for you, a great pity.'

That told Carrie that Tim could give as good as he got.

CHAPTER SEVEN

ARCHIE AND MARION HEARD from Rod several times. His mother was in hospital; she'd needed an operation but was recovering. He'd managed to book passages on the *Arundel Castle* so he could take her to Cape Town when he went back. Things had gone well in Amsterdam and he'd be coming to spend a couple more days with them before he left.

Archie was not looking forward to that. He'd had a few weeks alone with Marion and felt very close to her. She'd encouraged his love, welcomed it. He'd been stupidly jealous to think she cared more for Rod than she did for him. He grew more passionate and thought about her all the time. Marion was perfection.

He'd known in Johannesburg that he was in love with her, but now she was showing her love for him. 'I do love you, Archie,' she'd said, and it had lifted him to the clouds. She had asked him to stay; she'd promised they'd leave together just as soon as they'd done the work Rod had arranged for them.

Archie was determined to settle down, though he felt dissatisfied with the actual work expected of him. It was the sort of work he'd done years ago when he'd first started making jewellery. He'd enjoyed it then, but ever since had been trying to improve the standard of what he turned out.

When Carl Fabergé had died in 1920 and there had been a flood of newspaper articles about him, and many illustrated books published showing his work, Archie had been fascinated, considering him to be the greatest jeweller and goldsmith the world had known.

Fabergé had altered what was considered to be fashionable in jewellery by concentrating on craftsmanship rather than relying on the beauty of large gemstones set in heavy gold. When he started making delicate brooches and Easter ornaments, he was appointed jeweller to the tsars of Russia and went on to make his famous eggs, each one containing a minute surprise fashioned in gold.

Archie greatly admired Fabergé's work, and saw it as the standard for which he must strive even if he couldn't reach it. He wanted his own reputation to be based on his craftsmanship; what Rod was providing was simple stuff that didn't use the skills he had.

Bill was quicker and better at the work than Archie was, and very good at removing assay marks and leaving no trace that they had ever been there. Archie could see that he'd had a lot of experience. Marion was also doing her fair share and jollying him along to work faster.

Rod had signed up a large circle of jewellers to his scheme, and Marion telephoned ahead, organising where they would work. They did as much as they could at every session. Sometimes it meant working at night, when the shops were closed, and Archie knew that over the coming months they'd be travelling from shop to shop and from town to town, working a few days here and a week or so there. He closed his mind to the fact that they were breaking the law.

One night, Marion suggested at midnight that Bill make cups of tea for them, and she opened the package of sandwiches she and Archie had cut before coming. Bill was ravenous and almost fell on them.

'You've been trained as a jeweller,' Archie said to him, 'you're good at what you do. What made you sign up for a job like this?'

'It was the only thing I could get, and I have to eat.'

'Work is very difficult to get in England since the Depression,' Marion added, as though she wanted to stop any talk along personal lines, but Archie was curious about this man; he'd seen how he was living and felt sorry for him. Bill had long, slender fingers that could work deftly with tiny objects, and he too sought perfection in what he did. He also looked cowed by ill health and the burdens of the world.

'You're a master worker in a trade where there are many jewellery shops. You could find honest work if you wanted to,' he said.

Marion shot him a look that said *lay off this*.

'Didn't Rod tell you? I was caught doing exactly what we're doing here but in a smaller way. I had a shop of my own. It seemed an easy way to earn a little extra.'

Archie shivered; it felt as though someone had put an ice bag on his stomach. 'What happened?'

'I got careless. You know what it's like when you've been doing something for a few years. The police came to my shop with a search warrant, and . . . well, I ended up in jail.'

'Jail?' Archie froze in horror. He was moving the food round and round his mouth; he couldn't swallow it. 'Aren't you afraid it will happen again?'

'Yes, of course I am.' Bill was eyeing the last sandwich. Archie offered it to him and he took it. 'There's not much else I can do now. I've lost my shop, my home and my family, and no honest jeweller will choose to employ a jailbird if there are other applicants.'

Marion said firmly, 'Right, Bill, you take the cups back to the kitchen and we'll get on. No point sitting about talking.'

Bill stood up. 'Perhaps it's safer doing it this way, rather than working alone. I hope it is anyway, but right now I don't seem to have much choice.'

The minute he was out of hearing, Marion said, 'Don't talk to Bill about his problems. Rod has set this up to make it as safe as houses. We're moving about all the time; there are different police forces in Lancashire and Cheshire. We have no other connection with the jewellers we work for, and we can flit back to South Africa if anything seems to threaten. This is the one time in our lives we'll do it, and we'll get out as soon as we've earned enough money.'

When Bill came back, she said, 'Archie, write this down.' He had to scramble for his notebook and pencil as she picked up another ring.

Later that morning, when they'd dropped Bill off, Archie tried to talk to her about how she would know when danger threatened and it was time to get out.

She was cross with him. 'I knew Bill would frighten the life out of you. Come on, Archie, you've more backbone than this. Everything's going well. Nobody is suspicious about what we're doing.'

'But once they are, it could be too late.'

'Rod would be furious with you,' she said. 'He's paid our

passages and set us up in that house so we can do this work, and he's meeting all the running costs of that and the car. You agreed to it, and you've got six months' leave of absence. What is the point of going back before the time is up?'

That didn't settle Archie's nerves; he could feel himself trembling. 'We're breaking the law. Helping thieves get a reasonable price for stealing jewellery. Are they stealing to order? I'm afraid we'll get caught. If we are, it could mean prison, couldn't it?'

'It's as safe as it can possibly be, and surely you're pleased with what Rod's paying into your bank account at the end of each month?'

'I'm delighted with that,' Archie admitted.

'And he spoke of a bonus if our earnings are up to expectations. Anyway, I want to stay, and I want you to stay with me.'

Marion had told him she'd had a very hard upbringing: a father who drank and a mother who'd had to rely on taking in washing and whatever her eldest son could earn in order to support her five children. He couldn't blame her for wanting to do this so she could have a less penny-pinching life. For him, the best thing about the job was that he had Marion to himself. He told her often that he loved her, and wanted to be with her always. She promised that he would.

She kept all her things in her own bedroom but rarely used it except to dress and undress. Most nights she would slip into his bed and stay all night. If he felt he was dozing off and she hadn't appeared, he would go to see her, and she'd pull him into her bed and cuddle up with him. They were living as man and wife and he felt supremely happy about that.

Marion organised the shopping and the cooking, and for the most part they did it together. They took Saturday off each week, because the jewellery shops were at their busiest on that day. They often worked at night, and sometimes on Sundays, because the owners thought those to be the safest times.

Marion went out without him on Saturdays; she shopped for clothes, had her hair done, and he thought sometimes she met other people. Archie mostly met Bob or George in a pub, visited their homes, or went to the cinema by himself. Occasionally they took a half-day off on Sunday too, because that was when his children and Prue expected to see them.

Marion had painted a rosy picture of what they might do and earn once here, but he was finding his working life more nerve-racking than he'd expected. Even she couldn't ease that.

The weeks were passing, and one morning Archie received a letter from Tom Bennett, his boss at Gordon and Mayell in Johannesburg, reminding him that he'd agreed to send them more designs. Tom had approved his six months' leave of absence and he was being paid a retainer. It had been on his conscience for some time that he should do something about it, but he felt he'd had little time; he'd done nothing but rush round with Marion. Now he felt there was some urgency, as he might want to go back. Life there had suited him better than it did here.

Marion was working beside him on the bench, her face screwing with concentration. She was wearing a dark dress with a plain white Peter Pan collar; last Sunday, she'd worn a dress with a similar lace collar and he thought they suited her well. Peter Pan collars were very fashionable this year.

It came to him in a flash that he could design necklaces in that shape to be made in gold mesh. He pushed away the ring he'd been working on and reached for a sheet of paper. He'd drawn half a dozen similar designs in no time, some in mesh almost like cloth of gold, and some made from chain; plain, or with tiny gold pansies here and there.

'I like the idea,' Marion said. 'They should go down well. You could do daisies as well as pansies, or put a border round the edge. But come on, let's finish these dress rings we have left and go home. I'm tired.'

Archie always made up his designs himself before offering them to Tom. It was the only way he could be sure they would work out, and he knew then how many hours would be needed to make each piece, so he could estimate the cost.

It took him half a dozen attempts before he could get his collars to sit right; each was done in a different workshop and had to be melted down again. He gave one to Marion before posting the designs off to Tom Bennett, but he continued to tinker, trying out different patterns. Tom wrote back that he was delighted and the design would go into production at once.

Over the following months, his Peter Pan collar necklace became a best-seller. Archie sent all his variations on it to Gordon and Mayell, and they went on to make them up in gold and in silver, large collars and small collars, with different patterns on them, with and without borders. Within months Marion was telling him she'd seen copies made in base metals by other jewellery makers, with minimum changes. They were being sold everywhere, even in Woolworth's.

One Saturday, Marion bought a magazine and showed him illustrations of the necklace. Women were advised to wear it on a dark dress with a plain high neckline, as well as with off-the-shoulder evening gowns. Almost everybody had one. Archie thought it would look its best back in South Africa, gleaming against dark African skin.

Rod congratulated him. 'It's a winner,' he said, 'but I wish you had given me that design.'

One morning Archie and Marion were eating their breakfast when the phone rang. Marion got up to answer it. 'That was Rod,' she said when she returned to the table. 'He's coming up from London and wants us to pick him up at Lime Street station at three o'clock this afternoon.'

Archie groaned; he wasn't looking forward to Rod's visit. 'How long will he be staying?'

'A couple of days, he says. There are still five jewellers in his scheme that we haven't yet met. He's going to take us to see his friend Gerard Milner in Lord Street at ten tomorrow morning.'

'Rod expects to live like a lord, and the larder is almost bare.'

'We'll have to go shopping,' Marion said. 'We're late now so won't have time this morning before we pick Bill up, but we can do it this afternoon. Rod likes shopping. He's on his way back from Amsterdam, so he won't feel like work after so much travelling.'

Rod came breezily down the platform, hung about with parcels as well as a bag. He kissed Marion. 'How are you, Archie? I have a ready-for-the-oven duck for dinner tonight,' he said as he gave him a fancy carrier bag.

'Are the Dutch famous for their duck?' Archie asked.

'It was a present,' Rod laughed. 'I've spent the last three nights with Hans Hecht and his wife. She's a marvellous cook. You remember them?'

Archie had no idea who he was talking about.

'Well, because I praised Leila's duck dinner, she presented me with this.' He opened the car boot to toss his parcels and overnight bag inside; Archie hastily pushed the duck in too. 'I'm not much of a cook myself, but you're good at it. You know how to cope with a duck, don't you?'

'I don't remember ever cooking one before,' Archie said resentfully, knowing he'd be expected to do it.

'I love duck,' Marion said. 'We'll have a good dinner tonight.'

'I'll drive,' Rod said, flinging his newspaper in first and getting into the driving seat. 'Where are we going?'

'Let's knock off early for once,' Marion said. 'We've done enough for today.'

Archie liked to drive; instead he had to get in the back with Bill, who was snoozing and taking up more than his fair share of space. Archie prodded him until he moved up.

'I've had a very successful trip.' Rod always liked to be centre stage. 'Very enjoyable too. So we'll drop Bill off and go home?'

'We need to buy more food on the way,' Marion said, 'and drink.'

'The duck . . .'

'That's fine, but we need oranges to go with it, and basics too. You eat us out of house and home when you come.'

'I've brought a bottle of Dutch gin too. Ginevra, they call it. It looks strong.'

'Head down here,' Marion said, 'then turn right towards Bill's place. In a quarter of a mile or so, there's a parade of shops where we've bought food before. Yes, it's round the next corner.'

Rod pulled up in front of a greengrocer's shop. Marion got out. 'Come on, Archie, can you remember what we need?'

Archie fished the list he'd made from his pocket as she led the way into the shop. 'Onions, carrots and a green vegetable for tonight.'

'They've got broad beans.'

Marion selected and paid, while Archie packed their purchases into the bags he'd brought and carried them round to the baker's. Once they had the bread, he said, 'We need butter and cheese. Rod likes gorgonzola.'

They were heading back along the pavement when Marion grabbed his arm and pulled him to a standstill. 'Oh my God! The police!'

She was staring at the car. Rod had wound the window down and the back of a uniformed police officer could be seen bending down to talk to him.

Archie felt transfixed. 'What can we do?'

'We've got to help Rod.' She was pulling him towards the car. All Archie's senses urged him to run the other way. 'Come on, get a move on.' She had a fixed smile on her face. 'Good afternoon, Constable.'

The policeman turned and straightened up. It took a moment, but then Archie felt his every pore sweating with relief. 'Hello, Bob.'

'Hello! Fancy seeing you here with all your friends.' Bob

pulled him into a brotherly hug and thumped a greeting on his shoulder. 'Lucky you, being on holiday in this summery weather.'

He turned back to Rod. 'Our Archie's very generous about letting others drive his car. He let me have a go. It's smashing, isn't it?'

Archie, now feverishly alert, introduced Marion and Rod. 'Friends from South Africa,' he said, 'in Liverpool for a short visit.' Even Bill was fully awake and peering at them from the back seat; Archie introduced him too.

Marion was opening the boot and urging Archie to put the bags in. 'Lovely to meet you, Bob,' she said, 'but we're in rather a hurry. Why don't you get together as a family sometime soon? I'd really like to get to know you all.'

Archie climbed in and Rod moved off, though not as smoothly as usual. As soon as they were safely away, he burst out, 'Oh my God, Archie! Why didn't you say you had a brother in the police? I was reading the paper when he came and rapped on the roof. I nearly wet myself.'

'I didn't think—'

'Well, damn it, you should have done. He is just a constable, isn't he? What exactly does he do?'

Marion turned round in her seat. 'He's not a detective?'

'I don't know. Traffic, I think. I saw him controlling that crossing in Hanover Street once.'

'Well, it doesn't look as though he's in traffic now.' Rod turned into a side street and pulled up. 'My knees are still shaking. I couldn't understand what I'd done to attract his attention, but I feared the worst.'

'So did I,' Bill said in heartfelt tones.

'You'd better drop him,' Rod said. 'Have nothing to do with him from now on.'

'How can I do that?' wailed Archie. 'He's my brother.'

'It wouldn't be safe.'

'I won't tell him anything. I'll keep a tight watch on my tongue and all that.'

'He'll pick things up. He's probably trained to do that. Not only from you, but from what you've told other members of your family. You shouldn't go near any of them.'

That was more than Archie would take. 'I have two daughters; they'll come looking for me if I stay out of their way. Anyway, they're young and innocent; they won't realise . . .'

'They really are, Rod,' Marion said. 'Very innocent. Lovely girls.'

Rod was still angry. 'Your brother! You've already introduced us all to him. He can put faces to names. All of that is bad.'

'We can't do anything about that now,' Marion told him firmly. 'Let's forget it.'

'I'll get out here,' Bill said. 'Do a bit of shopping for myself.'

'Half nine in the morning,' Marion told him.

Rod was still not over the shock he'd had. 'Honestly, Archie, I can't believe you have a brother in the police. Why didn't you tell us? Oh, for God's sake, let's go home.'

'No,' Archie protested, 'that cut short our shopping. We still need butter and cheese and stuff.'

'There's another shopping parade further on,' Marion said. 'You'll have to stop again, Rod.'

The encounter with Bob had really shaken Archie, and knowing it had scared the others made him feel worse. He was glad of Marion's help getting adequate supplies into the car. He always felt guilty if they were found to be short of something Rod wanted.

When they reached home, Archie was exhausted and even Marion was flagging. He still had to get that duck in the oven, but for once she came to help him. While Archie made them a cup of tea, Marion organised Rod to shell beans at the kitchen table and dealt with the duck and the oranges herself.

When the dinner preparations had been completed and the cooking was under way, Rod said, 'I must show you the diamonds I've had recut. They've done a marvellous job in Amsterdam; nobody to touch them back in Jo'burg. They've hardly lost any weight.'

He wiped the kitchen table with a tea cloth, put on the electric light and pulled a small pouch from his pocket. Archie was fascinated. Marion brought out her loupe and a small piece of black velvet, which she smoothed out on the table. Rod emptied the contents of the pouch on to it, and the gems glittered and sparkled up at them.

Archie drew back, knowing they must all have been stolen. Despite that, his eye was drawn to the largest one. 'What d'you think?' Rod asked, and handed over his loupe so Archie could take a closer look. It was fabulous workmanship; already he could see it as a pendant, with a dainty filigree surround of gold.

Rod put the diamonds away and opened the bottle of ginevra. 'I think they drink it neat over there,' he told them as he poured out a glass for each of them. 'Before I settle down, I ought to ring my mother to let her know I'm back in England, and that I'll be home in two or three days' time.'

He went out to the phone in the hall, barely closing the door behind him. Archie could hear his voice rising and falling, but not what he was saying.

Marion took a tentative sip from the glass Rod had poured for her, 'Ugh,' she said, 'this would knock my head off.' She tipped what remained into Rod's glass. 'It's neat gin, and we didn't buy any orange squash. I'm going to open some wine.'

Rod came back and took a large gulp from his glass. 'Bad news. Mum's in bed and not at all well; she more or less collapsed this afternoon. One of her neighbours is sitting with her, and she's called the doctor out to see her. They're waiting for him now. Poor old Mum. I've said I'll come home tonight.' He was frowning. 'I'd better ring Gerard Milner and cancel tomorrow's visit. You'll see to the others I fixed up, Marion? Now, how long before that duck's ready?'

'Twenty minutes or so.'

'Then I'll have my dinner before I go. I'm hungry.'

Archie sighed. 'I hope your mother will be well enough to travel down to the boat next week.' He wanted to see the back of Rod now. It was hard to believe that he'd once enjoyed his company.

'So do I, but I'm worried about her. I can't stay in England for much longer; I've a lot to do when I get back.'

Archie ran him down to the station in time to catch the last train home. 'My mother lives close to the station at Rainhill,' Rod said, 'so I don't have to rely on getting more transport at the other end. I'll have to come back to take you round those few shops you haven't seen, but perhaps I can do that without staying away overnight.'

When Archie returned home, Marion had cleared away and washed up. 'Come on,' she said, 'let's go straight to bed. I'm shattered. We'll have a quiet weekend.'

They curled up together in Archie's bed. He knew he wouldn't really be able to relax until Rod was on the mail boat and it had set sail for South Africa.

Carrie felt that her father and Marion encouraged her to come and visit them, and really wanted to hear how she was getting on. She made a point of telling them that she was settling down in her new place of work and was glad she'd made the change. She thanked Archie again for providing the money for her. She found that having more to do with him had broken the ice, and they were closer.

She really liked Marion; she was always good-humoured, smiley and bubbly, and ready to chat about clothes and make-up. Carrie felt they had interests in common. She told Marion that a fellow clerk had told her she still looked like a schoolgirl and needed to appear more mature before she'd be taken seriously.

Marion laughed. 'It's your hair, it looks out of control. It's a lovely colour, Carrie, but perhaps it would be neater if there was less of it.'

'I don't want it cut. Connie and I have tried it short and we didn't like it. I was wondering about drawing it all back in a bun. I had a go, but it made me look frumpy.'

'Sounds like you need to get it higher on your head. What about a French pleat? That would look sophisticated and glamorous but businesslike at the same time, though it would take a bit of effort to put it up every morning.'

'I know, but I wouldn't mind getting up ten minutes earlier if it did something for me. I wish it wasn't such a mop.' Carrie eyed Marion's neat dark head. 'You can do so much more with straight hair, and it must be easier to manage.'

'Come upstairs to my room and let me try now.'

Carrie followed her up; her bedroom seemed very feminine, with a pink carpet and curtains. The bed was big, with a matching bedspread. The dressing table was covered with expensive-looking creams, lotions and perfumes, as well as a cut-glass powder bowl and a silver-backed brush and comb. Marion pulled out the chair in front of it for her to sit down, and Carrie watched in the mirror as she ran a comb through her hair.

'It's very thick as well as curly, but it's a gorgeous colour. A French pleat would suit you, but I'm not doing a very good job on it. Why don't I make an appointment for you with my hairdresser for next Saturday afternoon? Zoe will know what needs to be done and we'll ask her to show you how to put it up.'

'Where do you have your hair done?' Carrie asked. It was a top salon in the city centre. 'I'd love to, but I can't afford expensive hairdressing just now. Dad would have a fit; I daren't ask for more money when he's already given me so much. Connie and I trim each other's hair when it gets too long; having tight curls means it doesn't show if it isn't exactly level.'

Marion was smiling. 'Leave it to me. I think this will make a big difference, and we don't need to tell Archie.'

The following Saturday afternoon, Carrie met Marion in town and was taken to her hairdresser. She watched as Zoe gathered up her hair and wound it round her head to see the

102

effect. 'It would suit you, and show off your neck and shoulders. It needs a little trimmed off the length, but thinning more than anything else. We'll start with a shampoo.'

It took the hairdresser an age to comb through the tight damp curls; then she took a brush to smooth them out. Marion was looking at a magazine but occasionally made a suggestion. Zoe demonstrated to Carrie how to achieve the same effect at home, and she couldn't believe the difference when it was finished. She felt like a new woman.

'Do I look more mature?' she asked Marion.

'You look like a stylish young lady. We can see more of your face now; it shows it off.'

'But I still look very young.' Carrie grimaced at her reflection.

'You don't know how lucky you are,' Marion laughed. 'I want to look younger and so does everybody else I know. You have a very pretty face.'

It was the hairdresser who said, 'Why don't you try wearing a large pair of spectacles?'

'I don't need them.'

'Of course you don't, but with your hair up like this, they'll suit your features. They'll really complement the look. A friend of mine bought a pair of sunglasses in Woolworth's for fourpence, and they've turned her into a different personality. She looks like a glamorous intellectual now. If it's a mature look you want, spectacles are the answer. Think of them as an accessory.'

'But I can't wear sunglasses all the time in the office; I wouldn't be able to see properly.'

'Oh, my friend said it was easy to rub the dye off the lenses.

She was told to use either bleach or white spirit on a soft cloth, but even vinegar will do it.'

'Really? I wouldn't mind trying that.'

They had to pass Woolworth's to reach the tram stop, so Carrie dragged Marion in. They found a choice of styles to choose from and Carrie tried them all on.

'Zoe is right,' Marion said. 'They do something for you. Look in the mirror.'

Carrie peered through the dark lenses and agreed. She let Marion choose the style she thought suited her best: a pair with heavy brown frames and round owlish lenses.

Outside on the pavement, she kissed the older woman. 'I can't thank you enough. You're so kind, just like a mother to me.'

Marion patted her shoulder. 'I don't have children of my own, so I'm more than happy to spend time with Archie's.'

Once home, Carrie cleaned the shading off the lenses and rushed up to her bedroom to try them on in front of her mirror. She was delighted. Zoe had completely transformed her; she really looked sophisticated, and yes, quite a bit older. She gave silent thanks to Marion for helping her.

That evening, she met Edna, the girl she used to work with, at a suburban cinema midway between their homes. Edna didn't recognise her to start with, but was loud in her praise. 'It's turned you into a real beauty.'

'Wearing these heavy spectacles is going to take some getting used to.' Carrie laughed and slipped them into her handbag once the lights went out.

'Well worth the effort,' Edna told her. 'You could get work as a model.'

They saw Marlene Dietrich in *The Blue Angel*, the story of Lola, a promiscuous dance hall singer, who first enslaved and then destroyed a stuffy schoolmaster. They thought it was sensational. Carrie felt she'd had an absolutely marvellous day.

But now that she no longer worked in the same office as Edna, it was not easy to arrange meetings. They had to telephone while they were at work, and personal calls were not encouraged by employers. They did meet up once more, but Edna was about to go on holiday and could talk of nothing else, so they didn't arrange to see each other the following week. Carrie received a postcard from Torquay and after that they drifted apart.

CHAPTER EIGHT

O<small>N SUNDAY AFTERNOON, CARRIE</small> walked round to see Connie, who squealed with delight at her improved image. 'Marion fixed it for you?' She wanted to hear how it had come about. 'I wish mine looked like that. Would you try to put it up like yours?'

'I don't know that I could.'

'Come to the bathroom and help me wash it first.' They always used to wash each other's hair before Connie got married.

Carrie shampooed Connie's hair in the washbasin, and when she'd rubbed it partly dry, she tried to put it up in a French pleat.

'It looks very nice,' John said, but Carrie hadn't Zoe's skills, and, disappointed, Connie unpinned it later in the evening.

'Get a hairdresser to thin it down and do it for you,' Carrie said. 'Mine is much more manageable now it's less of a bush.'

The next day, Carrie found that her new look had a dramatic effect in the office. She implied that her glasses were needed to correct a sight loss, and everybody sympathised but told her how well they suited her.

'Wow,' Tim said, 'what an improvement. You've been

hiding your light under the proverbial bushel. Looking like that, you'll knock out every fellow in the office.' His brown eyes were smiling at her.

'I didn't think you'd notice,' she said.

The very same day, one of Atherton's articled clerks invited her to go to the pictures, but she knew he was one of the gang that taunted Tim and declined. The next day, she received an invitation from another man and went to the pictures with him that Saturday, but she found they had nothing in common and he didn't ask her again.

Over the following weeks, a number of men in the office asked her out, and she agreed to go several times, but none of the dates resulted in a relationship that lasted, though she did feel more at home in their company. As time went on, she felt she had settled in at Atherton & Groves.

One Monday morning, Mr Heatherington sent Carrie as a member of a four-man team that included Tim Redwood to the shop of G. E. Milner, a prominent firm of Liverpool jewellers in the city centre, to audit their accounts. It was a private company owning four further shops in the suburbs, and their flagship store was in the main shopping centre, only a short walk from their own office.

She had never been inside the shop before; it stocked goods at the top end of the market. Her feet sank into the thick carpet as she gazed round at the polished mahogany counters and the many glass-fronted display units filled with expensive rings, bracelets and necklaces. Everything seemed to flash and glitter under the electric light. There was a hint of perfume in the air and the atmosphere seemed to radiate wealth and luxury.

They had to walk through the ground floor to reach the offices and storerooms, which were upstairs at the back of the premises. Carrie lingered, eyeing the jewellery, while the men strode purposefully through.

Tim was behind her and noticed her interest. 'They're just bits of rock dug out of the ground,' he said. 'Utterly useless; they do nothing but sparkle. At least we can burn coal to keep us warm, and use granite to build our houses.'

Carrie thought that dour and miserable. 'Precious stones are very beautiful,' she said, staring at them. 'Absolutely exquisite when mounted in gold.'

'And exorbitantly expensive,' he retorted.

The team leader, Bill Brown, who had trained with the firm and had recently qualified, was dealing with the jeweller's chief accountant, a somewhat dandified individual, with just the right amount of handkerchief peeping from the top pocket of his formal suit. They were shown to the office and storeroom: bleak, utilitarian places that customers did not see.

Carrie and Tim were put to work in the storeroom. There was little for Carrie to admire, as most of it was still boxed up: clocks, watches, hip flasks, silver dressing-table sets and fountain pens. They had to stocktake and check the boxes against the accounting documents.

That took until the middle of the afternoon, after which Carrie was glad to sit down and sort through the paperwork. She saw Gerard Milner, the owner of the shop, for the first time when he came to speak to Mr Brown. He was tall, with broad shoulders, and immaculate in a very smart and formal suit, wearing a red carnation in his buttonhole.

An outfit suitable for a wedding, she thought, and here he

was wearing it for work. He was a man who drew every eye. Even Tim was watching him as he rocked on his heels, stabbing his finger at some entry in a ledger. He had attractive good looks, with a square jaw, and dark hair brushed back from his forehead. There was a magnetic quality about him.

Carrie guessed he was almost her father's age, so not young, but he radiated good health, fitness and energy, and could only be described as being in the prime of life. Suddenly he turned and noticed her. She met his dark eyes and felt a surge that sent her heart racing.

'Hello,' he said with half a smile, and immediately turned back to listen to what their team leader was saying. Carrie couldn't drag her eyes away from him. Here was a real man at the top of his form; all others faded in comparison.

Tim jogged her elbow. 'Come on, let's get on with this.'

Gerard Milner came in and out several times, looking tense, but he gave Carrie a nod of recognition each time. She couldn't get him out of her mind.

They worked late that evening, stocktaking the jewellery as it was taken from the display cases to be locked in a big safe overnight. Carrie marvelled at the diamonds as she handled some of them, but Mr Brown allowed her little time; he set a brisk pace as he wanted to get home. That night she fell asleep thinking of diamonds and Gerard Milner.

Back at work on Tuesday morning, Carrie was looking out for Gerard Milner, but it was his chief accountant who was liaising with the team. Today, Mr Brown had her sitting at the next desk checking figures in a daybook under his supervision. He worked tirelessly and expected the same from her, but by lunchtime she could feel her energy flagging.

Milner's accountant came in and Mr Brown began questioning him about some figures that appeared not to satisfy him. They left the office together, taking the offending ledger with them. Carrie took off her spectacles to relax for a moment. The rest of the team sat back too; they all felt in need of a break.

A clock nearby struck one and Robbie Wilson, one of their team, said, 'Lunchtime, thank goodness.' He slammed his ledgers shut and locked them away. 'Bill Brown said he fancies going to Murphy's Refreshment Rooms today; he'll come on later. Let's go.'

The men stood up. Carrie was never invited to join them on their lunchtime trips out. She always brought a sandwich, which she ate with Phoebe and Ruth when she was in the office. She took her lunch out of her bag now and took a bite. She was hungry.

She had hardly swallowed it before Gerard Milner came rushing in with files in his arms. His unexpected appearance made Carrie feel somewhere between excited and flustered, but then she noticed he was frowning; she could see that he was not in a good mood.

'Has Mr Brown gone out?' he demanded.

'He went off with your accountant fifteen minutes ago, but I expect he's left for lunch by now.'

'Then give him these when he comes back.' He flung the files he was carrying on to her desk; they skidded across, sweeping her spectacles before them. Everything ended up on the floor.

'Oh dear.' He surveyed the mess for a moment. 'I apologise

– shocking bad manners. Things aren't going as well as I'd hoped.' As he stepped forward to pick up the files and the assortment of documents shed from them, she heard her glasses crunch under his foot.

'Oh! Oh, I am sorry.' He laid the spectacles in front of her. One lens had been forced out of the frame, and one of the arms was broken off. 'You'll have to forgive me.' His dark eyes were looking into hers. 'I'll replace them, of course. Get you a new pair. Who is your optician?'

'It doesn't matter.' Carrie was almost overcome with embarrassment. 'Really it doesn't. You don't have to do anything.'

'I do,' he insisted. 'Glasses can be expensive. You must let me get you a replacement pair.'

His eyes met hers again and his manner had changed. Was he teasing her? Again that half-smile. He must like her; in fact, she thought his eyes had that come-to-bed look, and that made her feel even more flustered. 'No, no.' She tossed the broken glasses into the waste-paper basket. 'They weren't expensive.'

'But you'll need another pair now; the least I can do is replace them.'

A hot flush ran up her cheeks. 'I don't really need them.' She could see he didn't understand. 'They're by way of being a fashion accessory.'

'What d'you mean?' He lifted them out of the waste basket to peer through the remaining lens. 'Wearing glasses when you don't have to? Oh, they're not prescription glasses. Well, I suppose they do suit you.'

Carrie tried to explain. 'I wanted to look older, more mature. Able to tackle more interesting jobs instead of being stuck with the easy stuff.' Her cheeks were on fire. 'They cost fourpence in Woolworths; I shall just have time in my lunch break to run down and get myself another pair. So you see, you don't have to worry.'

His hearty belly laugh rang round the office. 'You're the first woman I've met who wants to look older and do harder work.' He mopped at his eyes. 'In that case, I'll walk down with you. Woolworth's isn't far, and if you will allow me to replace them, then honour will be satisfied on both sides.'

'That's very kind.' Carrie was pleased. It seemed he couldn't stop looking at her. Did he want to be with her as much as she wanted to be with him? 'I'll get my coat.'

'Will you need it? It's a warm afternoon.'

'So it is. Let's go, then.'

Milner led her down some stairs and out through the back entrance. It felt wonderful to be out in the sunshine, and she was very conscious of him walking alongside her.

'I'm Gerard Milner,' he said. 'And I assume you are one of Atherton's clerks? What is your name?'

She told him. 'Gerard is a bit of a mouthful; are you usually known as Gerry?'

'No, but you can call me that if you want to.' Again he gave her that slow half-smile.

'I think I will. Gerard is so formal, so posh.'

He laughed. 'When I first saw you yesterday, I thought you were a very pretty girl; you don't need any accessories. But the good thing is, by breaking your glasses, I was able to speak to you, and now I can get to know you.'

Woolworth's was full of girls shopping in their lunchtime. Gerard followed her through them to the counter.

'Here they are,' she said. 'These are exactly the same as the pair you broke. Perhaps I'll get a spare while I'm here.' She picked up a slightly different style.

'Oh, sunglasses! But the pair I broke were of clear glass.'

'The tint rubs off quite easily with a little vinegar on a soft cloth.'

'Ah, that explains it,' he said. 'I couldn't think where you'd get plain glass. There are three different styles; get one of each. Then I won't feel too bad if I break another pair.'

Once back on his premises, Gerard said, 'Come to the kitchen; there'll be vinegar there. I'll help you clear the glass, then you can wear them this afternoon.'

Carrie followed him up to the top of the building and was surprised to find she was in a compact kitchen fitted with a refrigerator and a cooker.

'This is nice,' she said. 'I was expecting a rather bare room, with a large battered table and plenty of chairs.' That was what she'd seen in the other businesses she'd worked in.

'There's a room like that downstairs, with one large teapot and a huge collection of cups and saucers.' He smiled at her. 'This isn't for staff use; it's my private kitchen. I have a small flat here on the top floor, bachelor accommodation.'

'Oh, goodness! Mr Brown would not approve of me coming up here.' Neither would Aunt Pruc.

'There's no vinegar anywhere else in the building.' He smiled again. 'I have to discourage the staff from bringing in chips at lunchtime – it smells the shop out.'

Carrie felt she could hardly rush away like a scared rabbit after all his kindness. Besides, what was the harm? She sat down. 'Thank you, then I should feel honoured to be brought here.'

'Let me help you, but . . . oh dear, I don't have any malt vinegar either. What about bleach? That will probably work too, and here's some bits of cloth we can use.'

Gerard sat beside her at the kitchen table and they set to work in companionable silence. It was surprisingly easy, but no sooner had they cleared the lenses than Carrie had to say, 'My lunch hour is over. I have to go back to work. Now, which pair of glasses shall I wear this afternoon?'

He leaned back in his chair, gazing at her. 'You look absolutely beautiful in those,' he said, 'but you'd look wonderful in anything. You had it right: the pair similar to those I broke suits your face to perfection.'

Carrie was back in the cramped office allotted to the auditors before the men. As she'd eaten only half her lunch, she sat down and took out another sandwich as they came in.

'Not eaten yet?' Tim Redwood asked. 'What have you been doing all lunchtime?'

'I went out shopping.' She felt wide awake and more alert. She powered through the job she was doing and was given another. The men seemed soporific after their heavier lunch.

That afternoon, Carrie studied Gerard's files and ledgers more closely than she had any others. She was very interested in his business. Halfway through the afternoon, one of the shop's staff brought in a tray with a cup of tea for each of them. Afterwards, Carrie piled up the used crockery and set out to return it to the staff kitchen. She wanted to see more of Gerry's premises, find out more about him and everything he did.

It was a quite an old building, with a warren of narrow

passages. She was passing two doors marked PRIVATE in very large letters when she met the girl who'd brought them the tea.

'What goes on in these rooms?' she asked. She was curious, and had been told that a good auditor should question everything.

'Mr Milner does jewellery repairs in there. He can design jewellery for you if you want something special. Nobody else is allowed in; the rooms are kept locked because there's bits of gold lying about, and even a tiny bit is worth a lot of money.'

Later on, Gerard Milner came in to speak to Bill Brown. Some sixth sense seemed to tell Carrie he was near and make her look up. His dark eyes were watching her; was he flirting with her? Yes, she thought he must be. How could she help but smile at him?

But her colleagues had noticed. 'Wow, I think he fancies you,' Robbie Wilson chortled when he'd gone.

'Stay clear of him,' Mr Brown ordered sternly, conscious of his responsibility as team leader. 'He's off limits. Mr Groves would not want a clerk of his getting involved with a client. Understood?'

'Yes, sir,' Carrie said.

But when she went to bed that night, Gerard Milner was very much on her mind. She knew it was important to toe the Atherton & Groves line, and she wanted the senior staff to approve of what she did, but Gerard Milner had already bewitched her.

She felt strongly attracted to him, even though he was quite old. He was a successful man, the owner of a profitable business; surely he couldn't be interested in her? Perhaps she'd misread the signals he was sending out, and they did not mean what she'd supposed.

The next morning she took extra care with her hair and wore her best blue dress to work. All morning she looked out for him but didn't catch so much as a glimpse. At lunchtime, no sooner had the men gone out and she'd opened up the serviette in which Prue wrapped her sandwiches than Gerry came looking for her. She was delighted.

'How about bringing your lunch up to my kitchen,' he said, 'and I'll make us a cup of coffee. I enjoyed your company yesterday, so why not do it again?'

Carrie was eager to follow him up, but she could do no more than nod. She felt very daring, because she'd been warned off him, and she knew that going to his private quarters would bring down Mr Groves's wrath on her head. In the kitchen she sat down at the table again.

'I'm not as organised as you,' he began, cutting slices from a loaf to make himself a sandwich, then getting out a jar of Gentleman's Relish.

'I've never heard of that,' she said. 'What is it?'

'A good old-fashioned standby for sandwiches. Here, have a taste.' He seemed relaxed; it was as though they'd known each other for years.

'I think I prefer my bloater paste and lettuce,' she said. 'You must find it handy living here. It's very central for shopping and everything.'

'Very handy for doing more work,' he said, 'my office being just one floor down from my sitting room. I'll show you round when we've eaten.'

That made Carrie's cheeks burn. She knew she shouldn't be

chatting to him like this, and she certainly shouldn't see more of his flat, but she couldn't bear to turn down his invitation. There was nothing she wanted more than to see it all.

He asked her where she lived, and she told him about her aunts Prudence and Maud who had brought her up because her father was working abroad.

When he took her to his sitting room, a large square room with two big windows looking down five storeys to Lord Street, she said, 'It's lovely.' It was furnished with antiques and two enormous modern sofas, and the same thick carpet as the shop.

'You might as well see more of it now you're here,' he said, and threw open two more doors, revealing a very masculine bed covered with a heavy dark quilt, and a bathroom beyond. He closed the doors again quickly, as though understanding her embarrassment. 'Just bachelor accommodation,' he said, moving her back to the sitting room. 'I'll make that coffee and we'll have it in here. You can keep me company.'

'I can't,' she said, catching sight of the ormolu clock on the mantelpiece. 'I've got to get back to work. I'm only allowed an hour.'

'Sorry, tomorrow then? I mustn't upset Dougie Atherton.'

'It's Mr Brown who mustn't know,' Carrie said. 'He's my team leader. But we won't be here tomorrow, and possibly not the next day either; he's taking me to stocktake at your branches in Woolton and Aigburth.' Robbie Wilson and Tim were going to the other two branches.

'But you will be here on Friday?'

'Yes, we'll be back as soon as we've finished.'

Gerard walked with her to the door. Before she realised his

intention, she felt his arms pull her close and his mouth came down on hers in a real lovers' kiss. It left her breathless and wanting more. 'Friday, then?' he whispered.

Carrie knew she was falling in love. At last it was happening for her. It was what she'd dreamed of, what she'd longed for. She felt on top of the world.

CHAPTER NINE

A T THREE O'CLOCK ON THURSDAY afternoon, Archie was woken by the telephone ringing in the hall below. Beside him, he felt Marion stir, but he knew she wouldn't get up to answer it. He heaved himself off the bed, pulled the eiderdown round him and padded downstairs. It was Rod.

'I'll be back with you tomorrow,' he said. 'I've got to take you to meet those last few jewellers.'

'I'm afraid we've arranged to work tonight,' Archie said.

'Oh? Where?'

Archie had to think for a moment. 'Fletcher's in Manchester.'

'Good, then on your way home tomorrow morning you could come through Rainhill and pick me up. Two of the shops are near here, so we could do those.'

'We won't be on top form after working all night.'

'You'll be able to shake hands and smile, Archie. We can see Gerard Milner the next day.'

'How is your mother?' Archie asked. 'I hope she's doing well now.'

He heard Rod sigh. 'Not very. She's been up and down and went back to hospital once, but she's stable now and I think picking up. As you know, I've had to keep delaying my return to Jo'burg; I can't leave her here like this. I've booked us both

119

on next week's boat. Fortunately, everything seems to be ticking over well there.'

'You're lucky there's a weekly mail boat sailing,' Archie said.

'I am. Tomorrow morning, then, come and pick me up on your way home, but not before nine.' Archie wasn't pleased; they all hoped to be home early when they worked at night. 'You could get yourself some breakfast before collecting me,' Rod went on, as though reading his thoughts. 'There's a transport caff at the bottom of the East Lancs Road; it's open all hours and the food isn't bad.'

For Archie, it was bad news that Rod was coming back, and he crept upstairs miserably. It made him feel a fool that he'd totally misjudged the work Rod had intended him to do, and he was ashamed that they were getting rich by helping thieves to market their stolen goods. Engagement rings had a sentimental value for their owners that couldn't be replaced with a new ring.

He got back into bed alongside Marion, thinking she was still asleep, but her arms went round him and all his misgivings spilled out. 'You poor love,' Marion said. 'You're living on your nerves. You must learn to relax. Rod isn't here yet.' They spent the next hour or so making love, and Archie felt better when they got up to go to work.

They were eating scrambled eggs on toast before setting out when Rod rang again. 'Change of plan; don't pick me up tomorrow morning. Mother was sick all over her bed this afternoon, so I got the doctor out again. He says she isn't fit to travel and needs to rest this weekend.'

'I am sorry,' Archie said. 'She's having a hard time.'

'So am I. I've had to cancel our passage and rebook it a week later. I want to take you to meet Milner. We need to start on the work he's got for us. I'll fix a day and let you know.'

All went well during the stocktaking in the two branches, and today Carrie would be back in the Lord Street shop. She was looking forward to seeing Gerard Milner again, but she knew the audit was almost finished, and Mr Brown would soon be drawing up the final documents. Certainly her services would not be needed in the shop for much longer: perhaps an hour or two tomorrow morning, or the junior work might go on till mid afternoon.

The morning seemed long. Carrie left her desk several times to walk round the shop, but Gerry didn't seem to be about. She was afraid that he might not come to find her at lunchtime. She was in a dither. If she didn't see him today, they wouldn't meet again until next year's audit took place. Even then she might not be put in the team that was sent to his shop.

Lunchtime came and the men left, talking about trying a different café. Carrie had no sooner taken her sandwiches from her handbag than Gerard came. He pushed the door closed behind him and took her in his arms to kiss her. For Carrie it was bliss.

'Come upstairs,' he whispered. 'There's more privacy there.'

He led her to his sitting room to sit side by side on his sofa. 'This time I'm organised,' he said. He'd set a tray with his sandwiches and also some delicious-looking cakes. He held her close, and kissed her several times.

There was something Carrie had to know. 'Do you live here by yourself?' she asked.

'Yes, you can see I do. It's a small bachelor flat. I find it lonely here on my own.'

She fully understood that. She told him about her twin sister getting married and how lonely she'd felt since. But his flat was a lot bigger than the one Connie and John shared. He'd shown her only one bedroom, but that had a double bed in it, and there seemed to be more rooms. 'You aren't married then? You don't have any family?'

'No, not close family. I have relatives all over the place, but I need friends too.' He pulled her close for another kiss. 'I think you're gorgeous. I do hope I can see more of you.'

'We've just about finished the audit,' she said. 'It's probably my last day here.'

'I know. We could meet after work. Would you let me buy you dinner?'

Carrie's heart seemed to bounce. 'That would be lovely. When?'

'Tonight if you like.'

'Oh, I couldn't. Aunt Prue expects me straight home from work; she prepares a hot meal for me and Aunt Maud.'

'Or I could take you to the Royal Court. I've heard the show there is good.'

Carrie hesitated; there was nothing she wanted more. 'It's difficult when I haven't let her know. We don't have a phone at home.'

'You've probably got lots of boyfriends your own age,' he said, drawing away from her, disappointment on his face.

'Not at all. What about Saturday? I'll be free from lunchtime onwards.' Aunt Prue was used to her going out on Saturday nights; she wouldn't probe too deeply.

His face fell. 'I'm afraid I can't. Saturday is my busiest day and I'm tied up over the weekend. And next week – I'm afraid that is going to be very busy for me too. What about tomorrow?'

Carrie was not prepared to lose this chance. 'All right, tomorrow,' she said. 'I'd love to go to the theatre. That would be a real treat for me.'

He beamed at her. 'I'll get tickets.'

They made arrangements to meet and Carrie returned to her desk in the room allotted to the auditors. She'd almost finished the jobs she'd been given when Robbie Wilson said, 'Let's drag the work out a bit. If we finish too early, we'll have to go back to the office. If it isn't finalised until four, we'll probably be told to go home.'

Tim told the team leader he'd finished, and Carrie said, 'So have I.'

Bill Brown studied the documents they'd been working on. 'You can go back to the office now, and give these to Phoebe to type up. I need to finish my report and have a word with Mr Milner before I come. Mr Heatherington will want to talk to us all later on.'

At half four they squashed into his office for his summing-up. 'As you know, we're going to sign off the Milner accounts as correct,' Mr Heatherington said, 'but this has been a rather worrying audit, due partly to the fact that the stock is so valuable and none of us have the knowledge to value gems and jewellery accurately. Except for its size, one diamond looks pretty much like another to me.

'Mr Milner buys in stones and precious metals from various sources as raw materials, and he has the paperwork to support that. He's designing necklaces, rings and brooches and making them up himself. He has them assayed in Chester before selling them at greatly enhanced prices. All of that is normal business practice, but there's something about Mr Milner that makes me suspicious.'

Carrie burst out without thinking, 'Such as what?' Bill Brown had warned her off, but she mustn't let him see how much that had bothered her.

Brown thought about that. 'He seemed unusually edgy to me. The problem is that it's difficult to estimate how much of the precious metal is in the finished piece and how much is left to make up more rings. Mr Milner invited me to weigh them, and provided the scales, but by then stones and metal were inseparable, and diamonds are weighed in carats, pearls in grains and pure gold in grams. The situation is further complicated because sometimes he works in nine-carat and sometimes in eighteen-carat gold.

'I put Robbie on the job to check his figures, but there were dozens of pieces in stock, and Robbie said he wasn't certain he'd got it right. So with a few small corrections, and after discussing it with Mr Groves, I felt I had to take the client's paperwork as correct.'

Carrie was almost biting her tongue off. How could he be so suspicious of Gerry?

'Everything was so carefully locked up,' Robbie Wilson said.

'It has to be,' Carrie said. 'Even a little bit of gold has value.'

'And it's easy to steal, easy to hide on one's body,' Tim said.

'Yes, and equally easy in those locked rooms for Mr Milner to hide anything he wanted to amongst the tools in the cupboards and drawers,' Bill Brown said. 'He told me he had to lock everything up for security reasons. He let Robbie and me into both those rooms and watched us like a hawk as we tried to estimate the worth of what was there. In one room he was melting down gold.'

'Anyway,' Heatherington went on, 'we sampled one or two pieces, but not all. His business has made a good profit, bigger than ever before, when the Depression is resulting in lower profits in almost every other firm. I'm not too happy about that audit.'

'He looks a bit of a ladies' man and he's certainly a wide boy,' Robbie said, and Tim agreed.

Carrie could contain her anger no longer. 'Surely art plays a part once the article is made, and who can put a price on that?'

'Exactly,' Heatherington said, 'but everybody knows that, in work rooms like those, gold dust and tiny trimmings can lie on furniture and floors and the value can build up into a surprising amount. I should not say this, and it mustn't go beyond this room, but I wonder where he finds all these customers who can afford his high prices. I have a nagging feeling that Mr Milner is doing something he shouldn't.'

Carrie was furious with Heatherington for blackening Gerry's name without proof. He was wrong, wrong, wrong. She could not put her mind to anything else. Gerry had seemed so open and sincere; she'd seen no reason to think he was in any way dishonest. Surely she couldn't be wrong? Then she began to wonder whether she should tell him of Bill Brown and George Heatherington's professional opinion. It didn't take her long to decide she couldn't possibly do that.

By the next day, the auditor's report and the additional

documents were typed up and Carrie was able to study them.

'Milner employs a good accountant,' Heatherington told them. 'He knows how to put the best possible gloss on the figures in the balance sheet, but I do wonder if he's leaving any out.'

When Carrie told her aunts she was going out on Friday night, Prue was not too happy. 'You know I don't like you being out late on week nights,' she said firmly. 'You must get your sleep if you're to do your work the next day. And you need time to study.'

Maud marvelled, 'Lucky you, invited to go to the Royal Court to see a play about Sherlock Holmes? You'll have a lovely time. Is it being put on by the Repertory Players? It'll finish about half nine, Prue. You needn't worry about Carrie being out too late.'

Carrie found it difficult to decide what to wear. She'd worn her best dress to work, so it had to be her blue twinset and pencil skirt, because Gerard hadn't seen her in those. He'd offered to come and collect her, but if he rang the doorbell it would mean she'd have to ask him in and introduce him to her aunts. They'd expect him to be her age, and it would cause a barrage of questions she didn't want to face. She chose to meet him in town.

As she walked up to the theatre, she could see Gerry waiting for her outside the main entrance. What George Heatherington had told the team about him had upset her, and she thought her boss very much mistaken. Gerry looked so gentlemanly, so handsome as he came forward to meet her, threading his way through the crowd gathering for the performance.

'Hello, love.' He kissed her cheek and took her arm, and she was sure they'd got it all wrong.

He had seats on the front row of the balcony and he held her hand from the moment they sat down. The atmosphere of expectation excited her, and through the first act she was very conscious of his presence beside her. She knew that her attention was on him more than it was on the play.

As the interval drew near, the scent of coffee filled the auditorium, and when he took her to the bar, Carrie sipped hers watching him over the rim of her cup. He hardly took his eyes from her face and she was sure he was as much in love with her as she was with him.

Before the second act started, he said, 'I've prepared a cold supper for us for when this finishes. I hope you'll come back to my flat and share it with a glass of wine.'

'I can't,' she said. 'I really want to, but Aunt Prue expects me to be home before ten o'clock. That's one of her basic rules; I'd be in dire trouble if I was late.'

She knew he was disappointed and she desperately wanted to go to his flat. He tried hard to persuade her. 'Just for an hour; I'll run you home afterwards. You need only be half an hour late.'

It was very hard to say no, but she did. She immediately felt him cooling towards her, and she hated that. 'I'm sorry, I'd love to come, but it would upset Prue.'

He drove her home, but she made him stop the car a few doors from her house. Prue would quite possibly be lifting the curtains every ten minutes to see if she was coming.

'When can I see you again?' he pressed her. 'I have so much on over the next few days, I'm afraid it's going to be difficult for me to fit everything in. Monday lunchtime might be possible. How would it be if I drove round to your office and picked you up? I could park somewhere near and at least we could spend the lunch hour together.'

'Yes,' she said, 'that sounds lovely.'

'I'll bring a picnic lunch for us both.'

'No, I'll bring my sandwiches,' Carrie said. 'I don't want Prue to see I'm not taking any. She'll ask a lot of questions.'

'As you wish.'

He took her into his arms and didn't seem to care that it was quite a busy road and vehicles were passing all the time. Also, he'd parked near a street lamp, and she was nervous the neighbours might see them, but his kisses were bliss. He pushed his hand up under her twinset and that gave her the most delicious feeling of all. He told her several times that she was the most beautiful girl he'd ever seen.

Carrie heard firm footsteps coming along the pavement and struggled to break free of his arms. By the time she had, the person had passed and was a receding shadow she couldn't recognise. It made her jumpy, but Gerard's arms enfolded her again and quietened her heartbeat.

It was well after ten o'clock when she finally freed herself to go indoors. Prue was frowning and asked what time tram she'd caught. Fortunately, Maud was in a good mood; it seemed she'd just come home from some meeting with her teaching colleagues and she wanted to hear about the play. Carrie felt guilty and wondered if it had been Maud who had passed Gerard's car on her way from the tram stop, but her aunt's eyes were kind and gentle and she made no mention of it.

It felt wonderful to get into bed and relive that evening.

Carrie felt euphoric: she was in love with a man who was equally passionate about her. Gerry Milner was a man she could be proud of, a man who had already achieved something in life. She knew exactly what profit he'd made from the thriving business he'd built up, because she'd worked on his accounts. Connie had seemed to be streaking ahead of her on life experience, but now she had a chance of catching her up. She was bursting to tell her twin about Gerry, but it was no longer easy to talk to Connie without John being present, and John knew Gerard. She'd already asked him if he'd ever worked on his accounts, and it seemed that he'd been part of the team that had audited them last year.

She didn't want John to know that she and Gerry were in love, and she certainly didn't want anybody at Atherton & Groves to know. She'd told Mr Groves she had no intention of getting married, which at the time she'd believed to be true, but since then things had changed dramatically.

Gerard was really showing that he loved her and was forcing the pace; he was not going to hang back. In a dreamy haze she thought of being Mrs Milner one day, living in that splendid flat and being draped with gorgeous diamonds and pearls.

CHAPTER TEN

EVERY WEEKEND, AS SOON as Gerard Milner closed his shop on Saturday evening, he drove to Bryn Hafod, so he could relax all day on Sunday with his family. It meant he had to get up early on Mondays to be back in time to open up, but he counted it well worth it.

This weekend had been busier than usual because Megan's family had been staying with them, and he'd had to help and be sociable. He'd kept thinking of Carrie, the sensuous feel of her soft firm flesh and her springy curls. He'd been unable to get her out of his mind. Friday evening had not gone as well as he'd hoped, but he was not going to give up now. His mind went back to that delicious moment in his car when he'd thought he was getting somewhere with her.

He'd taken out all the pins from her sophisticated hair-do and let her hair hang loose, so he could run his fingers through it, but then she'd said she daren't go indoors with it like that, her aunts would be shocked. He'd held her little mirror and her handful of clips and watched her put it up again. Close to her in the car, he could smell her perfume. It was strong and heady and turning him on, yet it was not what was normally thought of as seductive.

'What is it?' he'd asked.

Carrie told him, but he'd never heard of it. 'Do you like it?'

'Yes, it's fresh and girlish, and, in a way, a little innocent. A bit like toilet soap.'

'That's putting me off it,' she'd laughed. 'It was a present from Maud last Christmas.'

'I shouldn't have said that,' he smiled. 'It suits you.'

He hadn't wanted to let her go, but she was determined, a well-behaved girl. He'd gone home alone, climbed the stairs to his flat and poured himself a whisky and soda in the sitting room. Then he'd snatched the cloth off the cold supper he'd prepared for her and filled a plate with his favourite delicacies.

He would like to be able to phone her and assure her of his affection, but even that was difficult because he could only contact her in her office, where she was surrounded by colleagues who would hear what she said.

Carrie set all his senses on fire, and he'd been hoping this would prove a long term alliance, but he found her frustrating too. He'd intended to bring this affair to a head, push this infatuation to the limit. She was a virginal teenager ripe for the picking, but ready and willing to move into the adult world.

Really, it was a process of wearing her down; sooner or later he was sure she'd give in. He longed to be her guide and teacher, but she was forcing him to wait.

Next week it would be difficult to see much of her because he'd arranged to bring his wife Megan and younger son Ivor back with him. They were hoping Ivor would be joining his older brother at Liverpool College in September. Megan was taking him there for what they called an entrance exam at eleven on Monday morning – really it was more of an assessment of his capabilities. The headmaster had invited them to have lunch at the school and see their older son play in a cricket match that afternoon.

Gerard had thought he could rely on them being out of the way for most of that day and it would be safe to see Carrie at lunchtime. On Tuesday Megan would need to rig the lad out in school uniform, and she'd probably want to stay for the best part of the week, to take him round the museums, enjoy a theatre show or two and buy more clothes for herself. It would be difficult to fit in the time to see Carrie.

Sunday night always came too quickly and, as planned, he drove his family back to Liverpool. No sooner had they unpacked and he'd settled down with a nightcap than the phone rang. He wasn't expecting anyone to call; could it be Carrie? She could have slipped out to a public phone. He leapt to his feet to answer it almost overcome with guilt and nerves that Megan might hear, but she was seeing Ivor into bed.

He was disappointed to hear a man's voice. 'Rod Reinhart, here.'

'Oh, yes, hello.' Gerard had been expecting a call from him for some time.

'How are you?' he asked. 'My team is ready and everything is in place now. I'll bring them round and introduce them tomorrow morning, and they'll be able to start work sometime next week.'

'Oh, my goodness, no! I'm sorry, Rod, I rather expected more notice.' He lowered his voice. 'I won't be able to show you all the goods tomorrow. I have some very special pieces that I don't keep here on the premises. It's safer not to, but I'll fetch them next weekend. I can have everything here by a week tomorrow.'

'Gerard, we don't work civil service hours, and I'll not be in England much longer.'

'I know and I'm sorry, I've been expecting you for ages and now is a particularly busy time. I've had the auditors in all last week, and my family will be with me most of this week.'

He heard Rod's sigh of resignation. 'Monday next week is all right though? I'll have to ring Marion and change it.'

'What time?'

'Early, say about ten? Shall I just bring them in and ask for you?'

'No, Rod, come to my private entrance at lunchtime. I close the shop at one o'clock, and I'd prefer my staff not to see you. I can lay on a little light lunch; there'll be four of you, yes?'

'Yes, thank you. How many days' work do you have for us?'

'Well, that depends how quickly your team works. There's quite a lot.'

'They'll come back to do the work after I've returned to Jo'burg. Right, and you'll have all these special pieces on hand to show us?'

'Yes, see you a week on Monday then. I'll look forward to that lunch.'

Gerard paused uneasily when he'd put the phone down. Suddenly it was all getting too much. He'd enjoyed the frisson of occasionally handling stolen goods or having a girl on the side, but not both at once. He felt on edge, it was making him nervous. Megan knew nothing about his little affairs or about him being involved in Rod's business. He wanted to keep it that way.

Suddenly he felt he couldn't cope with the complications of a double life. He wished now he had not spent so much time last week with Carrie; he'd had little chance to rest, but in a way she had breathed new energy into him. From now on, it was important that he kept alert and on top of things; he had to avoid being caught. He knew Rod, of course, but he didn't altogether trust him. Really he couldn't trust anybody.

He poured himself another whisky. He could bring back enough stuff to keep this team busy for weeks. A pity he couldn't see much of Carrie this week, but it couldn't be helped. Hopefully, he'd be able to pick up with her later; she'd seemed keen.

Usually on Saturdays Carrie went to work in the morning and then on to a lecture from the Liverpool Society of Chartered Accountants at eleven in their office in Fenchurch Street. But because she'd worked overtime on two evenings, she was given Saturday morning off, which meant she could sleep in. She had an exam coming up and needed to get down to some studying, but she found it a struggle because Gerard Milner was on her mind.

Maud had told Archie she'd pop round on Saturday morning with a sleeveless pullover she'd knitted for him, but Prue had involved her in baking for some church fund-raising occasion that afternoon and she'd asked Carrie to take it instead. As Carrie walked down to the tram stop, she spotted the phone box and decided to telephone her father to make sure he'd be at home.

'I'd be delighted to see you,' he said. 'Is Maud coming too?'

'No, she and Prue are preparing for some church fete this afternoon. She wants me to bring the pullover she's made for you.'

'Good,' he said. 'You come round and see us.'

Marion let her in, welcomed her warmly and ushered her into the sitting room.

'How are you getting on?' her father wanted to know. 'Are you still happy as an articled clerk?'

'Yes, very happy, I'm thoroughly enjoying it. It's a different life altogether.' Carrie caught the flash of Marion's diamonds and took hold of her hand to look more closely at them. 'You know all about diamonds, don't you? Tell me how they are valued. Valuation is what accountants are interested in.'

Marion laughed, took one of her rings off and pushed it on to Carrie's finger. 'This is a two-carat round diamond,' she told her, 'brilliant cut.' She explained about clarity and colour and brought out her loupe, the magnifying glass jewellers used to examine stones. 'See if you can see any imperfections, any cracks or foreign bodies. We call them inclusions, though not all inclusions are bad news; some enhance the value of a stone.'

Carrie tried. 'I can't,' she said. 'It looks perfect to me.'

'It takes a bit of practice,' Marion said. 'There is a small crack; it can be seen about here.' She prodded with her fingernail. 'Not many stones are perfect.'

'I don't think I can see it even now. It's a beautiful diamond. I ought to know more about precious stones and gold, seeing Dad is in the trade.'

'I love them and they provided me with an interesting means of earning a living in South Africa,' Marion smiled.

'Are you going to look for a job here?'

'Er . . . possibly, if I can find something to suit me.'

'I helped with an audit at a jeweller's shop last week.

I thought I'd never seen such large and dazzling stones before, but I'm sure yours are equally good, if not better.'

'What shop is that?'

'Milner's, in Lord Street.'

Marion gave a nervous laugh and leapt to her feet to go to the kitchen, where Archie was boiling the kettle. Carrie followed and watched from the doorway. 'Did you hear that, Archie?' Marion said. 'Carrie's been working in Milner's the jeweller's.'

'Do you know it, Dad? It's a gorgeous shop.' She saw them exchange uneasy glances, and then Marion carried the tea tray into the sitting room. Carrie followed, picking up the plate of chocolate biscuits that was to accompany it. 'Tell me more about diamonds,' she said, but Marion's enthusiasm seemed to have waned.

'Drink your tea before it goes cold,' Archie said.

'Don't give me the brush-off, Dad.' Carrie felt impatient. 'I've been working with this team in Milner's, and we all thought we should know more about the business. Come on, tell me all about gold and precious stones.'

'Diamond is the hardest substance on earth and yet it symbolises love,' Marion said with a sense of duty in her voice. 'I've yet to find a woman who doesn't love them. Even if the man who gives them lets her down, she might be able to console herself by selling them and getting a little cash back. Though there's practically no second-hand market in diamonds.'

'No second-hand market in diamonds? Surely there must be?' Carrie had learned from her bookkeeping work that everything had a value, however old, even second- or third-hand. 'There's always a value,' she said, 'though it can get less

136

and less over time. A diamond ring looks much the same if someone else has worn it; it doesn't wear out.'

Marion was shaking her head. 'Diamonds are different. Every woman wants them because not only are they beautiful ornaments, but they have come to signify wealth and status. Most diamonds are bought by men to give to women, and women prefer new ones.'

'Would they know the difference?'

'Possibly not by looking at them, but nowadays all jewellery is hallmarked with the date and place where it was made. Diamonds are cut differently now – we have learned how to make them sparkle more – and fashions change in jewellery as in everything else.'

'But there are some diamonds that are said to be worth a fortune,' Carrie protested. 'Think of all those in the Crown Jewels.'

'Yes, very big ones like the Hope or the Cullinan. They were cut up into lots of pieces but they were still big enough for a king's crown. There are fancy diamonds, too, in rare colours – yellow and green,' Marion said, 'and they'll always fetch high prices, but most diamonds mined today are clear little stones. Occasionally the work that has gone into making a necklace or a brooch is superb, and that adds to the value.'

She picked up a biscuit. 'When diamonds were first discovered, only the very rich could afford them, and the rarely seen glitter gave both the owner and the stone status. They commanded high prices because they were scarce, but over the years new diamond deposits were discovered and opened up.' Carrie thought it was beginning to sound like a lecture, but it was what she'd asked for.

'More jewellery was made that sparkled just as brightly, but it could be bought more cheaply,' Marion went on. 'The companies that had become rich and powerful selling to the rich were no longer able to make the profits they had. The rich didn't want diamonds now that they were no longer a luxury, and demand for diamond tiaras and extravagant jewellery almost disappeared.

'As long ago as the start of the Great War, De Beers persuaded the other big South African diamond mining companies to join together to stockpile diamonds and limit the amount offered for sale. They agreed to charge a high fixed price, and that helped to stabilise the market.

'De Beers understood that their future lay in selling to the masses while making diamonds appear to be an exclusive luxury. Second-hand diamonds are only rarely seen for sale, as this too would upset the agreed fixed price.'

Carrie's father smiled at her. 'Gold is different again. It has a publicly quoted international price, because governments use it to back the value of their currency.'

When she left to go home, Archie kissed her, and said, 'Come again, it's good to see you.'

Waiting at the tram stop, Carrie decided that something she'd said had made Dad nervous and changed Marion's manner, but she'd got what she'd wanted: a lecture on jewellery. She shared Marion's fascination with jewellery, and diamonds in particular. They had a lot in common.

CHAPTER ELEVEN

ON SATURDAY AFTERNOON, CARRIE went round to see Connie. Her sister had always been her confidante, and she was bursting to tell her about Gerard. She knew she could trust Connie with her secrets; they'd never kept things from each other.

She found Connie cleaning the living room and John helping her. 'Everything has to be done at the weekend,' he said as he pushed the carpet sweeper up and down. 'How are you getting on? I understand you've been at Milner's this week?'

'Yes,' Carrie said, hoping he'd go out and leave her alone with Connie. 'It's a lovely shop, and I saw the most marvellous diamond rings and necklaces. Out of this world.'

'I've got to go out,' Connie said. 'I lost a filling from my tooth on Thursday and I've got a dental appointment this afternoon.'

Carrie brightened up. 'My teeth are fine, but I'll come with you,' she offered.

'That's great. We've always gone together to the dentist, haven't we?'

'So Connie said,' John smiled. 'I offered to go with her, but I have plenty of other things to do. I need to fix up some shelves so I can unpack my books. It's not easy to find time for everything.'

'Good idea,' Carrie said enthusiastically. 'Connie and I can have a good natter.'

'Don't forget you need to go to the shops afterwards,' John said.

They set off. 'Life was a lot easier when Aunt Prue did all the shopping and cooking and cleaning,' Connie mused.

'Connie, I've been dying to tell you: I've got a boyfriend at last. I'm in love.'

'Marvellous news.' Connie was all smiles. 'Tell me about him; who is he?'

'Gerard Milner.'

'Milner as in that jewellery shop where you've been auditing this week? Some relative of the owner?'

'No, he *is* the owner. He's lovely, Connie.'

Connie's smile slipped. 'But isn't he old? John talked about him last year.'

'He's forty-four, but we get on like a house on fire.'

'Forty-four?' Connie was shocked. 'He's twice your age, nearly as old as Dad! A different generation.'

'I know, but age doesn't seem to come into it.'

'But it will. It's bound to.'

Carrie tried to explain. 'You and John have been trying to match me up for years, but I didn't hit it off with any of them. Now out of the blue . . .'

'But you hardly know this man.'

They reached the dentist's and Connie booked in. There was another patient in the waiting room. They sat down side by side as far away as they could, and Carrie continued to tell her sister in a near-whisper how Gerry had broken her spectacles, how he'd bought three more pairs for her and helped her clean the lenses, how he'd sought her out at lunchtimes and taken her up to his flat.

Connie looked shocked. 'Alone? Did he try anything on?'

'Shush. He kissed me. He makes me feel like a queen.'

'Nothing else? Just kisses?'

Carrie hesitated for an instant. There had been some heavy petting. 'No, not yet. He took me to the theatre on Friday night and asked me to go back to his flat afterwards. He said he'd prepared a cold supper for us.'

'You didn't go?' Connie was looking more concerned.

'No, I didn't. You remember what Prue was like when we went out at night? She used to lecture us regularly: we must not allow a man to lay a hand on us until he'd put a ring on our finger, and she meant a wedding ring.'

'So no sex yet?'

Carrie had to laugh. 'No, not yet, but I wouldn't mind. He's lovely.'

Connie looked horrified. 'For heaven's sake, Carrie! Thank goodness you haven't yet.'

'Why d'you say that? I seem to remember it was all right for you and John.'

'Shush! We were engaged and tired of waiting. I was totally sure of John and we'd known each other for ages. It was different for us.'

That irked Carrie. 'In what way was it different?'

The receptionist called Connie into the surgery; Carrie, who had always gone in with her before, tried to read one of the magazines but couldn't concentrate. This wasn't going as she'd expected. It would have been better not to tell Connie. Nothing was the same since she'd married.

The dentist followed Connie out to shake Carrie's hand. 'All is well with you, then? You have an appointment for your check-up?' They got away at last, but Connie was stony-faced.

'He just replaced your filling?' Carrie asked.

'Yes, I'd only lost half of it; he ground the other half out first.'

'Did it hurt?'

'I hardly noticed what he was doing. I was brooding about you.'

Carrie had difficulty keeping up with her twin; she could see Connie had not calmed down. 'I've never needed a filling in the front there.'

'Lucky you.' Connie strode on briskly. 'You hardly know this Gerard. He could be married already.'

'He isn't, I asked him.'

'What if he's lying? In fact,' Connie's brow was deeply furrowed, 'I think he's out to seduce you. Make you his mistress. If he's forty-four and hasn't yet been married, I'd say there's something the matter with him, and he's very unlikely to marry you.'

'Don't be silly. You don't know him at all.' Carrie had never been nearer losing her temper with her twin. 'Anyway, I can't get married for years and years, so what's wrong with being his mistress? I'd settle for that; I think it would be great fun.'

'Don't be ridiculous. You'll ruin your whole life.' Connie was angry too. 'Aunt Prue would have a fit at the very thought, and what would Dad say?'

'So it's all right for you and John, and Dad and Marion,

but not for me.' Carrie was furious now. This was horrible; she'd never fought with Connie like this before.

'He could get you pregnant, and where would you be then?'

'There are ways and means of avoiding that, as you've told me. Anyway, where would you have been if John had got you pregnant?'

'We'd have coped with it together. I'd have given in my notice at work before it showed. We'd have been hard up, but it wouldn't have been the end of the world. Anyway, with reasonable luck, John will soon be qualified, and now I wouldn't mind in the least. He thinks we should wait till next year but it would be nice not to have to. You are in a different position; there would be no guarantees for you. It would be a disaster. Hang on a minute.'

They had reached the greengrocer's shop. Connie was blindly collecting what she needed from the produce set up outside, while Carrie fumed. They walked on to the baker's in silence. 'Are you staying to have supper with us?' Connie demanded on the doorstep. 'If so, I'll get some cakes.'

'No, thank you.'

'Good, there's not much left to buy anyway.'

Her bags were filling with food; Carrie took one to carry for her.

'John thought Gerard Milner might be a bit dodgy; he didn't like him.'

'Well, I do. You've got it all wrong, Connie. We're in love, why can't you be pleased for me?'

'My advice would be to drop him, and John will say the same. If you get involved with him, what time would you have for going out with men of your own age?'

'Men of my age seem like callow youths. Gerard is a real man.'

'You'll never get a decent boyfriend if you stay with him.'

'I don't want a decent boyfriend. I want him. I love him.'

'You're mad.'

Carrie sighed. 'Isn't everybody supposed to be a little mad when they fall in love?' She'd expected Connie to be pleased at her news, and coming on top of what her manager had said, she was more than fazed by her reaction.

'I'll have to tell John.'

'No! You mustn't!'

'Perhaps he'll talk some sense into you.'

'No, Connie!'

'Yes, I feel I have to.'

'Nonsense! I forbid you to do any such thing. I told you because I've always told you everything, but you're not to tell anybody else. Here, take your shopping bag. I've had enough; I'm going straight home. Goodbye.'

Connie struggled back to her flat with her shopping, feeling more worried at every step. John came to help her put her purchases away. 'I've had a terrible quarrel with Carrie,' she burst out. 'She's got herself involved with a man. She says his name's Gerard Milner and they're in love. She thinks she's found her big romance.'

'With Gerard Milner?'

'Yes, she knows you know him and she's forbidden me to tell you or anyone else. He's forty-four, nearly as old as Dad, for heaven's sake.'

'Well, she knows she can't get married now,' John said,

'and d'you know, I've got the feeling he could already be married.'

'She's talking of being his mistress, quite openly. She thinks he'll give her a marvellous time. I told her she's a fool.'

'Don't upset yourself, Connie.' He tried to comfort her by putting his arms round her, but she wouldn't have it.

'She's going to ruin her life. I've got to stop her, but how?'

'Talk to her, make her see reason.'

'I've tried that, she won't listen to me.' Connie mopped at her eyes. 'We've never had a row like this before.'

They went to the pictures that evening and for a couple of hours Connie was distracted from the problem by Charlie Chaplin, but she didn't sleep well that night.

'I'm worried, I can't help it,' she told John in the morning. 'Carrie is going to make a mess of her life. She's not yet twenty and this dirty old man of forty-four has persuaded her that sex with him will be a wonderful experience. What am I going to do?'

'Tell your father.'

'She forbade me to do that, forbade me to tell anybody.'

'You've told me.'

'Yes, well . . .'

'Connie, if you're worried, you must do something about it. Let's go down to the phone box after breakfast and ask your dad if we can go round to see him this afternoon. He ought to know what she's up to.'

'Yes, I don't like being the only one in the family who knows. They'll blame me if things go terribly wrong for her. What if she gets pregnant?'

'Even more reason to tell your dad.'

'I thought you were taking me out this afternoon?'

'OK, ask him if we can come round for a cup of coffee this morning. Say there's something you want to tell him.'

When they arrived in Allerton later in the morning, Archie opened the door to them. 'I'm intrigued,' he said. 'What is it you want to tell me?'

Connie could smell the coffee as soon as she was in the hall. In the sitting room, with Marion handing round chocolate biscuits, she recounted the story. She was surprised at the effect her words had. Her father leapt to his feet, a crimson tide rushing up his cheeks, his fists clenched. 'The dirty rotter! He's a married man with children. Carrie's little more than a child. I'm going to punch him on the nose.'

'Calm down, Archie.' Marion took charge. 'Fighting talk will not help in this situation.'

'He's a criminal and he's taking advantage of a young girl who spent a few days working in his shop. And you, Marion, turned her into a raving beauty to catch his eye.'

'I know, I know. Come and sit down. You're angry and saying things you don't mean. Let's try and think of something that might help.'

'He needs frightening off. I can't believe Carrie is that naive. Wanting to be his mistress? She'll end up a gangster's moll if she doesn't watch out.'

'Archie, please! Connie, are you sure she meant it? She wasn't just saying . . .'

'She meant it all right; she was deadly serious. She thinks he's in love with her.'

'All right.' Marion was still standing. 'I think we should start by reasoning with her.'

'She won't listen to me,' Connie said.

'I'll talk some sense into her, the brainless fool,' growled Archie.

'Carrie is nobody's fool,' Marion said, 'and I don't think you are the best person to do this.'

'You do it then.'

'Archie, shush. I don't know this man, I've never met him, but you do, John. Would you be willing to have a word with Carrie?'

'Me?'

'I don't think young people want to take advice from their parents; they think we've lost touch with everything. But you're her generation; she'd be more likely to accept it from you.'

'Why would she? She wouldn't listen to Connie.'

'She took your advice about applying to Atherton and Groves,' Connie said. 'Somebody's got to talk to her. Please, John.'

'I think you're the best person,' Marion said. 'You know this Milner fellow and you've worked in his shop in the way Carrie has.'

'I did that twice, but I can't say I really know him.' John sounded reluctant. 'I'll try if you think it might help.'

'Thank you,' Marion said. 'You won't lose your temper as Archie would. Be persuasive and have your reasons worked out.'

'I'll do my best.'

'Connie, I've been meaning to ask if you'd like me to take you to my hairdresser. I want to treat you both the same; that's only fair.'

Connie's hand went up to touch her thick, unruly curls.

'Oh, Marion, I'd love that. We don't want to look exactly alike any more, but I want to be made over. I think I'd like mine cut short, really short.'

'Zoe will advise on what would suit you. Shall I try and get an appointment for you next Saturday?'

Connie was delighted. 'Oh, yes, please.' She felt much happier as she went home on the bus with John.

As soon as the front door had closed behind them, Marion turned angrily on Archie. 'What were you thinking of?' she demanded. 'You completely lost your head and said far too much about Milner. I thought you didn't want your family to know what we were up to.'

'I know, I lost my rag, I'm sorry. Connie won't have noticed.'

'John will, but there are no flies on either of them.'

'We're supposed to see Milner tomorrow. I can't possibly work with him.'

'Archie, you've got to. The last thing we need is a scrap between you two. It could upset the whole apple cart. Rod would be furious with you if you did that. You'll have to forget Carrie; anyway, what's all the fuss? I reckon she's the sort to take care of herself, and John will help her focus.'

'Milner's a criminal. What on earth can she see in him?'

Archie knew he couldn't let Marion down, couldn't manage without her now, but he didn't want to face Milner.

On Monday morning, Rod phoned again while they were having breakfast, asking to be picked up at the station in Lime Street. 'I'll catch the train that gets in at five past nine,' he said. 'Milner can't see us until lunchtime, but he's something of a friend and said he'd lay on a bit of lunch for us, so we need to be there at one. Tell Marion to fit in the other jewellers round that; we must try to get them all finished today.'

'That doesn't leave me much time to do it,' she complained to Archie when he told her what Rod had said.

'Two of the shops are on the outskirts of Liverpool,' Archie pointed out. 'One is in Prescot and the other in Whiston. We should be able to do those two before lunch.'

'Provided the owners are in their shops now,' Marion said. 'I have to be able to speak to them.'

'With a bit of luck they'll live over them.'

She managed to contact both owners, and as they set out to meet Rod, Marion said, 'Don't forget, Milner is a client of Starbright and is helping us turn over the extra penny. Nothing in your manner must tell him, or Rod, that you've anything against him. If you cause trouble, I'll never speak to you again.'

CHAPTER TWELVE

O N MONDAY MORNING, CARRIE went to work only to find that one of the junior clerks had phoned in to say he was sick. Leonard Groves came to her desk. 'I want you to take his place in the team,' he told her. 'They are to draw up the annual accounts of Patterson's, a large bespoke tailoring firm, who have several shops and also sewing rooms and offices in the dock area. The other three members have gone directly there this morning; it's not a long walk, or you can take a number 87 tram.' He put a faint copy of a street map giving the address of the firm on her desk. 'Go straight away,' he advised. 'They're just starting this morning; they'll need you.'

Carrie felt a little shocked; this meant she needed to ring Gerard urgently to let him know. All weekend she'd been looking forward to seeing him again, but while Mr Groves was smiling benignly at her, she couldn't lift the phone to change their arrangement. 'Yes, Mr Groves,' she said, and went back to the cloakroom to put on her hat and coat.

She saw a tram coming and got on, all the time worrying about how she could contact Gerard before lunchtime. It was never easy in a strange office, and she didn't want anybody to overhear what she said. Tim was one of the team, and none of her colleagues must know about it.

She breathed a sigh of relief when she saw a public phone booth outside the building – she could ring Gerard before she went in. She slid her pennies into the box and asked the operator to connect her. 'Gerry,' she said, 'I'm not working in the office today. I need you to come to Patterson's Bespoke Tailoring instead.'

'Carrie, darling.' The sound of his voice brought joy, but he went on, 'I'm terribly sorry, but I must cancel our lunchtime arrangement. My shop in Wavertree is in big trouble. I need to make an urgent visit.' He sounded tense.

'Oh! What sort of trouble? Nothing disastrous, I hope.'

'It's been broken into. I need to check what is missing.'

'That's awful, I am sorry. Can we fix another time? What about this evening?' She could ring Aunt Maud's school and ask the secretary to tell her she'd be late so they wouldn't be worried. She didn't like telling fibs, but really there was only one reason they'd accept without argument, and that was that she'd been asked to work late.

Gerry sounded anguished. 'I can't meet you today, I'm so sorry. I've missed you terribly all weekend, but I just can't.'

'When?' she choked. 'You said I could come any lunch-time.'

'It just isn't possible. I'm absolutely tied up today, and I'm afraid all tomorrow and possibly Wednesday too are off. It seems an age since I saw you. Look, I'll ring you on Wednesday; perhaps we can fix something up then.'

She was making excuses for him. 'You're a busy man, of course.'

'Yes.' She waited, expecting him to explain. After a long moment, he said, 'I think I'm a bit off colour, sickening for

151

something perhaps. Everything seems on top of me at the moment.'

Carrie was surprised by his change of attitude. 'I hope you'll find not too much of your stock has been stolen.'

She could hear he was struggling. 'Yes, I need to concentrate on my business – arrange to buy more stock. Look, Carrie, I'm terribly sorry.'

'I'll probably be working here for most of this week, but I don't know how long exactly.'

'You can always get me on this number and I can find you through Atherton's. Please forgive me. I don't want to lose touch. I couldn't bear that.'

Carrie was worried when she put the phone down. She must have got the wrong impression; it was almost as though he was trying to put her off. He'd sounded agitated. The theft from his shop must have upset him badly, poor dear; he was not at all like the confident and relaxed Gerry she knew and loved.

The day stretched ahead of her but for once it felt flat. She found it hard to settle down with Tim to do the job they'd been given, but no sooner had they started than she was told someone wanted to speak to her on the phone. She knew it couldn't be Gerry and was very surprised to hear John's voice. 'I want to see you at lunchtime,' he said. 'Connie says I must speak to you. You'll know what it's about.'

'Yes, I know,' she told him, 'and I don't think it's necessary.' She lowered her voice, 'I've heard what Mr Heatherington thinks, and I expect it'll be in much the same vein.'

'Have you dropped Milner?'

'Of course I haven't.'

There was a note of urgency in John's voice. 'You're going to see him again?'

'Yes, but it's none of your business. None of Connie's, either.'

'We think it is. Will you meet me at Pier Head? We could eat our sandwiches there. It looks like being a fine day.'

Carrie was cross with him. 'No, I don't want to. There's no reason for you to interfere.'

'We think there is. Connie's worried about you. If you prefer, I'll come to Patterson's and speak to you there. I've been in the team doing audits at Milner's over the last two years. There are facts about him you really should know.'

'What facts? They'll be half-truths, rumours and gossip. I don't want to hear them. People are envious because he's done so well.'

'If you've a grain of sense, you'll meet me and hear me out, then you can judge for yourself. So where shall I see you?'

She felt defeated. Gerard didn't want to see her and John was pressing. 'I'll walk along to Pier Head.'

'Good, about twenty to one?'

Carrie didn't have a good morning. She found it hard to concentrate on the work she was given, and was not in a good mood. John couldn't possibly have anything to tell her that she didn't already know. Nothing would make her change her mind about Gerard Milner.

John came to stand beside her while she was looking down the Mersey watching a tugboat fuss round the West African mail boat as it came into its berth in Princes Dock. 'There's a low wall over there we could sit on,' he said. 'It's not much of a picnic if we have to stand up.'

'What are these essential truths I have to hear?' she asked coldly, but she sat down, spread her handkerchief on the wall and took her sandwiches from her bag. 'He isn't very well at the moment.'

'I won't pretend to have any sympathy. Gerard Milner has a reputation for liking young girls, and he's a bit of a Lothario. He's also a married man.'

'No, he isn't. I asked him.'

'Then he lied. I've seen his wife in the shop. I've spoken to her. Did he tell you she'd died? Or they'd divorced? If he did, I think those must be lies too.'

Carrie could feel her heart beginning to pound like a drum. Surely this couldn't be true?

'He has three children too, two sons and a daughter. He bought a manor house in Wales, out in the country, where he visits his family. I don't suppose you see much of him at weekends?'

Carrie couldn't swallow the food in her mouth. For the first time she doubted what Gerry had told her.

'He goes home to his family on Saturday evenings and comes back to his business on Monday mornings.'

She could feel the strength ebbing from her knees.

'You're not the first, either. He'll spend a bit of money on you. Give you a good time. He can be very charming, but all he wants is a little fling. To put it bluntly, what he's after is a pretty companion to show off on his arm during the week, and a bit of sex on the side.'

Carrie felt ready to throw up. She pushed the rest of her sandwiches back in her bag.

'Milner is not the sort of man you think he is. Also, he is a long-term client of Atherton and Groves, and if your liaison became known, you could be putting your training and career at risk. Connie's worried stiff that you're going to get hurt. So am I, so you must forgive me for being so outspoken. You'll ruin your life and your reputation if you persist in seeing him.'

She could see the sincerity on John's face; hear the desperation in his voice.

'I'm fond of you, Carrie. I don't want you to be hurt. And I'm terribly afraid you're heading for trouble.'

She pushed herself suddenly off the wall and strode blindly away. She didn't want to hear any more. Had she been a complete fool over Gerard Milner? Even now she couldn't quite believe it of him. She trusted John and knew he was telling the truth as he saw it. He wouldn't want to cause trouble for her. But she'd asked Gerard if he was married and he'd said he was not, and he certainly hadn't acted as though he had a wife. She knew she wouldn't be able to believe ill of him until she heard it from his own lips.

She made it back to work in time by the skin of her teeth, but she couldn't keep her mind on the job. It took her a couple of hours to calm down enough to make a decision, and it was that she must see him as soon as possible and ask him face to face. He'd said he would be busy all this week, but she'd worry about this until she'd had it out with him.

She thought she'd found love, and now she ached inside at the possibility that he'd been deliberately deceiving her.

Archie had driven to Lime Street in time to meet Rod shortly after nine o'clock. Rod breezed out of the station full of energy and enthusiasm, and wanted to go straight to Prescot.

Unfortunately they'd arranged to pick Bill Dainty up at nine thirty, so they had to backtrack to collect him.

'How is your mother?' Marion could be relied upon to appear calm and collected.

'Far from well, but we're packing and I hope the sea voyage will do her good. Nothing must stop us getting on the boat on Thursday. I've been away too long already.'

The visits went like clockwork. Rod drove back into the city and parked in Lord Street, a yard or two down from Milner's shop. It was a wide thoroughfare, bustling with shoppers and traffic. Customers were still going in.

'High-class place,' Bill Dainty murmured. 'He'll be selling top-of-the-market stuff here.'

'We're to use his private entrance,' Rod said. 'He doesn't want his staff to recognise us. We need to drive round the back. It's round this block and there's an entry from another street. I know the way.'

Five minutes later, Archie was stifling his qualms as Marion led them up an outside staircase to Gerard Milner's private quarters above the shop. Milner met them at the door.

'Come in,' he said, taking them into a comfortable sitting room. He was a handsome fellow, too suave and a bit of a tailor's dummy, but of course he'd have to wear that dandified outfit in his shop. Archie couldn't bring himself to look him in the eye. Milner was a criminal, and the thought of him seducing Carrie made him feel sick. He would have liked to take him by the throat, but Marion kept giving him warning glances.

Gerard Milner was on edge as he waited for Rod Reinhart to bring his team to be introduced. His daily help had set out the lunch on his dining table in readiness, but he couldn't sit still. He poured himself a beer, and put out glasses for his guests. They arrived right on time; he'd just closed the shop.

'This is Marion Collard,' Rod said, 'an expert in gemstones.' Gerard liked the look of her: very womanly.

'Hello, I've worked with diamonds, so I know a bit about them,' she said disarmingly, 'but I'm not all that well up on other gems.'

'Bill Dainty, our general factotum, and this is Archie Courtney; he's by way of being our goldsmith.'

Gerard had put out his hand to greet him when he suddenly froze. 'Courtney?'

'Yes, that's right.'

An alarm bell went off in his head. 'Do you have a daughter?' he asked before he could stop himself.

'Yes, twin daughters.'

Milner needed to support himself against the sofa: the floor seemed to be opening up at his feet. Carrie Courtney! Oh my God, he hadn't foreseen this! What father would willingly shake the hand of a man who tried to seduce his daughter?

'You know Carrie, don't you?' Marion was smiling at him. That ratcheted up his fear another notch; his mouth was too dry to speak. He was thankful he didn't have to, as she went on, 'She told us last week that she'd been working on your audit.'

Gerard held his breath. Had Carrie mentioned that she was being wooed by him? Chased by him? How would a young girl describe the attention he'd given her? This was worse than he'd first supposed. The room was beginning to spin round him.

'Yes,' said Archie, 'she was very impressed with your shop.'

He felt a sweat of relief break out on his forehead. So Carrie had said nothing! Of course she had. It wasn't the sort of thing a young girl told her father.

'Do you have a family?' Archie was enquiring.

'Yes, two sons and a daughter.' He was flooding with dismay, knowing he should not have said that. He'd told Carrie he had no near family.

'He has a nice old manor house in Wales,' Rod said, 'all ready for when he retires.'

Gerard felt shaken; he'd had a real jolt to his nerves. Archie and the team would be working in his shop for several days, and they'd be returning from time to time. The implications of what that might bring scared him. He couldn't stop thinking about Carrie; he hoped she wouldn't tell anybody.

He must stay calm. 'A drink, Marion? What will you have?'

They were talking, but he took in little of what they said. He couldn't get the cork out of the wine bottle, and Archie had to help him. The men all asked for beer.

He hadn't really seduced Carrie; he'd tried, and failed. She'd been too well trained by her aunts. Carrie had nothing to complain about, but he'd have to make a clean break from her. That was a shame when they'd been getting on so well. He'd known he was playing with fire, but she'd turned out to be high explosive.

'Well, where's this stuff you have to show us?' Only Rod was his usual breezy self.

Gerard told himself he must keep his wits about him as he brought out the box he had ready. He needed these people to make this stolen property safe.

* * *

Archie could feel the tension rising as he ran his fingers through the stuff in the box. It was of a slightly higher quality than he was used to seeing, but it was nothing spectacular.

'What about these good pieces you had to bring from home?' Rod wanted to know.

Milner pushed some foolscap pages at him. 'These are the ones. Look at this month's police list,' he said.

Rod whistled through his teeth. 'Must be worth a bit. They even have pictures of them.' Archie knew it was a list of stolen jewellery that was circulated round the shops at regular intervals. Shopkeepers were asked to keep an eye open for the stuff and let the police know if they saw it offered for sale.

'Old-fashioned,' was Marion's opinion as she scanned the list. 'But the gems must be valuable.'

'What do you think of these?' Milner went to a cupboard and brought out several jewellery cases that were clearly quite old. The first he opened contained a ring, earrings and a necklace set with large gemstones, a mixture of sapphires and diamonds. The next contained a diamond necklace. Archie could feel the increased interest in the room.

'They're set directly into eighteen-carat gold,' Milner said. The pieces looked heavy, with little glitter in the gems due to the fact that no light could shine through them.

Rod picked one up. 'Ripe for a makeover, I'd say. What about you, Marion?' He swung the sapphire string in her direction. 'They're big stones; they'd stand recutting.'

'That would make them smaller,' Archie objected, picking up the diamond necklace. 'They'd lose some of their value.'

'It would make them a little smaller, but the market value

159

would go up, not down,' Rod said. 'I bet you could create something very nice out of these, Archie. Can't make out when this was assayed. Get out your loupe, Marion, and tell us.'

'This one is London 1854, and this . . . it's hardly visible, but I think 1862 in London again. They're both very heavy and old-fashioned. Their value would be in breakdown.'

Gerard said, 'I also have this, and it's extra special.' He opened a square leather case to display a magnificent necklace of baroque river pearls, with graduated strings of clear diamonds cascading from it. Archie gasped audibly with admiration.

'Wow,' said Rod, lifting it up to take a closer look. 'This is lighter and has magnificent diamonds, more fashionable. What's that other thing in the case?'

'It's a base-metal frame,' Gerard said, lifting it out. 'The necklace can be made to stand upright on it and become a tiara.' He demonstrated how it worked. 'What d'you reckon it's worth?'

'Hard to say.' Rod lifted it to catch the light. 'A great deal. More than the other two combined.'

'It's lovely,' Marion said. 'Assayed in . . . let me see . . . 1880. There's a lot of diamonds here. The biggest must be five carats, and there are several other big stones,' she was counting, 'six of them along the front here, and plenty of smaller ones.'

'The bigger ones all need recutting,' Gerard said firmly. 'That's the only way to make them safe.'

'Could you do that, Marion?' Rod asked.

She was screwing up her forehead. 'No, I wouldn't want to botch stones like these.'

Bill was fingering the necklace; he whistled through his teeth. 'Worth a king's ransom.'

Archie took it from him. 'It would be a shame to break this up. It's from a different era, and very beautiful. Original shagreen case, too.'

'It's too easily recognisable and will have been specially insured,' Gerard said. 'It'll have to be done.'

'Worth a lot more broken up,' Rod agreed. 'Why didn't you tell me you had these before now? I could have taken them to Amsterdam last month.'

'I only saw them myself two weeks ago.'

Archie shivered. 'Does that mean they're from a recent robbery? They'll be hot property.'

'They came from a big place in Wales. As far as I'm concerned, the sooner they're broken up, the better.'

'A shame to do that.' Archie let the necklace run through his fingers. 'It's a work of art.'

'You won't change my mind,' Milner said. 'That one in particular would be worth more broken up, and the stones would be unrecognisable. There's no other way to make it safe to handle.'

'It would be worth another trip to Amsterdam,' Rod mused. 'What else have you got? Anything else worth recutting?'

'Possibly.' Milner prodded around in his box and brought out a brooch and some earrings.

'I'm booked to return to South Africa on the *Transvaal Castle* next Thursday,' Rod said, 'and I've got to go. I've already been away too long. But I might be able to catch a train to Harwich in time for tonight's ferry and take them over.'

'There's a lot of work here,' Marion said. 'It will take a

couple of weeks at least, maybe a month.'

'Yes, one of you will have to fetch them back when they're ready. Best thing is to come with me now to learn the drill. What about you, Marion?'

She was frowning in concentration; Archie knew why. She didn't want to leave him with Milner, and she didn't trust him to keep his mouth shut with Rod either.

'What about both of us coming?' she suggested. 'We've been working hard and a break would do us good.'

'A quick trip to Amsterdam won't be a rest cure. No, better if Archie stays here with Bill; you'll get through quite a lot of work while we're away.'

Marion shot Archie a warning glance. 'OK,' she said. They both knew it was no good arguing.

Rod took a deep breath. 'Right, we need to get going. Time is of the essence. Archie, I want you to find out about train and ferry times for us,' he ordered.

'Use my phone there,' Gerard told him.

Obediently, Archie got up to ring Lime Street station. 'You've got an hour to catch a train,' he reported. 'It has a restaurant car and connects with a train that will get you to Harwich in time for the five o'clock ferry.'

'Good.' Rod was counting pound notes on to the coffee table. 'I've had to give Gerard a cheque to get more cash to fund this trip.'

Gerald smiled. 'There's always plenty of ready cash in a shop.'

Marion was stuffing the notes into her lizard-skin purse, which exactly matched her large and elegant handbag. She always took charge of the cash and acted as banker for them.

'You take Marion back to the house to pack an overnight bag,' Rod went on. 'Mine is in the car. Then you can pick me up and take us to the station.'

'What about this jewel case?' Milner was waving it towards Archie. 'It has the name of the retailer on it. It could be incriminating. Can you burn it? I have only an electric fire here.'

'Yes.' Archie was feeling like their lackey. 'What about that tiara frame?'

'It's base metal,' Marion said, 'and has no marks on it. You could drop that in our bin. Most people won't know what it is.'

'Bill can make a start on the more mundane stuff you have here, and Archie, you could come back after you've taken us to the train.' He smiled. 'The sooner the work's done, the better.'

Archie was not pleased that Marion was going with Rod to Amsterdam. He didn't want to go with them – that would drag him deeper into Rod's criminal schemes – but he didn't want to stay on Milner's premises either. He didn't want to be reminded of what that man had tried to do to Carrie. At least it would be restful at home with both of them away, but he wouldn't really be able to relax until he knew Rod was on his way back to South Africa.

CHAPTER THIRTEEN

GERARD MILNER STILL FELT shaky. It had come as a shock to find that Carrie's father was one of Rod's team. Of course, picking up a girl was always risky but he'd done it before without it causing problems. He prided himself on seeing a danger before it could possibly land him in trouble, but he hadn't foreseen this. At least Rod had taken that hot necklace and other jewellery away.

Earlier he'd asked his daily help to prepare lunch for five, but first Archie and Marion had shot away, and then Rod, leaving him with Bill Dainty. The last thing he wanted was to entertain that fellow for lunch, but he had to show he had no quarrel with him. He had thought Bill quiet, but once they started discussing the jewellery trade, he was surprised at his wide experience. Fortunately Bill had an enormous appetite, and Rod ate quickly and wrapped some up to take for Marion, which got rid of most of the food. They carried what remained down to the workroom; Gerard told Bill it was for Archie's lunch, but he wanted it out of his flat before Megan came back.

The last thing he wanted was to have them working in his shop this afternoon while Megan was about, but Rod had arranged that they would. He had to keep them apart at all costs.

The doorbell rang on his private entrance and, taking a deep breath, he went to face Carrie's father. 'They caught the train, got away all right,' Archie reported, 'but by the skin of their teeth.'

There was something aggressive in the way Archie looked at him. It bothered him, and made him wonder if Archie knew he'd been pursuing Carrie. He must be careful to treat him exactly as he would if he'd never seen her.

He took him straight downstairs and through one of the doors marked PRIVATE. Bill Dainty was already hard at work on an emerald ring.

'You think it's safe for us to work here when your shop is open?' Archie asked as he lifted the bag of tools he'd brought with him on to the workbench. 'A lot of jewellers prefer us to work at night.'

Gerard was feeling the strain. 'It's very difficult for me at the moment, as my wife and son are here, and will be for the next few days. You've probably noticed that these work-rooms are at the bottom of the stairs going up to my private quarters,' he said. 'Normally I'd want you to use them so my staff don't see you, but it's even more important that my family don't, so please don't come up looking for me, and use the shop entrance for now.'

He wanted to impress on them the need to take care. 'Did you notice that I've locked us in? It's just a precaution, and if I leave you I'll lock you in from the outside, but that is the key hanging up there, so you can get out if you want to. Needless to say, I'd prefer you to stay until I come back for you. I'll make sure the coast is clear then.'

'Don't worry, we will.'

'I was glad to see Rod take away those three necklaces,' Milner said. 'Keeping them on the premises is a risk; they'd be too easy to identify.'

'There's still all this,' Archie said, looking through the contents of the box of jewellery they were to work on. He selected a diamond brooch to start with.

'It's a question of reducing the risks. It would be much harder to prove where these came from, and soon it will be impossible.' Gerard tried to smile, tried to appear as normal as he could. 'I'll bring you a cup of tea in the middle of the afternoon.'

He left them to it. He needed to keep an eye on his shop. It soothed him to find that business was slow and the shop quiet. Everything was normal. He was working at his desk and had just settled some small problem with the manager of one of his suburban branches when the phone rang again. Hearing Carrie's voice made his frayed nerves jangle again.

Carrie felt thoroughly churned up by the rumours she'd been hearing about Gerry. She still only half believed them. Had something happened that had made him put her off?

At about three o'clock, she found herself temporarily alone in the office, so she picked up the phone and asked the operator to connect her with Gerry's private number. She was relieved to hear his voice, and know he was in his own office.

'Gerry, I have to see you.' The need for urgency was making her sound breathless. 'I know you said you were going to be busy all week, but something's come up and I have to talk to you. Please, can I come to your shop after you've closed it this afternoon?'

She knew he was making excuses to put her off; she had to interrupt him. 'I'll not stay long, I promise.' She couldn't bear to be left with these terrible doubts for a whole week. She was being torn in two. 'You could spare me an hour, couldn't you?'

He said nothing for a moment or two while she held her breath, and then he said soothingly, 'Carrie darling, of course. Though I'll have all the time in the world by Thursday; could it not wait till then? I hate putting you off like this. I'm really missing you.'

'It can't wait. I'm worried,' Carrie said firmly. 'Tonight, please.'

His head was spinning. Carrie's father was working downstairs, and Megan would be back within the hour, but he had to keep calm. 'All right, why don't you meet me outside the Royal Court, where we met last Friday? I know a quiet little café up a side street near there where we could have a cup of tea. I can't do it earlier than six fifteen, as I have to get the stock locked away. Is that all right?'

'Yes, thank you. I'll be there.' Carrie decided she'd phone Aunt Maud's school and ask the secretary to tell her she was meeting a friend to have a cup of tea before coming home, though she knew she'd face questions about that from Aunt Prue.

Later that afternoon, Gerard's hands were shaking as he took two cups of tea to the workroom. Megan and Ivor were back and having tea upstairs. Having Archie this close was altogether too nerve-racking.

He inspected the work Bill and Archie had done, and was pleased to see that they were careful workmen, perfectionists, and the jewellery looked as though it had just been made. 'All it needs now is a new assay mark,' he said.

'Marion will put that through the Chester assay office when she gets back,' Archie said.

'What time do you want to leave? I close the shop at five thirty,' Gerard told them, 'but the staff will be here for at least half an hour after that, locking everything away in the safes. Better to go just before half five, or when it all settles down afterwards.'

'What about it, Bill?' Archie asked. 'Shall we carry on working until later? Then we can have a bit of a lie-in in the morning. We'll come in about nine thirty. Is that all right with you?'

'Yes, fine.' Gerard's mind was whirling. 'I need to go out for a short time once I've closed the shop, but I'll be back by seven.'

He went back to his office thankful that he'd not allowed Carrie to come to his apartment. It was going to be a difficult interview anyway, and the thought of her father being down-stairs in the workroom while he tried to deal with her would paralyse his mind. She might shout and cry; she'd probably plead and try to cling to him. At least in a café, with other people around, she'd be more inhibited.

He stretched back in his chair with a groan as he remembered that the quiet tea shop he'd been thinking of closed its doors at five thirty. Whatever was the matter with him? He leapt to his feet to pace the floor. He'd have to take her to a pub instead, and he'd have to be very firm with her and finish this affair once and for all.

The danger as he saw it was that Rod had put time and effort into selecting this team and they must all remain on harmonious terms. It was important that nothing should interrupt the work. Archie must never know he'd had designs on his daughter. Any confrontation with him could blow things apart. If Archie turned nasty, he knew enough about what they were doing to have them all charged with handling stolen goods.

Gerard made himself sit down at his desk and open the ledger he'd been working on. Usually thinking of his success brought comfort, but not today. He knew he had to deal with this problem. It was more important to stay on good terms with Rod and his team and get the work in hand finished. He needed to brush Carrie off; he couldn't cope with her while her father was on his premises. She really turned him on, but in this situation she could be dangerous to their plans – veritable dynamite.

At five o'clock, as the office emptied, Carrie went to the ladies' cloakroom and spent time redoing her hair and putting on more lipstick before she left. She knew she'd have an hour or so to kill before Gerard would be able to get away, and she tried to fill it by walking around the streets. She found the waiting was heavy on her nerves.

The shops were closing and the pavements were full of people rushing for trams and buses at the end of the working day. She studied the displays of clothes in the shop windows, trying to decide what would suit her if only she could afford to buy. She came to a bookshop, but she got her books from the library. Time seemed to be standing still, and there was a chill in the evening breeze. Suddenly she pulled to a halt beside a gleaming new Austin 10/4 Lichfield saloon parked at the kerb.

She stared at the number plate; was this Dad's car? It looked like it. Yes, there was his mackintosh tossed on the back seat. That must mean he was somewhere close. She looked round, but saw no sign of him. The shops had all closed now, and she couldn't think where he might be. She glanced at her watch and found it was time to make her way to the rendezvous. It was too early for the theatre crowds to start gathering, and there were fewer people about on the main streets now.

As she neared the Royal Court, she thought she could make out Gerard's figure striding out ahead of her. She followed him and watched as he stood to wait, a lonely figure under the placards announcing that *An Inspector Calls* would be performed by the Liverpool Repertory Company tonight.

He had changed out of his formal working suit but looked even more elegant in a smart but casual jacket and slacks. She hung around for a few moments out of his sight on the other side of the road, rehearsing again what she meant to say. She still hoped that John and Connie had got it all wrong. He kept looking at his watch and she knew he felt uneasy too. She took a deep breath and ran across the road to his side. 'Hello, Gerry,' she said, trying to smile.

'Hello.' There was no sign of a smile from him. 'Change of plan,' he said, putting a hand on her elbow to steer her. 'There's a nice pub along here. It'll be quiet at this time, just the place for us.' They walked another few yards. 'Here we are,' he said, and she went in ahead of him and sat at a rickety table in the corner. There were not many customers, and the place reeked of stale beer. 'What would you like to drink? A glass of sherry?'

'No, thank you, nothing alcoholic.' Aunt Prue would smell it on her breath and she'd told her she'd be drinking tea. 'A soft drink, please.'

Gerry went to the bar and returned with a glass of lemonade for her and half a pint of beer for himself. He sat down on the opposite side of the table. 'Now then, what was it you wanted to see me about that's so urgent?'

'I've been hearing rumours about you that I don't like and don't believe.' She looked him straight in the face and thought she saw him tense. Her heart sank.

'What sort of rumours?'

'That you're married and have three children. Is it true?'

'Who told you that?' He was staring back at her, his face open and innocent. John must be wrong.

'My twin sister and her husband; he knows you slightly. You told me you weren't married and had no near family, that you were lonely. So which is true?'

He was hesitating, and any hope Carrie still had drained away. 'So you *are* married?'

He wouldn't meet her eyes now. 'Yes, you must have got the wrong impression.'

'No, it was the impression you meant to give me. In fact, you lied.'

He turned on the charm, but it seemed a little false. 'I wouldn't put it quite like that. I was so beguiled by your beauty that I wanted to see more of you. I couldn't help myself. You have the most wonderful eyes.'

He was staring into them now with the innocent look on his face again. Was it the expression assumed by the practised liar? 'You must forgive me; you don't understand the power that beauty gives you. I wanted so much to see you again.'

Her lips straightened. 'Flattery won't help.'

'I was afraid you'd go straight out of my life when the audit finished if I didn't do something. I couldn't resist that first impulse.'

'What first impulse?'

'I know I broke your glasses, but I always meant to replace them. I wouldn't have left you out of pocket. It was pure serendipity that they were sunglasses, wasn't it?' He smiled for the first time.

Carrie's stomach lurched. She'd never for one moment suspected that her broken glasses were not a pure accident. She felt sick. 'So you went out of your way to trap me? I thought you loved me in the way I love you.' She felt tears start to her eyes. 'Was I to be another scalp for your collection?'

'Of course not. It wasn't like that.'

'I trusted you.' She couldn't believe he was trying to make excuses. 'I didn't really believe John. I couldn't until I heard it straight from your lips.'

'You don't understand—'

She felt the heat run up her cheeks as anger gripped her. 'Gerard, I understand only too well. It's lust you feel, not love. You've been softening me up to be your mistress, just as Connie said. I suppose the wife and three children are real? Yes, I can see they are.'

'We could have made it work.'

'Oh, your wife doesn't mind? Or do you keep her in ignorance?'

She could see his patience had snapped. 'Carrie, you wanted it, you know you did. You were ripe and ready for it.'

'You're a dirty old man chasing young girls in the hope of getting them into your bed. You're despicable, a liar. You were using me for your own ends, with no thought about how I'd feel. Thank goodness I came to my senses in time.'

Carrie stood up with a jerk, picked up her untouched glass of lemonade and emptied it over his head. She heard his involuntary grunt of shock before she threw the glass at the wall behind him so that it crashed and shattered. She saw the other customers turn to look as she stormed out.

Gerard Milner took a shuddering breath, pulled out his handkerchief and mopped his face, then looked round furtively to find everybody was staring at him. The barman came over with a wide grin on his face. 'Fourpence,' he said, 'for breakages.'

Gerard slapped the coins on the table and took a few sips of his beer, but he felt wet and sticky and he knew he smelled of lemonade. Worse, he was worried now about how Carrie had learned about his wife and children. She'd said she'd been warned by her sister and her husband, but how had they found out? He didn't like people knowing his circumstances; there were things that had to be kept quiet.

He got up suddenly and strode out. She'd drenched his new jacket and it would never be quite so smart after this, and he'd have to wash his hair. He knew he'd seen the last of Carrie Courtney. It was not the way he'd expected it to end, but at least now he only had to deal with her father. And Megan, of course. He needed to get home and cleaned up before she or Ivor noticed he'd been drenched.

* * *

Carrie felt an utter loss of hope, a sense of futility, as she waited for a tram to take her home. She'd thought Gerard was showing love and passion for her. Intense passion, which she'd certainly felt for him. She'd thought she'd found the love of her life at last, but all the time he'd been blatantly trying to seduce her.

She could think of nothing else all evening. What a fool she'd been, what a stupid fool. Prue had kept her dinner hot for her, but it had dried out in the oven, and anyway, the last thing she wanted was food as she parried her aunt's questions.

By bedtime, Carrie knew she was angry not only with Gerard Milner, but with herself too. He'd been right when he'd said she was ready for love, but she should have known she wouldn't get it from him. How could she have been so easily taken in? She'd thought she was far too much a woman of the world to fall for that. She'd never doubted Gerard for a moment.

Connie had told her that the first taste of married love was the experience of a lifetime, and she'd wanted that for herself. She'd had a terrible row with Connie when her sister had tried to bring her to her senses, but now she'd calmed down, she was glad that John had warned her off before she'd succumbed to Gerry's endearments. She was older and wiser now, and would be more careful in future.

She was itching for revenge, but it gave her little pleasure to remember how she'd emptied her glass of lemonade over Gerry's head. That was not nearly enough. Fuming, she thought up all sorts of schemes to get even with him: she'd find out where his wife lived and let her know what he was up to. She'd go to his shop and break his windows, go inside and smash all those glass cases, scatter jewellery everywhere, make a scene in front of his customers.

She'd just thrown herself angrily into bed when there was a tap on her door and Aunt Maud came in wearing her flannelette pyjamas and ancient dressing gown. She put a small tray with two mugs on the bedside table.

'You seem upset tonight,' she said, 'so I've made us some cocoa to calm you down and help you sleep. Has something happened?'

Carrie shook her head miserably. She couldn't possibly explain what had happened, not to her aunt.

Maud sat on the end of the bed. 'I've been meaning to have a word with you for some time,' she said. 'I'm pretty sure you're troubled, and I'm wondering if it has anything to do with that man I saw you with in a parked car just down the road.'

Carrie was stricken. So it had been Aunt Maud who had passed them, and she'd never mentioned it until now! She felt another wave of guilt and her cheeks were suddenly burning.

'It has, hasn't it?' Maud said gently. 'I don't wish to pry, Carrie; I mention it only because I fear for you.'

She reached for her mug of cocoa, and Carrie took a few sips from her own; it gave her something to do. 'I'm all right, there's nothing for you to worry about,' she said.

Maud's blue eyes were soft and kindly. 'You're very young still, and Prue says I must tell you something so that you understand and protect yourself.'

Carrie was calmer now; she supposed Maud had heard of her trouble from Connie, and that Maud was about to say much the same as John had in order to reinforce the message.

'I was a bit older than you,' Maud began, 'when I met my

fiancé. He was in the army and we were very much in love.'

Carrie was instantly fascinated. 'Fiancé? I didn't know you'd been engaged.'

'Yes, we were engaged for two years and saving up to get married. We had even set the date. But the country went to war with the Boers in South Africa, and Daniel was sent out there to fight. I never saw him again.'

Carrie put out a hand to cover one of Maud's. 'That must have been terrible for you. I am sorry.'

'There's worse, Carrie, much worse. I did receive two letters from him, but they took a very long time to reach me. When I found I was with child, I wrote to tell him. I didn't say a word to anybody until his family informed me that he'd been killed. By that time my pregnancy was well advanced. I had to tell Prue.'

'Oh, Maud!' Carrie scrambled out of bed to hug her. 'How awful.'

'Prue arranged everything for me; she couldn't have been kinder.' Carrie could hear the anguish in Maud's voice. 'She told our mother, and between them they kept it as quiet as possible. It was a terrible time for the whole family. Dad had been killed in a mine accident a month earlier. I brought huge disgrace on them all, on top of everything else, but they were very good to me.' Maud mopped her face with the hem of her dressing gown.

'How did you manage? I've never heard so much as a breath of this. It must all have been kept absolutely within the family.'

'It was. Mother had grown up in Liverpool and had already decided she wanted to return, but she was waiting for the mining company to pay out compensation for Dad's death. I had to leave my job, of course, and Prue did the same. She rented a small house in Toxteth and we moved there, while Mum stayed in St Helens with our brothers, who were still working for the company.'

'What about the baby?'

'It was a boy, a healthy seven-pound boy. I called him Daniel after his father.'

'You had him adopted?'

'I had no choice. I couldn't work and look after a child, and after my family had done so much for me, I had to go along with what they thought best.'

Maud was sobbing on Carrie's shoulder now. She blew her nose. 'That's the worst part of it for me. I've heard nothing of him since I handed him over and signed the adoption papers. He would have been given a new name and a new family, but I have no idea where he is, or what happened to him. All I can do is hope that he's happy.'

'I hope so too,' Carrie said. 'It must be awful thinking of your own child, your flesh and blood, and knowing nothing about how he grew up.'

'He was Daniel's flesh and blood too,' she said. 'I think it would have comforted me to bring up his child. Over the years, I've longed to see him, to have news of him, but it was not to be.'

'I always thought that you'd had a quiet, uneventful life, Aunt Maud.'

'No.' She'd recovered her composure now, and brought out a small box and two letters still in their envelopes, though they looked as though they'd been handled a great deal over the years. 'This is the ring Daniel gave me.' She opened the box.

'A sapphire.'

'No, it's a blue topaz. I don't suppose Archie would rate it very highly, but Daniel didn't have much money.'

'Money doesn't come into it,' Carrie said. 'I've never seen you wear it.'

'His death, Daniel's birth and adoption . . . it was all too painful.'

'That was a long time ago now, Maud. Daniel has long grown up.'

'Perhaps I will wear it.' She slid it on to her finger and stretched out her hand to see it twinkle in the lamplight. Then she looked up and smiled sadly. 'That is why Prue insists that you must not be out late at night. She fears the same thing could happen to you.'

'It won't. It's all over in my case, over and finished. At least you know Daniel loved you and everything would have been fine if he'd lived. My story is very different. I was taken in by a womaniser, an older man who didn't love me but was after all he could get. You need have no fear that I shall be in the same boat; he didn't get near enough for that.'

'Prue and I are bound to worry about you, love.'

Carrie's eyes were prickling with tears as she hugged her aunt again. 'Thank you for telling me. I now understand exactly what a mess I could have got into, and I'll try to be kinder to Aunt Prue in future.'

When Maud had gone to her own bed, Carrie settled down for the night. She thought about the life Maud had had. She'd always felt closer to her than she had to Prue, and she knew Connie had too. She supposed that was because she was gentler and more used to dealing with children.

She remembered the anger and vengeance she'd wanted to shower on Gerard. She realised now that she must never do anything like that. It would have landed her in trouble with the police. Reports would have got into the newspapers, and the whole city would have been able to read about her being an easily led fool.

She must write Gerard Milner off as an embarrassing experience. But she wouldn't be able to forget him; it still hurt and would rankle. Perhaps she'd get even with him when the opportunity arose, though deep down she realised that it probably never would. No, she must be satisfied with the company of her family and workmates until such time as fate led her to someone worthy of her love.

Archie and Bill had worked hard all afternoon, though Archie kept thinking of Marion and Rod travelling to Amsterdam. He heard the staff leaving the premises, and shortly afterwards Gerard came to let them out through the shop, saying he still had to cash up. Archie dropped Bill off on the way home, and by that time he was hungry, but also tired. The last thing he felt like doing was cooking for himself.

He was held up at traffic lights in front of a suburban parade of shops, and saw that a fish and chip shop was open. That was exactly what he needed; he parked and walked back. Once he had the newspaper-covered parcel in his hands, the delicious scent fuelled his hunger. With his mouth watering, he drove home as quickly as he could and unwrapped it on the kitchen table to start eating.

The cod was succulent, while the batter on the outside was

crisp and savoury; the chips were crisp and hot. Archie ate slowly, relishing every mouthful. He'd done a good day's work and deserved a rest. Idly he smoothed out the newspaper that his meal had been wrapped in, and began to read:

ROBBERY AT CORS Y GEDOL HALL

On Sunday evening, while Sir Harold Quincey-Downes and his family were attending a church service at Pentrefelin village church, daring thieves got away with jewellery worth a fortune. Sir Harold was able to point out to the police paintings of the jewels that were stolen. They were being worn in the family portraits hanging in his home. 'This necklace,' he said, 'and that tiara have been worn by the ladies of my family for generations, and have great sentimental value.'

Archie felt suddenly sick and pushed the food away from him; it would choke him to eat another mouthful. His heart was thumping as he looked at the newspaper page again. It was from the *Liverpool Daily Post*, and there was a heavy grease spot over the date, making it almost illegible, but he thought it was only about two or three weeks old.

It had to be the jewellery Rod and Marion had taken out of the country. They and Milner had been so sure that would make it safe for them, but would it? He read on.

There have been several similar robberies recently in the north-west; they are thought to be the work of a Liverpool gang.

Sweating, Archie leaned back on the kitchen chair. The police were searching for the thieves; perhaps they'd already caught them. They could be forced to say what they'd done with their booty. That would give them a direct lead to Gerard Milner, and from him, it must surely be a small hop to the Starbright Jewellery Company.

He thought of the leather jewellery case that Milner had given him to burn. He jerked to his feet and went to the sitting room. He'd left it together with the tiara case in the hearth. Marion had told him to put that in the bin, but now it seemed too risky. He didn't intend to light a fire tonight, and probably wouldn't until Marion returned. He rushed upstairs and pushed them under his suitcase on top of the wardrobe, where they wouldn't be seen.

Archie had been afraid from the beginning that Rod was overconfident. Now he spoke aloud. 'How can you be so sure? Sooner or later you'll be caught, and so will the rest of us. Look what happened to Bill Dainty.'

Realising that he was talking to himself, he groaned. Then he went downstairs again to get himself a bottle of beer. His knees felt weak, as though they could no longer support his weight.

He hardly slept that night in his lonely bed, and got up the next morning feeling exhausted. He wished Rod was here; he wanted him to heed the warning and be more careful.

He knew he should not show the page to Bill, or tell him about it – Marion didn't want Bill to know too much about their affairs – but once he'd picked him up, he had to talk about it. He could think of nothing else.

'No need to panic yet,' Bill said easily. 'The police have to have proof.'

'But if they catch the thieves . . .'

'They're unlikely to get a full confession.'

'They'd only have to prove a connection to Milner to throw suspicion on us.'

'They won't say anything about him. They might want to use his services again. They can't get everybody to talk, you know. Anyway, the diamonds are no longer in this country.'

As soon as Milner let them in, Archie had to tell him about it too. He pulled out the crumpled page of newspaper, still smelling of fried food, to show him. Milner smoothed it out to read on the bench in the workroom, and it seemed to induce the same feeling of foreboding in him.

'Oh my God,' he said. 'I was afraid that tiara came from a recent robbery.'

Archie couldn't get it out of his mind, and when he tried to work, he couldn't concentrate. Bill was working at twice the speed he was managing today, but eventually the familiar job soothed his nerves.

He'd cut sandwiches for the two of them to eat at lunchtime, as he couldn't believe Gerard Milner was going to continue being hospitable throughout the time they were here, but shortly after one o'clock, Milner came to the door with a tray of tea and some fancy food. 'I've closed the shop for the lunch break, and I can recommend the raised pork pie. Do help yourselves.'

Bill didn't need to be invited twice; he was on his feet in a moment, helping himself. 'This is very kind of you. Thank you, you're doing us proud. We don't usually eat this well at lunchtime.'

Archie's appetite had returned now, and he thanked Milner reluctantly, as Marion had made him promise not to upset the man, but he worried and fumed. Gerard Milner was a criminal; he must be to need the services Starbright was providing. He was also an adulterous seducer, but he was bending over backwards to be pleasant. Archie must try to do the same while he was working in his shop. It wouldn't be for much longer. Milner asked about the jewellery market in South Africa; drew from Archie his opinion of the gold and mining industry there. He felt he was being placated.

He and Bill worked all day. Milner continued to be attentive with cups of tea, and in the evening, Archie brought out the sandwiches he'd made that morning and they were able to work on. It had gone seven o'clock when Milner came to let them out. He urged them to be quiet as he led them to his private entrance.

Archie felt the tone of their relationship had now been set, and he felt a little less aggressive towards Milner. He suspected that Milner kept chatting to him because he wanted to know more about Rod and Marion, and their part in the Starbright venture. Rod had prepared him for questions of this sort, and he kept his wits about him and delivered the edited story.

CHAPTER FOURTEEN

Archie was getting ready for bed that night when Marion telephoned. 'We've arrived back at Euston,' she said. He was pleased to hear her voice and started to tell her of his worries. 'Not now, Archie, that can wait until I'm home. We're coming up on the milk train. It gets into Lime Street at a quarter to six in the morning and we want you to meet us, as there'll be no public transport running at that hour, and not much chance of getting a taxi.'

'I'll be there.'

'Good. Everything has gone well for us, except we couldn't get sleepers on the train. I think Rod might want you to drive him home.'

'That's OK.'

'Looking forward to being back with you,' she said.

Archie hardly slept all night. He was afraid he might not hear his alarm and oversleep. His fear of them being picked up by the police was now a nagging anxiety. He would unload that on Rod, and perhaps he'd decide they should all leave in a hurry.

He was awake and dressed in plenty of time the next morning, but left without making any breakfast. It was not yet light, and he shivered as he went out to the car. He was at the station twenty minutes before the train was due. The place seemed silent and empty; there was no sign that a train would ever come.

He went back outside to the small car park, where he'd seen a refreshment van. A newspaper vendor was leaning against it, drinking a mug of tea. Archie ordered one for himself, and now that he was up close, he could see that there was bacon cooking too. 'That smells good,' he said.

'You'll have a hot bacon sandwich as well?'

'Yes, please.'

'Goes down well on a cold morning,' the man said when he handed it over a few moments later, balanced on a bit of paper.

'Do you do much business here?' asked Archie.

'A little, while the cafeteria inside is closed. Can be quite busy when the train comes in.'

Archie finished his tea and took the sandwich back to his car. He was glad he'd not be seeing much more of Rod. He would have to return to his mother's house to get her ready to take the train to Southampton. They were booked on the *Transvaal Castle*, which would depart for South Africa on Thursday afternoon.

He heard the train approaching and had to rush back to the platform. The passengers came off slowly, travel-stained and weary. Rod and Marion looked spent, but she threw her arms round him and kissed him. Rod slapped him on the shoulder, but with none of his usual heartiness, and for once he didn't want to drive.

'I'm shattered,' he said. 'Plays havoc with me to spend a whole night without a bed.'

'I am too,' Marion said.

Archie made a small detour to drop her off at home first. It gave him plenty of time to explain his worries to them, but they took them as lightly as Milner and Bill Dainty had.

Once on the way to Rainhill, Rod dozed fitfully. 'I hope your mother is feeling better,' Archie said, wanting no further delay to his plans.

'So do I,' Rod yawned. 'I've booked rooms for us tonight in a hotel close to Euston station. The ship doesn't start loading passengers until midday, so we'll have plenty of time tomorrow morning to get down to Southampton.'

On the way home, Archie had to stop at the parade of shops, as he knew there was little food in the house. He'd expected Marion to be asleep in bed by the time he got back, but she was up and looking much more like herself. He was delighted that everything seemed to have returned to normal, and he took her in his arms to welcome her with kisses.

'I'm so glad to be back with you,' she told him as she helped him put the household supplies away. 'I got into bed and thought I'd go out like a light, but it was our usual time for getting up and I didn't feel sleepy any more, so I had a bath instead. But I don't think I'll come to work with you; there's plenty I can be getting on with here.'

Archie wanted to hear more about how things had gone in Amsterdam and was disappointed when she said, 'Isn't it time you were picking Bill Dainty up? We've got to keep at it if we are to get the work finished.'

He and Bill worked hard all day, and when they left, there were only three more rings waiting to be done at Milner's.

When Archie let himself into the kitchen, there was a delicious scent of roasting pork and Marion came to greet him with a glass of wine. She was in a happy mood and free with her kisses. He drew her into the sitting room. 'I'm dying to hear how you and Rod got on in Amsterdam,' he said.

'It was exhausting. A few days in Rod's company would frazzle anybody; he has the energy of a powerhouse. We had dinner with the men who will recut the stones we took. Do you remember Eddie Jurgens from Jo'burg? He was in Amsterdam, too; they entertained us well and kept us up late, talking. We enjoyed their company, enjoyed it all.'

'When the diamonds are recut, I could come with you to pick them up.'

'No, I can manage perfectly well on my own.'

'I suppose you'll just put them in your handbag?' Archie nodded towards her large lizard bag now standing on the bookcase. 'That could easily be snatched from you. How do you know somebody won't be watching when you leave the diamond cutter's premises?'

'What are you trying to do, Archie, frighten me?'

He groaned. 'I want you to be careful. I want you to come safely back to me.'

'Don't worry, I'll be very careful, but I'm more concerned about getting this fortune in diamonds out of Holland and safely through Customs.'

'How did Rod manage to get the necklaces out of England and into Holland?'

'He inserted them into the shoulder pads of his jacket. He wears hand-sewn bespoke suits and he unpicked the sewing in the lining. He said both shoulders must look equal and it must be impossible to feel anything from the outside. He got me to painstakingly stitch the lining up again. It had to look as though it hadn't been touched. He reckons trouser turn-ups is another good place for a man to hide things.'

'Where are you going to hide them?'

'I shall have to think about it. Rod says they must be hidden in a garment that's worn all the time. Come on,' she said, 'dinner will be ready to dish up.'

But at the table, he went and spoiled it all by unburdening on her more of his fears about being caught.

'You mustn't worry like this,' Marion assured him, 'Rod has made sure there is nothing to connect us with that robbery.'

He was sure it had been Rod's original intention that he should be in charge in England, but that Marion had done her best to convince him she was the right person to further his plans. They had a lot in common: they were both sociable and liked a good time. Rod was flamboyant by nature, too confident in his own powers and too fond of his own opinion. At times, Archie found him difficult to live with. Rod gave orders and expected his team to jump to carry them out without questioning anything. He was not always right. As he couldn't leave his business in South Africa indefinitely, they both knew he had to trust somebody, and Marion had done her best to make him feel she was the one.

Archie suspected that Rod had made a play for her favours; she was attractive as well as capable. He himself had fallen head over heels in love with her from the moment he'd seen her, but he was not always sure that he was the man Marion wanted.

Rod had made Marion both the manager and the accountant of the Starbright Jewellery Company. She made out the bills and collected the money. She paid it into the firm's bank account and he knew that every few months she sent regular payments to Rod's account.

Archie was being left more and more with Bill Dainty to alter or remove the assay marks and polish the jewellery up to look like new. He felt he'd been downgraded, but it didn't matter as long as he could be with Marion. Rod trusted her, and Archie was falling over himself to love and trust her too.

It had become routine for Archie and Marion to go shopping two or three times a week before picking Bill Dainty up. Archie always made a list and discussed what they needed to buy, but once in the shop, it was she who usually made the decisions and paid. Archie saw it as his job to drive and help carry their purchases.

One morning, as he followed her into the local baker's shop, sniffing at the lovely scent of fresh bread, he saw that she'd become suddenly agitated. She hurried him back to the car and slammed the door shut. 'Archie, I'm worried. I think somebody is taking money from my purse.'

Her large and expensive lizard-skin handbag was on her knee and she was waving the matching purse at him. 'It isn't the first time.' Her face was anguished. 'I had the same feeling last week that there should be more in here. But I wasn't sure, and told myself I must have spent it on something.'

'How much has gone?'

'I'm not sure about that either. Not a lot – two or three pounds.'

'Well, it wasn't me.'

She gave him a wan smile. 'I know it wasn't. I keep that red purse in the kitchen topped up so you can buy petrol and pay for our lunches. It would be easier for you to take money from that, or to ask me for more. Rod is generous with expenses.'

'Yes, and it won't be Milner, though I've seen you leave your bag on the workbench in his shop. He wouldn't be interested in small amounts; he's aiming for more than a couple of pounds. Could you be mistaken? Could you have spent it on something and forgotten?'

He could see her thinking about that. 'No, I don't think so. This isn't the first time. I don't think I'm mistaken.'

'That only leaves Bill.'

Marion gave a gusty sigh. 'He's a good jeweller but an ex-con; he'll have learned all the tricks of the trade inside. I think we must take it that it's him.'

'Nobody else has had the opportunity.'

'I'm careful with my handbag.'

'In shops and cafés you are. You hang on to it like a limpet.'

'If it's happened more than once, then it has to be Bill. But I don't know what to do about it.'

'Sack him. It's petty thieving. Isn't there supposed to be honour amongst thieves?'

'That gives us another problem. Bill is a quick worker, and he works hard. It won't be easy to find a replacement. I know Rod went to a lot of trouble to get him.'

Archie remembered the morning Bill had overslept and

he'd gone to his rooms to find him. He'd felt sympathy for him having to live in such a dire place. Two or three pounds would be a useful addition to his income. 'It can't be easy for him to find work, and we pay him well for what he does. You'd think he'd show some loyalty.'

'He can see this job won't last, and it could land him back in prison.'

'What are you going to do?'

'Let's go to that butcher's shop over there and see if he has any fillet steak. We need something to buck us up.'

'I meant about Bill.' Archie got out of the car.

Marion leaned against it for a moment. 'If we sack him, it'll take weeks for us to clear the work we've got. That means we'll have to stay even longer before Rod reckons it's time for us to get out. I think it might be better for us to carry on and pretend it hasn't happened.'

'You'll have to be very careful or you'll lose more.'

'I'll keep only one or two pounds in my purse, and a further cash supply in an inside zip pocket of my handbag. He won't have the luxury of time to search through my things.'

Archie shivered; the situation added to his feelings of insecurity, of threatening danger. 'It has to be Bill.'

'I would like to sack him. If we can't trust him not to steal cash from my purse, can we trust him with anything? He already knows a great deal about how we work; possibly he knows too much. I don't want to upset him by accusing him and throwing him out. Better if we say nothing and pretend we haven't noticed.'

Archie sighed. 'We'll both have to be more security-conscious.'

'A lot more,' Marion said. 'Watch your tongue; try not to tell him anything he doesn't already know.'

Archie sighed. 'I suppose we shouldn't blame him for trying to put a little aside while he can. It's what the rest of us are doing after all.'

One evening later that week, Carrie went round to see Connie and John to thank them for bringing her to her senses, and to update them on what had happened. 'Don't say anything about it to Dad and Aunt Prue,' she said. 'I don't want the family to know what a fool I made of myself.'

'I've already told Dad,' Connie admitted. 'I had to do something, I was worried about you.'

'Oh no!' Carrie covered her face with her hands. 'What did he say?'

'He suggested that John try to talk some sense into you.'

'No,' John said, 'that was Marion. He was raring to go and punch Milner on the nose.'

'Oh, goodness,' Carrie groaned. 'You haven't said anything to the people at work, have you? I mean, they know Gerard. I don't want them to talk and the rumours to get back to Mr Groves.'

'Of course not,' John assured her. 'They'll hear nothing from me, I promise.'

That didn't soothe her. 'I hope I can rely on that.'

Connie burst out, 'You can trust John, he'd never let you down.' There was an uncomfortable silence until she said, 'John's mother has made us a sandwich cake. I'll make a cup of tea to go with it.'

Carrie felt things were back to normal when John said, 'You

must know that the men in the office talk about you a lot. You're the only girl they know who's been taken on as an articled clerk, and you're a real hit since you had that makeover from Marion.'

Connie giggled. 'John says he doesn't need to fix any more blind dates with his friends. You've got the pick of the office now.'

'I'm getting asked out quite a lot,' Carrie said, 'but I haven't been out with anyone I'm particularly keen on.'

'You must keep going,' Connie told her. 'Isn't there anyone you fancy?'

'No! You know who I fancied.'

'Don't let him put you off everyone else,' John said. 'That way he'll do you lasting damage. You've got to accept invitations from people you work with. Get out and have some fun. If you find you've made a mistake and don't like the person, you don't have to go again.'

In the office the next morning, Carrie heard the men talking about a swimming competition at Guinea Gap Baths in Wallasey, where two of them were going to compete. Charlie Tate, a fourth-year articled clerk, asked if she'd like to go with him on Saturday afternoon to watch. She liked him and it might be fun, and so it turned out.

It was a lovely sunny afternoon and Charlie was good company. He never stopped chatting; mostly gossip about the staff. Neither of their colleagues was placed in the competition, but they joined up with them later and walked into New Brighton to buy fish and chips. They sat and ate them on the promenade and then went to the show at the end of the pier. They voted it first rate, but by the time they came out, they'd missed the last boat back to Liverpool and had to return by train.

The buses and trams had stopped running when they reached Lime Street, so they all piled into a taxi. Charlie got out early on and Carrie wasn't the last, but they wouldn't let her pay her share. Aunt Prue was still up, and cross with her for being so late.

On Monday, Charlie said, 'It was a good day out, wasn't it?'

'Great, I really enjoyed it,' Carrie agreed. 'Thank you for inviting me.'

'Shall we do it again this weekend?' he asked.

She was pleased. The weather wasn't so kind to them, but the summer crowds were still thronging the beach. They went to a small café on the front for fish and chips again, and afterwards he took her dancing in the Tower Ballroom. He was an excellent dancer and Carrie felt ready to be swept off her feet. He saw her home and kissed her several times at her gate.

John approved of him. 'A decent chap; he was on my list to introduce to you, but you've managed to get together without any help.'

Carrie went out with Charlie a number of times, but somehow she didn't feel the pull of attraction she'd felt for Gerard. It just didn't come.

Adam Winters was a manager in the firm and nine years older than her. She was thrilled when he suggested taking her to a variety show at the Empire Theatre. She thoroughly enjoyed that. His manner was restrained and his kisses brief pecks, and she liked that too; Gerard Milner had put her off too much fondling. Adam lasted only a couple of weeks. He was too stiff and reserved in every way; he seemed an old man already.

Clive Dance was the office comedian, and Carrie found him a laugh a minute, but that didn't develop far either. The best thing about being more sociable was that she was getting to know the people she worked with, hearing all the office gossip and feeling at home in their company.

When Robbie Wilson began paying her more attention, she held back for a time, but the job kept throwing them together. He was a leading member of the gang Tim had told her about. She thought he was lazy and didn't like him very much. He was quite good-looking, but he'd mocked her for being too keen on the job and he never did more work than was absolutely necessary. He was a cost accountant and had been working for the firm for five years, and was thus experienced, but his status was below that of a chartered accountant. One morning he came to her desk and said, 'D'you fancy coming out for a drink sometime?'

'I'm afraid I don't drink very much.' Aunt Prue had said she mustn't drink in a pub, as she thought it gave young ladies a reputation for being too racy. And of course, they must never set foot inside a pub without a man to escort them.

'All right,' he smiled, 'the pictures if you'd rather.'

She hesitated, but bearing in mind what John had said, and still with no boyfriend in sight, she felt she should accept. 'Thank you,' she said. 'I'd like that.'

'Tonight?'

'I'm afraid Saturday is the only night I go out. My family think I should stay home to study on week nights.'

'All right, Saturday then, it's a date. I'll find out what's on.'

He came back from lunch with last night's *Echo*. 'Not a lot, I'm afraid. There's W. C. Fields in *David Copperfield*, or the film version of *Chu Chin Chow*. I can't say I fancy either.' Both appealed to Carrie, but before she could say anything, he went on, 'At the Regal, there's Peter Lorre in *The Man Who Knew Too Much*. That sounds much the best bet; what d'you think?'

'Yes, if it appeals to you.'

Carrie made a great effort to look nice. When she met Robbie outside the cinema, he immediately kissed her cheek and put an arm round her waist to draw her up the steps. He was treating her with more familiarity than he ever had in the office.

He paid for the best seats, and once the programme started, he put his arm round her shoulders, pulled her closer and tried to kiss and paw her.

'Go easy, Robbie, I hardly know you.'

'Course you do, we see each other every day. I fancied you from the day you walked into the office.'

When the lights went on for the interval, he insisted on buying her ice cream and chocolates. When they dimmed again for the big film, his arm came round her shoulders again. His lips went down on hers and she felt his tongue push into her mouth. She could hardly believe it when his hand slid up her thigh under her skirt. Angrily she pulled back far enough from him to free her arm and take a hard swipe at his face. The loud slap made some in the audience turn to look.

Robbie jerked away and in the half-light she saw that his mouth had dropped open. She got to her feet and without another word eased her way along the row and out of the cinema. He seemed to think that paying for her seat gave him the right to neck her throughout the performance. He'd certainly gone too far by pushing his hand almost up to her knickers.

Nothing would induce her to go out with him again.

Carrie had spent her lunchtime in Bunney's with Ruth and Phoebe, looking over their selection of dresses. Ruth was going to a cousin's wedding and had asked for their advice. She'd received plenty of that but had not had time to try anything on. Even so, when they returned to the office, they found that the men had returned before them. They were gathered round Tim's desk and were creating a noisy disturbance. Horrified, the girls stood at the door and watched.

'How come you can get out of travelling to Warrington every day?' one shouted. 'We have to go where we're sent even if it means we have to get up early to spend hours on the train. We don't get featherbedded like you. No wonder you're a sissy. Where did you get to today? You're always sneaking off on your own. I'd say you were up to something if you weren't such a sissy.' It wasn't difficult to understand that the men were trying to bully Tim.

But he turned on them. 'What makes you think you're such scintillating company?' he demanded. 'Anyway, I don't want to spend my lunch hour guzzling beer and chips like you slobs. It makes you doze off in the afternoon.'

Carrie realised that somebody had come up behind her, and suddenly an authoritative voice rang out above the noise. 'Gentlemen, stop making this noise! Go back to your desks and sit down immediately. This is an office, not a bear garden.'

Old Mr Atherton pushed between her and Ruth to confront the men, his bald head shining under the lights. In the deathly silence that followed, his voice seemed even louder. 'What do you think you're doing? I'll not have rowdy behaviour like this in my office. You're behaving like louts, not professional men. Mr Devereaux, I'd have thought you would understand that by now.'

'I'm sorry, sir. It won't happen again.'

Carrie glanced at Tim; his head was down and his shoulders were bent.

'Mr Redwood, perhaps you would explain what this is about?'

Tim stood up slowly and turned round. He took a deep breath and looked straight at Danny Devereaux. Carrie held her breath, but Tim said calmly, 'Just juvenile behaviour, I'm afraid, Mr Atherton.'

'Very juvenile.'

'High spirits that got out of hand; they forgot where they were. Nothing I can't handle, sir.'

'I see. Get on with your work, all of you, and I want no more horseplay here.' The office door swung shut behind him.

Carrie shot to her desk and got out the files she'd been working on, as did everybody else. The silence was intense, but she said into it, 'You did well there, Tim, acted with dignity in the face of provocation.'

'You should have dropped the fools in the mire,' Ruth said, 'told Mr Atherton that they're ganging up on you. It would have served them right.'

'It certainly sorted the men from the boys,' Phoebe giggled. 'That's a great help to us girls, isn't it?'

'Perhaps they'll grow up soon,' Tim said in a resigned voice.

Carrie opened a ledger, glad to find that Tim could cope, and full of admiration. She thought he'd handled that in exactly the right way.

CHAPTER FIFTEEN

ONE AFTERNOON THE FOLLOWING week, Carrie looked up from her work to see Mr Heatherington at Tim Redwood's desk. Tim seemed to be in trouble. All their work was checked for errors in basic maths by the girls working on the tabulating machines, but she heard Mr Heatherington saying in the sort of whisper that carried far, 'This is a more fundamental mistake. Your figures don't make sense. Either you've put something in twice or you've added something in that shouldn't be there. It'll be good practice for you to trawl through what you've done, to find it and put it right.'

Carrie heard a chortle from Danny Devereaux's desk, but she ignored it and settled down to do her own work. Later in the afternoon, she noticed that Tim was still struggling. 'This is awful.' His face was agonised. 'I've searched through these figures three times and my head is spinning. I can't think straight any more.'

The trolley with afternoon tea had just been pushed into the office. Carrie got up to fetch two cups. 'Have this and ten minutes' rest,' she said, and put a brimming cup on the corner of his desk.

He took a gulp and swung round to talk to her. 'Thanks, I'm certainly in need of it. I can't believe it's half three already.'

'You're tired.' She could see other jobs building up in his in-tray. 'Wouldn't it be better to leave that until tomorrow? If you're fresh, you'll probably see the problem straight away.'

'No. Heathers expects it now. I must seem to be competent. I ought to be able to do it.'

'He's in with Mr Groves at the moment.' She pulled her chair up beside his. 'All right, start at the beginning and talk me through what you've done. Perhaps I can spot it.'

It took her twenty minutes to find the problem and recalculate the figures.

'Gosh, Carrie, I'm very grateful. How do you do it?'

'I stop and take a break when my head gets woolly. There's no point in carrying on when you feel like that. You just drive yourself up the wall.'

The very next day, Tim told her that word was going round the office that she was easy on the eye but completely untouchable. 'You're said to be strait-laced and frigid, absolutely no fun at all, a bit of a pain.'

'Oh!' She was taken aback but had to smile. 'I know who started that story,' she said, and told him about her outing with Robbie.

'Perhaps that'll put the men off you.' Tim grinned at her. 'They're round you like bees round a honeypot. The only time I have a chance to speak to you is on Saturday mornings, when we go to the lectures in Fenchurch Street. OK, two of Atherton's clerks go too, but they leave us alone. We keep being thrown together, and on the whole we rub along pretty well, don't we?'

'On the whole,' she smiled.

'How about coming out on a date with me? I have to keep

my nose to the grindstone during the week, but I allow myself a night off on Saturdays.'

'Same here. Yes, I'd like to.'

'Good, how about next Saturday? Since we go to the lecture in the morning, I'd love to suggest a spot of lunch and staying in town, but I can't. I'm afraid a trip to the cinema is about my limit.'

'That's fine, Tim.'

'Good, this is going to be one in the eye for the other men.' His slow half-smile widened into a grin. 'They'll probably be envious. They talk about spending a lot of cash on girls, giving them a good time in the hope that it will buy favours for them.'

'They don't throw money at me,' Carrie said firmly, but then she remembered the best seats and the ice cream she'd received from Robbie, not to mention all the luxuries Gerard had showered on her. 'Well, perhaps they do.'

'I'd like to do that too,' Tim admitted. 'Everybody thinks I come from a well-heeled family, but my mother is a widow and we live in straitened circumstances.'

Carrie frowned. 'But I understood old Mr Groves was your uncle?'

'Yes, my mother is his sister. He accepted me as an articled clerk without the usual down payment, and he put money in so that I'd have the same pocket money as the other clerks, but some of them have an additional allowance from their families.'

'I suppose I do too. My dad gives me an allowance for clothes, and he pays Aunt Prudence for my keep.'

'That's what I mean.'

'But Tim, you go out at lunchtime with the rest of the men and eat in cafés and drink in pubs.'

'No, I don't. I may leave the office with them, but I don't stay with them. My mother cuts me a sandwich, and I eat it on the hoof or on a park bench if I can find one. I go round the shops or to the market once or twice a week, because Mum thinks food is cheaper there. Everybody thinks I'm weird.'

'That's the gossip I hear on the grapevine,' Carrie smiled.

'Oh Lord!' He looked embarrassed.

'Why don't you stay in the office to eat? Surely you'd prefer to do that on wet days?'

He sighed. 'I did try it, but the girls teased me and they kept talking about clothes and lipsticks. It's considered normal here for the men to go out and the women to stay in. To stay in would mark me out as even more weird.'

'I'd have thought the lads would want to stay in to chat up the girls. Ruth is good fun, and Phoebe is very pretty.'

'My problem is that I don't fit in anywhere.'

Carrie smiled. 'You know that isn't true. As you said, you and I rub along all right together. You could stay in, and we'd eat at my desk and talk about anything you like.'

'Honestly? Is that an offer?' He laughed. 'Or even better, would you come and eat at my desk?'

'Right, tomorrow I will.'

'Excellent. You're very kind, and so is Uncle Jeremy. He says he's doing this for me so I'll end up with a means of earning a reasonable living.'

Carrie hesitated. 'Is accounting what you'd have chosen as a career?'

'I'm one of those hopeless creatures who's never had the slightest idea what they want to do. I don't seem to have much aptitude for maths, but then I don't seem to have much aptitude for anything. My mother is relieved because she couldn't afford to put me through any other sort of training, but you can see why I have to appear bright, alert and keen on accounting. I have to take advantage of what I'm offered.'

'Oh, Tim, you're doing fine. Today is just an off day.'

'I'm having quite a lot of those.'

Carrie was glad he'd opened up to her. 'Right, so now I understand. We're friends, and I want to go to the pictures with you, providing you don't paw me and want to neck throughout the performance.'

'I wouldn't have the nerve to do that.'

'And I want to pay for myself.'

'No, no, that's not what I meant.' He threw up his hands in horror. 'I've said it all wrong again. I can afford to take a girl out once in a while.'

'No, I mean it. It might hurt your pride,' Carrie said, 'but I know what straitened circumstances are. Habit makes my Aunt Prue economise whether she needs to or not. I count myself very lucky to have a father who is willing and able to give me money.'

On Saturday morning, they were required to be in the office at nine as usual, but they left in time to walk to the offices of the Liverpool Society of Chartered Accountants for the lecture at eleven o'clock.

Instead of the suit Tim always wore to work, he wore slacks and a tweed sports jacket. He seemed different, more relaxed. They both had to concentrate on the lecture, but afterwards he said, 'I hope it's still on for tonight? We made a date to go to the pictures.'

'Yes, of course, providing you're happy for me to pay my way.'

Again he gave that slow half-smile, 'Not entirely happy, but if you really meant what you said . . .'

'I did.'

'I'll agree to anything to have you come. What's on, do you know?'

'No,' she said. 'I should have looked in the paper.'

'Here's our tram, and it goes past the Odeon. If we keep a lookout, we might see what's on there.'

As the tram clanged past, Tim said, 'It's *The Informer*, with Victor McLaglen and Heather Angel. Have you ever heard of it?'

'Oh, yes,' Carrie said. 'Phoebe and Ruth went to see it on Thursday. They said it was very good, a low-budget film that's turned out to be a real winner.'

'Shall we go and see that, then?' Tim asked. 'Perhaps we could stretch to having a drink as well, either before or after.'

'Before,' she said. 'Aunt Prue likes me home by ten.'

'Good. I'll catch the half past six tram and hope to see you get on at your stop.'

Carrie took great care to be at the stop on time, and she saw him waving to her before she got on. She counted the evening a huge success: they both enjoyed the film, and got on like a house on fire. On the tram going home afterwards, Tim said, 'How about doing this again?'

'I'd like to.' Carrie was keen. 'We saw trailers of the films showing next week; on Monday, Tuesday and Wednesday it will be *Cavalcade*. I'd love to see that.' *Cavalcade* was the film of

Noël Coward's play, which had been a huge success in the West End; now an old film, it was having a second run.

'At the end of the week it will be Shirley Temple in *Curly Top*,' Tim said. 'Would you like to see that?'

'I'd prefer to see *Cavalcade*,' she said. 'It's said to be a pageant of patriotism, the story of one family from the Boer War to the present, taking in the sinking of the *Titanic* and the Great War.'

'It would mean going on Wednesday night,' Tim said, 'but I would like to see it. I missed it the first time it came round.'

'I'm tempted,' Carrie said.

'Why not?' he smiled. 'We can spend more time studying at the weekend.'

'Then it would be sensible to go straight from work and have a bite to eat beforehand,' Carrie said. 'No point in going home and coming back into town. Could we stretch to that?'

'I think so, yes, let's make it a special occasion.'

Carrie looked forward to it, and on Wednesday she wore her best dress to work. Just before five she went to the cloakroom to powder her nose, apply a little lipstick and redo her hair.

'I've had a scout round for a café,' Tim said. 'There aren't many that stay open in the evening, but Robbie recommends this one.'

They had cheese on toast followed by cakes. 'A treat for me,' Carrie said. 'I hardly ever eat out.'

'I never do,' Tim said. 'I can't remember the last time.'

His brown eyes had gold specks in them, and when he smiled at her, she decided that she liked him very much. It was also a treat to take his arm on the walk to the Odeon. It was a dark and chilly night, but the city-centre lights lit everything with a warm golden glow.

Suddenly she pulled him to a halt. 'I think that's my dad's car,' she said, peering closely at a parked vehicle. 'Yes, that looks like his number.'

'Very smart,' Tim said. 'This year's model, an Austin 10/4 Lichfield saloon.'

Carrie remembered seeing it parked in almost the same place when she'd been killing time waiting for Gerard Milner to meet her. 'Gosh, yes, and here he is.' She waited until he was nearer. 'Hello, Dad.' She reached up to peck a kiss on his cheek.

'Fancy seeing you here,' he said awkwardly.

Carrie caught sight of Marion then, who was a little behind, and for a moment she thought the older woman looked put out to see her, but then she was smiling and came to kiss her cheek.

'This is Tim Redwood,' Carrie told them. 'He's another articled clerk at Atherton and Groves. In fact, he's Mr Groves's nephew.' She knew Tim would shrink at that. 'Tim and I are going to the Odeon.'

'I'm pleased to meet any friend of Carrie's,' her father said, and shook Tim's hand.

Carrie introduced Marion. 'She's like a fairy godmother to me. She tamed my hair for me.' They all laughed and she went on, 'What are you both doing here at this time of night? Dad, I've seen your car parked here before. Are you working at Milner's shop? We're behind it here, aren't we?'

'Yes,' he mumbled, 'that's right.'

'Sorry, we can't stop now, we're in a bit of a hurry.' Marion was edging Archie towards the car. 'Why don't you come and see us on Sunday, Carrie?' Then they got in and were gone in an instant.

Tim took her arm and they walked on. 'Milner's shop is closed at this time of night,' he said.

'Yes, but Dad does design work for him. I think he and Marion do that sort of thing for several different jewellers. They'd need their shops to be closed so they can confer without interruption.' But something hadn't been quite right. 'Did they seem on edge?' she asked.

'Yes, a little,' Tim said. 'I do wish you'd forget about Jeremy Groves being my uncle.'

They both enjoyed *Cavalcade*, and Tim insisted on treating her to an ice cream in the interval, but Carrie couldn't help thinking about her father. She felt quite differently about Milner now, and she didn't like the thought of Archie working for him. Her father seemed to cloak his life in mystery, and she couldn't help wondering why, and feeling curious about what he and Marion were really doing. Even Prue and Maud talked about that from time to time.

The next morning, the chartered accountants' examination results came out, and Carrie heard that the two men put in by Atherton & Groves had passed. John Bradshaw was one of them. She took the news home to Prue and Maud, but he and Connie came round that evening anyway to tell them.

Connie was excited. 'Marion rang me,' she said with a smile. 'She's made an appointment for me to have my hair done by her hairdresser; she said ages ago that it was only fair to treat us both alike. I thought she'd forgotten all about me, but it was just that she's been really busy. It isn't easy to get an appointment on a Saturday, so it isn't until next week. Then I asked to speak to Dad and told him about John. It's all happening for us now.'

'We're so happy for you both,' Maud said. She liked a glass of sherry before her Sunday lunch and got out the bottle so they could drink to John's success.

'Does that mean you'll have to leave and look for another job?' Prue wanted to know.

'No, some of us are promoted to team leader once we're qualified, and Mr Atherton has already told me that he wants me to stay on,' John chortled. It was easy to see he was up on cloud nine. 'At least now I'll be earning a salary.'

CHAPTER SIXTEEN

I T WAS THE SUNDAY BEFORE Prudence's birthday, and Archie was feeling guilty. He owed Prue a lot, but he'd been tied up with Marion and had almost ignored her recently. Carrie came round on a Sunday from time to time, but she didn't bring her aunts. She got on well with Marion, and there'd been some talk of a meeting in town on a Saturday to choose a new dress.

Carrie rang up while he was thinking about her to ask if he'd be home this afternoon. 'Yes,' he said. 'Bring Gladys and the aunts with you and we'll have a real Sunday tea.'

When he put the phone down, Marion said, 'Sunday tea is hardly enough to celebrate her birthday.'

'She'll be sixty-eight. It's not an occasion for a huge celebration.'

'Give her that new Peter Pan collar you've made up,' Marion suggested. 'She'll love it; it's an example of your very successful design, and made with your own hands . . . though it might be better if you don't mention that – she might ask where you made it and you don't have a workroom here.'

Archie swallowed hard. The gold he'd used for the collar had been melted down from stolen goods, and he'd made it in a workshop belonging to a jeweller hoping to fence them at a profit. 'It hasn't been assayed,' he said.

'Prue will understand why not. You can offer to have it done for her.'

'The gold I used wasn't mine. Really the collar isn't mine to give.'

'You gave me one,' Marion laughed, 'and the workmanship is certainly yours. You made that in Ormskirk, at Calthorpe's shop. He might or might not realise that some of his gold has gone missing, but there's nothing he can do about it either way. He can hardly report it to the police.'

Archie recoiled with horror at the thought of giving stolen goods to his sister.

'If you feel that badly about it,' Marion said, 'you could offer to pay Calthorpe for what you used.'

'I could take Prue out for a meal instead,' he said. 'Take all the family out to celebrate. After all, my son-in-law has successfully passed a big landmark; he can afford to keep a wife now.'

'A good idea,' Marion said, 'and you've had great success with your designs and cemented your relationship with Gordon and Mayell. They'll welcome you back with open arms if and when you want to go back.'

When they arrived that afternoon, Prue said, 'Well, you may be living in this country now, but we've seen precious little of you. You must be working really hard.'

'Yes,' Archie managed. He was taken aback. He'd meant to play the work angle down; he was ashamed of helping thieves to fence their goods.

'So what is it that keeps you so busy you can't find time to visit your sisters?' Prue had always had an acid tongue. He felt her gaze boring into him.

Marion came to his aid. 'Archie's been designing for his firm in South Africa. He's had marvellous success, I'm very proud of him.' She was speaking rather more quickly than usual. 'Have you seen those Peter Pan collars? His design has spread everywhere.'

'Yes,' Carrie said eagerly, 'they're very pretty and suit everyone.'

'I have, too,' Maud said. 'One of the teachers at my school has one.'

'It's my birthday next Saturday,' Prue said. 'I don't suppose you've got one for me?'

Archie saw the warning glance Marion gave him. 'Actually, he has,' she said. 'He's had one made especially for you.' She'd wanted to get that in before he could tell Prue he'd made it himself. 'Shall we give it to her now, Archie? After all, we've whetted her curiosity.'

He had to struggle to get the words out. 'Why not?'

Marion shot off to get it. 'Luckily, I wrapped it up the other day. Here you are, Prue.' She put the package on the drinks table beside her. 'Do open it now.'

Slowly Prue removed the wrapping paper and folded it carefully. Marion had put the necklace in a cardboard box that had held a bottle of her perfume. 'Sorry there's no case for it,' Archie said.

'Well, I can't expect everything.' Prue took off the lid and gasped with pleasure. 'It's very nice, thank you.'

'It's nine-carat gold,' Marion informed her, 'and very good workmanship.'

'It's lovely, let's try it on you.' Carrie was on her feet and arranging it round Prue's neck. 'It fits fine, but your dress has a collar, so it doesn't look good with that.'

'I'll buy you a black jumper for your birthday,' Maud said. 'Collarless, of course. That would be just the thing.'

Prue had the necklace off and was cradling it in her hands. 'You don't think I'm too old to wear something like this?'

'No,' Marion confirmed, 'everyone's wearing them.'

'I'm also thinking of taking the whole family out for a celebratory meal on Saturday evening,' Archie said. 'Are you up for it, Prue?'

'What a marvellous idea, Dad,' Carrie enthused. 'Wonderful.'

Later, when their guests had gone, Archie and Marion went to the kitchen to start preparations for their supper. Archie was carving some ham when Marion announced, 'I won't be coming with you next Saturday.'

He didn't like doing anything without her. 'Why not? They see you as part of the family.'

'I often go out without you on Saturdays, and I've arranged to see a cousin in the evening.'

'I didn't know you had any relatives here. Can't you bring him too? Or put him off for a week?' Was it really her cousin she was meeting, or was this just an excuse? Why was he always so suspicious?

'Isn't it safer to keep our families apart?'

'I can't see what difference that would make,' he said irritably. He had never met any of her family. It seemed she didn't want to introduce him to them.

She was spending time in the week apart from him too. 'I have to keep the books up to date,' she'd explained, 'make out bills and look after the cash. It all takes time.'

There were periods when only Archie and Bill were altering the assay marks. He wanted to be closer to Marion, and he resented these barriers she was erecting, but on those days she always prepared a meal for when he returned, and she was giving no sign of being bored by his lovemaking.

She asked now, 'Where do you want to take your family?'

Archie frowned. 'Perhaps I should cook for them here? Rod said he wanted us to stay away from restaurants; he doesn't want us to get our faces known in any of them.'

'Nonsense,' she protested. 'It won't be much of a celebration for you if you have to cook for everyone. Rod meant that we shouldn't eat out together in the same place every night. Waiters overhear bits of conversation, you know, and get interested in regular customers. He was afraid they might pick up the name Starbright.

'It's a different matter if you and your family are having a celebration meal out. I think you should take them to the Adelphi. It's Liverpool's best hotel, and they'll see that as a real treat. It's a Saturday, so you'll need to book a table. I'll do that for you if you like.'

'I can do it myself, thank you,' he said stiffly. He felt miffed because she wouldn't come with him.

In the end, he decided to take his family to the Exchange Hotel rather than the Adelphi; he'd had a meal there with Rod once and they'd both enjoyed it. If Marion didn't want to come with them, he'd see to the arrangements himself and do things his way.

He saw that as one of their little differences; they'd get over it, as they always did, but it left a sour taste in his mouth. He loved her, he could forgive her almost anything, and he knew she'd be her sunny self again by tomorrow.

On Friday night, she gave him a wad of banknotes. Rod had advised them to pay cash for everything. 'In the unlikely event of trouble,' he'd said, 'it will make it harder for anyone to trace us, and harder to collect evidence of what we're doing.'

They'd had their instructions from Rod at the beginning. If they heard that the police were asking questions about activities that involved them, they were to pack up everything they wanted to take, drain the company bank account, and drive down to Southampton to take the first passage they could get to Cape Town. If none was immediately available, they should cross the Channel to France.

Marion thought Rod had been wrong to say such things, and blamed that for making Archie unnecessarily nervous. 'It's unlikely that anything will go wrong, and even more unlikely that we'll need to move with urgency,' she'd said.

For Archie's family, the invitation to a celebratory dinner at the Exchange caused considerable excitement and preparation. Prue met Maud one lunchtime and took her Peter Pan collar with her to choose a black top for the occasion. She chose a velvet one as Maud's gift, and treated herself to a black jumper as well so she could wear it on everyday occasions too.

After conferring with Connie on Saturday morning and hearing that she did not intend to buy anything new, Carrie decided to wear her best blue dress. Connie was bubbling with excitement on the telephone. 'I've had my hair done by Marion's hairdresser and it looks absolutely terrific.'

'She's put it up like mine?'

'No, I don't have time to put it up before I go to work every morning; she's cut it short. I'm a busy housewife too now, Carrie, I hardly have a minute to myself.'

'I thought we'd decided it didn't suit us short?'

'It does the way Zoe's cut it. But that's not all. I'm going to announce the most wonderful piece of news to the family tonight, but I've got to tell you first. I can't keep it to myself a moment longer. I'm pregnant, Carrie! Isn't that marvellous? And it's come at just the right moment, now that John is qualified.'

Carrie said all the right things, and even managed to sound thrilled and excited, but she couldn't help feeling it would move Connie further away from her. Her twin was experiencing all life's big moments now, and she was being left further behind. But no, after more thought, she decided that she herself wasn't ready to have babies yet, and she didn't feel envious about that.

On Saturday night, Carrie and her aunts went into town on the tram. She found Connie and John with her father waiting for them in the bar.

'Connie!' she said when she saw her. 'I can't believe the difference that haircut has made. You look absolutely beautiful.'

'Connie was always beautiful,' John said.

'I've had it thinned, too; she's cut a lot of the volume out.'

'She's set it in bigger, looser curls and it really suits you.' Carrie was tempted to have hers done the same way; getting it up into a French pleat every morning was a bit of a bind. 'But won't it all go back to frizzy curls when you wash it?'

'I hope not. Yours hasn't, except for the tight waves at the front.'

'Yes, but I have to pull my hair back hard at the sides and pin it,' Carrie said. She turned to Archie. 'Where is Marion? Isn't she coming?'

'No, she isn't well,' Archie said. 'She wishes Prue a happy birthday and sends her best wishes to you all.'

'She said she wasn't well this afternoon,' Connie agreed. 'She met me and took me to the hairdresser's, but she didn't stay.'

'What a shame she's missing this. I hope she's better soon.' Carrie was sympathetic; she enjoyed Marion's company.

It was rare to see all her family together like this. Prue was wearing her new black velvet blouse with Dad's gold collar, and a hat to complement her outfit. Dad was in the suit he'd bought for Connie's wedding, while John's suit was the one he wore to work.

'Yes, poor Marion, she was looking forward to this,' Archie said. 'Ah, here comes the bottle of champagne I ordered.'

'Champagne? Wow!' As the waiter poured it, bubbles raced up to sparkle above the brim of Carrie's glass.

Archie raised his own glass. 'We've a lot to celebrate,' he said. 'You've qualified as a chartered accountant, John. Prue, it's your birthday, and I've had success with my collar design.'

They all drank to that, and Carrie felt the bubbles rush up her nose.

John said quietly, 'Connie and I have another reason to celebrate, so I ask you to raise your glasses again. We are expecting our first baby.'

The family exploded with pleasure and excitement. There was an outburst of good wishes and congratulations, and questions were fired at the couple. 'Connie, are you going to

217

give up work now? Will you be able to manage in that flat with a baby?'

The head waiter came to tell them their table was ready, and Archie ordered another bottle. Carrie followed her family into the dining room, where they were shown to a round table with a low bowl of fresh flowers in the centre. Her chair was pulled out for her and she looked with pleasure at the sparkling cutlery set on starched white damask.

More champagne was being poured for them and they were still settling down when Carrie looked up to see Marion come to the restaurant door. She was smiling up at her companion, a handsome gentleman who was holding the door open for her. Carrie tried to attract her father's attention, but he was laughing with Connie, and within the split second it took her to turn back, Marion had vanished.

Carrie was perplexed. Had it really been Marion, or was she mistaken? Had anyone else seen her? She looked round: they all seemed to be talking and laughing. Aunt Maud, though, sitting next to her, looked surprised if not a little shocked. Her eyes came up to meet her niece's, and Carrie knew she'd seen Marion too. She'd ask her about it later, when they were alone. She was becoming increasingly suspicious about her father and Marion. There was something odd about the way they lived. Theirs was not a normal household. Did the designs for jewellery that he sold allow them to live at this luxury level?

Carrie didn't need to ask Maud. When they reached home that night, they all went straight up to bed. Carrie was hanging her dress in her wardrobe when Maud tapped on the door and came in. 'Did you see Marion come into the restaurant with another man? Yes, I thought you did. Whatever can be going on?'

'She didn't expect us to be there, couldn't have done.'

'She shot off like a scared rabbit as soon as she caught sight of us. Archie said she was sick.'

'They're hiding something.'

'But what?'

Neither of them had an answer.

Archie decided the dinner had gone well, even without Marion, but he'd really missed her tonight. He'd come to rely on her keeping social occasions on the rails. He'd not only bought too much champagne, but had drunk rather too much of it as well. Marion would not have let that happen.

Still, they'd all enjoyed themselves. He'd managed his last duty by asking the waiter to call two taxis. He'd put Prue, Maud and Carrie into one, and Connie and John into the other, and paid the drivers to take them home. He had no trouble finding his own car; it was just about the only one left parked in the street. There was hardly any traffic on the road at this time of night, so driving was easy, and he got home with no trouble.

He heard Marion's voice, and he knew she was angry. 'Archie! Archie, wake up.' She wrenched the car door open. 'What are you doing out here? It's four o'clock in the morning and I've been worried stiff. I didn't know where you'd got to. Come on, let's get you to bed.'

Wearily, he got out of the car. He knew what he'd done. He'd pulled into his own drive and fallen asleep at the wheel. He felt terrible.

'What a silly thing to do.' Marion was half dragging him upstairs. 'You've drunk too much.'

'I'd have been all right if you'd come with me,' he said.

CHAPTER SEVENTEEN

ARCHIE DIDN'T FEEL MUCH better by Sunday afternoon. Prue had invited them round to her birthday party. 'I made the cake before I knew about the celebration dinner,' she told Archie. 'So the party is going ahead. Besides, it's a way of saying thank you for last night. I don't often eat in a posh restaurant like that. I enjoyed it.'

He knew Prue would have invited almost everybody she knew, near neighbours and more distant family members, assorted uncles, cousins and in-laws that he hadn't seen for years. He knew exactly the form it would take; she'd held parties for them all over the years.

There would be dainty sandwiches without crusts, small cakes, and jellies in little bowls set out on the dining table for the guests to help themselves. Maud would be in charge of making enough tea to keep up a ready supply in the four family teapots. Carrie would be pouring it out and handing it round. Every one of their cups and saucers would be laid out for use and more would have been borrowed from next door. Archie did not feel sociable enough for that.

'We're supposed to be there by three o'clock,' Marion reminded him. They were late, but Carrie must have been watching for him, because she had the front door open as they came up the path.

'Hello, Dad.' She kissed them both. 'Marion, I was afraid you might not be well enough to come. A shame you had to miss Dad's treat at the Exchange Hotel. Were you hit by something nasty?'

'Just a tummy upset.'

'I'm glad you're better and were able to come this afternoon.'

'I really wanted to.' Marion was all smiles. 'I wanted to see where Archie used to live, and meet all your relatives. Happy birthday, Prue.' She presented her with a small indoor rose bush in a bowl.

'Thank you, it smells lovely. Come on in,' Prue said.

'I see you've done some redecorating,' Archie said.

'You haven't been near since Connie's wedding,' Prue said. 'You might as well be living in Timbuktu for the number of times you've come here to see us.'

'I'm sorry, we've been really busy.'

'Dad, come and see all our new paintwork,' Carrie said. She led him up to the landing, leaving Marion with Prue to be introduced to the wider family.

'You've done a good job with this wallpaper, but it needed doing anyway; the old paper must have been up for twenty years,' Archie said.

'It was a lovely do last night. I really enjoyed it.'

'Wasn't it marvellous news from Connie and John?'

'Wonderful, but what about you and Marion? I was hoping you'd announce your wedding before now.'

Archie was shaken out of his lethargy; he was afraid she'd led him up here to ask awkward questions in private. He tried to edge downstairs. 'I'm waiting for Marion to say yes. As a husband, I'm not the best catch.'

'Oh, I don't know. You're not bad-looking, in a battered and well-used way.'

Archie smiled. 'Marion says I look younger than I am.'

'Dad, you've got to accept that you're getting on a bit, but you've got a new car and enough money to provide a smart house and luxury such as we enjoyed last night. And you're still very generous to your daughters.'

His toes curled with embarrassment. 'I want you both to have a better start in life than I had.'

'You're doing pretty well for yourself now.' Her face was open and honest, but her eyes were watching him closely. He knew what she was doing: in her innocent way, she was seeking information that he couldn't possibly give her. He broke away to rush downstairs. Her voice followed, so he knew she was on his heels. 'You've done marvellously well, but I still don't understand what it is you actually do. I wish you'd explain.'

He needed help. He was looking for Marion across the crowded sitting room, but she was nowhere to be seen.

'I know you're still designing jewellery for the firm in South Africa, but what are you doing here? Prue says there must be some reason for you to stay. I know you and Marion did a job for . . . you know, Gerard Milner . . .'

Archie's hands clenched at the mention of his name. That rogue was everywhere! He'd like to wring his neck.

'It's all right, Dad, I know I made a fool of myself over him, but I've come to my senses now.'

Archie felt his own senses were deserting him. 'Not

everything works out exactly as we intend,' he said. 'Shall we get something to eat before it all goes?'

'There's plenty; nobody will go hungry.' Carrie led the way to the dining room and put a plate in his hand. 'I made these fairy cakes, they're good, and so are those scones, but I know you like sandwiches; those are tinned salmon and lettuce.'

Archie had a plateful of food before he realised what was happening. His mouth was dry, and when he tried to eat, he couldn't swallow.

Carrie was hanging on to him like a leech. 'I'm afraid you won't stay in England long unless you find a proper job here. I thought Marion said she wanted . . . Well, she did imply she'd like a job with a jewellery firm too. I've seen your car parked near Milner's shop on a couple of occasions; in fact I met you there that time I was going to the pictures with Tim.'

That took Archie's breath away. Of course she had, but he didn't want anybody else to hear what they were talking about. Worse, he was now thinking about designs into which he could set the diamonds from that tiara. The plan was that he'd make them up in Milner's workroom, and they'd be sold through his shop. The very last thing he needed was for Carrie or anybody else to know of the real connection between him and Gerard Milner.

'As I said, not everything works out as we'd like it to.' He knew he'd made a mess of that. Why hadn't he told her there was a restaurant near there that Marion liked? That might have put her off the scent.

'Hello, Dad.' Connie came over and kissed him. 'Thanks for last night, it was a wonderful evening.'

'How are you keeping? Nobody seemed to ask that last

night. Should you still be working and be out and about so much?'

'Dad, I'm fine. It's all so exciting; we're full of plans.'

'Are you thinking of moving house?' Carrie asked.

Archie was sweating with relief; Connie had deflected Carrie's attention at last. He caught sight of Marion talking to his brothers and made haste to join them. He wasn't going to leave her side in case Carrie came back with more questions. He offered her some of the food on his plate and she took it, but she was deep in conversation with George and his wife, and that left Archie with Bob.

Bob drew him away from the others. 'Let's get a breath of air,' he said, and led him out to the back yard. It was drizzling, and they had to find what shelter they could against the back door. Bob made sure it was firmly shut.

'I feel I have to warn you,' he said, 'that fellow you had in your car the other day, Bill Dainty, he's got a criminal record as long as your arm. He fenced stolen jewellery, amongst other crimes.'

Archie shivered; his brother's eyes, full of suspicion, were scrutinising his face. Bob was just two years older and his favourite brother. He'd always been so friendly before.

'Why are you associating with him?'

'I didn't know.' He couldn't meet Bob's gaze. 'He's an experienced jeweller, he's knowledgeable about gold . . .'

'Knowledgeable about a lot of wrong things, too. You shouldn't have anything to do with him. It could land you in difficulties.'

Archie took a deep breath; he had to do what Rod and Marion would do, keep his wits about him. 'Thanks for the tip-off. I didn't realise . . . didn't know Bill had form. And I thought you were on traffic duties, not detective work.'

'I've been on general duties, an ordinary area plod, for the last few years, but we all know him and keep an eye on him. He's been in and out a few times, and he's now reduced to doing almost anything to keep body and soul together. Any shoplifting, petty pilfering in the district and we take a look at what Bill Dainty and his friends have been up to. Often we need look no further.'

'Oh, hell.' Archie felt weak at the knees. Marion would have a fit if she knew that. How had Rod managed to recruit him?

'I'd stay clear of him if I were you,' Bob went on. 'You don't want his reputation to rub off on you. But I'm through with all that; I applied to go on a course at the police driving school a few months ago, and I've just heard I've been given a place to do it next month. I'm really looking forward to it. I've had a taste for driving since Connie's wedding day, when you let me have a go on your new car. I'll be doing car chases in future.' He opened the back door and let them into the kitchen. 'Quite nasty out there now; we mustn't get wet.'

Archie couldn't get his breath; he felt ready to collapse. He leaned against the sideboard and closed his eyes while the others watched Prue cut her birthday cake. Nobody seemed to notice that he didn't sing 'Happy Birthday' with them. As soon as he decently could, he said his goodbyes and took Marion away.

Once in the car, she said, 'You weren't in the party mood in there. George said you looked as though you had the worries of the world on your shoulders.'

After what Bob had said, he felt as though he had. 'Bob told me—' A woman stepped off the pavement in front of him and he had to slam on the brakes.

'The fool,' Marion said. 'Why can't she look before she does that?' They were moving again. 'What did Bob tell you?'

'That he's going on a course at the police driving school. He's pleased he'll be patrolling in a car in future instead of on foot. I think he's looking forward to car chases and all that.'

Archie had had time to consider what he'd been about to say. It had terrified him to hear the police opinion of Bill Dainty, but they already knew what he was like. He and Marion had discussed it and decided they needed to keep his services. No point in frightening Marion all over again.

She said, 'Bob clearly isn't a detective then; Rod will be glad to hear that. And one less thing for you to worry about, Archie.'

'I don't know about that.' For once he hadn't told her the full story. 'Carrie was asking awkward questions too.'

'She's bound to be curious, but you did all right. You said you didn't tell her anything new. Just keep stalling her.'

'That's easier said than done. Once Carrie gets her teeth into something, she's like a ferret.' He'd tried to keep a grip on himself, but he couldn't go on hiding his worries from her. 'And I hate having to work with that Gerard Milner and pretend he's a friend. He's a terrible man, a cad, trying to get off with Carrie like that.'

Marion laughed. 'She's over it even if you aren't. Just relax. Everything is going well, ticking over quietly.'

But Archie couldn't relax, and he wished Marion wasn't so confident about it being safe to carry on. He felt he was falling apart.

She was sympathetic. 'Perhaps we should ease back. Not

work so hard. No more night shifts. It's getting to you, Archie. We need to eat out more too. Whatever Rod says, we haven't the energy to cook for ourselves, not working the hours we do. There are lots of small cafés in town that do a reasonable lunch, and they're so busy that nobody is likely to notice us. We won't keep going to the same one, but we'll eat lunch out in future.'

After a breakfast of only tea and toast, Archie was usually hungry by one o'clock. To keep them going late in the afternoon, Marion organised two tins to be kept in the car for use when needed, one of cream crackers and another with cheese. When they reached home, it would be getting on for eight o'clock, and the first thing Marion did was to open a bottle of wine. 'This is our time,' she'd say. 'Let's forget the treadmill for a few hours.'

It had always been Archie's chore to provide their evening meal, but she began to help him more. 'We only need a light supper,' she said. They'd noticed a shop selling steak pies, and once a week they bought two at lunchtime to reheat for supper with a little salad. Occasionally they bought fish and chips on the way home, and they always kept plenty of eggs, bacon and sausage for other evenings.

Archie enjoyed his evenings, and he thought Marion did too. They each kept their separate room, but these days they always slept together. One night, when they went to his room, she found he hadn't made his bed. She screwed up her face. 'I'm not getting into that mess.' He thought for a moment he was being rebuffed, but she chuckled and took his hand. 'It'll have to be my place tonight.'

After that, Archie was always careful to make his bed and

keep his room fresh and tidy. When the alarm went in the morning, she'd drift quietly away, or if he was in her room, she'd shoo him out.

'There's no sense in having our own rooms,' he said. 'It doubles the laundry.'

'Who cares about that?' The laundry van called on Saturday mornings to collect and deliver, and it was another of Archie's chores to deal with that. There was always money available for expenses; Marion kept a full purse in a kitchen drawer and told him to take what he needed. She always undertook more than her share, not only of the jewellery work but also of the housework.

'We're partners in this, aren't we?' she asked. 'We have to make life as easy as we can for ourselves.'

He loved everything about Marion, but he thought she wasn't taking his worries seriously enough.

'Pull yourself together, Archie. Get a grip. You mustn't let your nerves get the better of you.'

The following Saturday, Prue and Carrie were having their bedtime cocoa in front of the dying fire when Maud came home. She'd been to the theatre with a fellow teacher to see *Swan Lake* performed by a touring ballet company.

'It was marvellous,' she exclaimed. 'They're doing *Les Sylphides* next week, and I'd really love to go again. But guess what? When we came out, we were waiting at the stop for the bus home and I saw Marion. She wasn't with Archie.'

'I bet she wasn't alone,' Prue said sourly.

'She was with another man. He walked to the edge of the pavement to hail a taxi and helped her in. Very gentlemanly.'

'Very posh. I've never liked her.' Prue was vehement. 'She'll never be any good for our Archie, but you can't tell him.'

'Was it the man we saw her with last week?' Carrie asked.

'I'm not sure, but I don't think it was.' Then they had to tell Prue about seeing Marion come to the door of the restaurant.

'Our Archie is telling us they're going to be married, but it doesn't sound likely. I think there's something very fishy going on.'

'Theirs isn't a normal life.' Maud shivered. 'I'm scared for Archie.'

'He's a fool to get mixed up with a woman like that,' Prue said. 'All those diamonds and fancy ways, not his sort at all.'

'Marion has been very good to me and Connie,' Carrie said. 'I like her.'

'Then you're a fool too. If you want cocoa, Maud, you'll have to make it yourself. I'm going to bed.'

Archie hadn't been sleeping well, but suddenly not only was Tom Bennett at Gordon and Mayell asking for more designs, but Rod was too, and he knew they would both pay well for the most original. Milner would want something very similar to what he was displaying in his shop, so Archie felt he could please everybody.

Now when he woke in the night, he made himself think of designs for bangles, brooches and rings, and he began to sleep better. He had to make time to sit down and start sketching them out, but Marion said, 'This is more important to you than rubbing off assay marks,' and arranged things so he had more time to do it.

This was work he enjoyed doing, and he was surprised and

pleased when a design worked out well. He also found that if he concentrated on that, it soothed him.

Marion was delighted and praised his work. 'Who would have thought you could create designs like this when you were almost a nervous wreck?'

'I feel much better,' he told her, 'since I added that tin of chocolate biscuits to our emergency supplies in the car.'

'Thank goodness for that. You were beginning to make me nervous. Next time you have half a chance, show these designs to Carrie. Once you settle her mind about how you earn a crust, she'll not bother you with questions. It will get Prue off your back too.'

CHAPTER EIGHTEEN

EVERY MONTH MR LEONARD Groves sent for Carrie and she spent an hour or so in his office discussing her studies and the increasing complexity of the work she was given to do. He invited questions from her and told her she was making good progress. She felt happily settled with Atherton & Groves and was enjoying going to the pictures regularly with Tim.

Aunt Prue took a great interest in the time she spent away from her: what she was doing, where she was going, who she was going with, and what films they saw. It didn't take her long to extract everything there was to know about Tim Redwood, and to pass it on to the rest of the family.

'There you are,' Connie said. 'I knew if you gave it a little more time, you'd have no trouble finding a boyfriend for yourself.'

'He's not a boyfriend in the sense you mean,' Carrie retorted. 'Just a friend.'

'It's a start,' Connie laughed.

Tim felt his life was getting better generally. His mother was keeping in good health and encouraging him to go out and about with his friends. She had been getting on in life when she married, and had been forty-three when he was born. Because his father had died when he was four, they had been all in all to each other. He felt very close to her.

Jane Redwood was sixty-four now, but had been suffering from rheumatoid arthritis for the last decade. Her health was fragile, but miraculously the disease seemed to have gone into recession over the last few years, and she'd been able to do more. Tim helped her where he could with the heavier housework, carrying in the coals and lighting fires.

They had very little income and both felt grateful to Uncle Jeremy for providing a training by which he could eventually earn his living. It made Tim feel he had to work hard to show his uncle how much he appreciated his help, but it also increased the daily pressure and stress.

His mother had inherited some of the family talent for figures, and was now doing a small bookkeeping job for a recent widow who had taken over the running of her husband's business, a shop selling general groceries in a nearby suburban parade.

At the same time, things had improved for Tim at work. The men in the office had seemed to look down on him; they thought because Jeremy Groves was his uncle that everything was made easy for him, that he didn't have the brains to make a good accountant. They couldn't believe Carrie had taken up with him, and kept asking him what he'd had to do to achieve that. Really he didn't know, but he was absolutely delighted that she was going out with him at least once or twice a week, and seemed to enjoy it.

The men all agreed that Carrie was stunningly good-looking and should be aiming to be a model rather than an accountant, but also that she was a cold fish. They said she brushed off all kisses and cuddles and had not allowed anyone to touch her, or even get within yards of her.

Tim didn't rate her as cold. She was friendly and had gone out of her way to help him in the office, and there was nothing in her attitude that showed she thought any the less of him. She made excuses for his lapses, while Robbie told him he was thick.

All the same, Carrie had made it very clear that her complaint about the other men in the office was that they were too ready to kiss and paw her, and that he was to be just a friend. He was not to think of her as his girlfriend and heading for romance. Of course, none of them would have the wherewithal to marry until they were qualified – or be allowed to – but that didn't stop the other men from seeking love in the office. Mabel, the telephone operator, was said to be the most obliging.

Tim knew that at the time of Gerard Milner's audit there had been something between Carrie and the jeweller. It had been discussed in detail in the office. Since then, Tim had tried to talk to her about it, but she was saying little, except that it was over. It led him to think that if Carrie was seeking romance, she'd be aiming higher than him. In the meantime, though, he was enjoying her company, and it made the men in the office look at him in a different light. They'd stopped harassing him.

All in all, Tim felt he was finding his feet at work and was more content than he had been for a long time. The autumn had been cold and cloudy, but one Saturday, when he and Carrie spent the afternoon in the museum and the evening in the cinema, they found it had suddenly turned bright and sunny.

As they waited for the tram home, Carrie said, 'It might be October, but I heard on the wireless this morning that we can expect an Indian summer this year.'

'Yes, it looks as though we're in for a spell of sunny weather. How about taking a sandwich with us and going for a long walk tomorrow?'

'I'd love to.' Carrie's eyes were shining. 'Do you know a nice place for a walk?'

'Yes, years ago my mother used to take me on the train to Ainsdale. There are sand dunes there; it's a lovely place for a picnic. We used to walk the coastal path along by the golf course and see the squirrels in the trees.'

'And get back on the train at Birkdale to come home? I've never done that, but it sounds great.'

'I'll bring the sandwiches and come round to your place after breakfast.'

'You might have to walk; there aren't many trams on Sundays.'

'That's all right.'

'I'll bring some cake. Prue keeps our cake tins full.'

When Carrie drew her bedroom curtains the next morning, she found there had been a touch of overnight frost and the air still felt a little sharp, but already the sun was climbing into a deep blue sky and it promised to be a day of mellow autumn sunshine. Prue was already downstairs preparing their breakfast of boiled eggs with toast and tea. She had arranged to go to the ten o'clock church service with Gladys as she usually did.

When Tim rang their doorbell, Prue let him in. 'Hello, Tim, I thought you might be Gladys. Come in, Carrie won't be a minute.' She took him to the kitchen and poured him a cup of tea before going upstairs to get ready. As it was half term, Maud had gone to the Lake District with a colleague for a couple of nights, and Carrie felt she couldn't leave without first clearing the breakfast dishes.

Prue came downstairs wearing her new winter hat with red feathers. 'Is Gladys not here yet?' She adjusted it and her fox fur in front of the mirror over the fireplace.

'It's a very nice hat,' Carrie told her. 'It suits you.'

'She must have overslept. I'll go and knock on her door. How long have the church bells been ringing? Have a good walk, you two.' The front door clicked shut behind her.

'No need for us to hurry, Carrie,' Tim was saying when Prue made an urgent return, rattling the letter box as she let herself in. She looked anxious.

'Gladys isn't answering her door. Surely she can't still be asleep?'

'Don't you have her key?' Carrie asked.

'I hope she's all right.' Prue was rummaging in the drawer of the hall stand. 'I know it's here somewhere, yes.' She rushed out again.

Carrie followed her. Gladys's house adjoined theirs, and the two front doors were close together; only a two-foot-high brick wall separated the two paths. Prue was frantically knocking on Gladys's door and ringing her bell. 'I can turn the key, but the door won't open,' she cried.

'She must have bolted it,' Carrie said, which was what Prue did every night before going up to bed.

'Gladys!' Prue was calling with her mouth to the open letter box. 'Gladys, open the door.' She turned back to Carrie.

'Something dreadful must have happened.' She was almost in tears.

'The back door?' Tim suggested.

'That could be difficult. I know she bolts the gate to her back yard. Oh my goodness, do you think she's fallen and can't get up?' Prue was really alarmed now.

'Is there an open window?' Carrie suggested. One glance upwards told her that the front ones were all firmly shut.

Prue was shaking her head. 'We've got to get in. Either she's fallen, or she's ill. Oh, poor Gladys.'

'We'll have to break a window,' Tim said.

At that moment the church bells stopped and Prue let out a despairing cry, her face running with tears. 'I do hope she isn't hurt.'

'Round the back,' Carrie said. 'Let's get the stepladder out.'

They had an outhouse in the back yard with a coal cellar attached to one end and a lavatory to the other. Tim got out the ladder and set it up against the six-foot-high brick wall that divided the two yards. A few moments later he said, 'The kitchen window is open a little at the top, but the curtains are still drawn. It doesn't look as though she got up this morning.'

He dropped down into the adjoining yard and slid the bolts off the back gate to let Carrie and Prue in. 'Tim!' exclaimed Carrie. 'Look at the mess you've made of your trousers. That wall is covered with soot.'

'I'll need the ladder,' Tim said, going back to fetch it. 'I can't reach the window; it's too high.'

'Thank goodness it's open,' Prue said. 'Gladys would be cross if we broke the glass.'

Tim didn't find it easy to force the sash window up. 'It's

really stiff,' he said. 'Goodness knows when this bottom part was last opened.'

He managed it eventually and climbed in on to the draining board; moments later, he'd taken the bolts off the back door and they were inside.

Prue went to the kitchen door. 'Gladys!' she called. 'Are you all right?'

Carrie threw open the living room door. The curtains were drawn here too and it was in semi-darkness. She switched on the light to make sure Gladys wasn't there. Tim looked in the parlour while Prue was stumbling upstairs. Moments later they heard her say, 'She's not in bed.' Her voice was almost a scream. 'It hasn't been slept in.'

They shot up after her. 'She must have gone out last night,' Tim said, 'and not come home.'

'She never goes out after dark these days.' There was anguish on Prue's face.

'She's here,' Carrie said, trying to keep the rising panic from her voice, 'in the bath.' Gladys's stout limbs were paper-white and she was partly covered by a thin towel. 'She isn't moving!'

Carrie caught her breath. 'Auntie Gladys?' She touched her bare shoulder and it felt so cold, she recoiled in horror. 'She's like ice.'

'Gladys!' Prue pushed past her. 'What is the matter? Oh my God! Is she dead?'

Tim said, 'I don't think so. I think I can see her breathing, can't you?'

'Just. Tiny breaths,' Carrie said, 'but she's unconscious.' The bathroom felt cold, and moisture glistened on the tiles.

'She must have taken a bath last night,' Tim said. 'She'd

have been tired and found she hadn't the strength to lift herself out.'

The huge figure seemed almost to fill the bath. Carrie said, 'She must have been like this all night. How terribly cold and uncomfortable she must have felt, lying naked on that hard surface and knowing nobody would come before morning. Oh my goodness.'

'When the water went cold, she must have pulled the plug out. The only thing within her reach would have been that towel.'

Prue let out a piercing scream and collapsed in a torrent of tears. Tim took both her hands in his. 'Oh God, Prue, please calm down. Gladys needs your help. Who is her doctor?'

She gulped. 'Same as ours, Dr Harris.'

'We'll have to fetch him.' Carrie felt like weeping too.

'Let's see if we can get Gladys out first,' Tim said.

'We'll never get her as far as her bed,' Carrie pointed out. 'She's very heavy.'

'Sixteen stone,' Prue said.

'Get her bedside mat in here to cover this lino, and all the pillows and cushions you can find. Her eiderdown too; we must try and warm her up.'

With those in place, Tim went behind Gladys's head to try to lift her out. Carrie was at her feet. 'Come and help us, Prue,' he urged. They heaved and panted but could barely lift her at all, never mind over the rim of the bath.

'We're wasting time,' Carrie said. 'We're never going to manage it. You go for the doctor, Prue.'

Prue let out another wail of agony. 'His surgery is nearly a mile from here.'

'The phone box,' Carrie reminded her.

'I'll go,' Tim said, feeling in his pocket for pennies. 'What is his number?'

Prue made two attempts to tell him. 'Maud made me learn it by heart, but I can't . . . Oh dear.'

'I'll go,' Carrie said. 'Dr Harris in Lombard Street. I'll get the operator to put me through.'

Prue was on the landing with her purse and offering her more pennies. 'Put your coat on,' Prue said.

'Don't forget to tell him we can't get her out of the bath,' Tim called after her. 'We'll need help.'

Carrie ran. The nearest phone box was two bus stops away; she was almost in tears by the time she reached it. Gladys had been a source of love and support to her and Connie when they were growing up. She hated to see her suffering like this.

Dr Harris's wife answered the phone, and Carrie was very relieved to hear that he was at home and would come and speak to her. She found it a struggle to get the words out to tell him, but he said calmly, 'Try and warm her up. I'll come straight away.'

Carrie jogged back, and minutes later the doctor's car was pulling up at the front gate. She took him up to the bathroom and found that Tim had covered Gladys with her eiderdown and tucked it round her as best he could.

'You've done just about all you can here,' the doctor told them, feeling for Gladys's pulse. 'She'll need to go to hospital. I'll go and ring for an ambulance and some strong men from the fire brigade.'

By then Prue had had as much as she could take. Her best

hat was askew and her face was ravaged with tears and anxiety. She was sobbing audibly. 'Poor Gladys, will she ever get over this?'

Carrie tried to pacify her and persuade her to go home. When Dr Harris returned, Prue let out another of her piercing screams, and then another and another. He turned her round. 'Miss Courtney, you've had a bad shock. You need to go and lie down.'

Carrie and Tim helped her next door to her own bedroom. The doctor followed. Carrie removed Prue's hat and coat, and Tim her shoes. They tried to get her between the sheets, but she let out another wail of distress. 'Not in my best frock. I don't want to spoil it.'

'It won't hurt it,' Carrie said, but they helped her remove it anyway and tucked her in.

'I'll leave you a sedative,' the doctor said. 'You'll feel better when you've taken that.'

Prue struggled to sit up again. 'But will Gladys be all right?'

'I'm afraid that remains to be seen,' he said gravely. 'She's very ill. Hospital is what she needs now.' On the stairs he confided to Carrie, 'Mrs Nesbitt is hypothermic. We must hope for the best.'

Once outside, he went to his car and put two pills in a small envelope. 'These are for Miss Courtney; see she takes them. They'll calm her down.'

'Aunt Prue's highly strung,' Carrie told him. That was what she'd heard Dad say.

The ambulance drew up behind the doctor's car, and twenty minutes later, everybody had gone. Carrie locked up Gladys's house, then went home and put the kettle on. 'I'm sure we could all do with a cup of tea. I'll take one up to Prue with this sedative.'

Tim sat down at the kitchen table and unwrapped the sandwiches he'd brought. 'You do realise it's lunchtime?'

'The last thing I want is food,' Carrie said. 'I feel sick when I think of what's happened to Gladys.'

Prue was fast asleep when she went up to see her. 'You won't want to leave your aunt alone after that,' Tim said. 'Had we better put off our walk to next Sunday?'

'Yes, of course. Thank goodness you were here, Tim,' she said. 'I don't know what I'd have done without you.'

A few days later, Aunt Prue went to see Gladys in hospital and reported that she'd recovered consciousness but that she felt anything but well. She no longer seemed to have any strength, and it had affected her mobility as well as her rheumatics. She was full of aches and pains and would not be coming home until she felt better. Prue said she didn't like having an empty house next door; she felt lonely, and they all missed Gladys popping in to see them.

They enjoyed almost a month of pleasant autumn weather, but early December brought the storms of winter: high winds, grey skies and lashing rain. One Saturday morning Carrie and Tim went to the lecture as usual, and when they came out, for once the weather seemed a little brighter.

'Thank goodness,' Carrie said. 'It's hardly been fit to go out.'

'Still a bit windy,' Tim said, 'but how about catching the ferry and having a walk along the prom at New Brighton? That should blow the cobwebs away.'

They were now in the habit of bringing a sandwich with them on Saturdays, just as they did in the week, so they need buy only a cup of coffee to stay in town all afternoon. When they reached the Pier Head, they ate their lunch in the waiting room, but Carrie wasn't sure that a trip on the ferry was what she really wanted.

It was high tide and she'd never seen such gigantic waves in the Mersey before. They were hurtling against the landing stage, sending spray high into the air, so that it was running with water. It was also rising and falling in the swell, and Carrie could feel the wind buffeting against her. She lifted her scarf over her head to safeguard her French pleat before the gale blew her hair clips into the river. The *Royal Daffodil* ferry had difficulty coming against the landing stage, but it tied up on the second attempt.

There were very few passengers when the gangplank crashed down, and Carrie wondered if it were safe to get on, but two frail and elderly men were ahead of them and Tim still seemed enthusiastic, so she said nothing.

'It's a bit slippery underfoot,' he said as they were boarding. 'Hold on to me.' Carrie was glad to. He took her hand and wrapped her arm round his. The touch of his fingers sent a thrill down her spine. She felt secure and comforted. Tim was firm, strong and upright, and she could rely on him to do the right thing.

The few other passengers headed straight for the shelter of the saloon, but Tim led her up to the top deck to stand against the rail as the boat ploughed through the waves towards the mouth of the Mersey.

Carrie watched him as he stood staring at the docks along

the riverbank. He wore no hat, and the wind was whipping his chestnut hair in every direction. He seemed to draw energy from the raging wind; his cheeks were pink and his face shone with life. She was still hanging on to him, but they'd both anchored themselves to the ship's rail with their other hand. It wasn't just windy up here; it was a howling gale.

She looked up and met his gaze. His brown eyes were full of golden light, and slowly his achingly familiar half-smile came. She felt a burst of love for him. Why hadn't she realised that for her, he was the one? She was about to throw her arms round him and tell him so when an elderly man with a walking stick came haltingly along the deck towards them, battling the wind.

She heard the old man's stick clatter to the deck, his exclamation as he slithered, but he saved himself from falling and ended up spread-eagled on a bench.

Tim reached him first; he was trying to get up. 'Let me help you,' he said. 'Carrie, give me a hand, would you?' Between them they got the man to his feet and retrieved his walking stick from under a nearby bench. 'Are you all right, sir?'

'Just a bit shaken up.'

'Safer for you downstairs in the saloon,' Carrie said, 'and warmer too.'

'But full of cigarette smoke. I wanted a breath of fresh air, but it seems I'm not up to hurricane conditions any more.'

'Let us see you safely down,' Tim said.

By the time the old man was ensconced in the saloon, having thanked them many times, there was no point in going back to the top deck; they were nearing New Brighton, and anyway it was more sheltered here.

With her arm in a grip that said he meant to stop her having a similar accident, Tim led her to the ship's rail to watch the boat tie up, but for Carrie that magic moment had been shattered and was gone. She was left wondering what she'd seen on his face. Joy in a shared moment, certainly, but had it been love?

She'd been wrong to think it was love she'd felt for Gerard Milner. He'd shown her passion and she'd responded to that. It was what he'd intended her to do, what he was aiming for. She found it hard to believe now that she'd been naive enough to believe she was in love with a man like that. He'd been too old and too flashy, and not at all the sort she admired.

Tim had just shown her that he was a very caring person, but she'd already seen that when he'd tried to help Gladys. She'd known it since he'd told her of his struggle to care for his mother. She knew she could depend on him. She'd always thought him attractive and good company, but it hadn't been love at first sight. Love for Tim had seeped into her soul over time. He was honest and somehow exactly right for her.

Yes, she was in love with him, but he didn't seem to feel that way about her. He'd never attempted to kiss her goodbye and only rarely touched her. It made her wonder if she was doomed to search for the right man for the rest of her life.

After more than a month, Gladys was brought home by ambulance. She'd spent the last ten days in a convalescent home to get her back on her feet, but even so, she was still very unsteady and had lost a lot of weight. Carrie welcomed her with a big hug. 'You really scared us all,' she said.

'No more baths for you,' Prue told her.

'I don't think I could get into the bath now even if I wanted to,' Gladys said, 'and the doctors tell me I'm lucky to be alive after a bad bout of hypothermia like that. My rheumatics have been terrible ever since.'

'We'll get you better,' Prue said. 'You must spend more time with me until you're fully recovered.'

Carrie visited her father and Marion frequently at weekends, and this Sunday, her aunts went with her. Prue was full of the latest facts about Tim.

'We've already met him,' her father said, 'haven't we, Marion? Not news to us.' He smiled wanly at Carrie, and seemed weary.

When Carrie helped Maud wash the teacups they'd used, she found her aunts were as concerned about Archie as she was. 'He's really changed,' Maud whispered. 'At Connie's wedding he took charge when the water tank burst, but now he's making no decisions at all. Did you notice that he refers everything to Marion, even whether he should open a packet of chocolate biscuits as well as the shortbread to have with our tea?'

When they were leaving, Prue said, 'What's the matter with you, Archie? Aren't you well? You look half dead.'

'I'm fine,' he assured her. 'Nothing wrong with me.'

Marion smiled at her. 'He's in good health,' she agreed. 'He's working very hard; perhaps too hard.'

'At what?' Prue demanded, but any mention of a job seemed to make Archie evasive. As far as Carrie could see, he was doing very little that could be called work, and she'd really embarrassed him by asking. Now even her aunts were curious.

On the bus going home they talked about his lack of a job, and wondered where he got all his money from.

'I wouldn't trust that woman,' Prue breathed. 'I really don't know what our Archie sees in her.'

Another week went by, and today Carrie meant to go alone to see her father. Was there a mystery, something Dad wanted to hide? Prue thought there was.

Once seated on the sofa in his house, she asked him again about his work, but today her father's eyes were smiling at her openly. 'You all know I design jewellery – the Peter Pan collar, for instance.'

'You mean you're doing it all the time?'

'Yes,' Marion said. 'Since he did that collar, everybody in the trade wants his designs. Why don't you take Carrie upstairs and show her?'

She followed him up to the front bedroom. The bed did not appear to be in use and he'd pulled a deal table into the bay window. 'Come and sit here beside me.' The chairs were already in place.

'You're using this as a workroom?'

'Well, a sort of study. The light is better here than downstairs. What d'you think of this?' He was unrolling intricate patterns drawn oversized so the detail could be appreciated, with the exact measurements marked. 'This one is for a necklace to be made in different shades of gold.' It was a delicate circlet of linked daisies with white gold for the petals and yellow gold for the stamens in the centre. Carrie gazed at it with delight.

'That's marvellous. It'll look fantastic.'

'Here's another; I want the stones in this to be cabochon-cut rubies set within a foliage of gold twigs and leaves so they look like berries. The rubies would need to be big, of course, which will make this expensive.'

Carrie almost whistled through her teeth with amazement. 'It'll be gorgeous, Dad. I didn't realise you were creating jewellery like this.'

'Mostly I'm not these days. I sell the designs for others to make up. I used to make the whole thing in Johannesburg, but even there they were employing others to help with the easy bits.'

'Gosh, Dad, I imagined the Peter Pan collar to be a one-off.'

'No,' he said. 'Do you like these rings? I've put the gemstones in a perpendicular frame at right angles to a plain gold band, instead of going round it.'

'They're lovely. And very different to anything I've seen in the shops, even Milner's.'

'This one is to have four stones in different colours: ruby, emerald, diamond and sapphire in the most expensive version. I shall send this design to the firm that employed me in South Africa. They'll like it because they can do cheaper versions with semi-precious stones.'

'And they make them up and sell them round the world,' Carrie marvelled. 'Can you sell your designs anywhere else?'

'Yes, there are jewellers in this country who want to buy them.'

'You are clever, Dad.'

'These are my patterns for brooches. I've put little springs under these dragonflies and birds, so that when they're worn, the stones move slightly with the body of the wearer and catch the light. They'll appear to flutter.'

'That's a wonderful idea. I love all your designs.'

'Tell me what you like best, and then I won't have to think too hard when Christmas comes. But you haven't seen my bracelets yet, or my earrings.'

Carrie felt much happier now she understood how Dad made his living. She went home and told Prue and Maud.

'Why couldn't he have told us this in the beginning?' Prue demanded fiercely. 'It's just like Archie to play his cards close to his chest. And to think we worried about him not being able to find a job!'

That evening Carrie went round to see Connie and John and told them what she'd discovered.

'He could have done all that in South Africa,' Connie said. 'Why did he need to come home?'

'He wanted to come for your wedding,' Carrie pointed out. 'He wanted to give you away.'

CHAPTER NINETEEN

THE NEXT MORNING, WHEN Archie and Marion got back from an early shopping expedition, there were letters waiting for them on the mat. Archie picked them up. 'There's one for you,' he said with a sinking heart. 'It's from Amsterdam.'

Marion ripped it open. 'From the diamond cutters,' she said, and read it out to him. '*We have completed the work and your order is ready for collection.*' She started to put their shopping away.

Archie felt things were happening too quickly. 'Do you want me to come with you?'

'No, I'll go by myself at the beginning of next week.'

'You'll be carrying stones worth a fortune. Aren't you afraid they could be stolen from you? That you could be attacked?'

'Archie, you know I've given a lot of thought to bringing those diamonds back. I've got it all organised: I'm going to do what Rod did and hide them in my clothes.'

Marion always bought clothes that were stylish. Now, in the mid 1930s, the fashion was for longer skirts and a silhouette that was slim and closely fitted but which flared out at the knee to mid calf. She had several softly tailored dresses with little or no padding, a very feminine style, and outdoors she wore a full-length coat over them.

'Your clothes are different to Rod's,' Archie said. 'Clearly you can't hide the stones in your coat, as you might want to slip that off in a restaurant or the lounge on the ferry.'

'I've decided that the safest place would be to hide them in my underwear.'

Archie was familiar with her underwear; she liked pure silk garments, which he understood were top of the market, but his mind boggled at the thought of where she could hide gemstones in that soft, slinky material.

With this in mind, one Saturday she brought home two identical pink silk petticoats; they were full-length and traditional in style, with three inches of lace round the bottom. She started by removing the lace from one and stitching them together so that one acted as a lining to the other. Then she opened the side seam on the left-hand side and inserted some small coins between the two layers.

She was sewing in their sitting room, and he'd watched her wriggle out of her dress and current slip to try the new garment on. Her skin was still suntanned, and it had sent a frisson of lust down his spine to see her stripped down to bra and pants. 'I'll wear it for the rest of the evening,' she'd said, 'to see how it feels.'

But ten minutes was enough. 'Although they can't be seen,' she said, 'I can feel the coins rolling around the hem. They're uncomfortable and distracting.'

'I can hear them,' Archie said, 'the rattle of cash. What have you put in there?'

'Four farthings and two halfpennies to represent the weight of the stones and the gold they'll return to me.'

'Stones won't roll round as easily, but if they keep touching, they'll make a noise that could give you away.'

'I need to give this more thought.'

By the following week, she had decided to sew the two layers together up the seams on both sides almost to the waist. 'Then if I run another seam down about an inch away, that will give me two long, narrow pockets. I'm going to attach the two bodices together to give the garment more stability, and with some adjustment of the lace round the top it won't be too obvious that it isn't a normal underslip.'

She had reinserted the coins, this time wrapped in cotton wool, and found she could wear the slip all day and hardly notice the weight when it was equally balanced.

Now Archie sighed. 'It's dangerous, carrying that fortune. Of course I'm worried.'

'I'll be all right. Only you will know I have the stones on me.' She paused. 'Be careful not to tell Bill.'

'But he knows about the tiara being broken up, about where it came from, and that you and Rod took it to Amsterdam,' he said. 'He was with us when Milner produced the thing. He won't have missed that you will be fetching the stones back.'

'But he won't know they're ready for collection or that I've gone to get them. He won't be able to pass the news on to any of the rogues he knows.' She patted his shoulder. 'Do stop worrying, Archie. Come on, let's go and pick him up and get to work. Act as you normally would; be your usual friendly self. Just don't let him know another thing about what we're doing.'

Marion went out alone and took an hour longer over her lunch that day. In the car going home she said, 'I've booked first-class tickets for the train and the ferry, and telegraphed to the diamond cutting company the date and time of my arrival. You remember Eddie Jurgens, don't you?'

'No, I don't think I do.'

'He was a good friend of Rod's in Jo'burg, and a good friend of mine too. He looked after us when we went to Amsterdam, and put us up in his flat. He's offered to put me up again.'

All Archie's suspicions flooded back into his mind. 'In his flat?'

'He has a live-in girlfriend. He'll give me a slant on how things are progressing in Jo'burg. I'm looking forward to seeing him again.'

'I think I should come with you. To make it safer.'

'It's as safe as houses. Eddie will meet me off the ferry, take me to his place and come with me to the diamond cutters the next morning. He says they'll provide lunch and he'll drive me back to the ferry terminal for my return journey.'

'All the same . . .'

'Archie, you poor dear, you're a nervous wreck: too intense, and worried stiff about what might go wrong. You've reached the state when it's affecting everything, even your health.' Even his prowess in bed. 'I should be thinking more of you. I know exactly what you need; really you're not cut out for this sort of life. I should arrange for you to go back to South Africa now. I should pay Bill off and get rid of him – both of you have become weak links – but if I did that, it would bring all activity here to an end. I couldn't finish the work Rod has lined up for us on my own; it would take too long and wouldn't be worth my while.'

'I'm sorry.'

'Poor old Archie.' She felt sorry for him; he needed more and more reassurance and encouragement to keep going, and he was not nearly so much fun as he'd been in Jo'burg.

'I hate the thought of you going away,' he told her. 'I'm not looking forward to being left on my own. I'll miss you terribly.'

'You'll hardly notice I'm gone,' she told him briskly. 'You know Milner wants to make new jewellery from these stones. Have you drawn up any designs for them?'

'You keep me so busy, I don't have time for anything else.'

'Well, you'll have time while I'm away. You should keep Milner in the picture; discuss your designs with him, as they'll be made up in his workroom.'

Archie was pulling a face. 'He'll want what he thinks will sell best.'

'He knows what will sell best in his own shop. Come on, Archie, this is work you say you enjoy.'

On Monday morning, Marion had to make an early start to go to Amsterdam. For Archie, it was not enough to drive her to the station; he insisted on escorting her to the platform and carrying her overnight case for her. Lime Street was the terminus and the train was waiting. He opened a door for her. 'A carriage to yourself.'

'No need to wait and wave me off,' she said, reaching up to kiss his cheek.

'I'll go and pick Bill up, then.'

'Work him hard. Thanks, Archie.' He clung to her for a moment. 'It's only for two nights.' She smiled and patted his arm.

'I'll come and meet you. Ring me from London . . .'

'I've got a sleeper this time. I won't feel so tired when I get back.'

'Right, I look forward to seeing you again before dawn on Wednesday.'

'Goodbye, Archie.' She sank into the corner seat with a sigh; there was relief on her face.

He couldn't bring himself to walk away. 'You look as though you'll be glad to see the back of me.'

'I'm just glad to get here on time. That's the first hurdle accomplished, isn't it? The journey will give me a chance to think and plan ahead, but I'll miss you.'

'Goodbye, love.' He leaned over to kiss her again.

He was early picking Bill Dainty up, and had to read his newspaper for ten minutes before he came. Ever since Marion had told him money was missing from her purse, he'd not felt at ease with Bill, and was very conscious of things he mustn't talk about. But he felt pity for the man. He'd never looked well, but now he appeared positively ill. Archie was afraid he wasn't looking after himself as he should.

Bill was chatty by nature, but only until he settled down to work, then they both concentrated almost in silence on what they were doing. At lunchtime, Archie suggested they go to a small basement café in a side street, where they'd been before. The tea urn permanently hissed and the place was full of steam and smoke, but the food was good and the service quick.

Archie felt he couldn't talk about his current concerns, and now that it was just the two of them, he decided that the best plan was get Bill talking about his own difficulties. 'You had a shop once, didn't you?' he asked tentatively, cutting into the pork cutlet on his plate.

'Yes, in Lord Street in Southport. I had it for over ten years.'

'High-class, then?'

'It would have outclassed Milner's.'

'You've obviously had plenty of experience in the trade.'

'I've worked in it all my life, ever since I left school.'

'How did everything go wrong?'

Bill pulled a face; he hadn't shaved properly this morning. 'I was running a similar scheme to the one you're using here, but in a smaller way. I'd been doing it for years; I suppose I became overconfident that I'd not be caught.'

'Bad luck, then. How did it happen?'

'The police were investigating a large theft, the proceeds of which I had fenced.' He looked up from his plate with a sad smile. 'It had happened two years earlier. Somebody must have let slip something to involve me. The first I knew about it was when two detectives came to question me. Just routine, they said, and I thought I'd got away with it. I heard no more for ages.'

Archie's fork was shaking in his hand. 'But you hadn't?'

'No. I didn't know it, but they went on quietly watching me. Eventually they came with a search warrant and caught me with stolen jewellery on my premises. They were investigating a different robbery by then, and brought in an expert, who went through everything in my shop with a fine-tooth comb. I went to prison.'

'For the first offence?' Archie was pushing food round his mouth; he couldn't swallow it.

'That wasn't the first. I'd had a few fines for other things, but that time they turned up enough evidence to give me a prison sentence. They figured I'd been doing it for years.'

'What was prison like?'

'Well, I didn't enjoy it, if that's what you're asking, but it wasn't actually being inside that wrecked my life. It was the outcome, the result.' Bill had cleared his plate; he laid down his knife and fork and pushed it away.

Archie gave up on his meal and followed suit. 'What was that?'

'I couldn't run my business from jail. My wife put in a manager, but he was no good.' He shrugged, and turned to study the blackboard on which the day's menu had been chalked.

The busy waitress reached their table and crashed their used plates together. 'What'll you have for pudding?' she demanded.

'Bread and butter pudding, please,' Bill said.

'And you, sir?'

Archie felt he'd choke if he ate another mouthful. 'Nothing for me, just a cup of tea.'

'I'll have tea too,' Bill said. When the girl had gone, he went on quietly, 'I went bankrupt. I lost my shop, my wife, my son and my home. It was never worth it.'

Bill's pudding was slid in front of him, and Archie watched him eat with gusto. He'd not been able to put out of his mind the report of the robbery that he'd read in the newspaper round his fish and chips. Couldn't that lead to them being caught in much the same way as had happened to Bill?

The waitress removed Bill's plate. 'Very nice,' he said. She slapped two cups of tea and the bill on their table. 'The problem is, Archie, that although I've served my prison sentence, there's no end to the trouble it's brought.

'No honest jeweller wants to employ me. Why should they when there are plenty of other men seeking work? They don't trust me not to lift their stock. The only work I get is from folks like you, and that could land me back behind bars.'

Archie had a nightmare that night. Hadn't he always been scared that something similar would happen to him and Marion?

He worried his way through the next day and night, with every moment without Marion seeming twice as long. He was back on the station platform twenty minutes before the milk train was due in. He was expecting trouble – even disaster – but there was none. Marion stepped off the train and threw her arms round him.

'Everything went exactly as planned. Absolutely no trouble with Customs,' she whispered. 'The stones have been beautifully cut, they're unbelievably improved. I can't wait to show them to you.'

'Let's get you home,' he said. 'Did you manage to sleep on the train?'

'Yes, not as well as I do at home, but better than sitting up all night.'

Archie cooked a breakfast of eggs and bacon for them while Marion changed out of her bespoke petticoat. They ate at the kitchen table with the stones and her loupe spread out on a bit of black velvet. He was fascinated by them. 'Magnificent workmanship,' he said, putting the biggest sapphire down.

'Has Milner decided on what he wants you to do with them?'

'He's got clients for two grand necklaces. I've given him a few designs but he has to show them to his customers and they haven't decided yet. I want to hear how your trip went. Every detail.'

She smiled. 'I dozed and had lunch on the train going down. I enjoyed the ferry crossing.'

'Did that man you know meet you off the boat?'

'Eddie Jurgens, yes,' she gave him another smile, 'with his partner, Kristen.'

'They're Dutch?'

'Well, Kristen is, but he's from New York, and talking of returning there soon.'

'He probably has Dutch antecedents, with a name like that.'

'Are you sure you don't know him?'

Archie shook his head. 'I don't think I've ever met him. What's he like?'

'I remember him having a series of partners in Jo'burg, but he never married. He's a good-looking man, positive, and full of energy. Like Rod, he knows how to enjoy the best that life can offer, and can be relied upon to give his guests a good time. They took me to a restaurant for dinner, and then back to their flat to spend the night. We were up late talking, of course, and had a few drinks.

'He hasn't changed a bit, good fun. What with catching up with the gossip from Jo'burg and discussing future plans, there seemed to be precious little time left for sleep.' She chuckled. 'I haven't told him how old I am, but I know he's fourteen years younger than me. It took me all my time to keep up with him.'

'You haven't told me how old you are either,' he said.

'No, it's one of those feminine little secrets I don't tell anybody. I had to take a long hot shower to get me going the next morning, but they were perfect hosts and provided coffee and a breakfast of warm bread, cheese and ham.'

'Very Continental.'

'Then it was a short drive to the diamond-cutting premises, where we were taken under the wing of one of the directors. He told us that Rod had booked a radio telephone call, and it came through while we were there, so we were both able to have a word with him.'

'How is he?'

'Fine. It was soothing to hear him say he's fully in control at his end and to know all is going well in Jo'burg.

'We were shown the diamonds I'd come to collect and I inserted them into my underskirt in the ladies' cloakroom; nothing could have been easier. The director took us out to lunch and Eddie drove me back to the ferry.'

'I'm glad that's over,' Archie said with relief.

CHAPTER TWENTY

TIM REDWOOD WAS FEELING very low. He was worried about his mother. She didn't complain, but over the last few months she'd looked increasingly ill, and he could see she was in pain and trying to hide it from him.

He and Carrie had completed this term's course of Saturday lectures and, now, like everybody else, they spent the morning at work. A week ago he'd had to say to her, 'Do you mind if we don't go out on Saturday night? I have problems at home.'

Her big green eyes had met his. 'What sort of problems? You haven't been yourself recently. I can't help but notice.'

'It's not me. My mother isn't well. Do you mind?'

'Of course not, we can go to the pictures next week.'

But the following week she was no better. Tim was afraid Carrie might think he'd grown tired of going out with her and was making excuses to avoid it. She'd surely wonder why he wanted to stay in with his mother on a Saturday night. As she had already been going Dutch with him, he was worried she wouldn't understand why the arrangement couldn't continue. He was also afraid she might find another friend to take his place. He'd tried to explain that really he wanted to be with her, but he just couldn't tell his mother he was going out again after being at work all week; he knew her face would fall.

Worse, he knew that Carrie had noticed what a zombie he'd become in the office. Several times she'd completed her own task and then taken over a job that had been allotted to him, finishing it without saying a word to anyone.

But on the tram going to work on Tuesday, she asked, 'Is your mother feeling better now?'

He shook his head. 'I think she's worse. I had to call the doctor out to her last night. I'm sorry, Carrie.'

'Tim, it's only right that you stay with your mother when she's not feeling well. You never tell me much about your home life. I hope it isn't serious.'

'She was diagnosed with rheumatoid arthritis years ago, but recently she's felt better and been able to do more. I'd come to believe that would be permanent.'

'Oh no! You mean her illness has suddenly come back?'

'It's come back but it hasn't been sudden; her strength has been draining away over the past months. I've had to call out the doctor several times.' He was glad he'd told Carrie; he wanted her to understand.

Her green eyes were studying him. 'You have to help more about the house?'

'Yes.' He shook his head. 'It upsets Mum to see me struggling with the cooking and the cleaning. She wants to do it, and when she finds she can't finish a job it makes her feel worse. She's losing her confidence as well as her strength.'

'Can I do anything to help?' Carrie asked.

'I don't think anybody can,' he said miserably.

The following week she said, 'I'm worried about you; you don't look well. It must be possible to do something that will help you both. Come on, talk to me, I want to know what's happening. Your mother's an invalid now?'

'Yes, I'm afraid she is. All through my schooldays she felt ill, but miraculously five years ago she began to feel better, do more about the house and get out and about. I'm sure much of her stiffness remained, but she learned to live with it, and though her gnarled fingers couldn't do fine work, they grew no more twisted. She was cheerful and even took on a little job to help a friend when she was widowed.

'Mum found it handy to buy most of our weekly food from Harrison's, a family business selling general groceries in a parade near us; Ethel Harrison provided a chair and a chat, and over the years they became friendly.

'Ethel lives over the shop, and since her husband died she's been running it, but she didn't know how to keep the books. Mum does that for her and helps with stock control and reordering, that sort of thing, and we plough back the wage she pays us into more food.

'We both expected that happy state to continue, but the doctor has told us that mother has had a flare-up of her old disease. I hate to see her in pain; it's almost constant, and it leaves her weak and disheartened and unable to do very much at all.'

Tim knew how to manage on very little money – it was what they'd always done – but it was getting harder. He could feel Carrie's sympathy and went on to explain further.

'When I was very small, we had a daily cleaning woman, but over the years we found we could no longer afford such a luxury. Now the extra expense of medicines and doctor's bills is upsetting our budget. I learned to do a share of the housework when I was a child, and now I'm getting up earlier to reset the fire in the grate and make breakfast for us both before I go to work. I have to make sure there's something ready for her lunch, and I cook an evening meal for us both when I get home.'

'Tim, it must be very hard to find time to do all that. I'm so sorry.'

His eyes burned and he had to struggle to stay in control. 'When Mum became really ill, I had to take over her job because it's our only source of income other than my allowance as an articled clerk. I now spend my Sundays keeping Ethel's books up to date.'

'Tim! You can't possibly do everything. There are only so many hours in the day!'

He sucked at his lip. He'd felt he could cope with these setbacks in the short term, but his mother wasn't getting any better, and he'd been warned as to how her illness was likely to progress. He dreaded to think of his present workload as permanent. He knew his work at Atherton & Groves was suffering; he had no energy and was slower than he had been. He'd stopped studying or even reading his accounting-related books.

During the weeks leading up to Christmas, he and Carrie were part of a four-man team drawing up the annual accounts for a restaurant in the city centre. They'd been invited to have an early lunch with the staff before they opened for business at midday.

Mr Stott, their leader on this occasion, raised his water glass to the owner. 'Thank you, sir. This is very generous of you.'

They began talking about Christmas. 'It really gets going

for me by the middle of December,' Carrie told them. 'Every year Aunt Maud takes us to her school to see the children in their nativity play, and Aunt Prue takes us to a carol concert at her church.'

Tim had nothing to say – the festive season was creating more difficulties for him – but Carrie caught his eye and asked, 'Do you have anything planned?'

'Not really. My mother and I are invited to have lunch with my Uncle Jeremy on Christmas Day. It happens every year; you know, family tradition.'

'We have family traditions too. Aunt Prue does turkey and plum pudding for Gladys and Uncle Bob's family, and then Gladys invites us all to her house for tea, and on Boxing Day it's Uncle Bob's turn to have us all over to a big lunch at his place.' Today in the restaurant it was sausage and mash, followed by rice pudding and prunes. 'I'm quite looking forward to the feasting.'

'So am I,' Tim said, 'but we won't be able to walk to Uncle Jeremy's as we've done in the past. It would be too much for Mum now.' Uncle Jeremy usually ordered a taxi to take them home in the early evening, as it was getting dark by then. 'And my mother's worried that she'll not be able to last out for the whole afternoon.'

Tim was also worried about how he would produce the little presents they traditionally took with them; worried about finding presents for anybody.

When work was over that afternoon and he was walking with Carrie to the nearest tram stop, the Salvation Army band was playing carols in the street. It was a longer journey home than from their office, and the city seemed full of life and light.

The shop windows they passed were full of festive glitter. The spirit of Christmas was all round him; everybody else was in good cheer.

'You don't seem to be looking forward to it,' Carrie said.

'I can't cope with any more of this,' he burst out, and was immediately sorry he'd let that slip.

He felt her take his hand. 'Can't cope with Christmas? Tim, it's not something to be coped with, it's something to be enjoyed. What's the matter? You've seemed a bit down in the mouth for the last week or two. Is your mother no better?'

'She isn't likely to get better,' he said. 'It's not that sort of illness. As time goes on, she's likely to get worse.' He went on to explain about having no money to spare for a taxi fare on Christmas Day.

'You'll just have to tell your uncle,' she said. 'I don't see your difficulty there. You see him almost every day, don't you?'

'Uncle Jeremy is very good to us, very generous. He's been keeping us going for the last few years. Mum doesn't like to keep asking for more.'

'But he'd expect you to tell him that she isn't as well as she was last year, and why it's difficult to accept his invitation. And if your mother tires more easily than she did, he'll understand and call the taxi early. He might even think it strange if you didn't tell him. You aren't thinking straight, Tim. You're making mountains out of molehills. You seem exhausted, almost too tired to do anything.'

'I am tired – well, you know why.'

'Coming to work and doing more about the house, yes. You're trying to do everything. You can't.'

He couldn't stop his troubles bubbling out. 'There's worse,' he went on. 'On New Year's Day, the family has always come to us for afternoon tea, and I dread asking them round, though Mum talks as though it's all going to go ahead as usual.'

'It'll take you both out of yourselves, raise your spirits, so why not?'

He couldn't look at her. 'Our relatives all have plenty of money, but we've no cash to spare for fancy cakes and presents, not now that it has to cover her medicines and doctor's bills. Mum used to bake but she can't any more, and I wouldn't know where to start on that.'

'I can make cakes,' Carrie said. 'I could bake for you and I'll have plenty of time before New Year. It could be my Christmas present to you.'

'Carrie, you're very kind, too kind, and I can't buy you a present. Besides, Mum can no longer act as hostess.' The tram was approaching her stop. He stood up to let her get off.

'I could come and fill teacups for you if you want help,' she said. 'Aunt Prue gives large family parties so I'm practised at that. Except . . . Your Uncle Jeremy is the boss. Will Leonard be coming? Oh golly, they'll all know me!'

'Of course they will. Does that matter?'

'Well . . . I'm articled to Leonard. He's my mentor and he controls my future prospects. It makes me feel differently about him.'

'My Great-Uncle William will be coming too. He's Jeremy's father and Len's grandfather. You won't know him; he retired from the firm years ago.'

'Quite a family gathering.' Carrie wasn't sure she'd done the right thing by offering to help.

Tim watched her turn to wave from the pavement as the

tram moved on, and was almost overcome. He mopped his face with his handkerchief, fighting down the emotion that threatened to engulf him. Carrie was offering more help in addition to all she did for him at work. He told himself it was gratitude and friendship he felt for her, but at this moment it was tenderness too.

He knew she didn't want love. Hadn't she said she'd had to fight off the attentions of other men in the firm? She'd wanted no more outings with Robbie and that lot, so Tim hadn't allowed himself to show any romantic affection. If friendship was all she wanted, friendship would be what he gave. He wasn't going to do anything that might put her off.

Over the last few weeks, all the time he was doing little things to help his mother, his mind had been on Carrie. He was in no doubt it was love on his side, but whatever his feelings, he could see no way forward. It would be three or four years before they were both qualified and could afford to even think of marriage. He needed to put thoughts like that right out of his mind.

His mother would always have to be supported, and he couldn't possibly desert her. They had the house, but it was too big for them, and as he walked up the road, he could see that it was easily the one most in need of a coat of paint. In fact, it looked decidedly shabby; since his father had died, it had had little maintenance. Mum was too proud to tell Uncle Jeremy they were no longer able to cope and ask for more help, and she didn't want Tim to do that either. 'Jeremy has a family of his own to look after,' she told him. 'He's already providing us with a great deal.'

As soon as he let himself into the hall, Tim could hear a

choir singing 'God Rest Ye Merry, Gentlemen'. His mother always made an effort to dress and come down by lunchtime, and she had the wireless on and the fire blazing up to welcome him home. He held out his hands to warm them; there was a row of cards along the mantelpiece.

'Two more cards came today,' she said cheerfully. She wanted to send cards in return, though her handwriting was uneven and spidery. Tim had to write out the envelopes, and he delivered them by hand if he could.

His mother went on talking about the festive season. She no longer ate very much, but he thought she was looking forward to having Christmas lunch at her brother's and seeing all the family again. It must be lonely for her now she couldn't get out and about. She used to have a lot of friends, but not many came round to see her.

'We'll be able to manage afternoon tea for them on New Year's Day, won't we? They won't expect much; if you bought a cake and a few biscuits, that would do.'

Tim told her of Carrie's offer.

'That's marvellous, and your friend will come and help too?'

'She said so, but I think she's somewhat uncomfortable at the idea. She's articled to Leonard and knows Uncle Jeremy professionally too.'

'What difference does that make?'

'She's afraid they'll be embarrassed, Mum.'

'Nonsense, why should they be?'

Tim grimaced; he wasn't looking forward to any of this.

'Only five more days and it'll be Christmas. It'll be a rest for you, Tim.'

A rest was a different matter; he *was* looking forward to that. 'But what are we going to do about presents?' he asked. 'It certainly is embarrassing when we receive gifts and have nothing to give in return.' He felt he was nearing the end of his tether.

By Christmas Eve, Tim and the team had completed their work at the restaurant and had only to tidy up small jobs in the office. He could see that nobody was in the mood for work, and little was being done. Spirits were high, and became even more buoyant when they were told they could all go home and start their holiday at lunchtime.

Last week it had been agreed that instead of buying gifts for all their colleagues, they would put their names into a hat and each would draw out another name and give a gift, costing about one shilling in value, to that person. This way, everybody would have a small gift at little expense.

Tim had drawn Miss Woodford, their receptionist, and had ready a box of six lace-trimmed handkerchiefs. The office was noisy with excitement and *joie de vivre* when they were getting ready to leave and were giving out their cards and gifts. Miss Woodford seemed very pleased with the handkerchiefs, and they were admired by the other ladies. 'Very expensive,' she said. 'Hand-made lace. I bet you paid more than a shilling for these.'

Carrie's eyes were shining as she came over to Tim's desk wearing her hat and coat. She'd been laughing with the typists and he could see they were all excited now that Christmas was close. It made him feel even more downhearted. 'Are you ready to go home?' she asked.

Tim was glad to escape. On the tram, he felt awkward about the gift he'd prepared for her. It wasn't quite what he wanted to give her, but he handed it over as her journey neared its end. 'Happy Christmas, Carrie.'

'Another present? Lovely, but I thought it was agreed the lucky dip in the office would be enough.'

'I wanted to give you something myself.'

She turned the package over in her hands; it was neatly gift-wrapped and tied with ribbon. She gave him a wide smile and asked, 'Am I allowed to open it now?' They'd done that with the office gifts.

'Of course.'

She gasped with delight as she shook out a gossamer silk scarf in swirling shades of blue. 'Tim, it's beautiful, and made of real silk. Almost everything in the big shops is now made of what they call art silk – that means artificial – but this is so much nicer, the real thing. Thank you, I love it. It will go beautifully with my best coat.'

He couldn't doubt her pleasure in it, but her enormous eyes looked searchingly into his. 'It's very generous of you. Miss Woodford reckons you did her proud too. But didn't you say you had no money for Christmas presents?'

He took a deep breath and sucked in his lips; he should have expected this. 'Money is short. I didn't mean to tell you, but . . . Well, the scarf was a present to my mother last Christmas. She's never used it.'

He could see Carrie biting her lip. 'And the hankies too?'

'Yes, Mum said it was sensible to use the gifts in some way, and I wanted to give you a present.'

He could see tears glistening in her eyes. 'I'm afraid I've no present to give you now.' She took a Christmas card out of her bag and put it into his hand. 'I shall bake cakes for you and bring them on New Year's Day when I come to help at your party. Happy Christmas, to you and your mother. Try to enjoy it, Tim.'

She skipped off the tram and turned to wave and smile as she always did, and Tim felt his heart turn over.

CHAPTER TWENTY-ONE

C ARRIE ENJOYED THE TWO-DAY Christmas holiday with her family, but she missed Tim. She couldn't stop thinking about him, wondering how he was getting on and whether he was enjoying the festivities. Surely he must find it hard not to?

She looked round her own living room, bright with the decorations Prue brought out each year, the Christmas cards set out along the mantelpiece along with the holly Uncle Bob had given them when they'd last gone to his house. The leaves still shone and it had lots of red berries. Bob had a holly tree in his garden and had sent her home with a big armful, so she'd given some to Tim to spark up his home. When she closed her eyes to sleep, she could see him standing before her with his tousled chestnut hair and his slow half-smile.

When she returned to work, everybody was relaxed and happily anticipating the next break for New Year, and even Tim seemed better. 'Yes, I enjoyed it,' he said briefly, 'but you haven't forgotten about coming to help at Mum's tea party?' Carrie could see he was still anxious about that.

'Of course I haven't. Aunt Prue is doing some baking for you today,' she said. 'She wants to know how many people will be coming, and I didn't ask you about that.'

'Five adults and two children, and there'll be us three. Mum doesn't eat much.'

'Prue was expecting it to be many more. She gives huge parties, but it won't matter if some of it is left; it'll keep for a day or two. You can eat it later.'

On New Year's Day, Carrie knew she'd have to walk to Tim's house because no trams would be running. He'd offered to come and help her carry the cakes, but she'd said that wouldn't be necessary, she could manage. An hour and a half before his guests were expected, she was ready to set off. She wore the scarf he'd given her; it felt cosy on this dark, raw day, and not only suited her coat but gave her best blue dress a lift and filled in the neckline.

She knew Tim travelled five stops further on the tram. He'd drawn a map for her and explained how to find his house, but she was sorry now he wasn't with her as she struggled to follow his directions. He lived further out from the city and it was a different sort of district. These were bigger and older houses in large gardens set further back from the road.

She checked twice that she'd found the right house. Her first impression was that it was imposing. It was a large Victorian detached villa, but the front garden looked seriously in need of attention: it had become overgrown in the summer and the borders had died back in tangled masses. The paint on the large front door was peeling.

Tim opened it before she had time to ring the bell. 'I was watching for you,' he said, taking her bags. 'Come on in. I'm very grateful for what you're doing. Gosh, these are heavy. I should have come to help you carry them.'

The hall was huge and chilly. 'Here, let's have your hat and coat.' He paused by the hall stand to hang them up, and Carrie saw his eyes widen with horror. 'You can't wear that scarf,' he hissed under his breath. 'My Aunt Enid is coming. She gave it to my mother last year; she might recognise it. Sorry, Carrie. I should have said.'

Hurriedly she whipped it off and folded it into her handbag, shivering as she did so.

'Oh dear!' He looked disconcerted. '"Beware thy sins will find thee out." Sorry, sorry. Come and meet my mother.'

Jane Redwood was small, hunched, grey-faced and gaunt. She was sitting in a large armchair drawn close to the fire, and struggled to get to her feet.

'Don't get up, Mrs Redwood,' Carrie said, going forward to shake the hand she offered. She saw it was misshapen and twisted, and it filled her with pity.

'It's very good of you to come and help Tim like this. Help us both really, I suppose. I'm very grateful.' Her voice shook.

The sitting room seemed vast, but a grand piano took up a lot of the space, and the rest was filled with sofas, armchairs and small tables. There was a six-foot-high gilt mirror over the fireplace, a little foxed in one corner.

Tim was urging Carrie to the kitchen. 'We need to get things ready, set the cakes out on plates,' he told his mother. It was downright cold as well as draughty out there, but she saw he had set out plenty of cake stands and plates in several sizes, all of good-quality gold-rimmed china. She began to unpack the cakes while Tim produced linen and lace doilies to go under them.

'Mum made me wash and starch these,' he said.

'Aunt Prue uses paper doilies, it's much less trouble. And

paper serviettes,' Carrie added when she saw him getting out lace-edged tea napkins.

'Mum thinks these are better. Besides, we already have them, so don't have to buy paper ones. Gosh, cherry cake, that's one of my favourites.'

'Prue made it, and this chocolate log is her speciality. I did the fairy cakes. Maud made the scones, while I cut the sandwiches this morning.'

'This is an enormous spread,' Tim said, beaming with gratitude, 'the best I've seen for years.'

He'd already set the table in the dining room, and it seemed they were all to sit round it. Carrie had expected to hand the food round; afternoon tea, after all, was not a formal meal.

Tim poked the fire into a blaze and put more coal on. 'Is it cold in here? We don't often light this fire.'

Carrie suppressed a shiver: it was freezing, and the room smelled of damp and disuse. 'Not as warm as in the sitting room,' she said diplomatically, and it hadn't exactly been cosy there.

'The family haven't been here since last New Year,' Tim said, 'and that afternoon didn't go well. I spilled tea on Uncle Jeremy's suit, and there was hardly enough of anything to go round; a frugal tea compared with the feast you've brought us. They'll be impressed.'

Carrie trailed behind him back to the kitchen, feeling at a loose end now her offerings were set out. He'd already filled a huge kettle and boiled it on the ancient gas cooker. It stood steaming with two silver teapots beside it.

'Everything's ready now,' he said. 'Let's go back and talk to

Mum.' But at that moment the doorbell rang, and Tim went to let the newcomers in. They brought a blast of freezing air with them as they helped in a very elderly and doddery gentleman. The ladies kissed Tim, and his mother appeared at the sitting room doorway to hug the children. They were filling the hall with noise and movement as they hung up their coats.

Tim came to Carrie's side. 'This is my Uncle William, my great-uncle, really. He's ninety-five and hard of hearing, so you'll have to speak up.

'I'm pleased to meet you, Mr Groves,' Carrie said at the top of her voice, offering her hand. 'I wish you all the best for the new year.'

He took her hand between both of his; they were icy cold. 'One year is pretty much like another to me, my dear.'

To the other menfolk Tim said, 'You know Caroline Courtney.'

The other two Mr Groves seemed to notice her for the first time and appeared surprised, but they smiled encouragingly at her. 'Of course, of course.'

To the ladies he explained, 'She's articled to Len, and she's come to help so that this year I can avoid the embarrassment of pouring tea down Uncle Jeremy's best suit. Carrie, this is my Aunt Enid, and Mary is married to Len. These are their two children, Robert and Polly.'

They all greeted her in a kind and friendly manner, but Carrie couldn't help feeling a little overawed. She was used to being summoned to the offices of the two Mr Groves, and until now she'd discussed only business matters with them. It made her feel stiff, awkward and out of place.

'Are you going to be an accountant like my dad?' the boy

asked. 'You must be very clever if you can do that. I'm going to be one too if I can, but I'll have to work hard at school.'

Carrie was relieved; she felt better able to cope with the children. 'How old are you?'

'I'm ten and Polly is seven.'

'No, you're not. You won't be ten till next week,' the girl retorted.

Tim came to sit beside her and she thought he seemed anxious and on edge. The next hour passed slowly for Carrie. The adults tried to talk to her, but she felt she lacked Connie's ready chatter. Old Uncle William dozed off.

'I think he finds this rather tiring,' Mary said, 'but we couldn't leave him at home by himself, not today. He still keeps up his household, but of course he relies much more on his staff these days, especially his valet, who has to do almost everything for him.'

Tim's mother was clearly making an effort to be sociable. She was smiling and seemed more alive than she had before, but Carrie felt she was making a brave and determined attempt to appear at her best.

When at last Tim went out to boil up the kettle again, Carrie went too. With the teapots filled, he ushered his guests to the dining room table.

'My goodness, what a magnificent spread!' exclaimed Len Groves. The other adults echoed him.

'Carrie made these cakes to help me,' Tim told them. His family were beaming at her, and seemed to be seeing her in a new light.

'All of them?' asked Mary, Len's wife.

'Yes,' Tim said firmly. Carrie went round with a milk jug in one hand and a teapot in the other, filling the teacup in front of each guest.

'Thank you, Carrie, for acting as hostess for me,' Jane Redwood said. 'My hands aren't up to pouring out now, and Tim can be a little clumsy.'

'Where did you learn to bake like this?' Enid wanted to know.

'My aunts taught me,' Carrie said. 'They brought me up and they bake every week.'

Mrs Redwood's knotted hands were struggling with a sandwich. Carrie was touched with sympathy; Tim's mother was more disabled by her illness than she'd expected, and was doing her best to hide it.

Jeremy bit into his sandwich hungrily. 'They're absolutely delicious. What have you put in them?'

'Cottage cheese and grapes,' Carrie said. 'Aunt Prue made the wholemeal bread.' They were equally loud in their praise of the cakes. She thought Tim began to relax then, and with her food being so obviously appreciated, she was able to do the same.

It seemed Uncle Jeremy had brought two bottles of sherry with him; he opened one and Tim brought in the tray of glasses he'd set ready so they could drink to Jane's health.

There was a flurry as they prepared to leave. Carrie saw Jeremy Groves look at her. 'Can we offer you a lift home? We've come in two cars, so there's plenty of room.'

'Thank you, but it's all right. I don't live very far away.' She'd intended to help Tim wash up.

'It's very dark and cold outside,' Mr Groves said. 'It would be safer for you to come with us.'

'Yes,' said Tim, holding out her coat for her, then handing her the bags in which she'd brought the food. 'Much the best thing. Thank you for everything, Carrie.' He shot her an affectionate glance. 'I'll see you at work tomorrow.'

Carrie found herself on the back seat of a very large car. Enid Groves thanked her for helping Jane and Tim, and praised her baking over again. 'I wish I could make cakes like that,' she said.

To Carrie, it seemed only moments before she was back in her own living room. Prue and Maud were eating high tea in front of a blazing fire, and the warmth seemed to envelop her. They were full of questions and she tried to tell them all about it. She'd expected Tim to walk her home and felt as though she'd been cut off abruptly from him.

It was a long time before she felt really warm again.

CHAPTER TWENTY-TWO

AFTER THE JOLLITY OF the holidays, Carrie found it hard to settle down to serious work in the new year. The first time she had reason to speak to Leonard Groves, he said, 'I must congratulate you on your baking, Miss Courtney, I did enjoy your chocolate log.' And before she could tell him that her Aunt Prue had made it, he'd launched into business matters.

Old Mr Groves never mentioned seeing her at the New Year tea, but he was a more visible presence in the office, checking on everything. Several people attracted his displeasure for wasting time – Tim more than once. Carrie kept her head down and worked hard until the sound of Jeremy Groves's raised voice brought her back to what was happening near her.

'Timothy,' he was saying, with a face like thunder, 'what do you think you are doing?'

Carrie's view was of Tim's back, his head and shoulders bent and sinking lower. 'I'm sorry . . .'

Mr Groves carried on in that vein for five more minutes. Nobody in the office could fail to hear, and they all understood that Tim was getting a rollicking for ignoring some basic principle of accounting and making a complete hash of the job he was doing. His uncle was almost shouting with rage. Tim's back told Carrie he was in despair.

When she saw that Mr Groves had finished and was about to storm past her desk, Carrie stood up. 'May I have a word with you, sir?'

'Now?' he barked at her.

'Please, if you can spare a moment.' He didn't say no, so she followed him to the quiet of his own office, where he threw himself into the chair behind his desk. She closed the door softly behind her, now feeling a bit shocked at what she'd done.

She stepped forward and remained standing. 'Sir, I know I'm speaking out of turn, and I hope you'll forgive me. Timothy Redwood is battling with home circumstances that are almost beyond his control.'

'I'm fully aware of his home circumstances,' growled Mr Groves, his face twisting with anger.

'With due respect, sir, I don't think you quite understand. In recent weeks Tim has had to take on the part-time job his mother was doing, because she is no longer able to manage it.'

'Can't manage it? Why not? She said she was feeling better over Christmas. She looked a little better, and on New Year's Day she was in good form.'

'Tim says she's finding it increasingly difficult to do anything. She wanted to hold her usual New Year tea for you, and Tim felt he had to arrange it, so I offered to do the baking for them. He said his mother put on the best show she could in front of you, but she went to bed half an hour after you'd gone.'

'What?' He took off his heavy spectacles and rubbed his puffy eyes.

'Tim has no time to himself and he's exhausted. He's doing most of the housework as well as spending his weekends doing her job.'

'He's trying to do the impossible. What is he trying to prove? Why put himself through that?'

'Because it brings in the money they need to buy food. I know it's none of my business—'

'It isn't, Miss Courtney.'

'Tim says you already do a lot to support them, and his mother has told him not to ask for more. She's proud and sees that as a form of begging.'

His expression had softened. 'So you've taken it upon yourself to tell me?'

'I felt I had to. Tim can't carry on doing all this. Before coming here in the morning, he makes breakfast for them both and cleans out the grate and sets the fire ready for her. He cuts sandwiches for his lunch and makes sure there is something for his mother to eat. On days when she's feeling really ill, he fills a flask so she can have a hot drink. He can't keep this up and give proper attention to his—'

He held up his hand. 'I've got the idea, Miss Courtney, no need to go on.'

'With the shopping in his lunchtime and the hot meal he cooks when he gets home from the office, he can't possibly be at his most alert at work, and he doesn't have any time to study.'

'Yes, thank you; that will do.'

She dared not look at his face; instead she stared at his silver and cut-glass inkstand. 'I'm sorry, but I thought you should know.'

His dark eyes gleamed from between the folds of flesh. 'Am I to understand that Timothy is your boyfriend?'

That threw Carrie; it was her turn to be brusque. 'No, he is not.' She wished he was, and hoped he might be in time, but that wasn't how things were. She couldn't show her feelings, not to his uncle. She was overforceful. 'We are thrown together all the time, and we've learned to rub along without too much friction. I consider Tim to be a colleague and a friend, and that's how he sees me.'

She paused and took another deep breath. 'And while I'm at it, sir, I feel you're harder on Tim than you are on the rest of us. I mean, you expect more of him.' She got as far as the door and turned to say, 'Sorry, sir,' before whisking out without so much as another glance in his direction.

When she returned to the general office, every head was bent over its desk and, apart from the scratching of pen nibs, there was complete silence. Tim's back still signalled despair.

Nobody stirred as she sat down. Carrie mopped at her forehead, her knees suddenly weak. She'd spoken up without giving any thought as to how Mr Groves would take her intervention. She hoped he wouldn't hold it against her.

Later that afternoon, Carrie couldn't help but notice that Leonard Groves went to Tim's desk to have a word, and they left the office together. Tim had not returned at five o'clock. She cleared his desk, and slid the documents he'd been working on into his top drawer.

The next morning, he'd kept a seat for her on the tram. 'You told Uncle Jeremy about my problems,' he said.

'Yes, I thought somebody should,' she admitted. 'Please forgive me. You were like a zombie in the office and nobody can be on top of things when they're tired out. Besides, he was telling you off.'

'Thanks.' Tim gave her a rueful smile. 'You won't believe how kind he's been – the whole family have really. He took me home, and Auntie Enid had already made a hot casserole for our dinner.

'Leonard and Mary came later and we had a family conference round the table. Auntie Enid is going to find us a daily help to come in six mornings a week, and Len is arranging for Mum to visit her specialist again to see if more can be done to help her. It looks as though you've sorted me out.'

Carrie pulled a face. 'Sorted your Uncle Jeremy out, more like.'

'The family said I should thank you.'

'Good. I was afraid your uncle would be mad at me.'

'You did too good a job on New Year's Day. Between us we put on such an impressive show that they thought everything was fine.'

'Yes, I had to tell him, though I thought you'd be mad at me too. You would have dug a deeper and deeper hole for yourself and still be in the doghouse.'

'Yes, as I said, you've sorted me out.' The corners of his mouth curved into a half-smile. 'Mum's pleased; she says you've rescued me from drudgery and now I must get stuck into my books before I get left behind in the coursework.'

Over the following weeks, everybody noticed how much more alive Tim became. Robbie laughed and said the display of ire from his uncle had had a miraculous effect. Tim told Carrie, 'My family thoroughly approve of you.'

On Saturdays now, he took Carrie home with him to a lunch made for three by Mrs Beattie, the home help. She had been cooking and cleaning for other people for the past thirty years and had a wide repertoire of tasty meals. Tim's favourite was scouse.

After they'd eaten and cleared away, Carrie and Tim settled down at the table with their books for an afternoon of study. After that, they felt they'd earned an evening out, and usually had a drink in a pub before going to the pictures or to one of the many theatre shows in the city. Carrie still insisted on paying for her seat, but Tim liked to treat her to the drink, and to the coffee or ice cream they had in the interval.

Carrie felt Tim was much happier, and now both of them were making progress in their studies. She was enjoying it all and thought he was too. Mrs Redwood spent a week in a nursing home, where her condition was assessed, and then Auntie Enid took her to Bath for a few days' holiday. When she returned home, she felt much better and was able to potter about the house again.

Archie felt he had to get out of England. 'I think we should book our passages back to Cape Town,' he said to Marion. 'If I had a date to look forward to, it would settle me down. And if we had to get out in a hurry, it—'

There was a look of pained forbearance on Marion's face. 'There is no reason to think we'll have to get out in a hurry,' she said. He knew he kept bringing this up, but she never wavered in her determination to see the job through.

'You'll have to be patient, if we're to get through the work Rod has organised. There's a lot more to do in Southport and in Chester, but when that's done, we'll take the maximum profit, and that will give us enough to live on comfortably for the rest of our lives. We'll never have to put ourselves in this position again.'

Archie sighed. 'Yes, but I still have to make these pieces for Milner. We have to use the stones you've had recut.'

Her deep brown eyes looked at him fondly. 'You'll enjoy doing that, you know you will.'

'I feel the net is closing round us, that—'

'You're obsessed with the idea. It's as safe as it can be. Just relax and go with it.'

Archie tried. On 20 January, the old king died, and he found everybody was talking about royalty. It caused endless interest and discussion, because they all hoped that the Prince of Wales would take his place as Edward VIII, but he was deeply involved with an American woman who had been twice divorced and was thought unsuitable to be Queen of England.

Archie was afraid that problem would be as difficult to settle as his own, and it added to his feelings of doubt and insecurity.

One dark, wet morning in February, Archie and Marion set off to pick up Bill Dainty, but today he wasn't waiting in his usual place on the corner of his road.

Archie halted the car while the rain lashed against its windows. 'Poor sod,' he said. 'Waiting here must be awful in a downpour like this.'

'But he isn't waiting here,' Marion pointed out. 'Drive down to his house. It looks as though you might have to go in and get him.' Archie backed the car up and turned into the road.

'Stop!' Marion's voice was almost a scream. 'Stop, I can see two policemen going into one of the houses. Is it Bill's? Archie, is that Bill's house?'

He was just in time to see a police helmet being taken off and, seconds later, the door swing shut behind a portly frame. He threw the gear lever into reverse and backed up as quickly as he could. Moments later he was speeding along their original route.

'What can Bill have done to be visited by the police?' Marion said.

'Something's happened.' Archie was agitated. 'I don't like this.'

'He knows where we'll be working today. Perhaps he'll come on later.' But they saw nothing of Bill that day, and Archie worried himself sick.

The next morning he was waiting in his usual place. 'What happened to you yesterday?' Marion barked at him as he got into the back of the car.

'I overslept. Sorry.'

'We saw the police going into that house where you have a room,' Archie told him. 'What have you done now?' Bill looked sheepish. 'Have you been charged with some offence?'

'Stealing from a parked car,' he admitted.

'What a damn fool thing to do,' Marion burst out. 'What did you steal?'

'A coat and a fruit cake.'

'Bill, you should have more sense,' Archie wailed as he drove on.

'All right,' Marion said. 'How and where? Let's hear what happened.' She had to dig the story from him; Bill was reluctant to say anything.

'The car was parked outside the Black Dog, my local pub. I was unlucky. The landlady was watching from an upstairs window and recognised me.'

'That was unbelievably careless of you. Stupid, in fact,' Marion told him. 'I have noticed before that you've got light fingers. You've got to stop thieving other people's belongings. Attracting police attention like this could get us all into trouble.'

'Sorry,' he said. 'I won't do it again.'

Once they reached the shop where they were to work, Bill took a brooch from the box and settled down without saying any more. Archie had the feeling that they still hadn't heard the full story. 'Come on, Bill,' he said. 'Tell us the rest.'

'I ate the cake,' he said. 'It was very good.'

A month or so later, Marion said, 'I'll not come to work with you today, Archie. I need to sort out the bills and get the books up to date.'

Archie liked Marion to be near; he felt safer when she was close, but he knew she'd be cooking dinner for him when he got home. The kitchen was full of savoury scents and added warmth, but Marion was not her usual happy self.

'D'you remember going to Edmund Cooper's, that jeweller in Birkenhead? I've had a bit of an argument with him today.'

Archie poured out two glasses of wine. 'What about?'

'He said he gave us seventeen pieces to work on but received only fifteen back. He's missing two dress rings. Both are clusters of small diamonds set in platinum. I've spent half the afternoon checking over our lists, and it seems we did have them.'

'I think I remember doing one; it had built-up shoulders with tiny stones there too.' Archie took a gulp of his wine. 'They couldn't have got mixed up with stuff for another shop?'

Marion shook her head. 'No, I've checked. We look after everything very carefully; we have to. I'm shattered.'

'Oh Lord, is it Bill again?'

She sighed. 'Apart from us two, nobody else had much opportunity.'

Archie exploded. 'Because we did nothing when we suspected he was taking cash from your purse, he thinks he can get away with anything. What are we going to do about this?'

'I don't know. I wish we could trust him.'

'We never should have. He's got a criminal record.'

'Mr Cooper has refused to pay our bill unless we return his rings or make recompense for them.'

'We ought to talk to Bill about this. Or sack him.'

'If we sack him, it will take us longer to finish. I don't want to stay here any longer than we have to, and I know you don't. That's why we said nothing to him the first time. It makes sense to do that again.'

That gave Archie several days of acute anxiety. How could he stay calm when the police had charged Bill with theft? 'It's coming too close to us,' he worried, 'and I don't think he's telling us the whole truth about what happened. It seems crazy to steal a fruit cake.'

'He must have been hungry because he ate the evidence, as the only thing he's been charged with stealing is a cashmere coat. He's not saying anything about taking those two rings, either.'

'Well, he wouldn't, would he? He'd expect to get the push from us if he admitted to that.'

Archie refilled their wine glasses and shivered. 'In one way it makes sense to say nothing, but I can't meet his eyes without thinking and wondering.' They discussed the pros and cons all evening and worried about it.

'OK,' Marion said, 'we can't make up our minds, so why don't we just leave things as they are, and see how he goes on?'

The following Tuesday, they were all tired after a long day working in Southport. Marion was yawning. Archie had driven them back to Liverpool and was about to drop Bill off near his rooms when he stirred on the back seat and said, 'I can't come to work tomorrow, boss.'

'Why not?' Marion demanded, instantly alert.

'I've got to go to court, but it's just the first hearing. I'm charged with stealing a coat. I told you.'

'Is that tomorrow? What time?'

'I've been told to be there for half nine.'

Archie felt his heart race, and his cheeks were on fire. Any mention of Bill being charged made him nervous.

Marion said calmly, 'Really, Bill, you might have given us more notice. Will you be available for work the next day?'

'I expect so. Yes, it's only the first hearing. I'll be tried later. Nothing will happen for a month or so.'

'Ring and let us know everything is all right,' Marion said. 'Tomorrow evening or early Thursday morning. Then we'll pick you up as usual.'

'Everything will be all right,' Bill said confidently.

Archie stopped the car to let him out. He could see his own hands trembling; it made him tighten his grip on the steering wheel. 'If we don't hear from you, we won't come,' he said. 'We need to know it's safe.'

'I'll ring you,' Bill said, 'but it'll be safe enough for you. Why shouldn't it be?'

'If they send you to prison again, I'd rather not be hanging about near your rooms,' Archie spat out angrily.

'Goodbye, Bill,' Marion said, and prodded Archie. 'Come on, let's go. For heaven's sake, calm down.'

'Bill's not telling the truth. I'm sure there's more to it than he's saying.'

'We don't know that. No need to panic.'

'If it was only a coat, surely there would be no first hearing? Doesn't that mean it's going to a higher court?'

'I don't know,' Marion said.

Archie couldn't calm down; he was filled with foreboding. Marion opened the wine and helped him cook dinner, but it didn't help.

'You need a nightcap tonight,' she said, and poured him some brandy before taking him to bed. She held him in her arms to soothe him, but all he wanted to do was sleep. He pushed her away, but his mind kept going round on the possible consequences of Bill being charged. Marion slept soundly, while he spent hours listening to her soft, regular breathing.

Often, now, Marion took Wednesdays off to work on the Starbright accounts. She'd not said whether she would tomorrow, because they'd talked of nothing but Bill's difficulties, but if she did, Archie decided he'd go to court and sit in the public gallery without telling her. He had to know exactly what was happening.

The next morning over breakfast, she said, 'You look worried stiff. I'll come to work with you today. I don't like to think of you being on your own.'

It spilled out before Archie could stop it. 'I'd like to go to court and hear what happens to Bill,' he said. 'It's the only thing that will settle my mind.'

'It'll make you more nervous. I don't think you should.'

'No, it won't.' He couldn't lift his gaze from his scrambled eggs.

'Shall I go instead?'

'Perhaps we should both go,' Archie said. 'I wouldn't be able to do any work anyway.'

'All right. At least his case is to be heard early. If all is well, we can all go to work afterwards.'

Archie found the formality of the court sobering. Marion led him to a seat in the public gallery where Bill would not be able to see them. Proceedings did not start promptly, and Archie felt impatient and restless, but when they did, he very quickly heard enough to be gasping with horror.

William Dainty was charged with breaking into a jewellery shop in Chester on 4 October last year and stealing a diamond ring and a brooch valued at two thousand pounds, and also on 7 March of stealing a camel-hair overcoat and a briefcase containing six hundred pounds in banknotes from a parked car. These items were recovered from his rooms, together with a silver and cut-glass hip flask, on 18 March.

Marion felt for Archie's hand. 'Let's go, we've heard enough. Oh, goodness! That was one of the shops we took him to.'

Once outside, Archie took deep breaths. 'The police have been there to investigate that theft! They could have found something to lead them to us.'

'But they haven't,' Marion pointed out firmly.

'I knew he was lying.' Archie could feel himself shivering. 'That's it; we can't work with him again after this.'

CHAPTER TWENTY-THREE

'**O**UR PROBLEM REMAINS THE same.' Marion's lips were set in a hard straight line. 'We put up with Bill, or we kick him out and do all the work ourselves.'

'If they send him to prison, that decision is out of our hands,' Archie said. 'I think we should pack up now and get out while we can.'

'He won't be going to prison until his case is tried. He can do a lot of work in the meantime.'

Archie felt he couldn't hold out against Marion's wishes, and as usual he gave in and agreed that Bill should stay. Over the next month or so they worked him as hard as they could. They managed to finish the work they were booked to do in Chester, and that left only Southport and a little more in Liverpool. They didn't mention the loss of the two rings to him, but Edmund Cooper continued to hassle them for recompense.

Archie thought he was reaching the end of his tether. His need for safety made him cling to Marion; she was strong, but even so, the future looked scary. They had been living as man and wife ever since Rod had gone, and getting on really well.

Just to see her smile at him could still send a thrill down his spine. He loved her, but the fact that they weren't married meant he didn't have the stability he needed. To feel secure, he had to know Marion would always be with him, that their relationship would be permanent.

He'd suggested once or twice that they get married, and though she'd humoured him and vaguely agreed, she'd sidetracked him and put off setting a definite date. He felt she'd not taken it too seriously.

They were both kept busy working long hours, and she too must have been stressed by this way of life. He made up his mind to propose marriage formally. He'd set all his cards out and make sure she understood that he was serious. They would decide together when this work for Rod had accumulated enough capital, and then get out and have a more normal life.

When she was going out the following Saturday morning, he said, 'Come home early from your jaunt into town. I'll cook dinner tonight, something nice, a little treat.'

Marion smiled. 'Is it a special occasion?'

'I hope it will be.'

'I know it isn't your birthday, so what is it?'

'Wait and see.'

Archie believed she'd be pleased to have their living arrangements made legal, that marriage would settle them both down and they'd feel better. He meant to make his proposal as romantic as possible. He bought a couple of bottles of champagne and some candles for the table; he wasn't much of a cook, but he could manage a roast, and as Marion was fond of chicken, he bought a large one. She came home early as arranged; the meal was almost ready and she ran upstairs to change into a new red dress she'd just bought.

He looked up from carving the chicken. 'You look lovely.'

'You have made an effort,' she said when she saw the candles. 'So what is this occasion?'

It came out in a rush and it wasn't how he'd planned it. 'I want us to be married. Do say we can go ahead on this now.' He could see her freezing and lost confidence. 'I love you. You must know I do, because I keep telling you.'

'I do, Archie, and you mean everything to me, but I don't know about getting married now.'

Heavy disappointment settled on him, leaving him frustrated and shaking. 'Surely living arrangements such as ours put you in a precarious position? Don't you want to have things made legal?' Her face was white and stony.

'Of course. Of course I do.' She was smiling again. 'I want it as much as you do, but we're in such a rush at the moment trying to finish off all this work we've started. I'd like us to have a big wedding with all the trimmings, and we haven't the time or energy to deal with that right now. Wouldn't it be better if we put it off until we're back in Jo'burg?'

'But when will that be?' Archie had had in mind a quick trip to the register office to make it legal. 'I want to get back there too. I've suggested before that we make a firm booking, but you never agree.'

'I do now,' she said and kissed his cheek. 'It should only take us another four or five weeks to finish what we want to do here. We'll go full tilt ahead and get as much done as we can, and you must get Milner's bespoke jewellery finished. Then I'll sack Bill Dainty and we'll go.'

'You'll book our passage?'

'First thing tomorrow morning. I'll go upstairs now and find out which ship it'll be.'

'Any cabin they have available,' Archie urged.

'Yes, the best they can give us. Archie, I'm very happy the way things are now, but I do understand it isn't enough for you.'

'I need more. I've had a few lonely years and I want to know you'll always be at my side. I'd like to design and make matching wedding and engagement rings for you. They can be any style you fancy; I've done a couple of designs to show you.'

She put out her hand to cover his; she already wore several rings with large, expensive diamonds. 'Archie, that's a lovely idea. You can make them up in Jo'burg. You'll have more time once we get there.'

'All right,' he said. 'We'll just get engaged now.'

'I'm sure that's the best thing. Is that champagne you've bought? Let's have a glass.'

Archie was mollified. 'We get on well together, don't we? We are as near married as we can get without the ceremony. I just want to tie the knot.'

'We will,' she said, 'just as soon as we have time. Anyway, now we're firmly engaged, we can start thinking about our wedding. All our friends are in Jo'burg, aren't they?'

She helped Archie dish up their dinner, which turned out to be excellent. Afterwards he took her to his workroom upstairs and showed her his designs for her wedding and engagement rings.

'Archie, they're both beautiful, but yes, I like this one best. I love it.'

'Good, I'd like the stone to be a princess-cut emerald, a big one that will stand out, about three carats. The ring is to be of platinum with built-up shoulders, as I've drawn here, in this pattern set with small diamonds.'

'It's a gorgeous design. I'm going to love it. Where's that timetable? Let's see what ship will be leaving in five weeks' time. Good, it's the one Rod travelled on, the *Transvaal Castle*. I'll make the booking in the morning. Would it be rather naughty to open another bottle of champagne tonight?'

'Why not?' Archie felt better. This was what he needed, to know that everything was moving in the right direction. 'We have two important things to celebrate.'

Already he felt more settled; he'd got Marion to make the booking and she'd agreed to marry him soon. He'd made some progress, even if she wasn't going to fix an early date for it.

Archie said nothing to his family about his plans, but he tried to involve himself in their affairs. He found quite a lot was happening for them, and he felt quite bucked at the prospect of becoming a grandfather.

Connie was all excited; things were moving fast for her. She had given in her notice at work, and she and John were looking round for a small house to buy. John was full of big ideas for their future, and as soon as they'd got married, they'd started saving for a home of their own.

Connie was haunting estate agents, and at the weekends Archie was driving them round to look at what had appealed to them on paper. Marion was interested too. When she saw a board outside a likely-looking property advertised for sale, she made him stop to assess the outside, and if she liked it she made a note to give to Connie. Prue and Maud were busy knitting matinee coats and mittens for the coming child.

Carrie had felt separated from her twin from the moment she had married, but now the gulf between them seemed to be getting wider and deeper. Undoubtedly Connie was moving more quickly through life's major experiences. She'd developed an interest in prams and cots, and was busy collecting a layette of clothes for her baby. Carrie was envious that she would be mistress of her own home.

Connie's cheeks became rounder and she had mauve shadows under her eyes that gave her an ethereal beauty. As the weeks went on she began to look decidedly pregnant. Carrie knew that she herself wasn't ready for that yet. She was more than happy learning to become an accountant. She had Tim to take her round and she was head over heals in love with him, but unlike all the other men she'd been out with, he showed not the slightest romantic interest. He was friendly but a little distant; she would have liked him to show more of his feelings.

Maud was getting excited; she was due to retire at the end of the summer term after her sixtieth birthday. Teachers were allowed to retire at the age of fifty-five, but she'd decided to work on in order to increase her pension. Prue had worked until she was sixty, and as they shared all the expenses, it seemed only fair.

She'd been teaching for thirty-six years without a break and loved the seven- to eight-year-old children in her charge. She'd appreciated the long school holidays that teachers enjoyed, but she'd craved more. She was planning to get away more often once she'd retired.

Already she had been invited to spend a few days in the

Lake District with Edith Warner, a friend who had retired last year. And Gladys MacNamara, another recently retired colleague, had invited her to spend a week with her in Connemara. She'd never been to Ireland before and was really looking forward to that.

Maud and Prue always spent a week of the summer holidays in Scarborough, and for the last few years they'd taken Gladys with them, but this year she'd said, 'I can't walk all that well, and I won't be able to keep up. I'd rather stay at home.'

She'd lost even more weight, and she needed a walking stick to get about. Prue was afraid she wouldn't be able to manage at home on her own, but she couldn't be persuaded to go with them. 'I don't want to be a drag on you two.'

'I shall cook for us both every evening,' Carrie had told them, and Connie said she'd come round during the day and take Gladys out if the weather was suitable.

Usually the sisters celebrated family milestones with a tea party at home and made cakes and jellies. But Maud counted this an important birthday and Archie had given her a taste for eating in the best hotels in the city. She'd asked his advice and booked a table at the Exchange Hotel for the family.

'I must give her a present,' Archie said to Marion when they received a formal invitation. 'Prue was very pleased with that Peter Pan collar I made for her; perhaps I should make another for Maud.'

'No,' Marion said, 'don't take on any more work. We want to finish what we're committed to doing. I thought you wanted to leave as soon as possible.'

'I do, but Prue gets all the limelight and everybody overlooks Maud. I'd like to give her a piece of jewellery too, something special. Perhaps we could buy her one of those collars.'

Marion grimaced. 'It wouldn't suit her. Prue has a thin neck but Maud is quite plump and her neck is getting thicker. If we bought one, it might be quite tight for her. Leave it to me; I'll get her something nice.'

'Not from Milner's. I don't want you to give him the trade.'

'All right, but he has the best jewellery in Liverpool.'

A week later she brought a small leather box to show Archie. 'I decided on a brooch for Maud. She doesn't wear much jewellery.'

'That's because she doesn't have much.'

Marion snapped open the box. 'It's your design, the dragonfly mounted on a tiny spring so that it moves slightly with the wearer, and that makes the stones flash with light. This one has been beautifully made: eighteen carat gold with diamonds, rubies and sapphires.'

'It's lovely, but if it's stolen property, I can't give it to Maud.'

Marion laughed. 'I knew you'd say that. I bought it in a top-class jeweller's in Southport. Here's the name on the case, and it's not one we've worked in. I kept the bill to show you.'

She unfolded it and held it out. Archie whistled through his teeth. 'Quite expensive.'

'We can afford it with our expense account from Rod.'

Archie thoroughly enjoyed Maud's birthday dinner, and seeing his brothers George and Bob again. George lived in Preston and so he saw little of him.

By the time Connie's wedding anniversary came round, she and John had moved into their little house, a newly built semi-detached in an outer suburb. Carrie thought it could be made lovely, but at the moment it was sparsely furnished. John took Connie out for a celebratory meal on the Saturday night, and on Sunday all the family were invited round to see the new house and have a meal of salad with tinned salmon, tinned peaches and cream, and fancy cakes made by Prue.

CHAPTER TWENTY-FOUR

O NE BRIGHT MORNING AT the end of May, Marion stayed home to work on the Starbright accounts. Archie was feeling increasingly alarmed but did what Marion asked of him: he picked up Bill Dainty and took him to Milner's shop. The alteration or removal of assay marks was almost completed, and they both wanted Bill to finish that off as soon as possible.

Archie didn't like Gerard Milner any better now he knew Carrie had broken off all contact with him. Marion had lost patience over this and told him to forget it, put it behind him and on no account ever mention it to Milner.

Gerard Milner let them into the workroom. 'Those stones Marion had recut – did she tell you? I have two orders that will use almost all of them.' This was one of those times when Archie could feel his fists clenching and he had to keep a careful watch on what he said. 'Two rich gentlemen who want to please their wives,' he chortled, 'and both customers have chosen which of your designs they want. They'll use up those stones very nicely.'

'One wants the necklace that is all diamonds?'

'Yes, and the other wants the necklace that has diamonds, sapphires and river pearls, and not only the necklace, but matching earrings and a brooch too.'

'Yes, I've started on that one, made six inches of it.' Archie took the centrepiece out of his workbox to show him, a lattice of platinum set with the precious stones.

'Very nice. She'll like that. This customer is happy with your designs and sketches, but she's quite elderly and has asked that the catch on the necklace be made larger because her fingers have stiffened with rheumatism and she can't manage small things.'

'I've already made two catches.'

'That doesn't matter. I can use one some other time.'

'If the fastening is to be larger, I probably need to alter the design slightly in keeping with that, otherwise it might look out of place.' Archie riffled though the designs he'd made to find the one. 'Yes, these are the large, heavy stones along the front, and then I've repeated the pattern but gradually reduced the size towards the fastener. With a larger catch, the last two or three links on each side would look better slightly larger.'

'Could you use more platinum instead?'

'A thicker rope of platinum would be the easiest, but whether I use larger stones or more platinum, it would make it heavier, and most ladies don't like too much weight round their necks.'

'It would also make it more expensive,' Milner said. 'Perhaps I'd better consult the customer. She's already approved your design for the earrings, but she's not sure about the brooch and wants more time to think about that.'

'I haven't done anything about the brooch, so no problem there. I'll wait to hear from you, but I'll have to give some thought to a larger catch, and how best to alter the necklace.'

'I'll phone her.'

'I'll work on the earrings today. What about the other necklace? Is that lady happy with the size of the catch?'

'Yes, she's young and beautiful.'

Milner popped in and out of the workroom all day. 'The lady doesn't want you to change the design of her necklace, just make the platinum links a bit larger near the catch if you think it needs it.' He seemed to be trying to appear interested in what Archie was doing. 'To watch you work is a masterclass in jewellery making,' he told him.

That sounded obsequious; he'd gone over the top with his praise. 'I've done a great deal of this sort of thing,' Archie grunted.

By three o'clock Bill had finished and Archie sent him home for the day. Milner packed the work Bill had done into a box and cleaned up his workbench.

'Marion will come in with me tomorrow,' Archie said. 'She'll want to check what's in the box against our paperwork, and bill you for what we've done. Then she'll decide with you what you'll send and what she'll send to be assayed as new.'

He was sure now that Milner understood how he felt, and was trying to disarm him by being friendly, but he was so obviously overdoing it. He was taking the same line as Marion: nothing must interfere with the work they were doing. When Milner closed his shop, he brought Archie a cup of tea and said, 'I've just been given a date for my annual audit. It's to be the second of June. I won't want you in while they are here.'

By seven, Archie had finished the earrings and they were both tired. 'I've had enough. Let's give up now,' he said, straightening his aching shoulders. 'I need to give more thought to the catch on this necklace. A big one will look out of place and it's got to be secure. I'll take it home and see what Marion thinks. I have to go to Chester with Bill tomorrow, so it might be a day or two before I come back to finish the job.'

'How about coming upstairs for a drink before you go home?' Archie hated all this pretence of friendliness, but as Marion wanted him to go along with it, he agreed. Milner was a good actor, but he could feel wariness in his manner and he couldn't relax with him.

He felt better by the time he was on his second bottle of beer. He thought Milner was trying to find out more about the other work Rod was involved in, but there was little he could tell him. He was just saying, 'Rod talks to Marion on the radio telephone once in a while. He's fine and so is his mother—' when he was interrupted by the strident ringing of the doorbell. It stopped for a moment, and then rang again. 'Are you expecting somebody?' he asked.

Milner was on his feet. 'No, stay here. I'll see who it is.'

Archie looked at his watch. It was time he went home; Marion would be making dinner. He was reaching for his drink, meaning to finish it and go, when he heard voices and steps coming up the stairs. Milner came into the room and shot him a warning glance. There were two men on his heels.

'Archie,' he said, 'these men are detectives. They want to ask a few questions.'

Archie's heart burst into overdrive. He felt the blood rush up his cheeks. Wasn't this what he'd been frightened might happen all along? His case of tools containing the half-made jewellery, set with those recut diamonds, was on the carpet at his feet. With his heel he pushed it backwards under his armchair.

'Then I'll leave you to it, Gerard,' he said, draining his glass and standing up.

'No, no, we don't want to disturb you,' one of the detectives said. 'We're just making a few routine enquiries. Perhaps you can help us too.' They flashed their identity cards at him and introduced themselves, then asked who he was. Archie felt cornered. He couldn't think, couldn't move, couldn't breathe.

'A friend,' Milner said, looking cool and collected, as though he hadn't a care in the world. 'We were just having a quiet drink.'

Thank goodness Milner had tidied up the workroom below and locked away that box full of stolen goods. Not to mention the materials they'd been working with. Had the detectives noticed Archie push the toolbox containing the necklaces and earrings under the chair? Was it really out of sight? He risked a glance but still wasn't sure.

'Do you have a business connection with Mr Milner?' The detective was looking straight into his eyes; Archie felt like a rabbit caught in the headlights of a car. He wanted to say no, but dare he?

'No,' Milner said firmly, 'he's just a friend but he is another jeweller; that's how we came to know each other.'

'You retail jewellery somewhere else? You have a shop?'

'No,' Archie managed. 'I work for a business that manufactures the stuff.'

He was immediately filled with doubt; should he have said that? What if they asked which business? He held his breath; the last thing he wanted was to mention South Africa. He wanted to go there and feel safe.

'Archie's here on holiday,' Milner volunteered, still without a vestige of nerves. 'He went to work in America a couple of years ago.'

'Yes,' Archie was sweating with relief, 'that's right. I've lost touch with the market here.'

'Oh, I have relatives in America. What part are you from?'

Archie gulped. He'd never set foot in America; what if he dropped himself in it by naming a city this man knew? But he couldn't think of any American city except . . . except . . . 'New York,' he said belatedly. Then, thinking he should add something to show he was familiar with the place, 'Home town of Franklin D. Roosevelt, thirty-second President of the United States. He's a Democrat . . . Not home town; I mean home city. Well, he was born there.'

They were all looking at him; he felt their surprise, saw concern on Milner's face. Don't say any more, he cautioned himself, you've overdone it already.

After a moment's pause, the detective took some photographs from the file case he'd brought. 'Ah, then it won't help to show you these.' He held them in front of Archie all the same.

Archie guessed they would be of stolen property, but when he saw the top one, he gasped audibly and gave such a jerk of shock that he knocked them out of the detective's hand. Making no comment, the man stooped to pick them up and repositioned them in front of Archie's face. 'This is a necklace, but it comes with a stand, so it can also be worn as a tiara,' he said.

It was their tiara. Archie was running with sweat. 'Don't see many of those in America,' he mumbled.

Then the photos were spread out in front of Milner. 'Do you handle used jewellery in your business?' he was asked.

'Occasionally, yes, for repairs and remodelling, that sort of thing.'

'You don't sell anything that is second-hand?'

'Well, not very often, and it would have to be something out of the ordinary. Something very special.'

'These are very special pieces, and they were stolen some months ago. Please look closely and tell me if you've seen them. Have they been offered to you through your business?' Milner put on his spectacles and took the photos to one of his table lights. 'They're made from eighteen-carat gold, large white diamonds and pale blue Ceylon sapphires, thirteen carats in all. This is a written description giving details of their cut and size.'

Archie couldn't believe how cool and collected Milner looked. He wished he was more like him. His mouth was as dry as a parrot cage; he reached for his glass, but it was empty.

'No,' Milner said, 'I haven't seen these pieces. Nice stuff, though.'

'Yes, top of the market. Would it be possible to see round your premises?'

Archie turned ramrod stiff against the cushions and couldn't get his breath.

Milner shrugged. 'Of course, if you want to, but there's nothing to see now. My staff lock everything away for the night before they leave.'

'Well,' the detectives stood up, 'just a glance round if you wouldn't mind.'

Archie watched Milner lead them out of the room,

undecided whether he should follow. Desperate to know what they would do, he rushed after them belatedly. Milner was flicking lights on as he went.

'The doors and windows are all shuttered and locked,' he said, 'and the more valuable pieces are locked away in safes, as advised by your security officer.'

'Quite right, it's as it should be.'

'How different it looks now the shop's closed,' Archie said inanely. 'It's the first time I've seen it like this.'

'Even the cleaners have gone now,' Milner added. 'There's really nothing to see.'

'No,' the detectives agreed, though they were both staring round at the empty display cases. One indicated the main shop entrance. 'We can't get out of this door now?'

'It would be easier if you used my private entrance,' Milner said, and led the way back upstairs towards it.

Thank God they were going. Archie was beginning to breathe normally again when they stopped outside the doors marked PRIVATE.

'Are these your workrooms?'

'Yes.' Milner unlocked the doors without being asked. He still looked innocent, but Archie was terrified and felt all his muscles tense. He'd been melting gold, and a blast of warmer air met them.

'I've been doing a few repairs today,' Milner said easily, 'but everything's been locked away here too.' There was nothing to be seen.

'Thank you, sir,' the older detective said as they prepared to leave. He took some sheets of paper from the case he carried. 'Here is our monthly list.'

Gerard smiled and waved it at them. 'I'll keep an eye open for this stuff,' he said.

'And one for you, sir, just in case. Sorry to have disturbed you for a routine enquiry.'

Archie stuffed the list into his pocket and didn't breathe again until he heard the detectives clattering down the outside staircase. The blast of cold night air felt wonderful on his face. 'Oh my God,' he whispered, 'they're on to us.'

Milner pushed him inside and slammed the door. 'You fool, you bloody fool,' he spat, and rushed back to his sitting room, where he gulped down the beer that remained in his glass.

Archie followed and retrieved his toolbox from under the chair. Milner was glowering at him; he'd gone white and his air of bonhomie had disappeared. 'Why did you have to spout all that drivel about Roosevelt? It made you look as guilty as hell. Made us both look guilty.'

Archie could feel his hackles rising; he'd done his best. 'I don't know. I tried to make it seem . . . as though I really knew about New York. You know, lived there.'

Milner's face no longer hid the fear and cold disdain he felt for him. 'You don't know when to keep your mouth shut. You told them a made-up story, a pack of lies, and it was perfectly obvious. Roosevelt has just announced he'll run for a second term, and we all read that stuff about him in the newspapers yesterday. They'll be watching us after that. What a crass, stupid fool you are.'

'You're blaming me?' Archie could no longer control himself; with all the venom he'd held back for days, he swung a right to Milner's face, then followed it up with more punches to his head and body. He straightened up to get his breath and saw that Milner had slumped to the floor. He picked up his toolbox and let himself out.

His hands were shaking as he unlocked his car. He was glad he'd done that; it evened the score. He'd given the man what he deserved. Done what he'd been aching to do since he'd heard how Milner had treated Carrie.

CHAPTER TWENTY-FIVE

'Y OU'RE LATE,' MARION SAID when he reached home. 'I'm afraid the dinner might be overcooked.' When she saw his face, she added, 'Has something happened?'

'Yes, the police are on to us. We have to get out now. Straight away; we can't carry on like this.' He started to recount what had happened, but she led the way to the kitchen, where he was met by savoury scents.

'We need to eat now or it will be spoiled. Fish pie with new carrots and spinach.' She began to dish up.

The last thing Archie wanted was food. He drank two glasses of cold water at the kitchen sink before he could go on. 'Marion, stop and listen to me, this is important. We need to get out of the country before the balloon goes up. The police came and searched Milner's shop. I was having a beer with him.'

'Did they have a search warrant?'

'No.'

'Did Milner refuse to let them look round?'

'No, he was surprisingly relaxed.'

'Sorry.' She was on the way to the dining room, carrying their plates. 'I can't concentrate on an empty stomach. Come and eat.'

'Milner let them see whatever they wanted, even into his workrooms, but we'd cleared everything away.'

'If they saw nothing incriminating, there's no immediate crisis.'

'Yes, there is.' Archie's stomach was churning; he couldn't eat. 'After this, my name will be on police files, and I'll be linked to Gerard Milner. Any evidence against him would incriminate me.'

'Not necessarily; they have to have proof. Archie, pull yourself together. You've got to calm down.'

'That's the trouble. I was a bag of nerves. Milner said I looked as guilty as hell, that I said too much. Gave the game away.'

'That is worrying,' she said, 'but we'll soon be able to sever our connection with Milner. I'll work out his bill tomorrow, and once he pays up, that's that.'

'But the police? That won't stop them.'

'They have to have evidence.'

'I know, but—'

'Was Milner worried?'

'Yes, of course, but he acted as though he was remarkably cool.'

'There you are then; you worry too much, Archie. I'll give him a ring and see what he thinks.' She stood up. 'You eat that dinner I made for you. Your nerves are always on edge when you don't eat.'

Archie did his best to clear his plate. It was some time before Marion came back, and she was frowning. 'Milner says it was a routine visit: they were giving out a new stolen property list.'

'Yes, they gave me one.' He pulled it out of his jacket pocket and pushed it towards her.

'He says you almost dropped him in it, said all the wrong things instead of keeping your mouth shut. And as soon as the police had gone, you went berserk, jumped on him like a wild animal and gave him a bloody nose. He thinks you're not safe to let out on your own.'

'Good, I hope I hurt him. The fellow's despicable. I can't cope with him.'

'Archie, he's doing his best. He sees no immediate urgency, and is hopeful there never will be. But we can't go in for a while; he told you, didn't he?'

'Oh yes, I forgot. He's expecting the audit team and doesn't want us there at the same time.'

'I should think not, though Carrie said she might not be going this year.'

'Milner suggested we work at night, but I told him no. We're both tired – we've been slogging away for months – and you can't be expected to do your best work in the middle of the night. We still have another three days' work at Edward Jones's in Southport, so we'll do that first. Apart from that, there are a few jewellers who haven't yet paid up, and odds and ends of work to finish off.'

Archie was relieved. 'That puts us off facing Milner for a few days. Jones has a good workshop; perhaps I can do some of that work there.'

'It depends on how quickly we finish the work he has for us.' Marion was frowning. 'I don't like you carrying those necklaces about in your toolbox. Bill Dainty will be with us, but it'll be the last place we have to take him.'

She was studying the police list. 'This is interesting reading. That tiara is not the only thing we've worked on. There's a signet ring here, and a watch chain you melted down.'

'There are pages of the stuff.'

'Of course, we're encouraging thieves to steal more by helping them get a good price for it. I'll have another look at this later. I have treacle tart to follow; I know it's your favourite.'

Archie didn't answer.

'You live on your nerves, that's your problem. We won't have to stay much longer; once we get the money out of these last few jewellers, we'll pack up and go.'

'But what about those necklaces I'm doing for Milner?'

'Well, you'll have to finish those first, of course.'

The following week, they collected Bill and drove out to Southport. Archie found there was more than enough work waiting for them at Edward Jones's shop. All three of them set to and worked hard, but Archie could see he wouldn't have time to do anything else. Facing Milner again was a weight hanging over him.

On their last day, Marion took them out for a decent lunch. She made out Jones's bill, checked over the paperwork with him and collected payment before they left that afternoon. Archie drove back to Liverpool, afraid that Bill was going to cause an embarrassing scene, though he must know their need of him was almost over.

As they approached the street where Bill lived, Marion half turned in her seat and said firmly, 'That completes all the work we have for you, Bill. We won't need your services any longer. Thank you for all the help you've given us; your workmanship is good and you work hard.'

Archie heard his sudden intake of breath. 'Is that it?' He

sounded quite shocked. 'You aren't giving me much notice.'

'I've worked out what we owe you,' Marion said briskly, 'and I've added an extra week's pay in lieu of notice.' She handed him an envelope.

Archie stopped the car at the end of the road. Bill was slow to get out and his face was truculent. 'It's goodbye, then,' he said, and slammed the door without another word.

'I hope that's the last we hear of him.' Marion's smile was a little grim. 'I kept telling you not to worry about him bringing trouble to our door. It was the right thing to keep him working, because once you've done these jobs for Milner, we're about finished; just payments to collect and odds and ends to clear up.'

'I'm not looking forward to facing Milner,' Archie said, but he could see that Marion was determined he would. 'When will that be?' Milner had given them a lot of work, and Archie would be well paid for this last job.

'I'll give him a ring tomorrow. It has to be done, but if all goes well, and we can pack and say goodbye to your family without much hanging about, we could bring our passage home forward by one week. What do you say to that?'

'Marvellous.' Archie was pleased. 'I reckon four days to do what Milner wants. I'm going to invite Carrie out to stay with us when she can tear herself away from her job.'

'Of course,' Marion said. 'She'll love it, and you'll enjoy seeing her again.'

Archie groaned. He was getting cold feet again. 'I don't know how I can face Milner after that showdown. I dread going near his shop. I hate him, and I think he feels the same about me.'

They spent all evening arguing the pros and cons. Marion had never looked more determined. 'I want you to finish the bespoke work you are doing for him. While those stones are loose, it doesn't take a big stretch of imagination to link them to the tiara. It makes it safer for us all to get them made up and being worn by one of Milner's clients.'

Archie shook his head. 'I can see the sense of that, but I can't do it. Gerard Milner and I know where we stand with each other. We've let our feelings show.'

'Come on, Archie. I'll stay with you. Be the oil on troubled waters. There'll be no more fighting.'

'He won't expect to see me again.'

'Then he'll be relieved when you turn up. He wants those necklaces finished more than anything else; we'll none of us get paid until they're done.'

Marion had an inner core of steel. Archie had seen her in action, and knew that he'd give in to her; it was what he always did. What everybody did.

'You know it makes sense,' she said. 'Come upstairs now and let's get the job out on your workbench to see what still needs to be done. Perhaps there's more you can do here at home, or perhaps I can help you.'

Marion got everything out of his case and studied the designs as well as his work in progress. 'How much bigger is this catch to be?'

Archie was enlarging the measurements on his diagram almost without realising it.

'I can make the catch for a start,' she told him. 'I don't want to sit there idle while you work. We've got to get this whole project finished now.'

That made Archie feel at fault that his work wasn't yet completed. 'You've got the Starbright paperwork to finish, haven't you?'

'I shall take it with me. I can do it there if I have to.' She smiled and repacked his case for him. 'Cheer up, Archie; we're on the last lap now. Let's have a nightcap and forget about our problems for tonight.'

Such was Marion's power that he did what she said, and afterwards he slept well.

Carrie was working at her desk that afternoon when her internal phone buzzed. She picked it up and a voice said, 'Mavis Cullimore here.' Mavis was Leonard Groves's new secretary. 'He wants you to come up now for your monthly discussion.'

'Right, I'm on my way.' Carrie had been expecting this summons and had prepared some questions she needed to ask. Now that she knew Mr Groves better, she quite enjoyed his monthly sessions, which could last for the best part of an hour. She knew she was his first articled clerk, and he took his responsibilities towards her seriously. He was kind, and talked her through what she was supposed to know by this time in her training, trying to be her tutor, guide, mentor and counsellor rolled into one.

When she reached his office, Miss Cullimore said, 'I'm afraid he's on the phone at the moment.' She rolled a sheet of paper out of her typewriter. 'This is the timetable of the work coming due; would you like to see it?'

Carrie picked it up. 'Well, I have to go where I'm sent, but it's good to know what's coming up.' The name *G. E. Milner,*

Jeweller jumped out at her. Only last night she'd been thinking about this. She was over Gerard Milner now, but she didn't fancy going to his shop to do his audit again this year.

Mr Groves opened the door of his office. 'Will you organise some tea, please, Miss Cullimore?' He smiled at Carrie. 'You'll have a cup, Caroline, won't you? Come on in.'

'Yes, please, sir.' He'd not offered her tea before New Year's Day. He was more relaxed with her now.

'I've typed up the list of clients with visits falling due now,' Miss Cullimore said, offering it to him.

He sat down behind his desk, studying it. He looked over his glasses at Carrie. 'You won't be going to Milner's this year,' he said. 'Mr Heatherington said he fixated on you last time. We can't have you bothered by that sort of thing. It's embarrassing all round, causes unnecessary difficulties.

'I see the Grey Goat Brewery need a team to draw up their accounts at about the same time. You can go there. Now, Caroline, your lectures have finished for the summer, but what have you learned from your correspondence course?'

Tim Redwood walked past the dazzling display of jewellery in G. E. Milner's jewellery shop in Lord Street, feeling full of suspicion. As John Bradshaw, their team leader, led the way upstairs to the office, the shop girls smiled at the team of four following behind him.

Milner leapt to his feet to shake John's hand and came down the line to shake Tim's. He wore a waistcoat with a gold pocket watch and a chain across his stomach, just like Uncle Jeremy. Hadn't he heard of wrist watches?

Tim thought him a flashy fellow with his little moustache

and formal suit, and he was old, very old for what he'd tried to do to Carrie. Tim knew she'd quietly put him out of her life afterwards but she'd not escaped unscathed: she wouldn't let another man near her now.

Whatever could she have seen in him? Tim found him repulsive and longed to pay him back for what he'd done. He knew that John was aware of what had happened between them, and he too would like to even the score if he could. They both knew they should be totally objective and free from prejudice when working on Milner's books, but in the past they'd suspected the accounts were not telling the whole story.

They all knew Milner could not avoid having an audit. His business was a limited company that had by law to lodge audited annual accounts with Companies House. His company taxes and his personal income tax were based on those figures. Neither could he just change his firm of auditors, as that would immediately cause them to question why he'd done it, and possibly raise their suspicions.

Before the visit, John had called the team into his office and told them he thought Gerard Milner a wily fellow. 'We've been doing his audit for years, and though we've suspected that all is not what it seems, we've been unable to put our finger on anything wrong. I think he may have had some training in accounting; he certainly knows all the tricks of the trade. His presentation of the accounts makes them look very satisfactory. Everything is shown in the most favourable light.'

'They all do that,' Robbie said.

'Yes, we must expect it,' John went on. 'But Milner employs an accountant to draw up his figures, and I think they go through them with a fine-tooth comb before we do the audit.

He's confident we'll pass them; he believes they're cast-iron.

'I predict that this year he'll have made a good profit, the top end for what would be expected in his trade. On our last audit, he had increased his previous year's retained profit and also his liabilities, but is he hiding something? Is he switching transactions either in or out of the current year? Is he showing all his expenses? Or is he selling goods that are not shown in his stock?

'Keep your eyes open for things like that. I'm going to question everything and I want you to do that too. If there's anything doubtful, we're going to ask why it's been done that way, and keep on asking.'

Tim had been taught that simplicity of presentation was almost as important as accuracy, and that the accounts should show not only the calculation of profit or loss, but how those results had been achieved. It was the way Milner did this that had caused doubts at previous audits. Also, the balance sheet should be presented so that it could be understood by people without a knowledge of accounting. The manager of any company being audited would be interested in the story the figures were telling rather than the figures themselves.

As usual, Tim was asked to start by checking the goods held in the stockroom, as well as those displayed for sale. Everything Milner bought went into stock, and if when they checked it was not there, the proceeds of the sale must be in his records. It took Tim and Frank Dawes, his fellow auditor, the best part of two days to get through that and find it correct, while Robbie and John started on the ledgers.

Tim was then given the job of checking that Milner's expenses for running the business for the year were correct.

With his five shops in the suburbs, they were many and complicated, but Tim was used to this sort of work now. He had only twenty minutes or so to glance through them before it was time to go home, but he saw that Milner's accounts were kept in an exemplary fashion; they were neat and clearly written. When he left the shop that evening, Tim was convinced that Gerard Milner was invincible; no problem would be found in his annual audit.

It was Sunday, and Archie and Marion were going to work. Gerard Milner had decided to stay in Liverpool over the weekend so that they could work on the bespoke necklaces. They all wanted that done as soon as possible. The shop would be closed; there would be no interruptions.

Archie stood two steps behind Marion as they waited at Milner's private entrance. When he opened the door, Archie couldn't look him in the face. Marion was doing her best to look relaxed. Archie was rigidly on guard and sensed the huge wall of tension between himself and Milner.

Marion started work on the larger clasp for his necklace and acted as his assistant all day. They saw less of Milner than they had on previous occasions, and when he did come to the workroom, his face was grim, and he spoke only to Marion. They worked on later than usual and Archie made substantial progress. 'Tonight we'll have dinner before going home,' Marion said. 'Neither of us has the energy to start cooking now. Let's see if we can get a table at the Adelphi.' She went off to use Milner's phone.

Archie felt exhausted and was surprised at how much energy Marion still had and how quickly she was able to shut off from work. She was sparklingly sociable and happy once they were eating, and he was able to relax and enjoy it.

They worked in the same way over the next two days, because the audit team were checking the stock in Milner's other branches. Archie felt he'd never worked harder, but with Marion's help he finished the bespoke work in three days. At last it was over.

'You've done an excellent job,' Marion said. 'You should be proud of it. This is top-class jewellery, and it bears no resemblance to that tiara.' She locked it into his workbox. 'But we aren't going to hand it over until Milner pays up. I'll make out his final bill, and come back to see him in a day or two.'

'I'm just thankful I don't have to come here again,' Archie said. 'Milner gives me the creeps.'

'Rod was friendly with him,' Marion pulled a face, 'but I can't say I took to him. I'll not be sorry to say goodbye.'

'He was our biggest customer,' Archie said, 'and he owes us a lot of money now.'

'I'll get it.' Marion smiled at him. 'You can depend on that.'

Marion made out the final bills for the Starbright work, and on Wednesday and Thursday Archie drove her round the shops where they still had odd jobs to finish off and those who had not yet paid. They covered a large area in Cheshire and Lancashire and Archie enjoyed it. 'It feels like a mopping-up exercise,' he said.

On Friday morning, Archie cooked sausages as well as eggs and bacon for breakfast; they were both on a high now the end was so near. He'd started to pack his belongings.

'I'm going to see Gerard Milner this morning,' Marion said,

'and I know you don't want to come with me. Why don't you go to that shop in Ormskirk? Puller's, it's called; I think we left three or four rings needing to be done there.'

'Fine by me,' Archie said.

'You'll get through the work easily in a day. I've made the bill out ready, and if you can collect the money, we can tie up our account with him too. That really will mark the end of our work here.'

Archie was still half expecting trouble from Milner; he knew he planned to pay in cash, and he found it hard to believe that things would go as smoothly as Marion assumed. 'What if Milner doesn't have enough money?'

'There's no reason to suppose he won't. He has plenty of cash customers and he's known this bill was coming for some time. Anyway, I won't give him the bespoke jewellery until he does.'

'I feel we're almost on our way,' Archie said, pushing his fears behind him. 'Next Thursday's ship is the *Arundel Castle*, yes?'

'Yes, I've changed our booking. The cabin is not as good as the one I originally booked, but we're getting out a week earlier. They say the tickets are in the post.'

Archie rubbed his hands together and smiled with satisfaction.

That same Friday, Tim was still checking the figures for the expenses that Milner had incurred in running his business.

Wages and salaries was easily the largest figure. He had a big staff and they were all listed on his payroll. In his office, Milner employed an accountant and several bookkeepers, a secretary and a typist. He had shop managers and many shop assistants, even a security guard cum driver; mostly they worked full time, except for the cleaners and some of the shop assistants.

He could find no fault with the figures; he checked and rechecked any additions or percentages. Everything was correct and his documents were meticulously neat. He'd stared at them for so long, he could almost see the numbers when he closed his eyes.

Tim had not seen Carrie over the last few days because she was working in the Grey Goat Brewery, but tomorrow was Saturday and her last day there. He wanted to remind her of their usual arrangement: that she was expected for lunch and he wanted them to spend the rest of the day together.

Though Uncle Jeremy had had a phone installed in the Redwoods' home to make it easier for Tim to keep in touch with his mother, Carrie's family didn't have one, and that meant he needed to ring her while she was at work. He was looking up the number of the Grey Goat Brewery when the phone rang. It was Carrie, wanting to speak to him for the same reason.

That settled, Tim put the phone down and returned to his figures, but his mind was on Carrie. He'd known her for a long time now, and she meant more to him with each month that passed. Suddenly he remembered an incident from their past, and Milner's expenses gave it a new importance. He straightened up with his heart beating faster.

Around him, the rest of his team were locking their work away for the night and preparing to go home. 'Good night, Tim,' John said to him as he left.

'No need to work overtime.' Robbie slapped his back as he passed his desk.

Tim sat almost paralysed, remembering how some months ago he'd been walking across town with Carrie on the way to the Odeon when she'd spotted her father's car. He'd met her father for the first time with his lady friend, whom Carrie thoroughly approved of and was hoping he'd marry.

Hadn't Carrie asked them if they'd been working at Milner's? The car was certainly parked in a convenient spot for his shop. But according to Milner's records, he employed all his staff permanently; there was no figure for any temporary staff. No figure for staff employed on contract.

Tim could feel excitement beginning to fizz in his stomach. If he was right, and Milner had employed Carrie's relatives, he'd come across something that ought to be shown in his records. He checked again, but it wasn't there. He felt a moment of triumph, then slowly began to clear his desk for the night and lock up the small office given over to the team.

The shop assistants were busy dismantling the displays of stock in the glass cases and putting everything of value into the safes for the night. The main shop door had already been locked and the manager had to be found to let him out.

Tim was in a daze; what could all this mean? What excited him most was that he seemed to have come across what John had told them all to search for. Had he found a means to pay Milner back for the passes he'd made at Carrie? And at the same time had he helped Atherton & Groves to get an honest view of what Milner was putting through his business? If so, it seemed too good to be true. Uncle Jeremy had been so good to him and his mother, and it would also show that he wasn't slacking during the time he was at work.

He'd pored over Milner's accounts for so long that he knew without looking again that the jeweller had made a good profit for the year. If he'd shown a higher figure for expenses it would have reduced that, but he'd probably still have made a good profit, so why hide what he'd spent on temporary labour? It didn't make any sense, but it cast suspicion on all his figures. He would have his reason, and it surely had to be fraud of some sort.

Tim's mind was in turmoil all that evening and for half the night.

Archie was anticipating a quiet day as he set off to the small shop in Ormskirk to finish the last of the work Rod had arranged for them. When he arrived, the owner wasn't exactly pleased to see him.

'I thought you'd have come back to finish off weeks ago,' he said. 'It's not safe to keep stuff like this on the premises.'

'Yes, I'm sorry. I think we took on too much work, but I'll finish it off today.'

'I've done some of it myself in quiet moments; there are just two rings left. I've even sold that heavy bangle you worked on; d'you remember that?'

Archie couldn't. 'Shall I do those rings now?'

'You might as well since you're here, though the assay mark has almost worn away on one.'

'I've brought the bill, but as you've done some of the work yourself, it'll have to be reduced.' Archie thought it hardly mattered whether Starbright was paid or not, because compared with all they'd earned elsewhere, this was peanuts. 'I'll start on the rings if you'll figure out what is a fair amount to reduce the bill by for the work you have done.'

'Right. Would you like a cup of tea before we start?'

'Yes, thank you.'

The owner paid in cash. They shook hands and parted on good terms just before midday. Archie was hungry but full of satisfaction; it was all over at last. He and Marion could now go back to Jo'burg. They had succeeded in doing what they'd set out to do. What a fool he'd been to worry about being caught; Marion had been right when she'd said they were safe enough.

He was passing a small café and caught the savoury scents as the door opened. On the spur of the moment he went in and had beef and ale pie followed by rice pudding.

He set off to drive home hoping Marion had managed to collect the large sum of money that Milner owed them. With that and what Rod had already paid them, they'd be set up for life and there'd be no need ever to break the law again. Archie felt triumphant. All they had to do was pack up the house and get down to Southampton by next Thursday to catch the mail boat to Cape Town. They were really going to enjoy themselves on the voyage.

As Archie edged the car up the drive, he was surprised to see a cabin trunk and several suitcases piled in the porch. His first thought was that they had an unexpected visitor. Had Rod come back?

He couldn't help but notice the colourful labels on the luggage: *Cunard Line. Flagship RMS Queen Mary*. He got out of the car and took a closer look, straightening out a smaller label tied to the handle of one of the cases. *Miss Marion Collard, voyage*

Liverpool to New York on . . . Wasn't that today's date?

Archie stood stock still, shocked to the core. There must be some mistake! He took another look at the label; it told him which deck her first-class cabin was on, and also the number.

'No,' he gasped aloud. 'No!' The future he was expecting had exploded in smithereens. He could hardly get his key into the lock, but at last he turned it and threw the front door open. 'Marion!' he cried out. 'Marion?'

She was coming slowly downstairs wearing her outdoor coat. There was a look of shocked surprise on her face. 'I didn't expect you back, not yet.'

'What are you doing? All your cases outside – why?'

She was biting her lip. 'Archie, I'm sorry. It wasn't supposed to happen like this.'

'I don't understand. What are you doing? You're not going to New York?'

He'd never seen Marion so put out. 'I'm sorry, yes.'

'But we're sailing to Cape Town on Thursday; you booked it. You can't . . .'

'I am, I'm sorry.'

'When will you be back?'

'Archie, I'm not coming back. You weren't supposed to know I was going to New York.'

That seemed to end everything he'd hoped for. 'But why?'

'You know I sold my house in Jo'burg.'

'Yes, but you're going to live with me.' He put his arms out to pull her close, but she stepped away from him. 'We're engaged; we'll be married as and when you like.'

'No! I don't want to get married. I've tried it and it was a bad experience.'

'It would be different with me, quite different.' Archie was still convinced of that. If he could just persuade her, all would be well. 'I'll come to New York with you if that's what you want. We'll have a holiday in America first.'

'No, I said no.'

He shook his head in despair. 'Why not? You seemed happy with me. I thought you were.'

'Archie, you were a nervous wreck. You needed a lot of encouragement to carry on.' She wouldn't even meet his eyes now. 'Look, I'm afraid I lied when I said Graham died of cancer. He was a rotter. I walked out on him, but we're still married.'

'Oh!' Archie was gulping down a deep sense of shock. Nothing was as he'd supposed. 'Couldn't you get a divorce?'

She was shaking her head. 'I've not seen Graham for years. I've lost touch with him.'

She'd lied! This must mean that she didn't want to marry him; that she never had and never would. She'd pretended to love him just to keep him here at work. And she'd been great in bed. Had she slept with him every night just so that he would finish what Rod had set up? He felt sick.

He heard a car horn blare outside. 'That'll be my taxi,' Marion said, moving to the hall mirror to put her hat on. 'I have to go.'

He could feel anger stirring within him. 'You were going to leave without even saying goodbye?'

She was biting her lip. 'I've left a letter for you on the mantelpiece.' The taxi sounded its horn again.

Archie was fighting back tears. 'I love you. Please don't end it like this.'

She opened the front door and waved to the driver. 'I have to go; the ship sails at six on the tide.'

'You won't be alone in New York, will you?' His voice was bitter. 'Who have you arranged to meet?'

The suitcases had gone from the porch. Marion turned to Archie. 'Do you remember Eddie Jurgens? He looked after me when I went to Amsterdam.'

'He was Dutch?'

'Originally, but he's an American now.'

She stretched up to kiss his cheek. 'Goodbye, Archie. You won't tell anyone where I've gone, will you?' The door slammed behind her and he heard the taxi drive away.

He stood stock still in the hall for five minutes, then groped his way to an armchair in the sitting room and sat staring at the blue envelope propped up on the mantelpiece. It could only confirm the bad news.

The clock on the mantelpiece struck six o'clock, and Archie thought of the *Queen Mary* edging her way off her moorings at the Princes landing stage and sailing down the Mersey.

He got up and poured himself a double whisky, then tore open the blue envelope. Marion's familiar scrawl told him little more than he already knew. She'd enclosed a cheque made out to him and added a postscript: *Your agreement with Rod was that he'd pay your fare back to Jo'burg.* It was generously more than that, but . . .

Archie recoiled. Did this mean she'd lied about booking their return passages for Thursday? Certainly no tickets had arrived.

It confirmed his loss and brought tears to his eyes. He ought to find the Union-Castle brochure and ring up to check, but without Marion he felt lost; he didn't know what he was going to do. Instead of going upstairs to the room she had used as an office, he poured himself more whisky and went back to his chair. All his expectations, all his hopes were crushed. He'd trusted Marion and she'd let him down. He felt she'd betrayed him.

He woke up at two in the morning feeling cold and stiff and told himself he was stupid to sleep in a chair when he could be in bed. He found the energy to climb up to his bedroom. The bed had not been made. Marion had taken over that job some time ago; she could whisk through domestic chores in minutes. It made his loss seem more acute. He took off his shoes and got under the blankets, feeling too cold and miserable to undress.

As he'd forgotten to draw the curtains, he woke to find the morning sun streaming into his room; it was nearly ten o'clock. He felt like a ship without a rudder. He needed to go back to Jo'burg, but without Marion it wouldn't be the same.

He must get up. His mouth was dry and he needed a cup of tea. He'd put his feet on the floor and was sitting on the edge of the bed when the phone began to ring in the hall below. He ignored it; eventually it stopped and he breathed a sigh of relief. Moments later it started to ring again.

He padded downstairs in his stockinged feet and lifted the receiver. 'Hello?'

'Gerard Milner here; can I speak to Marion Collard?'

Archie froze. 'She's . . . she's not here.'

'Is that you, Archie? I need to speak to her urgently. When will she be back?'

'I don't know.'

'Well, you must have some idea.' His voice was thick with impatience. 'Will she be back this afternoon?'

'No, she's gone.'

'What d'you mean, gone? Where to?'

Archie almost said New York, but remembered in time that she'd asked him not to tell anyone. 'I don't think she will be coming back here.'

'What? I paid her for the work you and Dainty did, and she agreed to give me that bespoke jewellery you made for me once I'd done that, but she didn't. She said it had been left in your toolbox by mistake and you'd gone off to Ormskirk with it. Can you bring it to the shop? I'm expecting one of the clients it was made for to come in this afternoon.'

Archie groped for the hall chair and sank down on to it. He was gripped by a new fear. 'Yes,' he managed, 'I'll look for it and bring it in.'

He had to sit still for a few minutes before his head stopped spinning. Had Marion taken that jewellery with her to New York? His gut feeling told him she had. She'd been planning this for months. She'd lied to him over and over just to keep him here. She'd never meant to share the spoils with him, or had the slightest intention of marrying him.

When he felt steadier on his feet, he went out to the car to look in his workbox. The tools were there just as he'd left them, but as he expected, the jewellery he'd made was not.

He went back indoors and flung himself into the armchair. He'd truly felt in love with Marion; he'd believed they'd spend the rest of their lives together. He'd trusted her, but it had all been an act to get what she wanted. She'd taken them all in. He felt engulfed in disappointment, dense, black and paralysing.

He heard the phone ringing again and guessed it would be Milner. He knew he'd keep on until he answered it. He picked up the receiver and told him that he couldn't find the jewellery; it was not in his toolbox.

Milner let out a string of swear words. 'The bitch!' he ranted. 'She's an out-and-out thief. I didn't think she was that sort of person.'

'She took us all in,' Archie said, and put the phone down. Milner sounded as desperate as he himself felt, but he had no sympathy for him.

It was another hour before he slowly climbed the stairs to the bedroom they'd used as an office and workroom. He sat at the desk Marion had used to do the Starbright accounts, and methodically pulled out each drawer in turn looking for them. There was no sign of them and no trace of the bank books and chequebooks she'd used. He had to assume she'd drawn out all the money that was supposed to belong to Rod. That she'd cheated on him too.

CHAPTER TWENTY-SIX

B Y SATURDAY MORNING, TIM WAS full of doubt. Was his memory playing tricks on him? Had he missed an entry for temporary staff? When he reached the shop and sat down at the desk, the first thing he did was to riffle through Milner's payroll records.

He was right, there was no indication that Milner ever employed any temporary staff, but had Carrie's father really said he'd been working there on the night they'd met? Was he right about the date? Carrie would know and he couldn't wait to ask her. He went home at lunchtime more excited than ever.

As she was working in the dock area, she couldn't catch their usual tram and had agreed to come straight to his home. She was ten minutes behind him and he waited full of impatience and heady with hope. He rushed to the door when she rang the bell and could hardly get his words out to ask, 'Did your father say he was working at Milner's shop? Do you remember? We saw him that Wednesday night when we went to the Odeon straight from the office.'

'What's all this about?' Carrie asked.

'I think I've found a hole in Milner's records. It could stop his accounts being signed off as correct.'

'What sort of a hole?'

'I believe he's hiding expenses. There's no record of payments to temporary staff. Didn't you ask your father if he was working at Milner's and he said yes?'

'He did,' Carrie confirmed, and laughed because, since then, she'd come to understand what he did. 'He designs jewellery for him.'

'Yes, but he did say he'd been working for him that evening?'

'I think he did, yes. Wouldn't it be marvellous if you've really—'

'And you said you'd seen his car parked there before, so he'd probably worked there on other evenings too?'

'Yes, I do remember.' Carrie's face puckered in thought. 'Dad's a marvellous designer; that Peter Pan collar is one of his. A huge success for him.'

'I know.' Tim caught at her hand. 'But did he do temporary work for Milner?'

'Oh gosh, yes. I think he and Marion do that in other jewellers' shops too.'

'Milner's shop would have been closed at that time of night.'

'Yes, but it wouldn't need to be open. Not to discuss designs.' Carrie was frowning. 'When Dad first came home from South Africa, he was a bit cagey about how he was earning his living. Prue and Maud used to talk about it, and kept asking him if he was surviving on fresh air.'

Tim mused on that. 'Designing jewellery is a big thing; perhaps he didn't want to boast about earning a living that way until he knew he could sell his designs. He'd have to find a market for them, wouldn't he?'

'Tim,' she took hold of his arm, 'could Dad be working for

Milner on a contract basis? Wouldn't that be more likely?'

'I thought of that too, but his accounts show nothing for contractual work either. I need to be quite certain about this. I don't want to get John involved unless I'm right.'

'Hello, Caroline, you're late today.' Tim's mother came out of the kitchen. 'What are you two dawdling in the hall for? Come on, your lunch will be getting cold.'

'Carrie,' Tim held on to her, 'you have to ask him. I need to know exactly what work he did for Milner and the dates on which he did it. And I need to know urgently.'

That afternoon, Carrie and Tim talked non-stop about Milner's business records, and though they tried to settle down to study, they found it impossible.

'Have you got a calendar?' Carrie asked. 'We could try and pinpoint the day we saw my father walking to his car. I don't suppose he'll remember.'

'I don't have a calendar for last year, but I think it was in October.'

'Hang on, I tore a page out of last year's diary that shows this year as well as last. It should be here in my handbag. Yes, look, it must have been Wednesday the sixteenth of October.'

'Goody.' Tim was all smiles. 'Why don't you ring your father and ask if we can come and see him?'

Carrie was as eager as Tim was to settle this, but the phone rang and rang until the operator's voice cut in to suggest she try again later. She put the receiver down. 'He's always there on a Saturday,' she said. 'Marion goes into town by herself.'

'I said nothing in the office this morning,' Tim said, 'and I ought to tell John about this as soon as I can. He's my team leader and needs to know. I'll give him a ring, and if he's in, we could go and see him instead.'

'Let me try Dad again first,' Carrie said. 'We really need to get him to confirm that he did work for Milner. He likes me to get in touch on a Saturday because he's by himself.'

Again the phone rang for a long time, and she was about to put it down when she heard it being lifted and a voice croaked, 'Hello?'

'Is that you, Dad?'

'Yes, Carrie.'

'Can Tim and I come round to see you? There's something we need to ask.' There was such a long pause that she added, 'Are you all right? Your voice sounds funny.'

Another long pause and he grunted, 'Yes, yes, come.'

'Has something happened?' she asked, but he'd put the phone down.

'What's the matter?' Tim asked her.

'I don't know, but let's get round there. Dad sounded quite strange.'

They had to ring the doorbell twice. Archie was a long time coming, and when he did, Carrie was shocked. He hadn't shaved and he looked dishevelled. There were beads of perspiration on his forehead.

'Dad, what's happened?' She could see into the sitting room. It no longer looked neat and tidy.

'Come in here.' He took them into the dining room, where an easy chair had been pulled up in front of the gas fire, which was full on. The temperature was like that of a greenhouse on this summer afternoon.

'It's very hot in here, Dad, can I turn it off? Tell me what's happened.'

'Marion isn't going to marry me after all. It's all over. I'm a bit upset.'

She stared at him, shocked. 'Very upset, I'd say. I'm sorry, Dad, I liked her.' Carrie wanted to know why, but it wasn't the sort of thing she could ask her father.

'What we want to talk to you about,' Tim said, 'is the work you did for Milner.' Carrie saw Archie's head jerk up, and he stared at them with glassy horror. Tim hastened to tell him about auditing Milner's accounts and finding what he thought was an omission. 'I understand that last year you did some design work for him, yes?'

Archie nodded vaguely.

'Did he give you a contract, or were you employed on a temporary basis?'

Archie continued to stare at them. 'I don't know,' he mumbled. 'Marion arranged all that.'

'But you did work for him, Dad? If we're to catch him out, we need to be sure about that.'

'Yes,' he admitted. He looked half dazed and pushed his fingers through his hair. It hadn't been combed this morning.

'Did Marion work for him too?' she asked. He nodded. 'Anybody else?'

'Yes, but forget about him.'

'Why? We need to be clear about who was working for Milner.'

'Bill is in trouble already, his own worst enemy. I can't make matters worse for him. I suppose I'm sorry for him.'

'All right. When did Marion go, Dad? I don't think you're

looking after yourself as you should. You aren't managing without her, are you? What do you want to do?'

'I don't know.'

Carrie could see his mouth was dry and crusted. 'Have you eaten today?'

'Shall I make a cup of tea?' Tim asked.

'I think it would be better if I took you home to Prue. She'll look after you. Why don't you pack a bag? Can you drive us there?'

'Prue has no room for me.'

'You can sleep in Maud's room. She's gone to stay with a friend in Ireland. I helped Prue make up her bed clean yesterday.'

'I'll be all right here.'

'No, I don't want to leave you by yourself. Let's put some overnight things into a bag and go. You can come back in a day or two when you feel better.'

The three of them went upstairs to his bedroom. Carrie screwed up her nose at the unmade bed and the general mess. The doors of the other rooms were open and she could see chaos in the one he'd used as an office, with drawers left open and papers strewn about.

'Can you reach an overnight bag down, Dad?' she asked, indicating the luggage piled on top of the wardrobe. As he did so, a large leather jewellery case crashed to the floor with it, and opened to show its satin interior.

'Oh! Oh!' Archie snatched it up, clicked it shut and put it back. His face had gone paper white.

'What was that?'

'Just an old jewellery case.'

Tim opened the overnight bag on the bed. 'Can you get your shaving tackle and toothbrush?' he asked, and steered Archie towards the bathroom.

Carrie opened the drawers in the tallboy and found plenty of freshly laundered clothes all neatly folded. She packed a generous amount of what she thought he'd need. She was concerned about her father; he seemed quite switched off.

Before leaving, she looked into the kitchen; it seemed that ingredients for a meal had been left out on the table for him to cook. She moved some of them to the refrigerator, and marvelled anew at the latest kitchen equipment. Tim locked up carefully and her father drove them home competently enough. Prue was welcoming.

When Carrie and Tim left to visit John and Connie, Prue saw them to the front door. 'I knew that Marion would be no good for him,' she said. 'All those flashing diamonds and expensive clothes. She made herself look like the fairy on the top of a Christmas tree.'

As they walked up the path to John and Connie's new home, Tim said, 'They are very lucky to be living here.' The evening sun was glinting on the fresh paintwork.

John let them in. 'Come on in, Carrie. I'm afraid Connie needs cheering up.'

Connie was lying on the sofa in their small sitting room. 'I'm not feeling too good,' she said, sitting up. 'I'll be glad when this baby is born; I've had enough. I feel too fat and too lazy to do anything. I can't wait to get my figure back.'

'You've nearly done your time,' Carrie said in cheery tones. 'You won't have to wait much longer.'

John smiled at them. 'The baby is due on Monday.'

'It's you we've come to see,' Tim said, and told him what he'd discovered in Milner's annual accounts. 'It has to be fraud.'

'Marvellous.' John understood immediately. He had the contents of Milner's paperwork clear in his mind, though the actual documents were in the office. 'And Archie confirms that?'

'Yes, we went to see him to make sure. He's very upset. Marion has gone away – left him. She's refused to marry him; he's quite depressed.'

'He was so sure that she would.' Connie was aghast. 'He thought she wanted it as much as he did. What's he going to do now?'

'I made him come to Prue's for a few days. He can't think straight at the moment, but I think he'll go back to South Africa.'

'I'm surprised he's stayed here so long,' Connie said. 'He never seemed that settled here. Come upstairs and see the new nursery. It's the smallest of our three bedrooms and we've just got it finished in time.' They all trooped up because John wanted to show off his workmanship.

'It's lovely,' Carrie said. 'Smart enough to be photographed for a magazine.'

'That's where we got the ideas,' Connie beamed. 'I made the curtains.'

'Gosh, John,' Tim said, 'did you build these shelves, and paint them too?'

'Yes, and I painted the cot and that little cupboard as well. Most of this stuff is second-hand; stuff that people have given to us.'

'I'm very impressed.'

Carrie thought Tim was getting restive now that he'd told John what he'd noticed in Milner's accounts. 'Tim and I usually go to the pictures on Saturday night; we'll still have time if we leave now.'

'We feel in a state of flux.' John was shaking his head. 'We won't be able to think of anything else until our baby arrives, but thanks for letting me know what you found, Tim.'

'We've had the phone put in too,' Connie said as they went through the hall. She scribbled the number on a scrap of paper.

'So she can let me know if things start while I'm at work.' John smiled at his wife. 'I'll ring Leonard Groves up right away and tell him the news. He'll be delighted if you've found a fault in those accounts. You know that last year they were thought to be a bit suspect?'

'It'll be one in the eye for Milner,' Connie said. 'I bet you'll be pleased about that, Carrie?'

'At the time, I made myself forget about revenge,' she smiled, 'but I won't be sorry if this lands him in the mire.'

'I wonder why he didn't show all his expenses,' John pondered. 'I can't see the point, but he'll have some reason, and it probably indicates fraud.'

'Perhaps investigations will reveal Milner to be at the centre of a criminal empire.' Tim grinned at him.

As they left Connie's house, Carrie said, 'It's been a very different Saturday afternoon, and we hardly have time to go into town for the last house at the Odeon.'

'I'm glad we went round to tell John,' Tim said. 'We could go to the Roxy; that's near where I live and will save us going into town. I noticed that the Marx brothers are on, but I've forgotten the name of the film. Do you like them?'

'Yes, it'll be a good laugh, but will we be in time to see the whole show?'

'Yes, with a bit of luck, if we go straight there. But we'll be starving when we come out, as we've had no tea.'

'We'll buy some chocolate as we go in.'

'Yes, and afterwards you can come home with me and I'll make us something quick, like eggs on toast. We might have the house to ourselves; Mum's going to see Ethel Harrison, the widowed friend she used to work for. She's teaching her to do her own accounts. Ethel's asked her round for a meal.'

They thoroughly enjoyed the film, which was called *A Night at the Opera*. When they came out, Carrie's sides ached with laughing. Tim's mother came home as they were eating their scratch meal, and they giggled together as they told her about the film.

Tim walked her home, and when Carrie let herself in, Prue was in the kitchen making a bedtime drink of cocoa. 'Will you have some too?' She got out another cup without waiting for a reply. 'How's Connie?'

'Tired of waiting. Wants it over.'

'She always was impatient. Your father's feeling very sorry for himself too,' she said. 'He's sunk in gloom and it's not like him. Go and cheer him up.'

Archie was sprawling in Maud's fireside chair, his legs half across the rug. He stared blankly at Carrie. She started to tell him how much she'd enjoyed the Marx brothers film.

'Don't like them. They're silly, not my sort of humour.'

'Dad, what is the matter with you? You used to be bouncing with life, game for anything. Happy.'

He sighed. 'I'm a bit depressed. Marion's gone.'

'I'm sorry about Marion, but you were switched off long before that. At Connie's wedding you took charge of Prue's plumbing disaster, sorted things out, but now you don't seem interested in doing anything. You've been going down the drain for months.'

He looked at her reproachfully, and Carrie remembered that she'd been asked to cheer him up.

'Sorry, Dad, but it's true. Before we went to the pictures, Tim and I went to see John. Once you'd confirmed that you did work for Milner, he wanted to tell John what he'd found in Milner's accounts.'

Archie jerked upright in his chair. 'What? Why?'

'John's his boss, he has to. John was delighted with the news and said he was going to ring Leonard Groves right away to let him know.'

Her father's eyes were no longer blank; he seemed gripped by a new shock wave. 'Oh my God! No, don't tell anyone. You mustn't.'

Prue came in with a tray of cocoa and biscuits. 'I'm taking mine up to bed,' she said. 'I've had more than enough of today. Archie, you go to bed as soon as you've had this, and I hope you'll feel better in the morning. Good night.'

Carrie waited until Aunt Prue closed the door. 'Dad, it's Tim's job to report things like that, and we're all keen to catch Gerard Milner out. We don't understand why he's hiding this. It doesn't make sense, but we mean to find out.'

'No, no, you mustn't.' Her father threw himself forward to

grip her wrist. 'Nobody must know.' He knocked the cup that Prue had placed on a low table beside him, and a wave of cocoa slopped into the saucer.

Carrie ignored it. 'Dad, I thought you were on my side, angry with Milner for leading me on. We all thought you'd be pleased if we could catch him out in some criminal scheme.'

'No, no.' Perspiration was standing out on his forehead. 'To start an investigation into Milner's affairs is the worst possible thing. You must stop John doing that.'

Carrie was staring back at him nonplussed. 'It's probably too late. John was going to ring Leonard Groves straight away. I don't understand what all this is about, Dad.'

He'd sunk back into the armchair. 'Without Marion, everything is going wrong. I feel I'm losing control.'

His whole attitude was telling Carrie that he thought she was stronger than he was. 'Come on, Dad, you've got to tell me. What's been going on?'

He gazed into the dying fire, looking defeated. 'Milner has been fencing stolen jewellery, in a big way. Marion and I have been helping him.'

Carrie's mouth fell open; she could feel herself shaking with shock. He wouldn't look at her now.

'Milner had to hide the expenses of fencing. He couldn't possibly show those in his business accounts.'

She could feel herself cringing with horror. 'You're saying you helped him? You've been involved with him? And if we prove he's engaged in criminal activity, will that also prove that you . . . ?'

'Yes, I've been scared stiff for months that we would be caught.'

'Oh my goodness! You and Marion?' Archie nodded. 'And now Tim and I have . . .'

'Yes, and not just Milner. We've been helping Rod Reinhart set up a big ring all over the north-west, Lancashire and Cheshire.'

Carrie gasped. 'Dad – the police . . .'

'They'll be after me too. I don't know what to do.'

'You've been helping criminals. I can't believe it. You've always seemed so honest. So upright.'

'You don't know the half of it. I did a lot of bespoke work for Milner using stolen diamonds, valuable stones, and Marion has left and taken the finished goods with her. So she's given him his comeuppance.'

'You mean she's stolen them from Milner?'

'Yes, and I think she's also stolen much of the money we made for Rod. She's drained what was building up in the bank accounts.'

'Stolen your money?'

'Mostly it belonged to Rod – he bankrolled the scheme – but some would have been mine.'

'Marion has done that? How much would it be?'

Archie shook his head. 'I don't know exactly; she kept all our accounts, and she seems to have burned the paperwork before she went.'

'But I really liked her; I thought she'd be good for you.'

'So did I. I loved her. I've been a fool; I let her talk me into doing things that I knew were wrong. She could convince me that black was white.'

'What on earth will Prue say?'

'I don't want the family to know.'

'Dad, everybody is going to know. Tim was out to catch Gerard Milner; we all were. John will have started the ball rolling. The police will be called in, and they're bound to investigate. We thought you were honest; it never occurred to me or Tim that you could be involved like this. Oh my goodness, what have we done?'

'Carrie, you've got to help me. What should I do now? I'm in a terrible mess.'

Although her father had freely admitted his guilt, she wanted to protect him from the law. 'Can't you go back to South Africa? You've been talking about it.'

'Back to Jo'burg?'

'Yes, as soon as possible. You said Marion had booked your passage?'

'I don't know for certain, but I think she might have lied about doing that.'

'Perhaps we can stop John telling Leonard Groves.'

'But then I could get you and John in trouble with the police, and also with your firm, your careers . . . I mustn't involve you.'

'Dad, you already have.' Carrie drained her cup of cocoa, now gone cold. 'We need to think carefully about this.' She reached for a biscuit. 'Drink your cocoa and we'll go to bed. We can't do anything now; it's after midnight.'

Carrie spent half the night tossing and turning, horrified that her father had admitted being engaged in fencing stolen jewellery. He had asked for her help, something he'd never done before, which just showed how low he felt.

Without Marion, he couldn't cope here. He wanted to return to Jo'burg. He had a house there, and work that he said was legal and above board; booking him a passage on the mail boat as soon as possible seemed the best plan. It would get him away from any investigation here. But wouldn't the police consider him a wanted man? Could they insist on his coming back from South Africa?

Carrie groaned into her pillow. She'd made it worse by encouraging Tim and John to look into Gerard Milner's affairs. Soon they would all know that Dad was a criminal.

CHAPTER TWENTY-SEVEN

B Y THE TIME SHE WAS dressing the next morning, Carrie's mind was on practical ways to help her father get out of the country. Prue was already down in the kitchen, preparing to take Gladys to the early morning service at church. Carrie poured two cups of tea from the pot her aunt had made and took them up to Maud's room. Archie was awake, but just as gloomy. 'What am I going to do?' he asked.

She sat on the bed. 'It's Sunday, so I don't know whether you'll be able to find out if you're booked on next Thursday's mail boat.'

He shook his head in despair. 'I don't think Marion will have done that, she booked herself to—'

'Then you need to do it yourself. I don't have to go to work today, so we'll go to that house you rented and pack all your belongings, empty it of everything that wasn't there when you took it over.'

'That'll be a big job; we've been living there for over fifteen months.'

'That's why it has to be done today. Tomorrow you can take the keys back to the estate agent and end your tenancy.'

Below them, the front door banged shut. Archie sat up with a jerk. 'What's that?'

'Only Prue on her way to church.' She went to the window. 'Can't you hear the bells?'

Below her she could see Prue, tall and stringy, with Gladys, much shorter and still not fully recovered from her misadventure in the bath. She felt a surge of sympathy for Gladys, who was finding it none too easy to walk. Prue was fond of her too, and was slowing her step so Gladys could keep up.

Carrie closed the window. 'Get up now, Dad. I'm going to make us egg and bacon for breakfast.'

He was a long time coming down, but she could hear him walking about upstairs. When he did come, he said, 'I can't ring the Union-Castle office. Prue doesn't have a phone.'

'We'll be going to Allerton as soon as we've had breakfast. You can ring from there.'

'Of course,' he said miserably.

'Poor Dad, you're not thinking straight. I need to talk to Tim; he might have a better idea.'

At least the car was parked outside, and Archie drove them to Allerton without wasting any more time. As soon as they arrived, Carrie rang Tim. 'I have a problem,' she said. 'My father is telling me he and Marion have been helping Milner fence stolen jewellery.'

'What?' There was no mistaking the horror in Tim's voice. She repeated what she'd said.

'Oh my goodness! That means your father has broken the law. He's admitting this? Heavens, Carrie, Uncle Jeremy will go ballistic. He'll be afraid that some whiff of criminality will attach itself to you and John, and because you are employees, to the firm of Atherton and Groves.'

Carrie's heart was sinking. 'I'm afraid it might.'

'Uncle Jeremy sees it as imperative that his company remains squeaky clean. Nothing must tarnish its name, because it acts as a sort of policeman, pointing out to its clients where they could fall foul of the law.'

'Dad's asking for my advice, Tim. What d'you think is the best thing for him to do?'

'Go straight to the police and tell them exactly how he's involved.'

'I'm helping him pack up his house and he's hoping to get back to South Africa before the trouble starts.'

'He mustn't do that! It could make him a wanted man.'

'Yes, I know. Would they be able to bring him back from South Africa to face charges?'

'I haven't the slightest idea. In any case, you shouldn't get involved in this. You could be charged with helping a criminal escape the law.'

'Well, I understand that, but—'

'If he won't go to the police and insists on leaving the country, tell him he's on his own. Do nothing to help him.'

'Tim, he's my dad. He's asked for my help, as I have just asked for yours.'

'I'm sorry.'

'Clearly you don't want to help me, though I've done my best to help you in the past.'

'Carrie, I'm sorry. So terribly sorry, but I can't involve myself in this. I too could be charged with helping a criminal. Uncle Jeremy would see that as—'

'To hell with you and your Uncle Jeremy,' she said and put the phone down. Tears were scalding her eyes; she'd expected sympathy from Tim, even if he couldn't help. She was glad her father was upstairs and not able to see her reduced to tears like this.

She wiped her eyes. She was disappointed in Tim, but this had certainly shown her just how much Dad needed her support. She couldn't cut herself off from him, regardless of the cost.

Carrie shivered. The house felt cold and had an air of being abandoned in a hurry. She was used to seeing it impeccably tidy, and it certainly wasn't that now.

'Dad,' she called, 'where are you?' Archie came downstairs looking numb. 'Why don't you get on the phone now and see if you can talk to the Union-Castle office today?' She watched as he did so, but it seemed nobody was there to speak to him.

'Try again later,' she said. 'It's still early to be at work on a Sunday. Let's make a start on packing.'

'Where?' He had no energy and looked as though he didn't care what happened.

'We'll begin with your clothes. Let's go up to your bedroom.'

He led the way up to his room. Carrie opened the window and turned her attention to the wardrobe. 'You're not short of clothes. How many suitcases do you have?'

'Three here on top of the wardrobe,' he pulled them down, 'and a cabin trunk in the spare room.'

He was opening one of the suitcases on his bed when Carrie asked, 'What's that thing that's still on top?'

He had to stretch up to reach it, and as he edged it towards him, something else fell with it.

'Oh, hell. I was supposed to get rid of these things, but I forgot.'

Carrie picked up a square jewellery case and opened it.

'There's nothing inside. What's that other thing?'

'I told you I made some bespoke jewellery for Milner? This belonged to the original necklace. If it was mounted on this thing, it could also be worn as a tiara.' He tapped it. 'Just base metal.'

'Let me see it,' Carrie said. 'And the necklace it goes with was stolen property?'

'Yes, a lovely thing; beautifully made. A real shame to break it up, but Milner wanted it melted down and the stones recut to make them safe to sell on. Marion took them to Amsterdam to be done.'

'Great Scott, Dad, you went along with that?' Carrie felt her heart flutter; this had been a bigger operation than she'd realised. It was scary.

'I had to. Marion and Rod thought it was the only way to make those stones safe to handle.'

'Then we've got to get rid of these things.' Carrie was staring at them in horror. 'You don't want to be caught with them in your possession. The police would see it as proof that you handled the diamonds.'

'I know.' He opened the leather jewellery case. 'The name of the original maker is on the satin lining inside. It can be tied to that particular necklace.'

She took it from him gingerly; it gave her the collywobbles to look at it. 'Let's burn that straight away.' She ran down to the sitting room grate to do it, but it was full of charred paper. 'What's all this?' she asked.

Archie had followed more slowly. 'Before she left, Marion burned all the records she'd kept for Starbright, the company Rod set up to fence the jewellery.'

Carrie felt herself cringing; the more she knew about what had gone on, the worse it seemed. Maybe Tim had been right. She picked up the poker and raked through the brittle burned paper, breaking it into tiny fragments.

'I remember now,' Archie said. 'Milner gave me that case to burn when Marion was going to Amsterdam. I didn't bother lighting fires when she was away and forgot all about it.'

'It's not easy to do it now. We'll take both things home and get rid of them there.' Her eyes went round the room. 'She hasn't burned everything, though. We must make sure we don't leave anything incriminating.' Carrie picked up several handwritten sheets of blue paper and a matching envelope from an armchair. 'What's this letter?'

'It's from Marion. She left it for me. To tell me . . . not to expect to see her again. Not ever. But I've already told you about that.' Carrie held it out to him, but he backed away. 'No, I don't want anything to do with it.'

'We can't leave it here.' Carrie pushed the pages into the envelope and put it in her pocket. Why had Marion gone without saying goodbye to the family? She still wasn't sure Dad had told her everything. 'Would you mind if I read it?'

'If you like.'

'I'll do it later. Better get back upstairs to the packing now,' she said.

They worked together, filling the cabin trunk and the suitcases and taking them down to the car. Then Archie went round the house with Carrie following, picking up odd items like books and bottles of wine and whisky that he wanted to take. She couldn't stop thinking about Tim's reaction, and how much it had hurt.

In the room Marion had used, the bed was neatly made. Carrie opened the wardrobes and found she'd left a few dresses, a hat and a handbag. She bundled them up and took them too. She'd admired Marion's outfits; perhaps these things would suit her or Connie.

They stripped both beds, collected the towels from the bathroom, filled up the laundry bag and made out the list ready to send to the laundry. Carrie was trying to work out how much it would cost as Archie carried it all down to the kitchen. 'It doesn't matter,' he told her. 'It will be deducted from the deposit I paid.'

'We ought to go soon,' she said. 'Prue wants us to be home by half twelve; she's making a roast dinner. Have another go at ringing Union-Castle before we go.'

He went to the phone while Carrie made herself look round to see what else they needed to do. There were a hundred and one things on her mind.

Her father came back. 'They don't work on Sundays,' he said. 'I didn't think they would.'

Carrie put on her coat. 'That'll have to wait until tomorrow morning then, and we'll have to come back here to finish off this afternoon. Perhaps Prue will help.'

As the car pulled up outside her home, she said, 'I'll help you carry your luggage up to Maud's bedroom. Prue will want it out of the way.'

When she opened the front door, she was met by delicious scents of dinner. Seconds later, Prue bounded out of the kitchen, her face sparkling with excitement. 'John has been round,' she said. 'He took Connie into hospital early this morning. The baby is coming.'

Carrie thought of Connie for the first time that day and was filled with compassion. She'd be in the throes of labour now, and it seemed all wrong that Carrie wasn't with her to comfort her. She had to remind herself that Connie had moved on; she had John now.

'Where is John now?' she asked. She needed to talk to him about Milner's audit, and Dad needed his support.

'He went back to the hospital to wait for news.'

'Goodness me.' Even her father had a smile. 'This will make me a grandfather.'

'And me an aunt.'

'Archie, you could get back in that car and go down to the phone box to see if the baby's here yet,' Prue told him. 'It was half ten when John came.'

'Let's empty it first,' Carrie said. 'It's stuffed full of luggage; I had a hundred things on my knee.' They both helped Archie carry his luggage upstairs to get it out of the way.

'I've put out clean linen for Connie's old bed,' Prue said. 'Let's get it made up now, while we're upstairs. Maud is due back this evening and we can't leave it for her to do, not when Archie's put her out of her own room.'

When Prue went downstairs to make the gravy, Carrie went to the bathroom to have a wash and get ready for lunch. She returned to comb her hair and remembered the blue envelope in her pocket. The letter inside was several pages long. Why would Marion be writing at such length when she'd been living with Dad until yesterday? Why had she upped and gone, apparently taking him by surprise?

She took the letter out of the envelope and sat down on her bed to read it.

Dear Archie,

I'm writing this by way of an apology, and to say goodbye. I'm not the person you supposed me to be, and neither is Rod. I'm afraid we have both deceived you.

We wanted you to come to England with us because you have skills in designing and making jewellery that we don't possess, and we knew how useful that might be to us. From the start, Rod was afraid you'd refuse to come if you knew we were planning to set up a company to help thieves fence the property they had stolen.

We could see you were far too honest for that, but as you wanted to come over for Connie's wedding and spend some time with your daughters, we set out to persuade you. When you found things were not as you'd supposed, it took a lot of persuasion to keep you with us. I'm afraid you are not cut out to lead the sort of life we do. Anyway, you don't need to, as you have the ability to earn the money to enjoy a generous lifestyle without sinking to our criminal methods.

I know you love me, and when I first met you, I wanted you to be the permanent man in my life. I found you very attractive and attentive, but you were too damned honest and your conscience bothered you. I had to drive you to carry on with Rod's plan. I'm afraid I've turned you into a nervous wreck, and you didn't deserve that.

I led you to believe I would return with you to South Africa and marry you. I can't do that. We are very different people, and in the long run it would not work out, but I want you to know that in my own way, I did and still do love you.

I know this is the last thing you're expecting and it will come as an almighty shock. Please forgive me for all my wrongdoing. I couldn't find the courage to tell you face to face. Eddie Jurgens and

I are going to new pastures where you won't find us. Don't even try. Forget us.

Go back to Jo'burg; you have friends there, a house, and an honest means of earning a living. You fitted into that life better than we did.

I hope you'll find happiness with someone else in the future.
Love from Marion

Carrie had a lump in her throat when she put the letter down. Poor Dad! Marion had taken them all in. At that moment, she heard him come home and shout in the hall that Connie had had a little girl. She felt a spurt of joy and instantly forgot the problems as she ran downstairs.

'Both are well.' Dad was certainly excited now. His cheeks were as red as Prue's and his eyes were shining; he seemed more alive than he had for ages. 'She weighs seven and a half pounds, and we can go in this afternoon to see them both.'

'Did you speak to John?' Carrie asked.

'No, I tried him at home but there was no answer, so I rang the hospital. It was the ward sister who told me. He's probably with Connie now.'

Carrie was left to lift the roasting pan out of the oven; for once, Prue was too excited for household tasks. She asked Dad to carve the joint while she dished up the vegetables. He waved the carving knife about dangerously while he and Prue laughed together.

They ate roast beef and Yorkshire pudding, but as Prue and Dad chattered on about the new baby, the contents of that letter were going round and round in Carrie's mind.

As soon as the washing-up had been done, they were off to

the Oxford Street maternity hospital. 'What a good job Connie's had her baby before you go back to Jo'burg,' Prue said, still in high spirits. 'Your granddaughter could have grown up before you saw her.'

'From now on, I'll keep in touch more. You must come out and visit me. I've plenty of room in my house to put you up.'

'I certainly will,' Carrie assured him, 'but it won't be for a few years.'

There were already visitors in the ward when they arrived at the hospital, and it was buzzing with chatter. Officially, visiting was from two to four on Sundays. They walked up the ward together to find John sitting at Connie's bedside. He stood up to offer his seat to Prue, but she was more interested in the new baby sleeping in a metal cradle swinging on hooks at the foot of the bed.

Carrie slid on to the chair. 'Connie, how are you? Was it awful?'

'Yes, I'm shattered but happy. Isn't she beautiful? I think she's going to have blond curly hair like us. We can't decide whether to call her Amelia or Arabella, with Mary as a second name after John's mother.'

Carrie peered into the cot and thought the baby looked like most newborns, rather red and wrinkled. But she was her niece!

'Connie's only allowed two visitors at a time,' John said anxiously. 'I'd better go out so you can stay with her for a bit.'

'I'll come with you,' Carrie said. 'Let's leave Dad and Prue to make a fuss of her.' Out in the stone-floored corridor, she brought him to a halt in front of a window looking out on to a brick wall a few feet away. 'I need to talk to you.'

'Connie's over the moon. A healthy little girl is exactly what she hoped for.'

'Did you ring Len Groves last night? What did he say about Milner's accounts?'

'I haven't spoken to him yet. He was out when I rang last night, and my mind has been on Connie and the baby since then.'

'Of course,' Carrie said.

'Connie's tired out now; they don't call it labour for nothing. She had her first pains around five this morning.'

'John, Dad is in trouble. We need your help.'

'Of course. I'll ring Len this afternoon.'

'No, don't, don't say anything to anybody until—'

He stared at her. 'I have to tell Len Groves; he expects me to tell him if we find anything out of the ordinary when we do an audit.'

'Surely there's no desperate urgency for you to tell him?'

'I can't put it off. It would be as much as my job's worth not to tell him. We can't think of signing off that audit as correct until we've had another close look at the accounts. Len will want to see them himself when he hears about this. Satisfy himself.'

'John, I've found out a lot more about what Milner has been doing, and Dad is involved too. He's in it up to his neck.'

'Involved with Milner? In what way? Not in anything criminal?'

'Yes.' She tried to explain about the Starbright business. 'Dad's name appears as a director and general manager on all their documents, and Marion has disappeared. I've been helping Dad pack so he can get out of the country before the police come looking for him.'

'Carrie, you mustn't help anybody to break the law. That would make you—'

She didn't want to hear this for a second time. 'It has reduced Dad to a nervous wreck. He hardly knows what he's doing. We've got to help him do the right thing now. Is it too much to ask for your support?'

'Of course not. What can I do?'

'Marion left him this letter. I want you to read it and tell me if, in your opinion, it could be considered proof of his innocence.'

John frowned and turned the letter over but didn't read it. 'Exactly what sort of work did Archie do for Milner?'

'He melted down gold and platinum jewellery, and reset diamonds into new necklaces of his own design knowing the original pieces were stolen. He removed assay marks, that sort of thing.'

John was shocked. 'Clearly, then, he can't be innocent.'

As Prue came bustling up the corridor, Carrie took the letter from John's hand and pushed it back in her pocket. 'Your turn now, Carrie,' Prue said. 'You've hardly seen the new addition to the family. I don't want to exclude you; I know how close you and Connie are.'

Not as close as we were, Carrie mused with regret, and she had a lot more to say to John. 'Thanks, Prue. Can we invite John round for supper tonight? He'll be on his own.'

'Of course. We'll eat about seven; just cold beef and salad on Sundays. We're going to Archie's house from here to help him clear it, but Maud is expected home around five.'

* * *

'Wow,' said Prue when she opened the cupboards in Archie's kitchen. 'There's enough here to feed a small army.' Marion hadn't meant to go short; she was a lavish housekeeper, and probably very wasteful.

'There's more in the fridge,' Carrie said. 'Clean it out and we'll take everything worth having with us.'

She went upstairs to the office, and read through every bit of paperwork that remained. There were still a lot of documents about the lease of the house, correspondence with Union-Castle, and a police list of stolen property.

Both she and Prue were sending Archie out to the car with load after load of anything they could use. When they started cleaning up, he was sent out to the bin with loads of rubbish.

All the time she worked, Carrie was trying to decide whether the new evidence she'd unearthed proved that Milner had committed criminal acts but that her father had not. She thought it did.

When she was satisfied there was no longer any trace of their occupation of the house, Archie locked up and drove them home. Prue had left a note for Maud, and she had supper ready on the table for them.

John arrived in time to help them carry the goods in from the car, and he and Maud were both in high spirits. Maud was full of the good time she'd had in Ireland, and wanted to hear from John every last detail about the birth.

Carrie had felt exhausted, but began to recover once she'd eaten. She was finding it difficult not to get sidetracked, but if she was to help Dad, she had to get on with it now.

'We need a family conference,' she told them round the

supper table. 'I'm sorry, Dad, we all want to help you, I'm sure, but your problem has come as a shock.'

'What's all this about?' Maud wanted to know. 'Have I missed something?'

Carrie was explaining what had happened, and how her father was involved with Milner, when the front doorbell rang.

Prue was irritated. 'Who can that be now?'

Carrie was nearest the door and got up to see. Tim was on the doorstep. 'I'm so sorry, Carrie. I had to come round to speak to you. I've been so worried since—'

'Tim, it's not a good moment. We're having a family conference about it and we have a lot to decide.'

'I feel terrible; I don't want you to think—'

'I'm all right, no need for you to worry.'

'But I want to help.'

'You can't. Things have moved on. You're right to stay out of it.'

'But—'

'Tim, I haven't time for this right now. I have to keep my mind on what I need to do. I'll see you tomorrow.' She was closing the door.

'No, you won't. I'll be at Milner's. I'll come over to see you at lunchtime.'

'No, Tim, don't—' The door clicked shut before she could stop it. Carrie sighed. That wasn't how she'd meant to treat him, but it was too late now. She returned to the dining room.

John was saying, 'The whole thing is going to be general knowledge very soon.'

Prue's lips were hard with condemnation. 'Archie, you say Marion has fled the country and taken a lot of the money you've earned here? You know my opinion of her.'

'Stolen from Archie?' Maud's jaw had dropped.

Carrie sat down and put her mind to the problem at hand. 'Today has been a full day and I've hardly had time to think,' she said. 'I did tell you, Dad, that I thought the wisest thing for you was to get out of the country as soon as you could.'

'I'll go just as soon as I can,' he burst out, 'and then you won't have to worry.'

'We will,' John said. 'The police will be involved. It will be in all the papers.'

'Archie,' Prue said, 'you must realise that this will reflect on the reputation of the whole family.'

'Yes,' John agreed. 'On Carrie's career with Atherton and Groves, not to mention mine.'

'What a load of nonsense,' Maud said. 'Archie is as honest as the day is long. His conscience troubles him if he takes more than his share of cake. You know it does.'

'Yes,' Carrie said. 'Hang on a minute; I'm going to fetch some things from my room that I think show the truth of that. I've been thinking of a better way for Dad to handle this.'

She was back in a few moments. 'Dad, I found these documents in your office.' She spread them out across the table. 'They prove that the car was bought in your name, and you did the same when you rented the house.'

'I wanted to come over before the others,' Archie said, 'so I could be at Connie's wedding. Rod asked me to set things up.'

'Exactly.' Carrie looked round at her family and took a deep breath. 'Would you have given details from which you could be traced if you'd known you were going to be involved in fencing stolen goods?'

'Of course he wouldn't,' Maud said. 'He thought he had nothing to hide.'

'They were using you from the start,' Carrie went on. 'This leather jewellery case and tiara stand – where did you get them from?'

'Milner, he asked me to get rid of them. The jewellery was stolen from a big house in Wales,' Archie said. 'I was with him when the police came to ask him to keep an eye out for it.'

Carrie said, 'If you go to the police and tell them all that, it will involve Milner. It will be a valuable lead for them into that theft. They'll certainly take your story seriously.'

'It'll involve Archie too,' Prue pointed out. 'It's proof that he's been handling stolen goods.'

'Yes, but we also have this letter written by Marion saying goodbye to Dad. It gives the correct slant on what happened.'

'No.' Archie put his hand out to take it. 'I don't want that to—'

'All right, Dad, it's embarrassing, I know, but what's a little embarrassment compared with being considered a criminal?'

'I designed and made jewellery for Milner. By then I knew the material I was using was stolen.'

'But you were in love with Marion and she was promising you the world to do it. Didn't she keep persuading you to stay and do this work?'

Archie didn't answer.

'Dad, I think you should go to the police tomorrow and take these things as evidence. Tell them exactly what happened, that you were hoodwinked by Marion and Rod to design for them. That you thought it was all going to be above board.'

'Not the letter.' His head had sunk into his hands. 'That's private. I wish I hadn't let you read it.'

'Dad, the letter is the most important part. Marion is saying goodbye to you, but she describes how she persuaded you to stay, and how worried you were about what you were doing. It was not her intention, but by setting things out as they really were, she clears your name.'

'Or provides mitigating circumstances,' John said grimly.

Her father couldn't look at her. 'I've been longing to get away for months, and as long as the police don't start questioning Milner again, I'll be in the clear.'

'Dad, I can't help wondering whether you're making yourself out to be more of a criminal than you are. And to run away will make you look guilty even if you aren't.'

He didn't answer. Carrie felt the family were all holding their breath. 'Do you really need to go on the run like a criminal? Rush off to Jo'burg without saying a word to the police when you have evidence that might help them solve a crime? Evidence they'll think is important?'

There was still no response. 'All right, can the rest of the family know what is in the letter? They knew Marion and were taken in by her too. We all were. May I read it to them?'

Archie hesitated. 'I suppose so.'

Carrie unfolded the sheets of blue paper and read the letter aloud. 'Do you all see what I mean now? Dad, do you?'

'I certainly do,' Maud said.

John nodded. 'So do I.'

Carrie picked up the letter again. 'Listen to the phrases Marion uses, she said, "*I'm not the person you supposed me to be, and neither is Rod. I'm afraid we have both deceived you. From the start, Rod was afraid you'd refuse to come if you knew we were planning to set up a company to help thieves fence the property they had stolen. We could see that you were far too honest for that, but – we were able to persuade you as you wanted to come over for Connie's wedding,"* and finally, *"When you found things were not as you'd supposed, it took a lot of persuasion to keep you. I'm afraid you are not cut out to lead the sort of life we do, your nerves couldn't stand it."'*

'You'd be a fool to turn yourself into a criminal when you have evidence to the contrary like that,' said Prue. 'Do be sensible, Archie, and do what Carrie suggests.'

'You really must,' John agreed. 'Also, if you do go to the police, it will mean Milner's activities come under their scrutiny. You want him to get his comeuppance for misleading Carrie, don't you?'

'I do,' Archie admitted.

'Then I'll talk to Tim and Leonard Groves in the morning. Tell them you've been inadvertently caught up with Milner's criminal activities and intend to make a statement to the police to explain how it happened, in order to clear your name. It'll certainly give the firm the green light to pull Milner's accounts apart and a reason to refuse to sign his audit as correct.'

CHAPTER TWENTY-EIGHT

CARRIE'S HEAD WAS STILL whirling when she got into bed. There were so many facts to consider and things to arrange, and she would have to go to work as well.

The next morning, they were all up early and ate breakfast with her.

'You should go down to the phone box at nine o'clock and find out if you have a cabin booked for Thursday,' Carrie reminded her father.

Maud agreed to go with him to return the keys of the Allerton house to the estate agent and close the tenancy.

'I want to be with you when you talk to the police,' Carrie told him. 'I'm going to ask for time off today, but if I'm not home by twelve, ring me. Maud will go with you if I can't.'

Carrie had finished her stint at the Grey Goat Brewery and, feeling on edge, she caught her usual tram to the office. John had told her that, instead of going to Milner's, he'd come in to tell Leonard Groves what Tim had noticed in the shop's accounts. 'Shall I tell him that you're worried about your father's part in this?' he'd asked. 'It'll save time and he'll probably send for you to hear your side of the story. Then you can ask him for a few hours off to go with your dad to the police station.'

'Thank you,' she said, 'that would be a help.' Now, ill at ease, she sat at her desk awaiting a summons.

It was John who came, smiling and friendly. 'Len will see you now. He's sympathetic.'

Carrie had been trying to work out how much to tell Leonard Groves, but he took over.

'Come and sit down, Caroline. John tells me – he's your brother-in-law, isn't he? – that your father has had business connections with Milner.'

'Yes, Tim heard Dad say he was doing work for him, and he noticed that no payment for the work appears in Milner's accounts.'

'Very strange, and John is afraid Milner may have a fraudulent reason for not showing it?'

'Yes, he says he can see no reason not to.'

'It could be an accidental omission.'

'John says his accounts are set out with great precision; he doesn't think he'd forget that sort of thing. Dad is very upset at being mixed up in something that could be illegal, especially when he's about to return to South Africa.'

'He's leaving this week, I'm told?'

'Yes, on Thursday, and it's all a bit of a rush.'

'I think he's quite right about wanting to go to the police today to give them the facts. We all need this to be cleared up as soon as possible. I understand you would like to go to the police station with him?'

'Dad's been doing too much, he's in the middle of packing up his home and he's a bit confused. I want to make sure he tells them all the facts.'

'Yes, quite, he needs a helping hand. Well, I see that you

haven't missed a day since you started, so I think you should certainly take the rest of the day off to settle this and help him with his packing. When did you say he was leaving?'

'He's hoping to catch the mail boat that sails on Thursday, so he'll be leaving early on Wednesday morning to go down to Southampton.'

'Once he goes, you'll not see him again for a long time; I think you should take Monday and Tuesday off to help him and say your goodbyes. We'll see you back here on Wednesday morning. Come and let me know how you get on.'

'Thank you, Mr Groves.' Carrie was all smiles. 'I'm very grateful.' She hurried out to catch a tram home, feeling grateful to John too for setting that up.

John walked rapidly to Milner's shop in a state of trepidation. In his experience, there had been very few occasions when the accounts audited by Atherton & Groves had not been signed off as true and fair. Only once had there been trouble with an account he was helping to audit, and since he'd been made team leader, this was the first time he'd had to deal with serious difficulties. He was having qualms about facing Milner and asking searching questions that could not avoid alerting him to the fact that his accounts were being viewed with suspicion.

Milner was behind the counter when he went in. Feeling very tense, John headed towards him. 'Could I have a word, sir, in your office?'

'Of course.' Milner led the way.

Once the door had closed behind them, John sat down at the desk and opened the file he carried. 'It has been noticed that you have no figure for temporary labour or contract work in your accounts. No expense at all for that sort of thing.'

'No.' Milner slid into his chair. 'All my staff are employed on a permanent basis.' He looked very much at ease. 'In a trade like mine, I need to trust my staff. I like to get to know them.'

'Yes,' John said, 'but I happen to know that Archie Courtney has done work for you, that he came here several times. I have some of the dates. He's my father-in-law, so I know the family well. I know that others worked for you too: Marion Collard, for one.'

He knew that that had poleaxed Milner; the colour was draining slowly from his face. He could not refute the facts.

Carrie reached home as Dad and Prue were having a minor crisis. Maud had been shopping and had bought herrings to fry for lunch. Prue had given Archie the job of gutting them; the knife had slipped, and he'd cut his hand quite badly.

'I don't know what's the matter with you,' Prue was complaining. 'You can't do anything without making a mess. Look, you're dripping blood over everything.'

Carrie turned the cold tap over the sink full on and held his hand under it. 'That hurts,' he said, trying to pull it away.

'Don't be such a baby,' Prue barked. 'That cut could get infected, and then it'll hurt more. There's a bottle of iodine in the bathroom cupboard; slip up and get it, Maud. Iodine will hurt you more than water too.'

'Don't be so hard on him,' Maud said. 'You can see he's upset.'

'Better bring that first-aid tin down while you're there.'

Carrie turned the jet of water on to the herrings and carried on gutting them, while Prue saturated the cut with iodine. Archie screamed.

Carrie felt Maud push her away from the sink and towards the sitting room. 'I'll see to the lunch,' she said. 'You look after your father.'

Carrie could see he was trembling but knew he was trying to pull himself together. 'Come on, Dad, let's sit down. How did you get on this morning?'

'I did what you asked me to do,' he said. 'I've ended the tenancy and returned the key to the estate agent.'

'Good. And everything's all right for Thursday?'

'No. I got through to Union-Castle, but it's as I thought.' His face was woebegone. 'Marion did nothing, and there are no first-class cabins left on Thursday's mail boat. I was offered a berth in a shared cabin, but I don't know.'

'Have you booked it?'

'No. Oh dear, I don't know what to do.'

'Dad, if you want to go on Thursday, you'd better make your mind up.'

'Of course I want to go.' His voice was irritable. 'But sharing with some stranger? I couldn't do with someone who snores or coughs. I need peace. And I might dislike him.'

'Did you ask about the following week?'

'They have no single cabins left then either, but they do have doubles. I suppose I could take one of those.'

'Then why don't you? It would be a headlong rush to get away this week.'

'I feel desperate to leave,' he groaned, pulling a face. 'The police might come . . .'

'It's your choice, Dad. A less than comfortable voyage, or

put it off for a week. If you put it off, you'd have time to get organised.'

He sighed. 'You could be right. I'll put it off.'

'Then hadn't you better go down to the phone and book it?'

'He can't think straight any more,' Prue said when he'd gone. 'What has that woman done to him?'

When he returned ten minutes later, he said, 'I've booked it. A double cabin to myself on the *Arundel Castle*, sailing a week on Thursday.' But he still looked down in the dumps and in no way excited at the prospect.

'If I was preparing to sail to Cape Town next week, I'd be absolutely thrilled,' Carrie told him.

'I really need to get away and put this mess behind me,' he said. 'All this talk of theft and the police – I'll be relieved when I do.'

Carrie shivered. She would be left to face any trouble that was coming on her own; she couldn't even rely on Tim. 'You've still got a lot to do before you leave,' she told him. 'At least there's no desperate urgency to get it done now. But since I've been given this afternoon off, we might as well go to the police and get that sorted.'

Prue said, 'Sit up, lunch is ready.' She brought their plates to the table and slid a fried herring in front of each of them.

'I don't like the idea of going to the police. It worries me,' Archie said. 'I've been trying to keep away from them for months. It feels a bit like putting my head into the lion's mouth.'

'Nonsense,' Prue said. 'Don't be such a coward! And come down to earth. You've put Marion on a pedestal, on a par with the Angel Gabriel, but she's a dishonest crook and she led you into that money-making racket. Now you're trying to take the blame for her criminal activities. My goodness, that woman certainly had her claws into you.'

He flinched. 'You're right,' he said, and seemed to shrink in misery.

Carrie ate steadily. 'You and I are going to the police this afternoon. I want you to get your story in before they come looking for you. I hope it will prevent too much stain attaching itself to your name,' she said.

'Does it matter? I'll be gone a week on Thursday.'

'I'm glad it isn't this Thursday; that would make it look suspicious, as though you're in a big rush to get away. Also, it will give the police time to ask more questions should they need to.' She saw him cringe at that. 'We're going to tell them the truth – the whole truth – and hide nothing.'

He looked beaten. Carrie could hardly believe the difference the last year had made in her father. 'Marion betrayed you,' she said. 'You weren't expecting it and it must have felt like a kick in the stomach.' She understood only too well; hadn't Gerard Milner done that to her?

He was staring at her, his eyes full of woe, and she went on, 'But she did more than that; she's made you doubt your own intelligence, your own worth. She has shattered your confidence.'

'I feel such a fool.' He was grinding his teeth. 'I thought she meant what she said. I must have been blind. Not for one moment did I suspect she was deliberately taking me in.'

'If it's any consolation, she took me in too. I was ready to welcome her as a stepmother. I thought she really liked me.'

Archie burst out, 'I asked her to marry me and she agreed. I thought I knew her.'

Carrie knew they had been man and wife already in every other sense, and could see his anger, his hurt and his fear of a future without Marion, but she didn't know how to comfort him. His distress robbed even Prue of words.

Half an hour later, they set off to walk to the nearest police station. Carrie had walked past it many times but had never looked at it closely. It was a very old building, and the front door always stood open to show a long, dark passage; she could see other doors opening off it, but they were all closed, and there was nobody about. Her father pulled her to a halt.

'Come on,' she urged, though her heart was pounding. 'Smile, Dad, try to look like the successful citizen you are.'

'What am I going to say?'

'We've been through that twice.' She'd made him think about what he needed to say, and schooled him in an opening sentence or two.

They turned a corner at the end of the passage and found themselves in a reception area with two policemen sitting behind a high counter. One stood up. 'Good afternoon, how can I help you?'

He seemed quite friendly. Carrie held her breath and waited for her father to speak.

His voice was scarcely above a whisper, but he gave his name and began, 'I design and make jewellery for other jewellers to sell, and I find myself in an awkward position. I'd like to talk to an officer to make my part clear. Set the record straight, so to speak.'

'You want to make a statement?' The officer hesitated. 'May I ask what it's about, sir?'

'While I was working ... I began to suspect that the

materials I was using were stolen. That I was handling stolen property.'

'Oh!' The policeman straightened up and gave Archie closer attention.

Carrie said, 'My father has been in this country for about sixteen months, but he's lived and worked in Johannesburg for many years. He's booked to return there a week on Thursday. He couldn't just—'

'I felt I should come here first,' Archie put in.

Carrie opened her bag and took out the tiara stand and the jewellery case, together with the other things she'd collected as evidence.

Immediately the policemen's attitude changed, and one of them said, 'Would you take a seat, please? I'll get an officer to come and talk to you.'

Carrie knew this wasn't the time to relax, but in her opinion Dad had at least put his problem over truthfully and honestly. They were taken by two detectives to a quiet room, and Archie was questioned minutely about what jewellery he'd made and for whom. The detectives asked for, and were given, dates and names and addresses. One man took notes.

Archie pointed to the relevant items on the stolen property list, and pushed the tiara stand and its case across the table. He hesitated over Marion's letter. 'This is very personal,' he said, 'but my daughter insists it's vital that I let you read it.' He pushed that across the table too.

'It supports what he's telling you,' Carrie said. 'It shows that Marion and Rod were in charge of the operation and considered him to be an innocent assistant.'

After studying the letter, the officer asked, 'The lady who

wrote this says she's going away. Do you have any idea where she went?'

Slowly Archie shook his head. He'd already made it clear to Carrie that he wouldn't say anything that might land Marion in trouble.

'And are you aware of anyone else who worked with this couple?'

Carrie held her breath. She'd heard about Bill Dainty and knew Archie felt sorry for him. He shook his head again. It seemed he couldn't actually say no – that would count as a lie, while a head shake was vague and possibly need not.

They were kept in the police station for more than two hours because the notes of their interview had to be typed up and signed by Archie. The detectives photographed the letter and also made typed copies.

Carrie gathered that her father had given the police evidence and proof that would solve an outstanding case for them, and though they didn't acknowledge that, they certainly appeared pleased and grateful.

'Should we have any further questions, may we come round to your address and see you?'

'Yes, of course,' he said, 'but I shall be leaving to travel to Southampton a week on Wednesday.'

'On his way to Johannesburg,' Carrie said, glad that Dad was able to allow them time to look into the matter before he went. She was also glad that although she had taken no revenge against Milner, and had put that hurt out of her mind, he was now heading for trouble, and it was of his own making. It gave her satisfaction that she'd helped to bring that about.

On the way home, their step was lighter and quicker. 'Am I glad that's over,' Archie said. 'It went well, but I was afraid it might go all wrong.'

'You took some persuading to do it.'

'You were clever to see the advantages. I feel better about the whole thing now. It's a load off my conscience. I think of Jo'burg as my home; I can go back now and be at peace. I wish I could take you with me, if only for a holiday.'

'I'd love to come, but that will have to wait until I'm qualified. I'm not allowed enough time off as holiday to cover the sea trip in both directions.'

'A pity, I could do with some company.'

They had reached the front gate when Carrie said, 'You want company? Why don't you ask Maud to go with you? She'd probably jump at the chance.'

He gave her a quick hug. 'You're right, that would be just the thing.' They were both rejoicing as she opened the front door.

Prue and Maud were drinking tea in front of the fire, and the scent of herrings still hung faintly in the air. Archie blurted out his invitation without a moment's thought. Maud's face showed incredulity and then delight. 'You mean that?'

'Of course I do. I want you to come. You're good company, and the last thing I want is to be on my own. But you'll have to be ready to leave here a week on Wednesday.'

Prue poured herself another cup of tea. 'He needs you to look after him, Maud.'

'But don't you have to book?' Maud was excited. 'Will they have a berth for me at such short notice?'

'If they haven't, I've got sole occupancy of a double cabin

and you can bunk in with me. I'll go down to the phone box now and see.'

'Ooh,' said Maud. 'I don't mind in the slightest. I'd sleep in the hold to get to South Africa. How long can I stay?'

Archie laughed. 'We'll have to see how we get on. Let's call it semi-permanent; certainly a few months.'

'Marvellous,' said Maud. 'I'm going upstairs to start packing, though I have only one evening dress and nothing much for the beach.'

'Don't worry,' Archie said, 'you can buy all that out there.'

'Come and help me decide what to take, Carrie. I have practically nothing for warm weather.'

They went upstairs together, and Carrie agreed her wardrobe was mostly pullovers and warm cardigans. 'Dad says you'll need those too; it can get chilly during their winter months, though nothing like it does here. She unpacked all the clothes that had once been Marion's to show her. 'This is the sort of stuff you'll need,' she said.

'Marion always looked so smart.' Maud stood in front of the mirror, holding dress after dress in front of her. 'Sadly, most of them won't fit me. I'm too fat; I ought to slim down,' but she took a beach wrap and a couple of sunhats. 'These dresses would fit you or Connie.'

Archie returned from the phone box to say, 'I've booked you a double cabin to yourself, Maud. It's all they had left.'

'Luxury,' she breathed. 'Thank you, Archie. I can't believe this is happening to me.'

CHAPTER TWENTY-NINE

SINCE HER FATHER WASN'T leaving for another week, Carrie felt she ought to return to work on Tuesday morning. She felt refreshed now his affairs were under control. She went straight to Leonard Groves's office to tell him what had taken place. 'I wasn't expecting you until tomorrow,' he said, and she explained about Archie's booking.

'My father made a statement to the police and they have no objections to his leaving the country,' she told him. 'Once we knew his problem was sorted and that he'd be staying for another week, everybody relaxed and there was no need to rush. I felt I'd be taking time off under false pretences.'

'Indeed. Well, we have refused to sign off Milner's audit and I understand the police are investigating. I'm pleased you've settled this matter, and I must congratulate you on the way you handled it. It was quite a tricky situation.' Carrie was rising to her feet when he added, 'My regards to your father; would you like to take time off on Wednesday morning to say goodbye and see him off?'

'Thank you, I would.'

As she walked across the floor of the main office to her desk, she could see many of the staff glancing up at her and knew they'd all discussed her problem. It didn't matter; everything had worked out well for Dad. She'd set out to help him and she'd managed it, but in doing that, she and Tim had clashed and she felt incredibly sad about that.

Tim's desk was in front of hers and usually he swung his chair round to face her, but today he got up and came closer. She understood this was a difficult moment for him too. 'Are you all right?'

'Fine,' she said. 'Everything has gone well and I hope will sort itself out satisfactorily.'

'I'm glad, but you were very unkind to me on Sunday night when I came round to apologise for my behaviour.'

'That's because you weren't very kind to me when I asked for your help.'

'You don't understand my difficulties.'

'Oh, but I do. I was struggling with difficulties of my own at that time, Tim.'

'You slammed the door on me.'

'You told me you wouldn't help. You could have listened and been sympathetic, especially as I've bent over backwards when you've had problems.'

'Oh my goodness, Carrie! Let's forget it.' He sat down and bent over his work. She felt terrible; she'd made things worse.

Before the afternoon was over, Bill Brown came to put some documents on her desk for her to read, and told her she'd be one of a team drawing up the accounts for a printing firm in Ormskirk and they were all to meet on Exchange station at nine tomorrow morning so they could travel together.

Tim was not to be one of the team, so that meant they wouldn't see each other for a few days. She stared at his hunched back, wondering if he'd say something. When the time came to go home, he disappeared without a word. Perhaps it would be just as well if they spent a few days apart.

That evening, Prue looked up from her lamb chop and said, 'What about your car, Archie? Shouldn't you be doing something about it?'

'I haven't forgotten it,' he said.

'You're leaving it a bit late to try and sell it. Are you taking it with you?'

'No, I did ask, but it would cost a lot to ship it out to Jo'burg, and I already have a good car there.'

'Has it all been paid for?' Prue wanted to know. 'Or did you get it on HP?'

'It's all paid for, no need to worry about that.'

'What a pity Carrie can't drive.'

Carrie had been about to say she'd love to learn, but Maud said, 'John can, and Bob; you'd better give it to one of them. They'd both appreciate it.'

'Bob,' Prue decided. 'John will soon be able to afford one himself.'

'I have been thinking about it,' Archie said. 'I'd like to give it to you, Carrie. You're the one who's tried hardest to help me. You've bent over backwards on my behalf. Would you like it? Well, anyway, if you don't want to drive it, you can always sell it. You're not going away, so you'll have plenty of time.'

Carrie was immensely cheered. 'I'd love to learn to drive it,' she said. 'That would be absolutely marvellous. Thank you, Dad.'

'Why don't we ask Bob if he'll teach you? For the last couple of years new drivers have had to sit a test and get a licence, but he'll know all about that.'

'We might see him this afternoon if he comes to the hospital to visit Connie and the baby.'

'We can tell him he can keep it at his place and use it until you get your licence; that will encourage him to teach you.'

Carrie breathed a sigh of satisfaction. 'That would be bliss, Dad. Absolute bliss.'

Carrie found that travelling to Ormskirk meant a longer than usual working day. John was leading the team and as the maternity hospital in Oxford Street allowed half an hour visiting for new fathers every evening, John usually went straight to see Connie before going home. It meant Carrie was kept up to date with news of her sister and niece, but she was longing to start learning to drive.

When she arrived home on Wednesday evening, she found the family had delayed eating until she got back. Maud and her father were in high spirits and talking twenty to the dozen about a plan to drive up to Preston to say goodbye to George.

'I haven't forgotten about asking Bob to teach you to drive,' her father said. 'It's difficult to know what he is doing because he works shifts, and he doesn't have a phone, so I went round to see him. I just caught him before he shot off to work; he's on two-to-tens this week so no chance yet. It's his day off on Saturday and I said I'd take you round to see him in the afternoon.'

'I'm glad you've fixed that. Saturday afternoon then.'

'It's not that long off,' Prue said. 'By Jove, you're keen.'

'I could take you out for a bit in the evenings to start you off. Do you want to come now? It'll be light for another couple of hours.'

Carrie was enthusiastic even though she was tired. 'Yes, please.'

He drove her to a bit of wasteland, a place of rough grass and deeply rutted hard-packed earth that gave a bumpy ride. Carrie found driving more difficult than she'd been led to believe and was disheartened. 'I'm afraid I don't have much aptitude for it,' she said.

'It takes practice, Carrie, not brainpower. You'll do it.'

'Of course I will.' She really fancied driving round in her own car and was determined to do it.

On Thursday evening, her father took her out again, but the result was much the same.

'We should get up early and come here before you go to work,' he told her. 'You'll be fresh then and find it easier.'

Carrie set her alarm clock and they tried it the next morning. She found she could concentrate better, but they lost track of the time. Archie had to drive her home to collect her handbag and the sandwiches Prue had cut for her lunch, and then run her to the station to join the team so she wouldn't be late.

She hadn't put her hair up in its customary French pleat and raced along the platform with a head of wild curls and a pocket full of hairpins. She caught the train by the skin of her teeth, sat down panting and noticed that the eyes of her three colleagues immediately fastened on her hair. 'Overslept this morning, did we?' Robbie Wilson asked. There was disapproval on Bill Brown's face.

Carrie felt a mess. 'I didn't oversleep,' she said. 'I've been up since half five. My father took me out for a driving lesson and we misjudged the time. He's going to give me his car.'

'Learning to drive?' Robbie said. 'By Jove, I wish somebody would do that for me.' There was admiration and envy in her colleagues' eyes now.

It was eleven o'clock before she found time to go to the cloakroom and put her hair up. Fortunately she was used to doing it now and it didn't take her long. They worked hard all day and by the end of the afternoon they'd about finished the job. Bill Brown told them to take Saturday morning off as recompense for the time they'd spent travelling. Carrie was delighted – that meant she'd have the whole weekend off – but when she got home that evening she felt shattered.

'I think we'd better leave it to Bob,' her father said. 'You really don't have the time and energy to learn to drive as well as going to work. There is a limit to what any of us can fit into one day.'

'I know, but thanks, Dad, for helping me do this.'

'Carrie, you've done so much for me, it's the very least I can do.' He smiled down at her, and she felt that the bond between them had tightened over the last week or two. She was going to miss him and would be sorry to say goodbye.

She was just waking up on Saturday morning when Prue brought her a cup of tea. 'You have a lie-in this morning,' she said. 'You deserve it.'

When she did get up, she found that Prue had made a

Victoria sandwich cake and a pork pie for John. 'Shall I take them round to him?' she asked.

She liked Connie's new home; it was exactly what she would have chosen for herself, and it still smelled of fresh paint. John was grateful. 'Thank Prue for me,' he said. 'I've got my parents coming to stay for a few days to help Connie when she comes out. But they won't be here until next weekend.'

He talked all the time about his new daughter, and took Carrie up to the nursery, where she admired all the recent additions to the baby's layette. The full-size cot had been made up ready, but there was also a cradle with pretty muslin frills that they intended to use while the baby was tiny.

She helped him put sheets and blankets on the new bed in the spare room; his parents would be the first people to use it. Then she dusted round and tried to make the room look as welcoming as possible.

She felt low as she walked home. Everything was going right for other members of her family. Connie was in seventh heaven with her new house, her new baby and a loving husband. The same could be said for Maud, who called her trip to South Africa the adventure of a lifetime, while Dad was relieved that he'd heard no more from the police and that it all seemed to be working out as they'd hoped. He was very much looking forward to going back to Jo'burg.

But Carrie was not happy; she was disappointed with Tim. Since that stormy trip on the ferry she hadn't been able to get him out of her mind. Every time they parted after a trip to the pictures, she hoped he'd kiss her. She would have liked him to show a little more affection for her, but he kept his hands in his pockets as though he didn't want to touch her.

Several times she'd been on the verge of telling him she loved him. At the very least she'd counted him a good friend and found it hard to believe that he'd refused to help her. It seemed she thought more of him than he did of her, and now there was this rift widening between them and it looked as though their friendship was about to peter out.

CHAPTER THIRTY

O VER LUNCH ON SATURDAY, Dad had been holding forth about how pleased he was that he'd heard no more from the police. 'It must mean they are satisfied with what you told them,' Carrie said. Afterwards he was getting ready to drive her over to see Uncle Bob when the front doorbell rang. When Carrie answered it, she found two men on the doorstep flashing identity permits at her.

They introduced themselves as detectives and said, 'Does Mr Archibald Courtney live here? He made a statement in the station last week and we'd like to ask him a few more questions.'

'Yes,' she said, afraid that some new problem had arisen. 'Come in and I'll get him.' As she showed them into the front room, her father came clattering down the stairs. 'There's a couple of detectives here wanting to talk to you,' she said softly.

She would have followed him into the front room, but the senior detective said to her, 'Do you mind if we speak to your father on his own?' He closed the door firmly, shutting her out, so she went to the kitchen to help Maud wash up, hoping Dad would be all right.

'What do they want?' Maud was anxious too. 'I hope they aren't going to stop us leaving.'

Carrie shivered, shook her head and continued to help with the chores. The interview seemed to go on for a long time and she was anxious to see Uncle Bob. She was ironing tablecloths for Prue when she heard the detectives being shown out. All three of them went into the hall. 'Is everything all right?' Carrie could see it was; her father was smiling and looked relieved. 'What did they want?'

'Those are the detectives working on Milner's case. They've been to see him and he doesn't seem to have told them about Marion. They wanted to talk through what we told them on Monday and pressed for the names of others involved.'

'You're daft to protect that woman,' Prue said. 'You mix with all the wrong people.'

'But we're still sailing on Thursday?' Maud wanted to know.

'Yes, of course. Come on, Carrie, let's go and see Bob.'

Carrie was relieved; it looked as though everything might work out as they'd planned after all. Bob and Dilys were expecting them and wanted to hear the latest news of Connie's baby.

Afterwards Bob said, 'I'll be more than happy to teach you to drive, Carrie, especially as you've offered me use of the car until you get your licence.'

'Carrie's clever, it won't take her long,' Archie told him.

'I'm not so sure about that,' she said. 'Dad has been trying to teach me, but I don't seem to be getting the hang of it.'

'It took me a while,' Bob laughed. 'Be patient, it'll come.'

Archie told him about the rutted tracks on the wasteland.

'I know a better place than that,' Bob said. 'How about having your first lesson now?'

Archie came too because Dilys wanted to go out to do the

weekend shop. Bob drove them to a building site where the roads were already in and the buildings pegged out but construction hadn't begun. There was nobody about. Carrie thought her uncle was very patient with her and that she got on a little better.

'When do you want your next lesson?' Bob asked. 'I'm working a late shift tomorrow so I could come over in the morning.'

Carrie agreed; she had to take every chance when they were both free.

Bob was as good as his word and arrived shortly after breakfast. After an hour going round the building site, he said, 'You're improving, you're doing all right.'

He drove her home and popped in to have a word with the family. 'I'll come round on Tuesday evening to say goodbye,' he told Maud.

'I'll give you the keys then,' Archie said, 'and you can take the car. Maud and I will be catching the eleven o'clock train down to London the next morning.'

'Excellent. I'll come on the tram and bring Dilys. She's looking forward to us having a car. She's been trying to persuade me to buy one, though I'm afraid it might not be as posh as yours. I'll take good care of it until Carrie can drive.'

Connie and baby Amelia were coming out of hospital that afternoon, but as John's parents were staying with them, Carrie felt she couldn't intrude. Prue had invited some of their neighbours round that afternoon to say goodbye to Maud and Archie, and she was kept busy handing round cakes and cups of tea.

* * *

Carrie waited anxiously for the tram to take her to work on Monday. She didn't know whether Tim would be on it. She hadn't seen him for ages and the rift between them seemed wider than ever because they'd parted on bad terms.

If he was on the tram and he'd kept her a seat, she would join him and hope they could get back to normal, but she dreaded seeing him on an outside seat hiding behind a morning paper.

They had not gone out on the last two Saturday nights. She'd really missed seeing him, and was afraid he meant the present stand-off to be permanent. With Connie engrossed in her baby and Dad and Maud leaving, she felt she was being deserted.

When the tram came, it was full. She could see Tim standing in a crush of passengers well away from the entrance. She had to stand too, but hesitated about pushing her way through to him. More passengers got on, but eventually he made his way through them and came to touch her arm. 'Carrie?'

He'd made the first move; she relaxed her clenched hands. 'Hello, Tim, haven't seen much of you recently.'

'No, and I'm standing in for Danny Devereaux at a chain of men's outfitters, so we won't see each other today either,' he said, his voice sounded strained. 'Devereaux is off sick.'

'I understand everybody's congratulating you,' Carrie said. 'What?'

'On finding the problem in Milner's accounts. The police are investigating him, but you know that?'

'Yes. How is your father?'

'Everything turned out well for him,' she said. 'Did your cousin Len tell you?'

'No, I haven't seen him.' In the crush he had to stand very close to her, and he seemed to be speaking into her hair.

'No blamc was attached to Dad after all. He's sailing to Cape Town on Thursday and taking my aunt with him for a holiday.' She was trying to be bright and breezy, as friendly as she could, but he continued to look stony.

They had reached the centre of the city and the shop workers were getting off. Tim stepped further away from her as soon as there was room. 'I'll be getting off one stop before you.'

'When will you be back in the office?'

'Tomorrow, I expect. Perhaps late this afternoon.' The tram came to a halt and the passengers surged off. 'See you.'

He was gone, and the tram clanked on. Carrie was left feeling even more unsettled. It was easier to cope with Dad's problems than her own.

During the morning, she heard welcome news: tomorrow she and Tim would be part of a team going to a jam factory. That meant she'd see more of him and they'd have time to settle things. She would try and put him out of her mind until then.

Next morning, when the tram came, she could see that Tim had a seat. He stood up to let her sit near the window, but he still looked withdrawn and unhappy. 'I'm sorry,' he said. 'We've been at odds since that Sunday. We need to talk. There's a lot I want to tell you.'

Carrie thought it sounded as though things might be all right after all. She told him about Connie's baby girl and John being over the moon. She'd already told the rest of the office, who had been full of questions and goodwill for John. When they reached their stop, Tim walked stiffly beside her and said little.

'You do know we're both to go to Johnson's jam factory today?'

'Yes, I was told. Who else is in the team?'

'Robbie Wilson and we're to be led by Douglas Davies. I've not worked with him before; what's he like?'

'He's all right.'

No sooner were they in the office than the team were summoned to Len Groves's office, where he outlined basic details of the Johnson business. Tim sat beside Carrie and looked withdrawn. Mr Davies had a car and drove them all to the factory, where they set about the work.

As usually happened, Mr Davies said to Carrie, 'You and Tim can start by physically checking the empty jars and ingredients waiting to be used in the stockroom. When you've done that, you can check the jars of conserve ready to leave the factory. Here's the paperwork.'

'Right,' Carrie said.

'The stockroom is on the top floor.'

A girl was waiting to take them up. It was a tightly packed and airless place, but they were alone at last.

'Shall we start at the far end with the jars?' Tim said. 'There's stacks and stacks of them and they're all different sizes.'

'There was something you wanted to tell me,' Carrie prompted.

'No time now. We've got to get on with this.'

Tim spoke to her when he had to about what they were doing, but never before had things been so stiff between them.

Carrie was filled with foreboding. A hooter sounded through the factory, signalling the lunch hour.

'Let's get out of here,' he said. 'It's no place to eat.'

They went downstairs to the table the team had been allotted in the main office. Many of the factory staff were getting to their feet and going out. Douglas Davies said, 'Robbie and I are on our way out to find a café.'

Carrie took out her sandwiches and watched Tim do the same. She pulled her chair closer to his and spoke in a whisper, as there were other staff eating sandwiches at their desks not far away. 'You said you had something to tell me, that we must talk?'

He was staring at his sandwich. 'Yes.' He paused. 'It's difficult.' He sighed heavily. 'I'm sorry I upset you. I'm sorry about your father.'

'No need to feel sorry for him. He's delighted his difficulties are over and he's going home.' He was also grateful for the help she'd given him, which was more than could be said of Tim.

'I need to tell you about *my* father.'

'Yours? You don't speak of him much.'

'No, he died when I was four so I don't really remember him, but he caused a split in the family and terrible trouble for my mother.'

'This is sort of family history?'

His eyes had been avoiding her, but he looked up now. 'Yes.'

Carrie chewed on her roast-beef sandwich and wondered why this was important to him now. 'Go on,' she said.

'My father was a gambler. Not just a man who had an

occasional flutter, but a habitual and obsessive gambler who was certain his next bet would be a big winner. He was addicted to it in the way some people are to drink, but he could hide it.

'My mother said she didn't realise the extent of his problem, though he'd told her he gambled. She understood that to mean he had a bet on races like the Grand National or the Derby. She thought he was saving money, but he gambled away every penny he earned.

'Dad was a chartered accountant, and to start with, Mum's family approved of him. Once they were married, they offered him a job in the business, and within a year or two he was made a director.'

Carrie was appalled; she could guess now where this was leading and why he was telling her.

'When money was found to be missing from some of the business accounts, it all came to light. Dad had been fleecing the business to back what he thought were sure winners. Needless to say, they mostly lost, and what little he did win was immediately put on another horse.' Tim sighed gustily again. 'Mum told me there was a humdinger of a family row about it.'

'Were the police called in?' Carrie could see why the trouble with her father had had such an effect on him.

'No, everything was kept quiet. Completely under wraps. Uncle Jeremy put the money back into the accounts, but after that, he wanted no more to do with us. Since then, he's been pathologically scared that a stain on the company name would hurt the business.'

'Oh, Tim, I am sorry.' She was full of sympathy for him now. 'What happened to your father?'

'He couldn't forgive himself for what he'd done to Mum and me. He committed suicide the following year.'

'Oh my goodness! Tim, that's dreadful. Your mother must have had a terrible life. Well, you too, of course.'

'We've had our problems.' He sighed again. 'We had nothing but the roof over our heads. That came to Dad from his family, but he'd also borrowed money against it. Once my father was dead, Uncle Jeremy relented. He paid off the debt against the house and offered to help train me, and thought that was enough. He neglected Mum until you brought our penniless state to his attention.' She saw a fleeting smile. 'You can see why we didn't want to ask for more. Really, the family have been very generous to us.'

'I can. I didn't know, Tim. I see now why you refused to help my dad. Any hint of criminality would be bound to scare you off.'

He was shaking his head. 'This is not something I can talk about. I've never told anybody else, but I had to put things straight with you.'

'I'm glad you have.' She could feel tears of sympathy prickling her eyes. 'Now we can get back together.'

'I couldn't let a spat like that come between us. I hated being shut out of your life.' Her heart seemed to turn over. 'Carrie, I want you to know I'd go to the ends of the earth for you.'

She beamed at him and would have said more if their colleagues had not come back from lunch at that moment. She was happier than she'd been for a long time. Things were coming right for her at last.

Tim put his hand on her arm. 'Stay in town with me for an

hour or so after work and let's have a drink somewhere. We have so much to talk about.'

'I'd love to, but I can't, not tonight. There's too much going on at home. Today is Dad's last day; he and Aunt Maud are leaving tomorrow morning. Prue has planned a big farewell dinner.'

CHAPTER THIRTY-ONE

THAT AFTERNOON, CARRIE AND Tim spent another busy session in the stockroom, but now that they'd started talking freely with each other, it was as though they'd opened the floodgates and couldn't stop. All they wanted to do was talk about their personal affairs. She could see affection shining out of his eyes.

She thought about what he'd said when they'd been downstairs, and was racked with sympathy all over again. 'Why didn't we discuss these things when we had plenty of time? We really have been taking each other for granted all these months, haven't we?'

'I've never taken you for granted,' he said, his brown eyes searching into hers. 'I've really appreciated your friendship. You've been marvellous to me, both at work and helping me and Mum at home. She thinks you're lovely too. I felt a real heel refusing to help you.'

'I understand why you did that now,' she said. 'You didn't intend to push me away.'

'Carrie, that's the last thing I'd ever want to do.' She could see a new intensity in his manner, and her heart missed a beat. 'Although I've been telling you that you're the best friend I've ever had, I've always wanted more from you.'

'More?' Her heart was bouncing.

'Of course more.' He reached for her hand. 'Carrie, I'm in love with you. Have been for ages – since the very beginning. Head over heels. I can't get enough of you.' He took her in his arms and his lips came down on hers.

Carrie felt as though she was melting. The sudden sound of footsteps outside followed by voices made them draw apart. 'I love you too,' she whispered. 'Why didn't you kiss me before? I hoped you might on our Saturday nights out.'

'Honestly? I didn't dare, not after you went out of your way to say we were to be just friends. Uncle Jeremy told me he'd asked you if I was your boyfriend and you were vehement that we were colleagues and friends and nothing more.'

'Oh dear!'

'And Robbie said you slapped his face and put him in the doghouse for good because he tried to kiss you.'

Carrie smiled. 'On our first date he did nothing but grope me. And he wouldn't stop when I asked him to; it put me right off him. Besides, he wasn't my type.'

Tim laughed. 'I've been struggling to keep my hands in my pockets for months. I didn't want the same thing to happen to me.'

'But you're not Robbie, you're completely different.'

'If I couldn't have you as my lover, I wasn't going to risk losing your friendship.'

That made Carrie catch her breath; he was saying he wanted her as his lover. His arms came round her again and she put her head on his shoulder. 'Oh, Tim, what blind fools we've been.'

'Yes,' he whispered. 'I've loved you all these months, and

I've been trying to decide what I could do about it. What I really want is for us to be married. I've imagined proposing to you in all sorts of romantic places, with a ring ready to slide on to your finger, and here I am telling you this in a stuffy jam factory stockroom.'

Carrie could hardly get the words out. 'Is this a proposal?'

'It's what I've wanted for a long time, but it isn't practical, is it? I'm not earning a proper wage, and I've agreed not to marry before I'm qualified, which is still two and a half years off.'

'I agreed to the same terms,' Carrie said, 'but now I wish I hadn't.'

'But we could be engaged,' he murmured. 'There are no rules about that. I have no ring to offer you, though, and no prospect of getting one for years.'

'That doesn't matter.'

'In fact all my prospects are in the distant future.'

'Knowing how we feel and having an understanding is what matters.'

'Yes, yes, it is.' His arms tightened round her and stayed there until the factory hooter sounded again to mark the end of the working day. They shot down to the office to lock their documents and files away for the night.

On the tram going home that evening, Tim held her hand and his eyes wouldn't leave her face. She could see he was excited and brimming with pleasure. 'I want to tell everybody that I love you, and that we have an understanding. My mother will be pleased. Are you going to tell your family?'

'I'd like to tell Dad before he goes. I will if I get half a chance, but the spotlight is going to be on him and Maud.' She gave a little laugh. 'Aunt Prue has assumed we reached this point ages ago. I do love you, Tim, and I'm thrilled to have a real boyfriend at last. No, you're more than a boyfriend: a fiancé. I've felt left behind since Connie got married. Did you know John kept trying to hook me up by arranging foursomes?'

Tim laughed. 'Did he? And you didn't like his friends?'

'I wanted to make my own choice.'

'We could go out for a walk tonight, couldn't we? Think about ourselves and not all the other things we're expected to be doing.'

'Tim, no, I'm sorry, I really can't. There's so much to be done before Dad leaves. Uncle Bob is coming round to take his car away.'

'He's giving it to him?'

'No, did I not tell you? He's giving it to me. Uncle Bob is going to teach me to drive it.'

'Heavens! How could you forget that? I'd be thinking of nothing else. It's a lovely car too.'

'Getting things straight between you and me was more important. I've been hankering for that for a long time too.'

'Carrie, here's your stop.'

'Nearly missed it,' she laughed as she got to her feet. 'I was delighted when Dad's problems were settled, but I'm totally thrilled that we've sorted ourselves out too. See you tomorrow.' She dropped a kiss on his forehead and skipped down the tram.

When she let herself into the house, the first thing she saw was the mountain of luggage building up in the hall. Maud came to the living room door. 'She's home, Archie,' she called.

'Hello, love, come in and have a glass of sherry,' he said. Uncle Bob and Auntie Dilys were already there, and so was Gladys, dressed from head to foot in black as she usually was these days. Something of a party atmosphere was already building up.

Archie had provided two ducks for the feast and Prue had roasted them to perfection. 'Maud and I have spent the afternoon round at Connie's place,' he told Carrie. 'We went to say goodbye to her and the baby.'

'She's absolutely gorgeous,' Maud said.

'I expect she'll be a demanding child before I see her again, but I'm inviting all of you to come out and see me.'

Gladys had made the dessert, a confection of sponge cake, fruit and cream, but Maud had to carry it in from the kitchen because Gladys couldn't manage without a stick now, and the heavy bowl needed two hands. As she was dishing it up, Archie decided it was the moment to open the champagne.

He raised his glass to Carrie. 'I can't thank you enough,' he said. 'You have been wonderful. You made everything turn out right for me.'

Carrie took a deep breath. 'Everything has turned out right for me too,' she said with a beaming smile. 'Today Tim asked me to marry him, and I said yes.'

'Congratulations,' Maud whooped, and the rest of the family joined in.

Archie was brimming with delight. 'That gives me a marvellous excuse to come back for another wedding.'

'I'm afraid it'll have to wait for a few years,' Carrie said.

'We all know that,' Prue said with her usual sniff. 'Tim hasn't exactly rushed to ask you, has he?'

It was quite late when Bob stood up and said, 'I'm afraid I have to break this party up. It's high time we workers were in bed. Good night, Carrie, I'll come round to take you for another lesson on Sunday.'

He kissed Maud. 'Lucky you, I wish I was coming with you. Goodbye, Archie.' The brothers shook hands. 'Don't stay away so long this time.'

'You and Dilys must come out for a holiday and see me.'

'We might keep you to that,' Bob said.

They all went outside to watch Bob and Dilys drive off. 'I really feel I'm on my way now he's taken my car,' Archie said. Gladys kissed Maud and hugged Archie goodbye, and Prue saw her into her own house and upstairs to her bedroom.

Carrie couldn't get to sleep. She felt high on excitement and it took her some time to calm down. It took the others a while to settle down too; she could hear them whispering and walking round until quite late.

Morning came all too soon. Everybody was out of bed at once and wanted to use the bathroom at the same moment. Breakfast was later than usual and seemed chaotic. Prue had hard-boiled the eggs and Maud said she couldn't possibly eat hers.

Carrie was fraught because she had to get off to work and at the last moment realised her lunchtime sandwiches had been forgotten. She pushed Maud's egg and a few Ryvita into a paper bag. Prue, all apologies, found her some triangles of cheese and her father scooped up a handful of the chocolates they hadn't eaten last night and dropped them into her pocket.

She was nearly in tears as she hugged Maud goodbye, and they overflowed as she gave her dad a final hug. He said, 'I'm so glad you're happy too.'

She ran to catch her usual tram, and when it came, she

could see that Tim had saved a seat for her. 'Bit of a rush this morning,' she said. He stood up to let her sit near the window, and she collapsed on the seat and closed her eyes for a moment to calm down and get her breath back. As soon as she was settled, Tim took a box from his pocket and flicked up the lid.

'Oh!' she gasped as she saw the three-stone diamond ring. 'An engagement ring after all?'

'Yes, this was my grandmother's – my mother's mother. I hope you like it.'

'It's absolutely gorgeous,' Carrie breathed. 'I love it.'

'You don't mind that it's this or nothing? That it isn't new?'

'Of course not! The fact that it's come down through your family makes it extra special.'

He took it out of the box and slid it on to her finger.

'Oh, I'm thrilled, thank you. And thank your mother too.'

He kissed her. 'She wanted you to have it. She told me she'd hidden it so that my father couldn't sell it.'

Carrie admired it on her hand, turning it slowly to see it flash with fire.

'It's going to shock Robbie Wilson that I've succeeded where he failed.' Tim dropped a butterfly kiss against her cheek.

'He needs taking down a peg or two,' Carrie smiled, 'but I doubt he ever thought of marrying me. Tim, on second thoughts, do you think we should just go in and tell everybody in the office?'

'Oh dear, no. It might be more diplomatic if I told Uncle Jeremy first; well, Len at least.'

'It wouldn't help if he heard it first from Robbie Wilson.' Carrie slid the ring off her finger and put it back in its leather case, and then safely into her handbag. 'They have funny ideas about marriage, and this clearly shows our intention. Ours had better be a secret engagement for the time being.' Her smile grew broader. 'Still, it is lovely to have this magnificent ring straight away, even if it isn't politic to wear it.'

CHAPTER THIRTY-TWO

HAVING TIM'S RING AND knowing he loved her changed Carrie's mood, even though they couldn't make it public knowledge just yet. She felt up on cloud nine, and being so happy filled her with energy. Tim's family invited her and Prue to a celebratory meal in a new restaurant, and Prue said, 'They seem pleasant enough people, and I really like Tim's mother.'

Carrie missed her father and found it much quieter at home without Maud. Bob continued to give her driving lessons, and soon she began to feel that she was getting the hang of it. He made her drive through the busy city streets after that, and finally he arranged for her to sit the test.

Maud had promised Carrie she would write to her, and in her first letter she told her that both she and Archie had enjoyed the voyage out. She was loving South Africa, but Archie had been upset to find that his friend Rod Reinhart had sold his house and his business and left without leaving any forwarding address. None of his many friends seemed to know where he'd gone.

Soon her letters were filled with glowing accounts of the social life in Johannesburg, and of how much she was enjoying the sun. She said that both she and Archie were bursting with good health in the better climate.

'I'm sure she's finding it very exciting,' Prue said disdainfully. 'That's her sort of thing.' Now that there were just the two of them, Prue continued to keep house as she always had, while Carrie studied hard.

Within months, Archie was writing to say that Maud had an admirer. *I introduced her to Tom Bennett, my boss at Gordon and Mayell, who is about to retire. He's a few years younger than Maud and has been a widower for five years. From the moment they met, they got on like a house on fire. Maud is very happy; she's looking younger than she used to and says she's having a marvellous time.*

'I suppose age hardly matters at her time of life,' Prue commented, 'though I wouldn't want to marry a man who was younger than me. I've had to bring up and discipline too many younger brothers; I know how tiresome men can be.'

Carrie arrived home one evening to find Prue quite agitated. 'I've had two letters today,' she sniffed. 'This one's from Maud telling us she's getting married. I hope she knows what she's doing; she's nearly sixty-one, for goodness' sake, and should have more sense. Ridiculous to think of it at her age; she hardly knows this man.'

'Dad knows him,' Carrie pointed out. 'He likes him, thinks highly of him.'

'Read what she says,' Prue held up the letter and pointed out the paragraph. *I'm too old for a fancy church wedding with white gown and orange blossom. It's going to be a quiet affair, very informal, just to make it legal for us to set up home together. Tom is talking about moving down to the coast once he retires. I'm afraid you won't approve but that's the way we want it.*

'You must be pleased,' Carrie said, sitting down on the sofa to change into her slippers. 'It'll be a new way of life for her, a completely fresh start.'

Prue sniffed again. 'And there's this one from your father inviting me to go out for the wedding.' She flung both letters on to Carrie's lap. 'You'd better read them.'

'You will go, won't you?'

'It hardly sounds worth the trouble if it's not to be a church wedding. They won't really be married.'

'Nonsense, Prue, of course they will.' Carrie read the letter from her father. *Come out for the wedding and have a decent holiday; you deserve it. I'll pay your fare and put you up. I've persuaded Bob and Dilys to come, so you'll have company on the journey out. Bob will take care of things.*

'You must go,' Carrie insisted. 'You can't miss a chance like this.'

'But you're not going, are you? He says he'll do the same for you if you want to.'

'He knows I can't go now, but I will as soon as I'm qualified. It would take a month to get to Cape Town and back, and then there's the long rail journey up to Johannesburg. If I'm going that far, I want to stay for a while and enjoy it.'

There was regret in Prue's voice. 'Maud will never come home again, you realise that?'

'All the more reason for you to go out for her wedding,' Carrie retorted.

Eventually Prue agreed to take up Archie's offer, though she said in doom-laden tones, 'It's against my better judgement.'

Gladys said, 'Of course you must go, though I'm going to miss you terribly. I expect you will too, Carrie.'

'I will. I'm so used to having Prue and Maud in the house, I'll feel lonely on my own.'

'I have a key to this place. I'll pop in and light a fire half an hour before you come home from work. Get it going for you and give the place time to warm up.'

'That's very kind of you, Gladys.'

The first night Prue was away, Gladys had a cottage pie ready to dish up when Carrie got home, and she ate a more than generous helping. Gladys went on to make a hot meal for her every evening. 'This is kindness beyond the call of duty,' Carrie told her. 'I'm more than grateful.'

'I know Prue did this for you, and you must be tired after working all day.'

'But I'm taking up all your time, and now I'm taking up even more sitting here talking to you.'

'I'm glad of your company,' Gladys said, 'and it gives me something to do. The place is very quiet without Prue.'

Prue wrote giving all the details of Maud's wedding, though her disapproval was obvious. She stayed in Johannesburg for three months, and later letters said she couldn't settle, it was too hot and she didn't like swimming pools. Archie kept a houseful of servants, so there was nothing for her to do, and she was bored. She wanted to come home to her own house and her friends.

CHAPTER THIRTY-THREE

PRUE SETTLED QUICKLY BACK into her old life. Carrie passed her driving test and took Prue and Gladys for little outings at the weekends. She drove Tim to the office, and when required, she ferried her audit team to wherever they were working. That earned her kudos from everybody. Tim laughed and told her that her status had gone up, and by association, so had his.

She was spending more and more time with Tim, and although she felt content with what she had, she still wanted what her twin had achieved. Connie told her she was very happy, and that marriage had given her everything she'd ever wanted. Within two years, Amelia had become an engaging toddler, and she had a baby brother.

Carrie longed to be married, although she knew it was hardly possible.

'It's what I want too,' Tim said. 'I want to feel settled with you.'

'But I also want to finish my time as an articled clerk and sit that exam,' Carrie reminded him. 'I don't want to be thrown out at this stage.'

'Of course you don't.'

'And I'll want to go on working after I'm married,' she

sighed. 'But none of us knows if that'll be possible. We must both buckle down and wait. After all, that's what we all agreed to do before we started.'

In the summer of 1938, Tim qualified as a chartered accountant. 'Now I'm earning a salary,' he said, 'I'm getting impatient. I feel we've waited long enough to get married.'

To hear him say things like that sent a thrill rippling down Carrie's spine. 'But I still have another year to wait, and there are any number of reasons to put it off even longer than that.'

'Yes, Mum's health is failing and she can't live on her own. I couldn't possibly leave her.' Jane Redwood was now confined to a wheelchair. 'There is one thing we might do,' Tim said. 'Would you be willing to come and live with us? It isn't much of a prospect for a bride-to-be, I'm afraid. Not only would you be taking me on, but also an invalid mother-in-law.'

'That wouldn't worry me,' Carrie laughed. Tim had been taking her home more and more often, and she'd grown fond of Jane Redwood and had been doing more to help her. Prue baked cakes for her regularly, and had invited her several times to high tea on a Sunday evening.

'Are you sure?' Tim was frowning. 'Marrying into my family seems a lot to ask of you. I feel I'd be unloading my responsibilities on you.'

'You can't shrug off your responsibilities, and I want to share your life, so yes, I'm quite sure. I'll be happy to share everything.'

Carrie felt his arms go round her in a loving hug. 'You're one in a million,' he whispered.

He explained his plan. 'Uncle Jeremy is concerned about Mum too; he and Aunt Enid have had to give more and more help. They know exactly how I'm placed. What if I can get him to agree to us being married? He knows what a help it would be if I had a wife, and he likes you.'

'We'll see him together. Or perhaps talk to Len first?' Carrie suggested. 'I'm articled to him, so it's his problem too.'

The next morning they went to Len's office together and Tim said, 'Carrie and I have been engaged for two years and we feel we've waited long enough. We want to get married.'

'You know that's against the rules,' Len replied. 'It would set a precedent for the business.'

'Not if we kept it quiet and only our families knew,' Tim said.

'I don't wear my engagement ring in the office,' Carrie pointed out. 'It isn't public knowledge that we are engaged.'

'You know how Mum is. The family helps her a lot, but Carrie does too in practical ways. Wouldn't it be a good thing if she moved in and lived with us? Mum isn't going to get any better.'

Carrie added, 'But after all this training you've given me, I want to have a career. That isn't usually possible for a married woman, so I'd need my marriage to be kept hidden anyway.'

Len said, 'I don't see how we could arrange that. An engagement is one thing, marriage is another.'

'My sister did it,' Carrie said. 'She was married to John Bradford before he qualified, and she carried on working for the council. They kept it quiet; you didn't know, did you?'

'No.' Len sank back in his chair in thought.

'And there's this growing fear of a coming war; that will change everything and women will be needed in the workforce,' Tim said.

'I'm not unsympathetic,' Len said. 'I'll put it to Father and see what he thinks.'

Carrie and Tim left his office in jubilant anticipation, and later that day Uncle Jeremy sent for them.

'Caroline,' he said, 'you know full well that it's national policy for a professional firm like ours not to employ married women, yet you're asking me as a director to collude with you to do so.'

'I'm afraid I am, sir,' Carrie admitted. She was quaking in her shoes. 'It isn't fair that because I'm a woman I can't—'

'Nothing is fair in this world,' he said, 'but in your case there are advantages for Tim and his mother. Though I feel I should point out that, like our male clerks, you agreed not to marry until you had qualified.'

'I did,' she said, 'but nobody wanted to marry me then.'

He smiled. 'You've fitted in well and been an asset to the business. An asset to the family too.'

'And a huge support to me and Mum,' Tim added.

'What does your mother think about this, Timothy? Have you discussed it with her?'

'No, I wanted to have your opinion first, though she has said she'd like to see me settled before . . . well, you know.'

'Yes. Poor Jane, I'm afraid she's suffered more than most, and I have to consider her best interests in this. Well, Caroline, I'd be sorry to lose your services here, so I agree to you and Tim being married, but only on condition that nobody except family members know about it. Not even the Athertons; you must be very careful about that.'

'We will, Uncle,' Tim said. 'We'll be very careful. Thank you.'

'Then I give you my blessing and my best wishes for your future.'

Carrie's head was in a joyous whirl and she could see Tim felt the same, but they carried on in the office as though nothing momentous had happened. That evening, Tim got off the tram with her so they could tell Aunt Prue together.

Her mouth opened in surprise. 'Married now? A secret wedding?'

'Just as soon as it can be arranged,' Tim said.

'I want it to be like Connie's wedding,' Carrie said. 'We'll have it in your church and afterwards hold the reception here. We'll only invite our two families.'

'Yes, but Tim, won't your family want to invite their friends? Have something grander, a big wedding breakfast in a large hotel?'

'No, what they really want is for us to keep it quiet, so that their friends and the staff in the business don't know. We'll arrange to be married on a weekday. There'll be no printed invitations, and a reception here would be ideal.'

'I shall enjoy arranging it all,' Prue smiled, 'though I hope there'll be no burst water tank this time.'

Carrie wrote to her father immediately to tell him of her plans, and he replied saying, *I came home to give Connie away, and I'm going to do the same for you. Maud and her husband will be coming too.*

When she told her twin sister, Connie hugged her in delight. 'When is it to be? I'm almost as excited as if I were getting married again.'

'At eleven o'clock on the Tuesday morning after the August bank holiday. Tim and I are going to take the rest of that week off. Uncle Jeremy is paying for five nights in a hotel in Southport as a wedding present.'

'I want to be your matron of honour.'

'Connie, it's not going to be a dress-up wedding. I've seen a pretty dress in Bunney's that I like, but I can't make up my mind about the colour. They have it in green or lavender.'

'No,' Connie wailed. 'You must be a proper bride and have a white gown; it'll be the only chance you'll get. Why don't you borrow mine; it's only been worn the once.' She suppressed a giggle. 'I haven't looked at it for years, but I packed it away carefully.'

'I'll start by baking the cake,' Prue said, 'and I'll ask Gladys if she'll ice it. Now help me draw up the menu for the wedding breakfast.'

Carrie knew exactly what she'd want to make. Prue laid out similar grand buffets for all her family parties, but this time she was unaccountably nervous. 'I hardly know Tim's family,' she said. 'Apart from his mother, we've only ever met the once at that restaurant.'

'They're very easy to get on with,' Carrie said. 'And his mother is thrilled. She's very frail now, and the doctor doesn't give her much longer. I'll be able to help if I go to live with them. All his family are in favour of us getting married.'

'I'm not surprised, but it hardly seems the best start for your life together,' Prue said. 'I hope he's worth it.'

'He is, Prue, and I want you to know that we'll look after you if the need arises.'

'It won't,' she said. 'I'll always be able to look after myself.' But Carrie could see that she was moved.

* * *

One Sunday morning, Tim came round to help her distemper the yard walls, and at lunchtime the next day, they went to the market and bought some plants that were already in bloom to put in the tubs.

They were very busy over the following days making cakes and trifles, made even busier when their visitors arrived from Johannesburg. Carrie had moved out of her bedroom so that Maud and her husband could use the twin beds. She would have gone to the camp bed in the box room, but Prue, stern as ever, put her foot down.

'You're the bride, everything must revolve round you. It won't hurt your dad to spend his first few nights on the camp bed. He can move to Maud's old room once you're gone.'

Carrie drove Prue down to Lime Street station to meet them. She could see her father waving at a window as the train came into the station; he had the door open in moments, leaving Maud to find a porter for their luggage. It was two years since Carrie had seen him, and he looked tanned and healthy and carefree. She felt his arms scoop her into a bear hug.

Maud seemed younger than she had, and her clothes were really smart. 'I knew your turn would come,' she whispered to Carrie. 'You haven't had to wait as long as I did. This is Tom, my husband.' He put out his hand to shake hers. Carrie liked the look of him.

On the morning of the wedding, the more distant members of the family gathered at the house. Everybody was talking about the leaking water tank that had flooded the dining room on Connie's big day. Bob now had a car of his own, and he and George were going to ferry people to the church just as they had for Connie. She and John came round early, bringing their babies and enough flowers to decorate every room in the house.

'Come on, let's get you into that wedding gown,' she said. She had had it dry-cleaned and pressed before bringing it round, and Carrie had tried it on and decided she liked the heavy ivory silk, the small stand-up collar and long sleeves. The princess style with a wide skirt fitted her perfectly; it was a very traditional wedding gown.

Carrie was used to putting her hair up now, and today she'd arranged it in a large bun on top of her head. She'd chosen a plain silver band to hold the veil in place.

'You look the perfect bride,' Connie breathed. 'Stylish yet demure, and very romantic.'

Her father said, 'I've ordered plenty of champagne; we aren't going to rely on Prue this time. She's good at catering for the food, but she hopelessly underestimates how much guests will drink. She thinks a glass of sherry is all the ladies could possibly want. I'm going to open a bottle now.' Carrie heard the cork come out with a resounding bang. 'You need just one glassful before you walk down that aisle,' he told her. She sipped it while bubbles danced up from the glass.

The last batch of guests caused a flurry as they left for the church, and now only Dad and Connie were left with her. 'I'll never be able to thank you enough for what you did for me,' her father told her. 'You're a daughter in a million.'

During the short car ride to church, Connie kept giving her hand a comforting squeeze. Then, as the organ soared, she clung to Dad and he walked her up the aisle. This time it was all for her.

The man she loved was waiting at the altar with his cousin

Leonard, who was acting as his best man. Tim turned as she approached, and gave her the slow half-smile she knew so well. She could see the love in his eyes, but suddenly everything went misty and there was a lump in her throat.

She heard the groom's strong, firm voice saying, 'I, Timothy, take thee, Caroline, to my wedded wife, to have and to hold from this day forward, for better for worse, for richer for poorer, in sickness and in health, to love and to cherish, till death us do part.'

And Carrie knew that now she too had everything she'd ever wanted in life.

Wartime Girls

Anne Baker

Set in Liverpool during the Depression and the Blitz of the Second World War, Anne Baker's dramatic saga brings a close-knit community vividly to life.

It is the day of the Grand National, 1933, when Susie Ingram's fiance, Danny, is killed in a tragic accident. In a cruel twist of Fate, Susie discovers she is carrying Danny's child and, shunned by his parents, she turns to her mother for support.

Louise Ingram, widowed during the First World War, knows how hard it is to bring up a family alone, but with the help of her eldest daughter, Martha, who lives next door, they manage to survive.

When little Rosie is born there is no doubt that she is Danny's daughter, but it is destined to take many more years of heartache before the two families are united again . . .

Praise for Anne Baker's gripping Merseyside sagas:

'A stirring tale of romance and passion, poverty and ambition' *Liverpool Echo*

'Baker's understanding and compassion for very human dilemmas makes her one of romantic fiction's most popular authors' *Lancashire Evening Post*

'With characters who are strong, warm and sincere, this is a joy to read' *Coventry Evening Telegraph*

978 1 4722 1226 9

headline

A Liverpool Legacy

Anne Baker

On a spring day in 1947, Millie and Pete Maynard take their daughter Sylvie on a boat trip that is to end in tragedy. Poor Sylvie blames herself for the accident and Millie needs all her strength to comfort her children and overcome her grief. Then Pete's will is read and further heartache lies in store . . .

Meanwhile, Pete's younger brother and his good-for-nothing sons try to take control of the family business, but they've underestimated Millie's indomitable spirit. She's worked in Maynard's perfume laboratory for eighteen years and is determined to protect her husband's legacy no matter what obstacles are thrown in her way . . .

Praise for Anne Baker's gripping Merseyside sagas:

'A stirring tale of romance and passion, poverty and ambition' *Liverpool Echo*

'Baker's understanding and compassion for very human dilemmas makes her one of romantic fiction's most popular authors' *Lancashire Evening Post*

'With characters who are strong, warm and sincere, this is a joy to read' *Coventry Evening Telegraph*

978 0 7553 9960 4

headline

Nancy's War

Anne Baker

As the Second World War looms, Nancy Seymour is told that her RAF pilot husband, Charles, has been killed. Devastated by her loss, she struggles to support their little girl, Caro, on her own. But, as bombs start to fall on Merseyside, Charles's father offers them sanctuary, in the form of a cottage in the countryside.

Meanwhile, Charles's mother Henrietta is hell-bent on making Nancy's life a misery. For dark secrets lurk in the Seymour family and Henrietta will stop at nothing to keep them hidden. With the danger of war ever-present, Nancy is determined to protect her loved ones from harm, knowing that if she can survive the years of peril ahead, then perhaps one day she will find happiness again . . .

Praise for Anne Baker's touching Merseyside sagas:

'A stirring tale of romance and passion, poverty and ambition' *Liverpool Echo*

'Truly compelling . . . rich in language and descriptive prose' *Newcastle Upon Tyne Evening Chronicle*

'A heart-warming saga' *Woman's Weekly*

978 0 7553 5667 6

headline

Now you can buy any of these other bestselling
books by **Anne Baker** from your bookshop
or direct from her publisher.

Liverpool Gems	£7.99
Wartime Girls	£6.99
A Liverpool Legacy	£8.99
Daughters of the Mersey	£8.99
Love is Blind	£8.99
Liverpool Love Song	£7.99
Nancy's War	£7.99
Through Rose-Coloured Glasses	£8.99
All That Glistens	£8.99
The Best of Fathers	£8.99
A Labour of Love	£8.99
The Wild Child	£8.99
Carousel of Secrets	£8.99
Let The Bells Ring	£8.99

TO ORDER SIMPLY CALL THIS NUMBER

01235 827 702

or visit our website: www.headline.co.uk

Prices and availability subject to change without notice.